Advance Praise

"Arthur Young will introduce you to a special world, East Baltimore, and its vacation spot, Ocean City, with his warm *Downeyoshun*. Not that life is perfect—not all mothers are kind, and the VietNam war casts a shadow. But you'll feel as if you've met new friends as you follow his characters through the challenges of growing up. In his skillful telling, the fabric of a family and a neighborhood comes to life. You may even find yourself becoming a Baltimore Hon!"

— Pamela Zerba, author of *Grace*, contributor for *Atheists in America*, Creative York Contest Winner

"Be prepared to fall in love with one of the most endearing literary characters of the century thus far. Ultimately, this is a book about family, the one you're stuck with and the one you make. By the end, Sally will feel like part of yours. You will thoroughly enjoy your trip *Downeyoshun*."

— Robert Akridge, writer, blurber

DOWNEYOSHUN

a novel

a novel

Art Young

First Edition

Casebound ISBN: 978-1-62720-602-0
Paperback ISBN: 978-1-62720-603-7
Ebook ISBN: 978-1-62720-604-4

Design by Apprentice House Press
Promotional Development by Rylee Miller
Editorial Development by Kyreeze Jones

Author photo by Paulette Flemmens
Cover painting by Paulette Flemmens

Published by Apprentice House Press

Loyola University Maryland
4501 N. Charles Street, Baltimore, MD 21210
410.617.5265
www.ApprenticeHouse.com
info@ApprenticeHouse.com

This story is for: Ms. Vicki Rae Wheeler –therapist, counselor, teacher, first reader, and friend. Without her gentle push for me to write, Sally would never have lived.

And for The Shrewsbury Writer's Group: Robert Akridge, Pamela Bromiley, Paulette Flemmens, and Pamela Zerba. Their encouragement, criticism, enthusiasm, and warm friendship finallygave me the courage to submit my stories as well as to write them.

And for Lily Young: Just because I love you. Thank you, Beautiful.

Downeyoshun: (down-ee-oh-shun) From Baltimore, Maryland dialect. Contraction of “down to the ocean” or “down to Ocean City.” Usage: “We’re going downeyoshun this summer.”

PROLOGUE

Aunt Sally's Downeyoshun, Summer 1955

My baby photos show that I had a "widow's peak", which thoroughly offended my mother's infallible sense of beauty.

"There was a little girl,
who had a little curl,
right in the middle of her forehead.
Her mother ripped it out and
slapped her when she shouted.
Now she wears her hair in bangs to hide the scar."

Want to know what my first happy memory was? Dropping and breaking a full glass of milk.

I was four, almost five, and Mother's sister Sally (whom I was named for) brought me all the way from Baltimore Maryland to spend the summer with her, my Uncle Bill, and my 5-year-old cousin Billy, "Downeyoshun"—Ocean City Maryland. It had been a long, hot drive. We got to their home around supper time, and had cold fried chicken, coleslaw, and potato salad.

And milk.

I don't know if it was too big of a glass, or the condensation made it slippery, but it fell off the table and onto the floor, where the glass broke, and pieces went everywhere.

Aunt Sally made a noise like a siren and said "Alright, Kitchen Police! Nobody moves!"

She carefully knelt and started sopping the milk up with a dish towel and picking up the pieces of glass.

"I'm sorry," I whispered.

"Hmm? S'okay, Hon, I'll get you some more. Just stay put for a few minutes."

"I'm sorry," I whispered again. "I broke your glass."

"S'okay, Hon, just a glass."

"No," I whispered. "Glasses are 'spensive. And I broke it. I'm sorry."

Aunt Sally made a snorting noise when she laughed. "These aren't expensive, Hon. I buy them at the A&P because they have grape and strawberry and pineapple jam in them." She laughed louder. "And these towels come in detergent boxes, and the plates come from the gas station when we get a fill-up." She kept on laughing. "And our 'silverware' is stainless steel from Sonny's Army-Navy Surplus, and—", she looked up when I started sobbing. "Honey? Sally Honey, don't cry, it's alright."

"No, it's not, I broke your glass, and I'm not crying, and I'm sorry, and now you hate me, and—" I started hiccupping, and when Aunt Sally stood up, I flinched away and held my arms in front of my face. "I'm sorry, I'm sorry, I'm sorry."

Aunt Sally slowly and gently put her arms around me and kissed me. "Oh, dear God, Honey, I don't hate you, I love you. Please, baby, it's okay."

My cousin Billy spoke. "Whasamatter with her?"

Aunt Sally picked me up and sat with me in her lap. "She's okay, she's just tired."

Billy turned in his chair. "Can I get down?"

Aunt Sally looked down at the floor. "Alright, but not over here."

Billy leaned over and said "I spill stuff all the time. It's okay."

Aunt Sally snorted again. "Yep, he sure does. We've got the best fed ants in town."

I imagined fat ants waddling across the kitchen floor, and I wanted to laugh, but all that came out were more tears. Aunt Sally held me closer and started to hum, and then sang to me about an Alleghany Moon in a kind of flat voice. I let her hold me while I cried and fell asleep.

I woke up when Uncle Bill came home. He was a Fireman and an Ambulance Driver for the City. Uncle Bill always smelled like scrubbing soap and car polish. He was a quiet man with sleepy-looking eyes and almost always had a smile. When he came into the room, he grabbed Billy and gave him a big raspberry on his neck and made him laugh, then tucked him under his arm, and leaned over and kissed Aunt Sally and then me. He saw the dish towel and glass on the floor and tipped his head to the side. Aunt Sally shook her head once. She kissed me and told all of us "I think we're going to keep Sally here with us *all* summer, *every* summer from now on. From the time school stops in June till school starts in September." She looked at Uncle Bill and hugged me tightly. "And I'd like to play some football right about now with a certain someone." There was a growl in her voice.

"Do you play football?" I asked.

Aunt Sally looked at me and shook her head. "No, Honey, I'm just kidding. But I'm not kidding about coming down for the summer. From now on, you're mine in the summertime, just so I can love you."

I looked at her. She didn't look or sound like Mother. I tried to hug her back, but I wasn't sure how. "Okay," I whispered. "Thank you."

We smiled, and I was happy.

CHAPTER ONE

Summer 1955

I probably should try to explain my family.

Mother and Aunt Sally were fraternal twins. Mother was a pale, blue-eyed, Nordic blonde like my grandparents. Aunt Sally had olive skin, dark brown eyes, and coal-black hair. NOT what people think of as Swedish.

When they were growing up, Mother was always their favorite. Aunt Sally... well, as she put it, "They acted like I was something the Gypsies left behind when they stole the real twin."

Mother went to dancing school, vocal classes, and sewing circles.

Aunt Sally—didn't.

Mother attended Goucher College and graduated with a Bachelor of Fine Arts.

Aunt Sally worked her way through Towson State Teacher's College as a waitress and a weekend domestic, received a teaching certificate, and taught English at Stephen Decator High School in Ocean City Maryland.

Aunt Sally met a very quiet and very nice man at the Diner she worked at during the summer months. Bill Palkin was a Marine who served in the Pacific during World War 2 and had joined the Fire Department when he came home. Aunt Sally always made it a point to take his order when he came in, not just to tease him because he rarely spoke, but also because he was a good-looking guy with a friendly smile. One day she asked him why he became a Fireman. He told her that after the war, he wanted to spend the rest of his life *saving* people.

She leaned over the counter and kissed him. They were married at St. Paul's By-the-Sea Episcopal Church over the Christmas school holiday.

Neither Mother nor my grandparents came. "Too far. Too cold."

Mother decided that *she* would get married. She met Dad at a Lutheran church social. Friedrich (Freddie) Osterhoff had served as an Army officer in an engineering battalion in Europe during the war and had been assigned to rebuilding the railroads in Germany afterwards. His commanding officer was a Reservist who had been an executive with the B&O railroad before the war. On his recommendation, Dad was hired at a mid-level position by them when he came back to the States.

Dad would speak lightly of his wartime experiences, but almost never about his life before the war. The few things I was able to piece together was that he'd been born into an Amish community in Ohio, could build anything from wood, be it a box or a barn; and during his "Wilding Time" before his choice between faith and the world, he joined the Army after Pearl Harbor. During training, he impressed his superiors enough to be sent to Officer Candidate School and finished his service as a Captain.

I've never met anyone in his family.

Mother somehow managed to get him to marry her after a six-month courtship.

I've never been able to find out why he did it.

The wedding was fancy, expensive, and very exclusive. In other words, not many RSVP'd: a testament to the lack of friends on the part of Mother and my grandparents. Grandmother was Matron of Honor. Aunt Sally "and guest" received an invitation to the wedding, but not the reception. Aunt Sally said she wanted to show up in patched bib overalls and bare feet, but Uncle Bill talked her out of it.

They both felt sorry for my father.

At the family Thanksgiving at Mother's house, nearly two years after their marriage, Aunt Sally and Uncle Bill announced that they were going to have a baby. After a long silence, Grandmother said "I KNEW you had to get married." She and Grandfather got up and walked out the door.

Two months later, Mother was pregnant.

My cousin Billy was born in May 1950.

I was born in August (almost a month premature). If Mother could have managed it, I would have been born in April.

I don't know why she named me Sally.

I do know that my grandparents never said my name. I was always "the child" when we visited them and was never spoken to directly. It was always "Why is the child fidgeting? Can't the child be still? Does the child have a weak bladder? Can't the child control herself till she gets home? Doesn't the child know how to speak? The child should at least say 'Hello Grandfather and Grandmother'. Tell the child to be quiet. Children should be seen and not heard."

Visits there were short and few. We entered the front door, walked the plastic path over the carpet through the living room with its plastic-covered furniture, and past the dark dining room into a small Pullman kitchen with a tiny table and two chairs. We stood, they sat. Mother would report on our lives, and we would listen to their criticism. Then we left the same way we entered. At Thanksgiving, they came to our house, complained, ate, complained some more, and left. They didn't visit for Christmas.

At Christmas, Aunt Sally, Uncle Bill and Billy would arrive at 11:00 AM, exchange gifts (a $5 bill for Billy, toys for me), eat dinner at noon, and leave for the drive home at 3:00. The next day, Mother would take the gifts to the Goodwill Store—I was always "too old to play with toys."

In August we would take the long drive to Ocean City to spend Dad's two-week vacation with them.

They lived in a small, two-bedroom house with gray asphalt-shingle siding, a front porch, and a yard of sawgrass. Just over the dune behind the house was the ocean. It was north of the city, nearly at the end of a line of other small gray houses between Ocean Highway and the beach. Mother called it a shack. Aunt Sally called it a home.

Every day, Mother and I would walk over the low dune to the beach and sit under a large beach umbrella so that I wouldn't get sunburned, wet, or covered with sand. Two weeks later, we would drive home.

Then, in my fifth summer, I went down in June, broke a glass of milk, and my life became wonderful.

Every morning, Uncle Bill's mother, Granny Annie, would come to the house and Aunt Sally would go to work at the Diner. Granny Annie would cook breakfast for Billy and I (*never* cold cereal—"You can't grow on bird-crumbs.") Then we'd go to the beach and look for seashells, dig for Sandcrabs and clams that would squirt at you, and build sandcastles. When the sun grew hot and high, we would go back home, eat lunch, and take a nap. When we woke, Granny Annie was gone, and Aunt Sally was home.

Uncle Bill would come home in time for supper unless he was working "The Shift" and stayed at the Firehouse. After we ate, Aunt Sally would give us baths, then she might read to us, or we'd play board games like Candyland, Chutes and Ladders, and Parcheesi. Then it was "Showtime!," and the radio would tell a story. Each night was different: cops and robbers, cowboys and Indians, monsters and spaceships. When the show was over, Aunt Sally would clap her hands twice, and say "Alright, that's it for today, bedtime!." We'd all hug and kiss (I didn't know how to at first), and everyone went to bed. Billy and I shared a room and a bed, and we learned to share a blanket on cool nights without tugging.

Summer almost lasted forever. One evening while Aunt Sally was combing Alberto VO5 into my hair (it got dry from the wind and sun), she stopped and hugged me tightly and told me "Your Mother and Dad will be here on Saturday."

I felt dizzy and started to cry.

Two weeks later we were back in Baltimore. When we walked up the steps to the porch, a girl's head popped up over the brick divider. She looked like Aunt Sally: black hair (only hers was curly), dark eyes and olive skin.

"Hi!" She had a loud voice. "I'm Marie! Who're you?"

I started to say, "I'm Sal—." Mother yanked me inside.

We lived in a rowhouse (Mother called it a "Townhouse") in the part of Baltimore called Highlandtown. I could hear Marie through the wall. "Ma! They got a girl! Her name's Sal!"

Another loud voice answered. "SHE's got a kid? Jeez! Poor kid!" A few seconds later, the second voice yelled out the back door. "Hey, Vince! They got a kid!"

A man's voice answered. "HER? Jeez. Poor kid. Boy or girl?"

"Girl. Name's Sal."

"How old?"

Marie answered. "She's as big as me!"

Mother hissed. "Common." Dad made a little cough. I think every time Dad coughed, he was hiding a laugh from Mother.

"Where's Mr. and Mrs. Weinmann?" I whispered to Dad.

"They moved a couple of days after you went to your aunt's. Mr. and Mrs. Giametti moved in the week after. Their little girl is five, too," he said softly.

"We don't need to talk about them," Mother said in that quiet, cold voice of hers. "It's bad enough they're there, we don't need to concern ourselves with them."

I spoke without thinking. "Maybe we'll be in Kindergarten together," I whispered.

Mother froze and turned to glare at me. "You will not speak to her." She squeezed my chin in her hand. "Well?"

I dropped my eyes. "Yes, Mother." But to myself I said, "Yes I will."

CHAPTER TWO

Marie

For the first day of school, Mother laid out the clothes I would wear: a yellow and white dress, black Mary Janes, white anklet socks with tiny flowers, and added what looked like a small briefcase in a gray and white plaid. "What's that for?" I whispered.

"That," Mother said, " is for carrying your schoolbooks and your lunch. It has your name inside here." She raised the flap. "Do not lose it or let it get it dirty."

"Yes, Mother," I whispered.

"Look at me," she commanded. "You will speak to no one except your teacher. And all that she needs to know is your name. Do you understand me?"

"Yes, Mother."

"You will especially not speak to that child next door if she is there. Is that understood?"

"Yes, Mother."

I really hoped Marie would be there.

After breakfast, Mother pulled me along down several blocks until we got to school. She stopped at the office to get directions to the classroom and marched me past a row of other kids and their mothers and through the door. Marie and her mother were at the front of the line. A smiling woman at a large desk said "We're not quite ready -"

Mother ignored her. "I am Mrs. Osterhoff. This is Sally Osterhoff. You will see to it that she stays clean and neat and away from the other children, especially that child just outside the door."

The teacher looked confused and annoyed. "Don't they get along?"

Mother stared at the teacher. "I do not want them to 'get along' at all. Keep them apart. I will return at 3 o'clock."

"Just a moment, Mrs....?" The teacher did not look happy.

"Mrs. Osterhoff."

"Mrs. Osterhoff. All the children in this class will learn together and play together—NO EXCEPTIONS." She caught Mother in mid-word. "They will also learn common politeness, if they haven't learned it at home." Mother's jaw was clenched. "One last thing, Mrs. Osterhoff: Kindergarten is half-day. You will be here at 11:45 to pick up your daughter."

I recognized the look Mother was giving the teacher, but the teacher ignored it as if it wasn't there, and walked past Mother, opened the door, and smiled. "And good morning to *you*, Mrs. Osterhoff."

An alarm bell rang and made me jump. The other kids and their mothers came in, and Mother fought against the tide and left. The teacher walked over to Marie and her mother. "Hello, I'm Mrs. Harris, and you are?"

"Carmella Giametti. And this is Marie." Marie smiled over to me and wiggled her fingers in a wave. I smiled back.

"Well, now, it looks like these two would like to sit together, don't you think?" asked Mrs. Harris.

Miss Carmella laughed. "Yeah, that's fine with me." She patted Marie on the shoulder. "Go say hi to her."

Marie rushed over, grabbed my hand, and shook it. "Hi Sal!"

"Hi Marie."

"I got an uncle named Sal," she told me.

"It's really Sally. Mother didn't let me finish."

Mrs. Harris clapped her hands together and we all looked at her. "Now, everyone choose a desk to sit at, and then it will be time for all the Mommies to go home until lunchtime." One boy started to cry and grabbed his mother. She turned pink and rolled her eyes.

After the mothers had left, I looked around me. I had never been with other kids before except Billy. Some were neatly dressed; others were a little rumpled. Two of them were very busy picking their noses. We were all quiet, and waiting to see what would happen next.

The teacher softly clapped her hands again, and said "Good Morning, Class! Welcome to Kindergarten. I'm Mrs. Harris, and when you need to talk to me, I'd like you to raise your hand in the air like this." She raised her arm straight up in the air. "When I point to you, you can ask me a question, or answer one of my questions, or get permission to go to the bathroom—and the bathrooms for kindergarten are right next door. The first door is for the girls, and the second for the boys. Does anyone need to go? Raise your hands, please." A few hands went up, and Mrs. Harris asked, "Anyone else?" Three more. She guided them to the doors and waited in the hallway until everyone came back.

"Now, then, let's find out who all of you are. Every day, I'll call your names, and you will raise your hands and say 'here'. Let's begin: Thomas Alban?"

"Here. My family calls me Tommy."

"Okay," she said. "Tommy it is, then. If there is anyone else who has a nickname or is called by another name at home, just let me know when I call you." She quickly went down a list of names until she got to the boy who had cried. "Steven MacTavish." He barely raised his hand and didn't answer. Mrs. Harris spoke softly and smiled. "Just raise your hand all the way up and say 'here'." His hand slowly rose, and a "here" was whispered.

"Oh, my," Mrs. Harris said. "Willie will never be able to hear you." She pointed to a drawing of a cat holding a paw behind his ear. "That's Willie. He doesn't hear too well, so you'll have to speak a little louder, so he'll know who you are. Now, let's try again. Steven MacTavish."

He slowly grinned and said "Here."

Mrs. Harris looked at the cat. "No, I don't think he heard you yet. Try again."

"HERE!"

A noise like a cat meowing came from somewhere. "Ah! He heard you." We giggled. "Does your family call you Steven or Steve?"

"Stevie." Mrs. Harris was about to call another name when his hand shot up and waved.

"Yes, Stevie?"

He turned pink and chewed his lips. "Can I be called Mac?" His face turned bright red. "I don't like being called Stevie."

Mrs. Harris smiled and answered him in a tough voice. "Okay, Mac. When you're in my place of business, I'll call you Mac." He laughed.

"Sally Osterhoff?"

I raised my hand and whispered "here."

Mrs. Harris pointed to Willie, and I loudly called out "HERE!"

A cat meowed, and we all giggled again. "Very good. Norma Poniatowski?"

A few more names and the roll call was finished. Mrs. Harris told us all the things we would do every morning, and some of the things we would learn that year. The alphabet, telling time, the Pledge of Allegiance, arithmetic games, the 23rd and 100th Psalms, "My Country 'Tis of Thee;" and every day if we behaved, Mrs. Harris would read us a story. There were going to be things to do besides sit and be quiet. School was going to be fun!

All too soon, the alarm bell rang again, and it was time to go. We lined up and Mrs. Harris opened the door and was nearly pushed aside by Mother. Somehow, Mrs. Harris blocked her from coming in. The other kids were let out one at a time. I was the last. Mother grabbed me and pulled me toward the door, and Mrs. Harris blocked her again. She smiled at Mother. "So, you found out all the other classes were full, hmm?" Mother's jaw muscles stood out on her face. Mrs. Harris stood aside. "I'm SO looking forward to teaching Sally this year AND seeing YOU at PTA meetings." Mrs. Harris winked at me as I was dragged out. "See you tomorrow!"

Outside the room, Mother spun me around and demanded "Did you talk to anyone?" I hesitated and whispered, "I said 'here.'"

"What?" Mother hissed.

"'Here'. When Mrs. Harris said my name, I raised my hand and said 'here.'"

She looked at me closely. "Did you speak to that child next door?"

I shook my head. "No, Mother."

She grabbed my hand and dragged me all the way home.

It was the first time I had ever lied to her.

CHAPTER THREE

Marie and I

I led a secret life that year in kindergarten. Marie and I would whisper back and forth during class—well, *I'd* whisper, Marie never quite got the hang of it. Mrs. Harris would suddenly appear with Willie's meow and hold a finger to her lips. Thinking back, Mrs. Harris might have been a lot firmer with the two of us, but instead she would lean down to say that she was glad we were friends, but "Shush, girls. I'm the teacher and I'm the one who can talk." Then she would wink and continue the lesson.

One thing that would keep us quiet and attentive was Mrs. Harris's arithmetic games. We learned to count—*really* count—up to one hundred, and there was "plus" and "take away" and Marie and I liked it so much that she taught the two of us the "times table" and how it could be used as a "goes-into table."

PTA meetings were very frustrating for Mother. Mrs. Harris could easily control the conversation and ignored Mother's commands and edicts as if she had never heard her. I was praised as "very bright," "polite," "attentive," and "a joy to teach."

My lack of "social skills" showed a real need for friends, and "Didn't you tell me on the first day of school that Marie Giametti lived next door? She's also very bright and has a strong talent for arithmetic just like Sally. I've been having them work together, and Sally seems so much happier than she was at the start of school."

Mother's teeth were grinding loud enough that Mrs. Harris told her "That's very bad for your teeth, Mrs. Osterhoff. Be careful you don't grind them away." Dad coughed.

When we got back to our house that evening, Mother paced back and forth like something in a cage, hissing about Mrs. Harris, the Giamettis and their child, and that "unspoken insinuation" that she was a bad mother when she was only raising her daughter properly as she had been raised. After he stopped coughing, Dad said "Susan, let the children be friends."

Mother bared her teeth at him and went upstairs. Mr. Vince next door would smoke a cigar on their porch every evening, and we heard him call "Hey, Carmella, c'mere. It's raining clothes." Mother was tossing Dad's clothes out the window again. Dad looked out the front door and sighed. When the last sock landed on the sidewalk, he went outside, picked everything up and brought them inside and started folding them. He looked at me. "Perhaps you should take a bath and go to bed."

After that night, Marie and I began to play together after school—but always on her porch or backyard. One day when they were both hanging laundry in the backyard, Miss Carmella called over the fence to Mother: "Hey, Susie, you ever need to go somewheres, I'll watch Sally for you."

Mother glared back and said, "My name is Mrs. Osterhoff."

Miss Carmella shrugged. "Okay, Susie."

In the 1950's, the whole country was hard at work. It wasn't unusual for Longshoremen like Mr. Vince or even salaried men like Dad to work on Saturdays. On the first Saturday of every month, Mother would go to the beauty parlor to have her hair "done." I hated going with her. It stank and was always crowded with no place for me to sit. One Saturday, Mother put on her coat, held mine in her hand, and looked at me. When I reached for it, she pulled it back and tugged me out the door, down our steps and up the Giametti's and rang the doorbell. Miss Carmella opened the door and grinned at Mother. "Hiya, Susie. What's up?"

Mother chewed her lips. "You offered to watch Sally if I had to go out," she said very quietly.

Miss Carmella grinned even wider and leaned against the doorpost. "I did?"

Mother chewed on her lips some more, and finally asked "Would you watch Sally for me? I need to go out." It was not quite her usual hiss.

Miss Carmella opened the door wide. "Yeah, sure, Susie. Take your time." She winked at me. "Come on in, kid." I hurried inside before Mother could change her mind. Miss Carmella closed the door and looked out the window as Mother walked up the street. Then she turned to me and grabbed me in a big hug and laughed. "You hungry, kid? We got some Grottoni, you know what that is?" She yelled up the stairs. "Hey Marie, look who's here!"

Marie galloped down the stairs (I had NEVER done that), stopped, grinned, and said "Hi Sal! Your Ma says you can come inside now?"

"Yes," I said. "She had to go to the beauty parlor."

Miss Carmella looked like she was going to say something about that, but changed her mind and said "C'mon, have some Grottoni."

I had never tasted anything like it. The cake was light, the cream filling was thick, and the brown dusting on top tasted like chocolate and coffee. "It's very good," I told her. "You must be a good cook."

Miss Carmella laughed and said "Ahh, Vince stops by Vaccaro's on the way home. I got enough to do cleaning and cooking meals." She stroked my cheek. "Boy, you're a quiet one. This one—" she pointed to Marie "- You can hear her down the street. You should teach her how to whisper."

"I tried in school. She can do it a little."

She laughed again. "Yeah? What, about three words?"

"No, Ma'am. She can do it a little longer than that."

She laughed even harder.

After we finished eating cake (Miss Carmella gave me a second slice), we cleared the table and she asked "Okay, what do you two want to play? Baby dolls?"

I felt my face grow warm. "I don't have dolls," I admitted. "Mother says I'm too big for toys."

Miss Carmella and Marie both looked shocked. Miss Carmella's mouth moved, and then she said "Boy, kid, your Ma—No, never mind." She waved her hand as though to chase the words away. "How about a game inside, then?"

Marie suddenly said, "How are you gonna know how to be a Mama if you don't play with babies?"

I looked down at the floor and whispered, "I don't think I want to be a mother when I grow up."

Again, they both looked shocked. I whispered, "I'm sorry."

Miss Carmella hugged me. "You're not the one who should be sorry." Marie squeezed in to hug me too. "Well, never mind, bambino Mio, you can decide that when you grow up."

"Don't worry about it," Marie agreed. "You wanna play Nopoly?"

"MONopoly," Miss Carmella corrected. "Hey, you like numbers, you'll be good at it. C'mon, we'll show you how."

We played three games. I was bankrupt in the first, fastest game, still had a couple of green houses at the end of the second and was really starting to understand the game when Mother came to take me home.

Miss Carmella tried to delay Mother. "Don't worry, Susie, I'll bring her home after the game's finished." Mother ignored her and said "Sally. Now." I thanked Miss Carmella and brushed past her down the steps. Mother turned and started to walk down Marie's steps.

"She was an angel, Susie," Miss Carmella said. "Oh, and Susie: YOU'RE WELCOME."

Mother hesitated on the street, and then said "Yes," and we went inside our house.

CHAPTER FOUR

Thanksgiving

Thanksgiving at our house was never anything to be thankful for.

Mother would get up while it was still dark outside and begin to cook. The menu was always the same: dried-out turkey with a watery gravy, doughy stuffing, gluey candied yams, broccoli and cauliflower boiled to mush, tasteless pumpkin pie, all to Grandmother's recipes. The best part was the brown-and-serve rolls from the grocery store.

At noon, my grandparents arrived, sat at the head and foot of the table, and waited in silence for dinner to be served. They would eat, complain that everything was too seasoned, and leave.

But things were different this year.

I could hear through the walls that Miss Carmella also got up early to cook. Refrigerator and stove doors slammed, pots clanged, and wonderful steamy smells somehow seeped through her kitchen into ours.

Other people began arriving at their home by eight o'clock. The kitchen got noisier as more women crowded into it. People yelled, laughed, argued, babies cried, and kids ran through the house as though they were wearing work boots. The smells became more and more fascinating. My stomach started to growl.

Mother made me leave the kitchen.

At noon, my grandparents walked up our front steps. The voices of the men on the porch called out "Happy Thanksgiving." My grandparents ignored them and came into our house. "What are THOSE doing there?" my grandfather demanded.

"The Giamettis moved in during the summer," Dad told him.

"They should go back to where they belong," Grandfather said.

They sat in the dining room and waited. "They probably have too many children." Grandmother looked vaguely in my direction. "The child doesn't associate with them?"

"No." Mother came in from the kitchen. "She does not." She gave me a warning look. I said nothing.

Mother brought in the dinner, and we began to eat. Grandfather put down his fork. "Everything smells like garlic." "And grease," added Grandmother.

Someone new must have arrived next door because the noise suddenly grew louder.

"They're probably all drunk," Grandfather said. "Disgusting," Grandmother agreed.

I bit down hard on my lips. I wanted to say something, anything. Marie and her family were so nice.

Dad saw my face, smiled, and said, "At least they are having fun."

Mother dropped her fork and sat there with her mouth open. I could see the yams nearly falling out.

My grandparents looked at each other, stood, and walked to the living room and put on their coats. Mother looked at Dad with death in her eyes. She got up and followed them, but too late: they slammed the front door behind them.

"Boy, that was quick!" came a voice on the porch. "Hey, you walk around with your noses in the air like that, you'll get run over by a streetcar!"

Mother came back into the room with her lips curled back in a snarl. Dad said, "Perhaps Sally and Bill could start coming up for Thanksgiving again." Mother's eyes bulged and her fingers were like claws. She spun and headed up the steps. Dad sighed and said, "Best to eat fast." Outside on their porch, the laughter stopped, and a voice said "What the Hell with the clothes? Hey, Vince! Look at this!"

Dad got up and walked to the door.

CHAPTER FIVE

Downeyoshun 1956

My kindergarten year went by quickly. We were always busy. Something new happened every day. We learned the alphabet and what sound each letter made. Word games—with changing one letter, "bat" became "cat" became fat, hat, mat, pat, rat, sat, vat. Reading might be as much fun as arithmetic.

Marie figured out what made Willie the Cat meow. Her Uncle Sal teased her with something in his hand that mooed like a cow. She guessed there must be something like it that meows. When we asked Mrs. Harris, she put her finger to her lips and asked us not to tell anyone else.

School ended for the summer, and I was going back Downeyoshun. I would miss Marie, so I asked Miss Carmella if she could come down too. Miss Carmella said "Nah, Vince don't like the ocean. He says it's full of sharks."

The morning after school ended, I sat on the porch and waited for Aunt Sally to get there. Mother had a mean smile on her face. When Aunt Sally drove up and parked in front of our house, Mother said "I've changed my mind. She's staying here. We'll come down in August."

I started to cry, and Mother said "Sally. Inside."

But Aunt Sally went right up to Mother and said "Forget it, Susan. She's going to be mine every summer. Sally Hon, get in the car with Billy."

She pushed Mother back into the house. I could hear Mother hiss at Aunt Sally, and Aunt Sally growl back at her. Miss Carmella came out onto her porch. "I like your aunt, kid. Introduce us when she comes out."

Aunt Sally came out of our house grinning and skipped down our steps with my suitcase. Mother slammed the door. Marie and I hugged and kissed, and I said the words "I love you" for the first time in my life. Miss Carmella grinned and stuck out her hand and Aunt Sally shook it and laughed. They agreed to play "pen-pal" for Marie and I through the summer. Marie and I hugged one more time and said goodbye. Billy stuck his head out the window and said he had to pee. Aunt Sally told him to hang onto it for a few more minutes until she got gas. Miss Carmella pointed to her home and said "You wanna?," but Aunt Sally said thanks, but she wanted to get out of here. Miss Carmella laughed, said she got it, kissed my cheek, and said, "Have fun, kid."

And off we went.

On the trip down to Ocean City, I told Aunt Sally all about my friend Marie, Kindergarten, and all the things I learned this year and what I would learn next year, all the different kinds of food that Marie's family ate and how good it all tasted, and how happy they were, and that I wished we could be that way too, but now I was going Downeyoshun where *I* would be happy, and—

Billy started laughing. "She talks a lot, now!" Aunt Sally snorted. "She's been saving it up for six years, it's about time it all came out." She looked at me in the rear-view mirror. "Talk all you want to, Hon, I'm glad to hear it."

I found out I knew a lot more arithmetic than Billy, but that he knew a lot more about reading. He read all the billboard signs all the way down, and Aunt Sally only corrected him twice. I wanted to learn this, too, so I asked him to teach me. "Sure," he said. "It's easy. I've even got my own books."

The trip down seemed to go much faster this time, and the smell of the ocean suddenly filled my nose. I didn't say so out loud, but THIS was home.

Billy's room was different: it had two beds, one stacked above the other. The mattresses were smaller, and the bed frame was made of metal and felt hard and cold. "Uncle Bill brought these home from the Firehouse so that you two could have your own beds this summer." She frowned at them. "We'll see how this works out."

Billy slept in the top bed the first night. He woke up to go to the bathroom, fell out of bed, onto the floor and started crying. I woke up and tried to sit up, hit my head on the bed frame above me, and I yelled and started to cry too. The light came on and Aunt Sally came in and made sure we were both okay. Uncle Bill brought out and unfolded the roll-away bed that Mother and Dad slept on and threw sheets, pillows, and a blanket on top of it. Uncle Bill said the bunks would go back tomorrow. Aunt Sally sighed and kissed both of us and they went back to bed. Billy and I each took our share of the blanket and went back to sleep.

When we woke up, Aunt Sally was standing with her back to us, looking into Billy's bedroom. Her arms were crossed, and she was frowning. "Oh, this is ridiculous!" she growled. "Her and her nasty mind. She's always been a pain in my—". She looked over her shoulder at me and pursed her lips, then grinned. "Hi kids. Any more bumps in the night?"

"No, ma'am."

"Right, then." She whipped the blanket off us. "Up, bathroom, dress, come to the table. French toast this morning. Syrup, butter, or jam?"

"All of them!," yelled Billy.

"Yuck," Aunt Sally said.

While we waited for breakfast, Uncle Bill came in the kitchen and hugged Aunt Sally from behind. She tipped her head back and kissed him.

Why didn't Mother and Dad do that?

"Thinking," Uncle Bill said. "Buy another bed 'on time'?"

"No. Costs too much. I'd sooner just buy a second mattress and put them both on the floor. But we can't afford that, either," Aunt Sally answered.

"Roll-away in there?"

"I don't think there's room."

"Take out the chest of drawers and sit it in our room."

Aunt Sally walked over and looked in Billy's room again. "Um. Maybe. But where will we put Susan and Freddie?"

"Freddie on the sofa," Uncle Bill grinned. "Greyhound for her."

Aunt Sally snorted. "I wish." She shrugged again. "Alright, we'll figure it out when they get here. I'm not going to let her ruin our summer."

She turned back to us. "Hey, we're both off this weekend! How about we go down to the boardwalk for the day? We'll have French Fries and ice cream for lunch."

Wow! This was a treat that usually came after Mother and Dad came down. And we could sit in front of the "Wurlitzer" down at the Rides and listen to the music. I loved Downeyoshun!

We spent the summer the same as last year: breakfast and beach with Granny Annie, lunch and a nap, but also reading lessons from Billy and Aunt Sally. By August I could read the "funny pages" by myself, *and* I could write a letter to Marie, with some help with spelling. Aunt Sally and Miss Carmella wrote back and forth all summer, and their letters got a lot longer than mine and Marie's. I missed Marie a whole lot, but at the same time, I didn't want to go back to Baltimore. Sometimes when we listened to the radio at night, Aunt Sally would hold me and Billy, and I think she wished that I could stay, too.

The day before Mother and Dad arrived, Granny Annie drove up with a mattress tied to the roof of her car. She gave me a hug and said "That's for you. Don't have a bed to go with it, but it's a good one and it'll last a good long while." Aunt Sally looked happy and sad at the same time. "Mom—" she began. "I don't want to hear it," Granny Annie interrupted. "That kid's the sweetest thing since cotton candy, and—well, you need it before SHE gets here." They untied the mattress and brought it inside Billy's room.

When they arrived, Mother swept past everyone without a word and looked in Billy's bedroom and saw both of our mattresses on the floor. She hissed something about sleeping on the floor like "beatniks." She looked at Aunt Sally. "I do not approve of them sleeping in the same room."

Aunt Sally ignored her and said "Hi, Freddie. Some ice water?"

"Thank you," he said. "I am glad that you invite us down."

Mother glared at Aunt Sally. " I said—"

"I heard you, Susan. There's only two bedrooms here."

Mother's jaw began to pulse. "I am concerned about the two of them—alone at night—I should think you would also be concerned."

"About what, Susan?"

Mother hissed through her teeth. "What if they—become curious?"

"If she takes after you, Susan, you have nothing to worry about."

Dad shot ice water through his nose and started coughing and choking.

After dinner, Mother sat on the sofa, hands folded, knees pressed together, staring at the wall. Aunt Sally did dishes while I dried, and Billy put away. Dad and Uncle Bill were out on the porch. Uncle Bill came in and got a yardstick and pencil and paper, and then took Aunt Sally outside. Billy and I followed.

Aunt Sally was talking to Dad. She looked worried. "Freddie, it sounds nice, and we'd like to, but I don't think we can afford—"

"Do not worry about how much it will cost," Dad said.

"How much?"

"Free, mostly," Uncle Bill said.

"How much, Freddie?"

Dad said "I did this growing up. Bill can help, wood is cheap, it will be roughed-in by Monday and finished on Saturday." He had an almost sad look on his face, like he was remembering something that he missed very much. "Sally, my people could put up barns in a day."

Aunt Sally frowned "No one's still saying anything about how much."

"I am buying the wood and shingles and such," Dad told her. "Bill is buying the paint and linoleum." He smiled. "This will be a 'thank you' for taking care of Sally and inviting us down every year."

Aunt Sally looked at Dad and finally gave him a small smile. "Thanks, Freddie," she said, and gave him a hug.

"What's going on?" Billy asked.

"Come this way, my nephew, and I will show you," Dad said. "This part of the porch will be a new bedroom. That window will come out and a door will go in, walls will be built here, here, and here, and the old window will be hung in this new wall."

Dad sounded different than he did at home. Happy. Excited.

"Your father tells me that Granny Annie still has all of your grandfather's tools that he used to build boats. I can teach you how to use them. Would you like to learn?"

"What are you talking about?" Mother came outside.

Aunt Sally looked at her. "The Protector and Defender of the Public and Private Morals will be pleased to learn that the Palkin Palais de Mer will be adding another wing, complete with ballroom, art gallery, arboretum and bedroom suite." She grinned at Mother. "And *you* can sew curtains for the window."

Dad coughed.

The next morning, Dad and Uncle Bill drove our station wagon to Granny Annie's house and a lumber yard. There was wood on the roof, and sticking out the windows, and more hanging out the back. Dad was grinning.

Some pieces of wood were made into "sawhorses," then wood was laid on them, measured and cut. By evening, Dad and Uncle Bill had the room "framed in." It looked like a skeleton of a room.

Billy got splinters, nicks, and a bruised thumb, but he learned how to saw a straight line, drill a hole with a "brace and bit," and drive a nail without bending it. I went with Aunt Sally so I could pick all the colors and patterns of the paint, fabric, and linoleum for my new room, but I wished I could help like Billy.

Mother silently sewed curtains and a matching bedspread on Granny Annie's old sewing machine. "Had to show her how to work the treadle," Granny Annie told Aunt Sally, "but once she got it, she 'went to town' on it. Got her to talk some. Says she makes all her own clothes and Sally's too." I realized I had never shopped for clothes except for shoes, socks, and underwear.

It wasn't finished until the next Tuesday because Dad built in a bed with drawers under it and a sort of closet with some more drawers and a place to hang clothes. There wasn't enough room for a closet door to open, so Mother sewed another curtain to cover it.

"The paint to dry and the room to air another day," Dad said at supper that evening, "and sleep there on Thursday she can." He talked funny all week. Aunt Sally said she bet that's what he sounded like when he was a kid. "And we have still three days for vacation."

"It's beautiful, Freddie," Aunt Sally said. "Why aren't you doing this instead of riding a desk?"

"Because he is not a common workman," Mother said. "He's an Executive."

No one said anything else for the rest of the meal.

So that was my second summer Downeyoshun. I learned to read, I got my very own room (and now it really *was* "Home"), and I was LOVED. And all that silly stuff Mother was afraid of: Granny Annie explained some about boys and girls last summer when she'd peel our bathing suits off and hose the sand off us. She said that if girls were made like boys, there wouldn't be Mommies, Grannies, Aunts, or sisters, and if boys were made like girls, there wouldn't be Daddies, Grampies, Uncles or brothers.

But Billy and I both think it all just looks funny. Anyway, she said when we get to be about eleven or twelve, we'll get the next surprise in life, and we'll keep on getting surprises no matter how old we get.

I wonder what it will be.

CHAPTER SIX

First Grade—Miss Ritter

I didn't want to leave Downeyoshun, especially since I had my own room now. I hugged and kissed everyone until Mother hissed "Stop that" and pulled me out to the car. Dad got hugged by Aunt Sally and Billy, and Uncle Bill shook his hand for a long time and said thanks, and that they'd be up for Christmas. They ignored Mother.

It was a long drive back to Baltimore, but Dad kept smiling and talked about building a "Club Basement" and some furniture. Mother didn't say anything.

When we got to our house, Marie was waiting for me. She ran down the steps and yelled "Hi, Sal! I missed you!" We started to hug, but Mother pulled me away and hissed "People will see."

I got to go over to Marie's the next day, and we told each other all the stuff we didn't write about. We were both ready for school to start on Tuesday and couldn't wait to find out what we were going to learn this year. 1st Grade goes all day, so we knew we'd be busy.

Then we met Miss Ritter, and school wasn't fun at all.

We would sit in alphabetical order.

"G" is NOT next to "O."

We would not speak. Not to each other. Not to her. We were there to listen.

We would follow a "strict order of curriculum." There would be no "extra" or "advanced" lessons. Those whose skills are ahead of others from the old-fashioned teaching of Mrs. Harris would not advance any further until the rest of the class caught up.

No arithmetic games. No reading except for "Fun with Dick and Jane."

This included reading at home (but how am I supposed to find out what happens to Dick Tracy and Lil' Abner and Smokey Stover and everybody else?)

Mother thought Miss Ritter was an excellent teacher.

Miss Carmella subscribed to all three newspapers and went to school and got a list of books from Mrs. Harris that she could get for us from the library, and she complained to the principal, the people at the School Board, and the mayor's office. They told her that City Councilman Joe Ritter was Miss Ritter's father.

Marie and I hated Miss Ritter.

We hated school.

It was going to be a long year.

On Thanksgiving, Mother got up early to prepare dinner. We sat and waited until two o'clock for my grandparents, but they never came. I didn't miss them at all, but I missed all the smells from Miss Carmella's kitchen. They had gone to another relative's home. Mother threw all our food in the trash and said it was all dad's fault. We didn't eat that day. I helped Dad pick up his clothes from the sidewalk.

Dad spent nearly all his time in the basement. You could smell sawdust, varnish, and paint every time he came upstairs for meals. Mother stopped talking to him. Dad would wink at me every time he said something, and she didn't answer.

On the 2nd Sunday of Advent, Reverend and Mrs. Lehmann came for dinner. Mother apologized for the horrible smell coming from the basement. Rev. Lehmann asked Dad if he was building something. Dad invited him downstairs to see. A couple of minutes later, Rev. Lehmann called up the steps for Mrs. Lehmann to come and see. I tried to go down, too, but Mother hissed "Stop. Sit."

When they came back upstairs, Mrs. Lehmann said "You must be *so* proud to have such a handy husband! It looks like something from 'Good Housekeeping' magazine. I know it will look perfect after you've made the cushions for the furniture.

I recognized the look on Mother's face and backed away fast. Mrs.

Lehmann saw it, and she stepped back too.

Mother's face slowly relaxed and she said, "I haven't decided on the color or pattern, yet."

Dad said he'd have it done by Christmas so that her sister's family could stay for Christmas Eve *and* Christmas this year.

It rained clothes after they left.

CHAPTER SEVEN

The Train

On Christmas Eve morning, I couldn't wait for Aunt Sally to come.

By noon I couldn't wait so badly that Mother sent me over to Marie's so that I could be underfoot there.

Miss Carmella opened the door and laughed. "I heard, kid. C'mon in, Marie can help you be underfoot." She started to close the door, and stopped and yelled "Hey, Amico!"

Aunt Sally was there. "Bueno Natale, Pen Pal!" They hugged, kissed, and laughed. Uncle Bill came up the steps with a big silver metal box. "Where do you want it?" he huffed. Miss Carmella said "Huh?" and Aunt Sally laughed and said it was something for her for Christmas. They brought it into the kitchen and Uncle Bill scooped some ice out of the box and showed us a big slab of something. "Blue Fin Tuna," he said. "Game fishers just want a trophy, so if you know someone, you can get something. Fresh this morning at eight o'clock."

Aunt Sally and Miss Carmella went back and forth over how to cook it, what ingredients to buy at the grocery, and go next door to invite Freddie (and *her*, too) for dinner. While they cooked, Uncle Bill and Mr. Vince talked about the War. I never heard Uncle Bill talk so much before. At suppertime, Dad came over and ate with us. Mother didn't.

We didn't go back to our house until nine o'clock. Mother gave us her icy look and said "So, you finally remembered where I live?"

Aunt Sally snorted and said "Yeah, next door to my girlfriend."

Dad started coughing.

Christmas morning started with cornflakes and the tangerines in my stocking. When we exchanged gifts, Aunt Sally gave me a big book of Fairy

Tales. I remembered Miss Ritter saying, "no reading outside of class," so I knew it would go to Goodwill tomorrow.

Dad got a gift from Aunt Sally too. "For the Executive," she said. Dad smiled and peeled the paper off. The box had a picture of a train on it. When he opened it, there was a diesel engine, a boxcar, and a caboose. Each one said "B&O." Dad laughed and put the pieces of track together and wound up the engine and let it run. "Now I am the President of the Line," he said. When it stopped, I asked him to wind it up again.

Mother said that was enough noise and to put it away.

I asked Dad if he wanted me to take it downstairs. Mother said no.

I thought that maybe since it was Dad's, she wouldn't give it to Goodwill tomorrow.

The day after Christmas was always the same. Mother took all the decorations off the tree that had been bought Christmas Eve. Dad would put it next to the garbage can when he came home, and no trace of Christmas would be left.

Mother took my book and set it by the door to go to Goodwill. But then she put Dad's train there too.

"That belongs to Dad," I whispered.

"No," Mother said. "Your Aunt was trying to be funny."

"But that's Dad's," I said, a little bit louder.

She looked at me. "It's going to Goodwill. Be quiet."

"But it's Dad's!" I felt myself getting angry.

She slapped me. "That's enough. Don't talk back to me."

"No!," I shouted. "You give everything away!" She slapped me again. "Everybody else in the whole world gets to play with toys!" The slap made my ears ring, and I could taste blood. "I bet you never had toys when you were little and that's why-"

She hit me so hard that I fell and couldn't get up. She jerked me up off the floor and pushed me out the door and onto the porch. She grabbed my hair and twisted my head around to face her. "Never talk back to me again," she hissed. "You're going to stay out here and freeze all day and all night until you apologize."

"I won't!"

She drew her arm back to slap me again but stopped when the door opened, and Miss Carmella stepped out. "Hiya, Susie." She waved at no one across the street. Mother dropped her arm and didn't turn around to see who might be there. She looked at me. "You'll stay out here until your father comes home." She went inside and locked the door.

Miss Carmella leaned over the porch wall to look at me. "Jesus!"

"Leave her alone," Mother's voice warned her.

Miss Carmella snapped her thumbnail off her front teeth at our door and went inside her house. I felt all alone, but then she came outside again with Marie's coat and went back in and got an electric heater. She looked at our windows. Mother pulled the curtains closed.

Miss Carmella touched my cheek very gently. "I'm sorry, bambino, I know you don't understand, but this is all I can do." She kissed me on the forehead. "If you need to go to the bathroom, just come in." Marie was watching through their window. Miss Carmella went inside and told Marie "You can't" and closed the door.

Marie's coat and the heater made the outside of me warm, but *inside* I was on fire. It wasn't fair, it *never was* fair. She's mean to me and Dad and Aunt Sally and Miss Carmella and everyone. Why is she like that?

It was dark when Dad came home. He looked confused when he saw me there, then he tilted my head to the light. "Gott in Himmel." He sat on the porch wall. "What happened?"

I told him about his train and that it was his and she couldn't just give it away like she always does with my presents.

"Oh, Sally." He looked at our window. "How long have you been out here?"

"Since nine." Miss Carmella was leaning out of her door. She wasn't smiling at Dad like she usually did.

Dad looked at the window again. "How would you like to go out for dinner tonight?"

We hardly ever went out for dinner. "Okay," I said, "But this is Marie's coat."

Dad sighed and looked at the window again. Miss Carmella said, "If you're that damned afraid of her, she can wear Marie's coat."

Dad stood up straight, opened our door and went in. Mother started telling him "What really happened," but he just got my coat and came back outside. I gave Marie's coat back to Miss Carmella. She looked at Dad and said "She's tougher than she looks. I wonder where she gets it from?" Dad looked like he wanted to say something, but she closed the door. We could hear the bedroom window open above us.

At the White Coffee Pot restaurant on Eastern Avenue, the waitress looked at me, and then Dad. She took us to a booth in the back, and I wondered what my face looked like. When she gave Dad a menu, I said I could read too, and she smiled and gave me a menu.

One of the things that I saw was "Roast Turkey and Bread Stuffing w/ Gravy and Cranberry Sauce plus two sides." I was curious, and asked Dad if it was like Mother's. He said no, so I tried it. It was good! We had cornbread instead of rolls. It's like cake, but not as sweet and it has butter instead of icing. I liked that too, and Dad said it's made differently in every part of the country.

We talked while we ate. Mother never let me speak when we ate. After we finished eating, Dad was quiet and looked down at the table. "I'm not a very good father, am I?"

He looked like he wanted to cry, so I reached over and patted his hand and said "There, there," like in a book that Aunt Sally had read to Billy and I in the summer. He tried to smile.

When we got home, Miss Carmella had folded Dad's clothes and left them in her laundry basket on the porch. Dad said to go upstairs and get a bath and go right to bed, and that it was good there was no school this week. I saw what he meant when I looked in the mirror. Wow.

"But I'm tougher than I look," I whispered.

And I NEVER apologized.

CHAPTER EIGHT

Aunt Viv

When we got back to school from Christmas vacation, there was a different teacher in the classroom. "Mrs. Hampden" was written on the blackboard. When the bell rang, everybody raised their hands and started yelling questions.

"Where's Miss Ritter?" "Is she sick?" "Is she gonna be sick for a long time?" Mac MacTavish yelled "Is she dead?"

Mrs. Hampden coughed like Dad did. "Miss Ritter won't be your teacher anymore—" We all yelled "YAY!" Mrs. Hampden raised her voice. "Quiet, please! Everyone please be quiet." She whispered, "Hoo boy" and rolled her eyes. "Now then, Miss Ritter has a new job as Vice Principal in another school and won't be coming back—*no more noise*, please!" She took a deep breath. "I will be your teacher for the rest of this year. I think that we will need some catching up– ""It's not our fault!," Mac MacTavish yelled. Mrs. Hampden frowned. "That's enough. For the next few days, we will find out what we need to work on."

Marie was waving her hand. "Can I sit next to Sal again?"

Mrs. Hampden laughed this time. "After I call the roll, we'll probably rearrange things." She sat on the corner of her desk. "Alright, kids, I shouldn't say this, but I know you're all happy she's gone, but you're probably not going to like ME very much, either, because I'm going to make you work so hard and give you so much homework that when school stops for the summer, you'll all have headaches for two weeks from all the things you had to learn for next year." We were all quiet now. "Don't worry, it's not as bad as it sounds."

It *was* hard, but she was a good teacher.

And Marie and I sat next to each other again.

Winter ended and Spring came, and Marie and I always brought home report cards that said "A" and "Excellent." The weather got warmer and stickier, and summer vacation was finally here!

When Marie and I came home on the last day of school, Aunt Sally and Miss Carmella were waiting for us on the porch. "You're early!" I said. "I thought you weren't coming down till Saturday."

"Well, I'm here early so I can have some more time with you. Miss Carmella let me know when school ended, and she told your father I'd be here." Aunt Sally and Miss Carmella grinned at each other. "And now I'll tell Susan."

Marie sat on the porch and waited with me while Aunt Sally packed my suitcase and argued with Mother.

"You wanted her gone in summer, Susan. This all started with you. Well, I'm not giving her up. She's mine till school starts."

"You only want her because you can't have another child of your own," Mother hissed.

"Oh, I thought that was what you told Freddie when you cut him off."

"Keep your voice down. I don't want that woman next door to hear you."

"She's mine in the summer, Susan. Somebody has to give her love. Mother and Father never showed us any, and God knows that's the truth."

"Maybe for you. Not me."

Aunt Sally snorted. "You probably believe that. Never mind. I'll just pack her bag and take her home."

"*This* is her home," Mother hissed.

I felt like I was doing something wrong by listening to them. Aunt Sally came out with my suitcase. Marie and I hugged and kissed and so did Aunt Sally and Miss Carmella. Aunt Sally said they all should come down too, and Marie and I yelled "Yeah!"

"Nah," Miss Carmella said. "Vince would be up all-night waiting for his sharks to break into the house." She looked at Marie. "But maybe I'll send this one down sometime."

Aunt Sally told her to just say when.

When we drove away, I started thinking about all that I had heard, and I didn't say much. "What's the matter, Honey? Don't you want to come down this year?"

"Yes!," I hurried to answer. "I want to go home with you!"

Aunt Sally looked at me and pulled the car over. "Okay, Hon, we've got plenty of time. Do you want to tell me now?"

I slid over and sat next to her. "She doesn't want me, does she?"

Aunt Sally sighed. "I grew up in a rowhouse, too. I should know how sound carries." She held me. "Okay, I won't make any excuses. I think she wanted to be a mother because I was going to be. What else did you hear?"

"You can't have any more kids."

"Boy, you got it all, didn't you? No, Hon, I wanted more, but... well, it's a doctor thing. I'll explain it to you when you're older. There's other things you'll have to learn first, but I *will* tell you."

There was one more thing, and I really wanted to say it the right way. "When I'm Downeyoshun with you, can I be your little girl?"

Aunt Sally held me tight, and I could feel my hair getting wet from her tears. "You already are, Honey. You already are."

When we got home, Uncle Bill was waiting there with Billy. We went down to the Boardwalk and ate Rib Eye sandwiches at the Alaska Stand. We sat in front of the Wurlitzer and Aunt Sally explained that it was just a big music box with an electric motor and a bellows that pushed air into the organ pipes and made the drum and cymbals bang. I had thought it had somebody inside playing it like the organ at church. I wished I had one, but Mother would just give it to Goodwill.

The radio was different this year. It had less stories and more music. But that was okay because we all liked to read books.

But the biggest thing that happened that summer was a week later. Billy's Aunt Viv "hit town like a hurricane!" Well, that's what Granny Annie said.

Aunt Sally was cooking dinner when a lady came to the door and yelled "Hey in there, Ding Dong, it's the Avon Lady!"

Aunt Sally laughed and turned the stove down low and said "Well, don't just stand there, come on in! How about supper with us?"

The lady came inside and hugged and kissed Aunt Sally, and turned to Uncle Bill with her hands on her hips and yelled "Well? You gonna give your big sister a hug and a kiss?"

Uncle Bill just grinned and said, "Wash that crap off your face first."

The lady did something I had NEVER seen a grownup do before: she pulled her mouth wide, stuck her tongue out and crossed her eyes at him. I laughed so hard I had to run for the bathroom. I could hear her yelling at Uncle Bill. "Crap? Crap? This 'crap' paid for my house and my car and these clothes, Buster, *and* is putting my baby girl through college. This 'crap' has made me the Regional Sales Director for Avon in D.C., Northern Virginia, and Southern Maryland. The only 'crap' I see around here is that stuff between your ears!"

I came out of the bathroom and watched her grab Uncle Bill and kiss him. Then she yelled "Where's the brat?" Billy was trying to sneak into his room. He looked scared. "There he is!," and she almost jumped across the room and grabbed him and started kissing him all over his face while he screamed "NOOO!"

"Whaddya mean 'no'? Don'tcha love me no more?" and kissed him even more. He finally got away from her. He had her lipstick all over his face. "Boy, look at all those kisses!" she said. "The girls are going to see those and want to give you even more!"

"MOM!" Billy ran over to Aunt Sally, and she started to wipe his face with a dish towel while she laughed.

Then the lady was in front of me. She looked like a movie star in the magazines at the beauty parlor, only bigger and strong. She had big shoulders and lots of muscles in her arms. She picked me up and held me at arm's length and turned me this way and that way and said, "You must be whatshername's kid."

"No ma'am," I said. "I belong to Aunt Sally in the summer."

She looked surprised and said "Well! I stand corrected. And I like you already. You can call me Aunt Viv." Then she kissed me the way she kissed

Billy, and I started laughing again. She flipped me under her arm and pulled a chair from under the table, plopped me onto her lap, and leaned back on the chair legs and made it creak. "When do we eat?"

Aunt Sally laughed some more. "Soon," she told her. "How long are you in town for?"

"Two weeks. I'm staying at Mom's. It'll be the first vacation I've had in years, but with my promotion I'm finally able to take some time off for myself."

During supper, Uncle Bill reached over and squeezed her arm. She smacked his hand away. "Don't you worry, Buster, I can still beat you at arm wrestling. The YWCA in Georgetown has a pool, and I use it every evening."

"Did you get all those muscles from swimming?" I asked her.

She laughed. "Yep. You know how to swim?"

"No, ma'am."

She looked at Billy. "How about him?"

"Teach them Bayside. Not the ocean."

"Tomorrow morning, then. I'll come over with Mom and get 'em in training. They'll be as good as Johnny Weissmuller in a week and swimming the Channel in two."

When Aunt Sally tucked me in that night, I asked "Is Aunt Viv a good swimmer?"

Aunt Sally snorted. "She sure is. She swam on the American Olympic Team in 1936."

I didn't know what that was, but it sounded important. "Did she win?"

Aunt Sally kissed me goodnight. "You can ask her all about it in the morning."

Aunt Viv came over with Granny Annie the next morning. She pulled both of us out of our beds. "Rise and shine! Lots to do and lots to learn!"

We ate breakfast, and then she started. She made us lie down on the floor and pulled our arms and legs to where she wanted them and had us move them back and forth. Billy said, "I thought we were going swimming?"

"We are," she said. "You're learning the backstroke, the easiest stroke to learn. Keep moving." She watched us and changed the way we moved a little, and she finally said "Okay, bathing suits on and let's go!"

She had a little red car with no roof and only two seats. "C'mon, get in, let's go! Sally sits on Billy's lap on the way there, and you can switch on the way back!"

We drove up Ocean Highway until we didn't see any more houses. "Here looks good." She spun the car around fast and parked on the sandy grass. She took off her dress and there was a swimsuit under it. We walked down to the water on the bay and waited while she waded and slowly felt around with her feet. She pulled up pieces of a broken beer bottle once and tossed them 'way out into the water. "Right. Out here with me."

The water was still cold. "Now," she said. "Deep breath, and—" She lay down on her back on top of the water like she was lying down on a bed with her arms and legs spread.

She raised her head, swept her arms behind her, and stood up. "You try."

We did, but we got water up our noses and sank. We kept trying and finally got it. "Now, breathe while you're floating." More water up our noses, but we got that right too. "Now, remember what we did on the floor?"

More water and more sinking, but then we got it, and we were swimming!

We swam back and forth the rest of the morning until we were both shivering, and our lips turned blue. Aunt Viv sent us up on the grass to warm up and dry out. "Stay put. Don't wander off." She started swimming farther out and faster and faster. I bet a boat couldn't catch her!

She finally came back and got out grinning and huffing, and the muscles on her arms and legs were really BIG! She sat down next to us and leaned back on her elbows. "I learned to swim down here in the bay when I was younger than you two. I loved it then and I still love it today." She smiled at the water. "Better than a pool."

I remembered what Aunt Sally said last night. "What's the American Olympic Team?"

Aunt Viv laughed. "The Olympics are sports that are played every four years. Only the best from every country can play to see who's the best in the whole world."

"Were you the best?"

"I was *one* of the best in America and I got invited to go to the Games in 1936—and don't ask how old I was 'cause I was only twenty and now I'm forty-one, so don't ask me." She laughed. "The Games were held in Germany that year. Berlin." She frowned. "Ugly city. Swastikas everywhere. People in Nazi Uniforms."

"Nazis?" Billy asked. "Like in the war?"

"Yep. But this was before the war. They were still trying to pretend they were nice."

"Did you see Hitler?" Billy asked.

"DID I? You bet I did! He snuck up behind me and pinched me right on my fanny!"

"He did?" I asked.

"Yep, he sure did. I got so mad at him I grabbed him by his moustaches, and I pulled the left one off and then the right one and all he had left was the little fuzzy part in the middle like you see in the pictures!"

Billy was giggling. "Whatcha do with them?"

"I gave them to two little puppy dogs who didn't have any tails and from then on, every time they saw Hitler, their tails would go—" and she raised her arm up in a Nazi salute.

"No, you didn't!" I was laughing now.

She put her nose up to mine and said in a funny voice "Vas you dere, Sharlie?" (*) She had a HUGE laugh![*From vaudeville and radio comedian Jack Pearl. Pearl portrayed Baron Munchhausen, and when he was called on for the truth of his fabulous tales by his straight man, he would reply with this tag line.]

She looked up at the sky and pulled us up on our feet. "Let's go home and get some lunch!"

On the way back, I asked "Did you win?"

"Nope. Closest I got was fourth place in the 400-meter freestyle. The other girls were—" she snapped her fingers. "- that much faster than me.

But I'm still an Olympian and still the only girl from little Ocean City that ever went to *any* Olympics. Nobody else here can say that." She smiled and looked proud.

When we got home, we went around to the back to get washed off with the hose and were sent inside to get dressed while she washed. Granny Annie looked out the door when we came in. "Vivian! VIVIAN! For Pete's sake!" We heard Aunt Viv laughing, and the lady from the rental house next door yelled something. Aunt Viv yelled back "Oh, yeah? Well, you know what, Sister? There's a whole beach right over that hill. Why don't you go pound sand up your -"

"VIVIAN!" Granny Annie was scolding her. "Get in here! Running around like that at your age! And the kids probably heard you, too."

"Running around like what?" Billy asked.

"Never you mind! And stay in there! Tomorrow I'll hang some sheets on the clothes lines when you get back home!"

Aunt Viv had the biggest laugh in the whole world!

Every day we would learn a new swimming stroke. We thought we were good enough to swim in the Ocean, but Aunt Viv said no. "The edge of the surf is close enough. You can feel the water trying to pull you in." A couple of days later, she brought in a newspaper that said, "Lifeguard Drowns." We didn't ask after that.

I asked Aunt Viv lots of questions: Are you married? "Yep, but he died in the war. I figure he's in Heaven, 'cause he's too ornery for the devil to try and keep him." Did he swim, too? "Yep, he swam for LSU and was on the men's Olympic team." Do you have any kids? "Yep, I got a daughter that's a Mermaid." I thought she was joking, but she showed me a photograph. "Adrienne has a summer job down in Florida at Crystal Lake. She wears a mermaid suit and swims around for all the 'Lookie-Loos'. That means tourists." Is she an Olympian too? "Wants to be. Came close to making the team last year. We'll see what happens in 1960." Do you think I could be an Olympian? That made her grin, and she poked me in the ribs. "That's up to you. It's hard work, don't think it isn't, and a lot never make it. But if you want to try—DO IT!"

On the last day of her vacation, she came "dressed to the nines," Granny Annie said, and chased Billy and I for kisses. I told her something I had thought about for a couple of days. "I want to be like you when I grow up." She looked at me and was quiet for the first time in two weeks. "Y'know, Honey, that's the nicest and best thing anybody ever said to me. I hope I deserve it." She gave me a big hug, and then told all of us "I won't make promises for next year, so maybe I'll be here, maybe not. We'll see."

She got into her little car and drove away.

CHAPTER NINE

Back in Baltimore (darn it)

Mother and Dad came down at the end of August, and Dad and Uncle Bill built a "two-stall cold water shower" on the back of the house out of scrap Teak wood from one of the boat yards. I got to help this time. I dug the "Footers" and learned how to mix concrete. Mother complained about my hands every chance she could.

Vacation was over, and we had to go back to Baltimore. At least Marie was there.

While I was away, Marie had started Catechism classes. That's when her Church teaches kids about God and Jesus and Mary and everything. She was supposed to go to St. Leo's, but something happened.

Marie said when Miss Carmella took her to get enrolled, one of the old Nuns came up to Miss Carmella and slapped Marie in the face and said, "That's because she's yours." Marie says Sister Jonata was her mother's teacher when she was a kid, and Miss Carmella got into trouble for saying "If you're a Bride of Christ, I bet He wants a divorce." Miss Carmella said that teachers like her were why Marie goes to public school. Marie says there was a BIG fight with the Priest, and another one with Mr. Vince, and an even bigger one with everybody else in her family, and that's why Miss Carmella and Marie go to Sacred Heart of Jesus right up the street now.

Some other things had changed too. Mr. Vince bought a Television set. Miss Carmella says it was so he could yell at the Orioles and the Colts at home instead of the VFW. I'd seen them in store windows, and lots of people have them, but theirs was the first one I got to sit and watch. I don't know if I like it or not. There're cartoons, but everyone keeps getting hurt. I like Laurel and Hardy sometimes until they get mad at each other. But I

LOVE Harpo and Senor Wences and Victor Borge and Peter Pan with all the singing, and I really, *really* liked Amahl and the Night Visitors when it came on at Christmas. But I think I still liked the radio best. Things look better when you hear them.

Mother says TVs are common and we will never own one.

Marie and I were in the 2nd Grade now, and Mrs. Hampden is still our teacher. When we saw her on the first day, Mac MacTavish thought we had all failed 1st Grade and had to do it over, but Mrs. Hampden says she usually taught 2nd Grade and last year was just an emergency. The big thing we learned that year was cursive writing by the "Palmer Method." Marie and I think the only thing it's good for is to read the "Babar the Elephant" books.

There was a colored girl in our class. Her name was Doris Johnson, and she didn't talk a lot, and only a few kids talked to her besides Marie and I. She was in our reading group, and Marie would tell her to read louder, and that even I didn't whisper anymore, but she was still always quiet. When some boy called her a name, she just looked at the floor. Mother hated that she was in our class. Mrs. Hampden told her at the first PTA meeting that the world was changing and to get used to it like most of us kids were doing. Mother never went to another PTA meeting that year.

I really wanted to go swimming again, and Miss Carmella said that the YWCA used the Patterson High School pool, and that she would ask about joining for me and Marie. Mother said that was "out of the question" for people like us. Dad said YWCA meant Young Women's Christian Association, and what was wrong with that? Mother looked at me and sent me out of the room, but I could hear her say that those places were full of Lizbonians. Dad said what do the Portuguese have to do with anything, and Mother went upstairs, and I heard the window open. I looked in the living room and Dad was grinning. He told me that we'd work something out and not worry about it.

Thanksgiving was like last year. Marie's family went to another relative's home again, but she said it would be their turn again next year. Mother got up and cooked, but my grandparents didn't show up. We waited only until one o'clock this time, then Mother got up, told Dad this was all his fault, took all the food off the table and threw it in the garbage can. We could hear her throwing other stuff out too, like the dishes, pots, and pans. Dad peeked in the kitchen and told me at least we wouldn't have to eat leftovers. He told me to get our coats and he would take me to get something to eat "somewhere."

We found out that the White Coffee Pot is open on Thanksgiving.

CHAPTER TEN

The "Y"

A few days before Christmas that year, Miss Carmella told me that Aunt Sally would be coming up without Uncle Bill this year. He was working for another man whose baby was having his first Christmas. Mother had never said anything, and I wondered if she even knew. I think Miss Carmella was the only one that Aunt Sally wrote to. Miss Carmella said Mr. Vince would miss talking to Uncle Bill.

When Aunt Sally and Billy arrived on Christmas Eve, Mother opened the door and hissed "Why don't you stay with your friend? You don't want to see me anyway." Miss Carmella grinned at her and said "Okay, Susie. I'll put them up if you ain't got the room." Mother yanked the suitcase out of Aunt Sally's hand and brought it into our house and slammed the door. Aunt Sally and Miss Carmella laughed, and we went inside their home. This year the silver box had swordfish in it. Dad came over for supper. Mother didn't.

For Christmas, Aunt Sally gave me a membership to the YWCA! I'll be able to swim every Saturday!

Mother said Aunt Sally wasted her money because she wasn't going to take me, but Miss Carmella said that *she* would because she got Marie a membership so she could learn how to swim and come Downeyshun too! Mother is really mad at Aunt Sally and said a lot of nasty things to her, but Dad said I was going to go anyway, and now she's mad at him too. And I don't care, because now Marie and I are both going Downeyoshun in the summer! And maybe we'll both be on the American Olympic team, too.

Well, I almost didn't get to go to the YWCA. Mother kept thinking up more reasons that I couldn't.

First, she said she couldn't find my bathing suit. But Dad had already asked Miss Carmella to buy me a new one from Monkey Wards when she got Marie's.

Then she said she didn't have time to go downtown to get my membership, so Dad took a day off work and took me.

And then she said that Dr. Dobihal told her that public pools were full of diseases and that HE said I couldn't go. Dad said he didn't care if it was the Pool of Bethesda in the Bible and was filled with the halt, the blind and the lame— *I* was going to go swimming. When Mother started going upstairs, Dad told her to just throw the clothes down the steps instead of outside and not make the bedroom any colder than it already was. That made her even madder, and she broke a window when she threw Dad's shoes through it. Dad only looked at his watch and said that the hardware store was closed now, and then he looked at the front page of the newspaper and said it was going to be 38 degrees outside tonight, but it was warm in his basement. Then he sat in the living room and watched his clothes come down. I went upstairs and was quiet.

I was teaching Marie different strokes on the floor, just like Aunt Viv taught me. Miss Carmella said if she dipped Marie in soapy water, she could clean the floor. Teaching Marie made me feel like Aunt Viv. I'd write her a letter and tell her so.

On the first Saturday morning we went swimming, I was careful not to say anything or do anything that would make Mother madder than she already was. Dad shooed me out the door when she went to the bathroom. I climbed over the porch wall, and Marie and Miss Carmella were waiting with their coats on inside their door, so we all ran down the street as quick and quiet as we could.

Pools smell like Clorox, but they're a lot warmer than the ocean.

There was a kind of balcony above the pool with benches on it, and Miss Carmella sat up there and watched us swim. Marie "caught the rhythm" faster than I had. We swam back and forth at the shallow end of the pool until our fingers and toes were all wrinkly and our eyes were red, and our legs were shaky. It was great! Miss Carmella took us to Arundel's for ice cream, and then home. Marie and I sat on the sofa while Miss Carmella made lunch, but we fell asleep before she was finished.

When I woke up, I heard her talking to Dad outside. "Tell Susie nobody ever died from my cooking, and she should come over sometime and try it. We eat at six, and you can come over earlier if you want." She laughed a little and said, "Here. One of your socks was on our porch."

When she came back in, she looked at us and laughed some more. "You two got hair like a rat's nest." She grinned at me and whispered "Next Saturday. Same time. Right?"

I grinned back. "Right!"

CHAPTER ELEVEN

Summer and Sharks

Marie and I went swimming every Saturday for longer and longer, until Miss Carmella finally just gave us a nickel and told us to call her when we were ready to come home. The only weekend we missed was when we had the blizzard. We made a snowman, and tried to make an igloo, but it wasn't as much fun as swimming (and it was a lot colder!)

Marie and I lost our front teeth the same day at suppertime. She lost her teeth chewing on a crusty piece of bread, and I lost mine on a piece of Mother's roast beef. Dad looked at me and said, "I thought the meat was tough" and started laughing and couldn't stop. Mother got up and took our plates away. When we got to school the next day, Mrs. Hampden looked at us and said "Bookends."

All Spring, our baby teeth kept falling out and new teeth grew in. My front teeth had sort of nubbly edges on them, and when Mother did her nails, she would look at me and rub her thumb across her nail file. I stayed away from her as much as I could.

Marie had her First Holy Communion, and Dad and I went to her party. Dad had made her a puzzle box for a present. It was made of all kinds of different colored wood, and you had to slide some parts and turn other parts to open it. Dad showed her the first two steps, and then handed it to her. He told Marie she could put jewelry and stuff inside of it— once she figured out how.

It took her almost an hour. Miss Carmella said that Dad had "missed his calling." I think she meant Dad should have been a carpenter like Aunt Sally said.

The weather got warmer and warmer, and Marie and I were counting the days till school was out and we could go down to Aunt Sally's. I hoped that Aunt Viv would be there so she could teach us more swimming.

The night before we were supposed to go, Mr. Vince said he'd changed his mind, and he didn't want Marie to go and get eaten by a shark. He and Miss Carmella got into a big fight, and I could hear Marie crying. Mother sat in the living room with a mean smile on her face and made this awful-sounding noise. She was laughing. It sounded so ugly, I ran upstairs and put my pillow over my head. Dad told her that she should pray to God for forgiveness and went down to the basement.

I went out on the porch the next morning after breakfast with my suitcase to wait for Aunt Sally. Marie came out, and I climbed over to her side and hugged her. Miss Carmella watched us, and then disappeared for a little while, and came outside with Marie's suitcase. We looked at her, and she said "You're going. I'll settle it with your father when he comes home. Him and his damned sharks."

We were happy, but we both felt a little scared too. When Aunt Sally and Billy got there, Aunt Sally looked at Miss Carmella and asked, "Is everything okay?" Miss Carmella said "Ahh, Vince wanted to change his mind, but I'm not letting him ruin her summer." Aunt Sally looked at her again, and Miss Carmella said "It's fine. Better get going," and hugged and kissed us all.

On the way home to Ocean City, we all talked about what we had done that year. Billy was reading at the 6th grade level, Aunt Sally was going to teach Summer School instead of working at the Diner, and Uncle Bill had taken a test and was a Lieutenant in the Fire Department. Aunt Sally looked at us in the rear-view mirror and said "Marie. Your dad's going to be mad, isn't he?"

Marie looked down and nodded. "Yes, ma'am. Pop's really afraid of sharks. He won't say why."

Aunt Sally sighed. "I might be taking you back tomorrow."

Marie nodded. "Yes ma'am."

When we got home, Uncle Bill was waiting on the porch. "Vince called. Coming down in the morning. Wanted to come tonight." Aunt Sally said

"Sorry, Bill." He looked at us and shrugged. "Water under the bridge. Let's eat."

We ate cold fried chicken and salads like we usually do on the first day home. Aunt Sally asked Uncle Bill if he knew "why" about Mr. Vince and sharks. He told her yeah and that she really didn't want to know about it. Then he looked at us and smiled a little. "Finish up and we'll go to the boardwalk."

The sun was still up, and the tide was high, and Marie just wanted to sit on a bench and watch and listen to the waves. Billy and I sat next to her. "You're not going to get punished, are you?" he asked. Marie looked down "I don't know." Billy held her hand. "I don't like girls" he told her. "But I like you." Marie smiled a little, and then started to giggle, and so did we.

Voices woke us up in the morning.

"Oh my God, what time did you leave this morning?"

"We couldn't sleep, so we just got in the car and drove."

"HE couldn't sleep. Sally, can I have some coffee? Please?"

"Where's she?"

Mr. Vince came into my room, picked up Marie and carried her out.

"Pop, you're squeezing too tight."

"Jeez, Vince, she's okay. Let her breathe."

I got up, went to the bathroom, got dressed, and made my bed. Marie came back in and whispered: "I don't think I'm getting punished."

We had pancakes with fresh strawberries and scrapple for breakfast. Mr. Vince had never had scrapple before and wanted to know what it was. Uncle Bill said don't ask, and Mr. Vince nodded and said, "Just like Navy chow."

Nobody talked a lot.

After breakfast, Aunt Sally gave Billy a deck of cards and told him to go out on the porch and teach us how to play Gin Rummy. They all went out the back and sat around the picnic table behind the rental house next door.

Playing cards is a lot like arithmetic. I won the most hands.

We heard them come back inside, and Mr. Vince came out and knelt next to Marie.

"You're staying" he told her. "Uncle Sal and Aunt Rose will bring you back home in a couple weeks like we planned. But NO SWIMMING in the ocean. Or the bay."

Marie nodded her head so hard I could hear her neck bones crackle. She hugged him. "Thanks, Pop."

Aunt Sally said we would go with her in the mornings, and she'd leave us with the lifeguard at the Santa Maria Hotel and we'd swim in their pool, and then she'd bring us home when classes ended at noon. Miss Carmella asked why the hotel would let us swim there, and Uncle Bill laughed and said "I'm the Fire Marshall. They owe me a favor."

Miss Carmella and Mr. Vince stayed for the weekend. It was quiet, but nobody was mad or scared or anything, so we just had a nice time.

Before we fell asleep that night, Marie and I could hear Uncle Bill and Mr. Vince talking on the porch about the war. Mr. Vince said "Bill. Gotta ask you. You're a Marine. Made a lot of landings and all that. And you're living... well, you're kinda living on a beachhead. Don't it bother you?"

Uncle Bill didn't say anything, then he said "Sometimes. Sometimes if I go down to the boardwalk, daytime. All those people lying there. Not moving. Yeah, sometimes it bothers me. But up here, no. No. This is home. This is home."

I didn't understand all of it, but he was right: this was home.

The first two weeks Marie stayed went by so fast. Most days Aunt Sally would take us to the pool, but sometimes she had teacher's meetings to go to, and Granny Annie would take us. The first time she came, Marie called her Miss Annie, but Granny Annie put her hands on her hips and leaned over with a fake frown and said "That's GRANNY Annie to you, MISS Marie. Humph! You'll have people thinking I'm a stranger from somewheres else."

We raced each other at the pool every day. Who won depended on what stroke we did. Billy was best with the butterfly, Marie with the backstroke, and I with the breaststroke. We all wished Aunt Viv was there.

Marie's Uncle Sal, Aunt Rose, and her cousins Vinnie, Tony and Johnny came on Saturday afternoon to get Marie and take her to their hotel for the third week. Marie asked Aunt Sally if she could stay just a few more days, and her cousins yelled "Yeah! Can she?" Aunt Sally said it was okay with her, and where were they staying? When they said The Santa Maria, Marie told them that's where we went swimming every day and if she stayed with us, she'd still see them and PLEEESE could she stay? Her cousins yelled "Let her stay!," and Aunt Sally and Marie's Aunt Rose called Miss Carmella LONG DISTANCE, and she said okay.

And right then, AUNT VIV banged on the door and yelled "Ding Dong!" and I knew it was going to be the best week ever!

When we got to the pool the next morning, Aunt Viv was already there. She was talking to Miss Jenny, the pool lifeguard.

"'Olympic Pool,' Jenny?" She was laughing. "'Olympic'?"

Miss Jenny was laughing too. "It doesn't say anything about size, Viv. It just looks good on the sign." She pointed to us. "Your 'team' is here."

Aunt Viv had a whistle and a big watch hanging around her neck on strings. She blew the whistle. "Alright, in line, heads up, shoulders back and tummies in." We started laughing. She looked at Marie. "Trying out for the team, huh? In the pool and show me what you got."

Marie swam back and forth doing everything I taught her.

"Okay, out." Aunt Viv pulled Marie out with one hand. I told Marie she was strong.

Aunt Viv sat on a lounge chair and looked at us. "I'm off ONE week, so we'll have to work hard and learn as much as we can." Miss Jenny laughed and said "Yes, Coach." Aunt Viv laughed too, and then looked serious. "What I'm going to do is teach you how to work together as a team, and... well, maybe relive the 'glory days' a little, same as I did when I taught my Adrienne how to swim."

"She's the mermaid" I whispered to Marie.

"First things first," Aunt Viv stood up. "Down to the deep end. You're going to learn how to dive-in the right way and the safe way, and that always means *only* diving in at the deep end."

By the end of the morning, our fronts were sore from all the "belly flops" we did, and it didn't feel like a lot of fun until Aunt Viv showed us how much faster we were, diving, instead of just pushing off the side of the pool. The next day, we learned how to turn around underwater when we reached the end of the pool. All week, we raced each other, and together as a relay team, and the best thing was when we raced some teenaged boys, and we won by a whole lap. When we did that, Miss Jenny cheered and clapped. "What d'ya think, Viv? 1968 or '72?"

We all laughed, but maybe one day, we *might* be on the Olympic team.

Neat o!

CHAPTER TWELVE

Sick

Marie went home with her aunt and Uncle, and Mother and Dad came down a month later, and two weeks after that we were back in hot, smelly, dirty, noisy Baltimore. At least I had Marie again.

Mrs. McGonigle was our teacher in 3rd grade. She kept Marie and I after school on the first day. She said she didn't know what to do with us because we were so far ahead of everybody else in Arithmetic. I guess she was right, because we could do fractions and decimals and change them back and forth (that's called "converting") and we could do it in our heads instead of having to figure them out on paper. Mrs. McGonigle said that in her class, we had to write everything, not just the answer. We told her that it was too slow, but she said if we did it her way, she'd get us mathematics books for older kids.

Marie and I spend almost all our time together. Sometimes I think the only time I was home was to eat and sleep. Mother didn't care as long as nobody "important" said anything to her (but she still didn't like Marie and her family).

One Saturday after swimming, Miss Carmella took Marie and I to the movies. I'd never been to a movie theatre before. They didn't have commercials like they did on Marie's TV.

We saw "Bambi." It was funny sometimes and scary sometimes. There was a part that made me feel weird inside. Bambi's mother got shot, and his father told him that his mother couldn't be with him anymore. Kids all over the theatre started crying, and Marie was crying too.

But I didn't cry.

Miss Carmella was hugging Marie, and she looked at me and said "Hey, bambino, come on over this side." She hugged me and she whispered that Marie loved me, and she loved me, and my dad loved me, and Aunt Sally loved me, and I thought about how I would feel if something ever happened to any of them.

And then I cried.

In October, a lot of kids in school got chicken pox. Marie and I got all the red spots and blisters the same day. Mother didn't say anything, but I knew she was mad. She put socks over my hands so I couldn't scratch, but then she took one off and traced my hand on a piece of paper. "I am going out" she said. "You will control yourself and not itch or scratch until I return."

When she got back, she unwrapped a pair of thin white gloves and told me to put them on. They looked like the kind of long gloves rich ladies wore in the movies on TV. She left me alone for a minute and came back with her sewing box. She sat down and looked at me. "You are eight" she said. "It is time you learned to sew."

Every day for ten days, she showed me how to measure, cut, baste, sew, and embroider. I watched her hands do all of it so easily, and I thought of all the clothes she made for herself and me.

She seemed different when she was sewing. It was the first time I had ever wanted to be with her. She told me there was a "sewing circle" at Church on Tuesday nights, and when I was better, I would start going with her.

One afternoon, I was watching her hands sew buttonholes— each one the same size as the next. I don't know why I did it, but I reached out and touched her arm.

She didn't stop sewing or even look at me, she just twitched my hand off like it was a fly.

I never, ever touched her again.

Thanksgiving that year was... well...

Miss Carmella was up early, and everything started to smell good, and I wondered what kind of food they'd be eating that year— especially when everybody else got there. More and more people came, and it was noisy again, too. Mother was quiet in the kitchen. At noon, Dad and I heard

Mother in the dining room, and we went in. Mother was sitting there with a bowl of tomato soup and a cheese sandwich and a cup of coffee. She ignored us.

Dad and I looked at each other and got our coats and left. We said "Happy Thanksgiving" to all the men on Marie's porch and walked up the street to the White Coffee Pot. About halfway there, Dad started laughing. When I asked what was funny, he said that Mother had probably cooked the best Thanksgiving meal of her life. I laughed too, but I don't think I should have.

At least Dad's clothes weren't on the sidewalk when we got home.

Mrs. McGonigle started teaching us extra mathematics during recess. That was fine with us, because it was cold outside. We learned about square roots and cube roots and "powers" (which just means a way to multiply until you get HUGE numbers). She said if we don't slow down, we'll have to learn geometry next, and that's all about measuring different shapes like triangles, rectangles, circles, and stuff. She said she wonders what we'll do with all of it when we grow up. Marie and I don't know either, but at least it's fun. Maybe we'll find jobs doing mathematics. Maybe we'll be teachers like Aunt Sally.

The Saturday before Christmas, Dad took us to Hausner's Restaurant for supper. We had to wait outside for almost an hour, and Mother stood and tapped her foot the whole time. I had always thought Hausner's was some kind of store, because it didn't look like any restaurant I'd ever seen from the outside. It didn't look like a restaurant inside either. There were statues and paintings all over the place, like the museum our class went to in the 2nd grade. The waitress took us to a table in a corner where two gigantic paintings were. One looked like Friar Tuck in Robin Hood, and the other was a lady. Friar Tuck was drinking beer in a big mug and laughing, and the lady was naked. She looked a little fat, but pretty.

Mother kept telling me to stop looking at the paintings and all the other stuff. Then she told the waitress that we had to sit at a different table away from all the filth. The waitress told her if we wanted another table, we'd have to stand outside again.

Dad grinned at me and said, "Do you know why we are here tonight?" Mother said "Shh." Dad ignored her. "Your Dad has received his master's degree in business administration." Mother said "Shh" a little louder.

I knew what a degree was, because Mother had hers in a frame in the living room. I asked Dad when he went to college. He said he'd gotten his Batchelor's Degree just before I was born, and that he'd taken night and weekend courses since then, and now he was finished. Mother started to hiss at Dad. "No one needs to know any of this, please be quiet." Dad just kept grinning and said he didn't think he had done too badly for a farm boy. Mother kicked him under the table. Dad only turned away and said he was now qualified to do the job he already had. Mother picked up her fork and looked like she was going to poke him with it, but the waitress came back and asked what we wanted to eat. Mother said we had changed our minds, and we were leaving, but Dad said he'd have the Westphalian Ham with spaetzle and red cabbage, and a pint of Dortmunder.

Mother got up and walked out. The waitress ignored her. "What about you, Honey?" she asked. I looked at the menu quickly and saw "fil-et mignon," and asked what that was. The waitress smiled and said it was a small steak. Dad said "Perfect! She will have that, medium, and a baked potato, and... hmm... peas?"

"Okay" I said. "And a glass of milk too, please."

"Got it" she said, winked at me, and left.

I sat with Dad for a while and then I said "Congratulations." Dad laughed and said thank you.

I thought about what Mother had just done and asked Dad what was the matter with her, and why wasn't she happy that he got a degree? Dad said Mother wanted people to think that he'd always been to college and was an important person at work.

Dad started talking about growing up on a farm, and what Amish were, and how he got picked to be an officer in the Army and came to Baltimore and started working for the B&O, and going to college, and when he first met Mother.

But then he stopped talking, and I didn't ask any more questions.

At the Church Christmas Bazaar, Mother bought a big box of Christmas tree ornaments from Mrs. Hoffmann's grandson (she's dead, and he didn't want them). Mother said they were from Germany and very old, and on Christmas Eve morning she sent me to Marie's so I wouldn't break any. I didn't care, because I knew Aunt Sally would be there soon, and she was!

Uncle Bill was there this time, and he had another tuna fish. Miss Carmella laughed and said she'd been hoping they'd bring a fish with them again. Aunt Sally went over to our house to see Mother, and I listened but I didn't hear any fighting, so I guess it was okay. Miss Carmella went over later and invited Mother and Dad to supper. Dad said yes. Mother didn't say anything.

Miss Carmella cooked all afternoon, and Aunt Sally helped when Miss Carmella let her. When they set the dining room table, they set it for eight, but then Miss Carmella got a funny look on her face and rubbed her arms like she was cold, and she set another place.

At six o'clock, Miss Carmella sent me to get Dad for supper. I was surprised to see Mother all dressed up. I wondered where she was going. Dad helped her put on her coat, and she walked out our door, down the steps and up Marie's steps and waited for Dad. Dad stepped over the porch wall and knocked. When Miss Carmella opened the door, she yelled "Hiya, Susie, c'mon in!"

Mother took her coat off and held it out. Miss Carmella took it and tossed it on the back of Mr. Vince's easy chair. "Hope you're hungry," Miss Carmella told her, "'cause I don't want to see no leftovers, capisce?" She grabbed Mother's arm and pulled her into the dining room.

Supper was delicious, noisy, and fun. Mother didn't say anything, but I noticed she took seconds when she thought no one was watching. Miss Carmella was watching though and made sure that when the bowls went around the table, they stopped in front of Mother. Aunt Sally saw what was going on, too, and was grinning at Miss Carmella and rolling her eyes. I stopped watching so I wouldn't laugh.

After supper, Mother got up and said, "Thank you" and walked to the door. Miss Carmella yelled "Hey Susie, I'll write you recipes for all the things you liked." Dad got up, grinned and said "Thank you, Carmella. Everything was delicious." He helped Mother with her coat, and they left. Aunt Sally lifted Mother's plate up and said, "No tip," and she and Miss Carmella put their hands over their mouths to keep from laughing.

Marie and Billy and I sat on the sofa all wrapped up in a blanket and watched "Amahl and the Night Visitors" on TV, and then we said good-night and went back to my house.

I couldn't wait for it to be Christmas morning. Not because I was going to get presents (Mother always took them to Goodwill anyway), but because this year I made presents to give to other people. When I told Mother what I wanted to sew, she looked at me for a long time. She nodded and said they would be a "good beginning" and then she frowned and looked at me even longer and said I might have "good fashion sense."

Here's what I made:

For Dad I embroidered a couple of white linen handkerchiefs with the letters "B&O" on a corner to wear in his suit jacket breast pocket. Mother had suggested small letters in white silk instead of color because "the silk would shine and catch the eye in an unobtrusive way that would leave an impression of refined personal style." I think that sounded snotty.

For Aunt Sally, I made a big scarf out of aquamarine satin with a two-inch border of white cotton. The satin was so it would look pretty, and the cotton was so she could tie it and the knot wouldn't slide open. That was *my* idea. Mother didn't say anything, but she made one for herself.

For Marie, I made the hardest one to do.

She and I were reading all the "Wizard of Oz" books, and we had just finished "The Patchwork Girl of Oz" and I made a doll of "Scraps" (that was the girl's name) out of little bits and pieces of material in Mother's scrap basket. I thought that "Scraps" looked just like her picture in the book. Mother said that it would do because it was only for that child next door.

I didn't make anything for Mother. Dad paid me a dollar every week to keep his workshop clean, so I bought her a "Coats & Clarke Silk Sampler" with 24 different colors of embroidery thread.

I didn't know what else to give her. I don't think there's anything that she really likes.

On Christmas morning we all had oatmeal, and then we opened our presents. Dad and Aunt Sally liked theirs, and Mother looked at hers and took it up to her sewing room.

Aunt Sally renewed my YWCA membership so I could keep on swimming, and I knew Miss Carmella did the same for Marie. Billy got $5 from Mother, and Dad gave him a puzzle box like the one he made for Marie. He sat on the sofa and figured it out in about 15 minutes. Dad said he was impressed, and Billy grinned and put his $5 in it. He looked sleepy. I guess he's getting too big to sleep on the sofa.

By eleven o'clock, Mother looked at me and hissed "Alright, go" and I ran next door. Marie really, really, REALLY liked "Scraps" and she ran upstairs to get the book to show Miss Carmella that the picture and the doll looked the same.

Marie gave me a book for my present. It was "The Wind in the Willows." I'll keep it at Marie's house.

When I went back to our house, Aunt Sally was looking at Billy and feeling his forehead, and then she tugged his shirt up. Billy said "Hey!" but there was a rash on Billy's tummy and his neck and behind his ears. Aunt Sally said, "Uh oh" and Mother looked disgusted and went upstairs and slammed her door.

"Does he have chicken pox like I did?" I asked. "No, Honey" Aunt Sally said. She took a deep breath and blew it out. "It's measles. And you haven't had them yet. But you're going to." She stood up and walked to the door. "I'd better tell Carmella."

CHAPTER THIRTEEN

Carpentress

It was almost the end of February, and since I wasn't "always disgustingly sick" anymore (according to Mother), I was down in the basement with Dad. He was at his workbench sliding pieces of wood back and forth, and flipping them over, and rubbing them with a damp sponge.

"What are you going to make?" I asked.

Dad flipped one piece of wood over and looked at it, and turned it end-for-end. "It is going to be an end table for Mrs. Lehmann. What I am doing now is trying to match grain and color for the tabletop to match the one that Reverend Lehmann brought over." He pointed to the little table in the corner. "He told me she always wanted to have a table at both ends of their sofa, and asked if I could make one." He wiped the wood with the sponge. "Ah" he said. "Look."

There were four pieces of wood, and when they were all wet, but not real wet, they all had the same color, and Dad ran his finger down the edges where they met, and I could see that together they almost looked like they had been cut from one big piece.

"I will drill, dowel, and glue them together, then cut them into an oval, plane them flat, and for the edge I—"

"Teach me how to make stuff" I interrupted.

Dad grinned at me, and then tried to look serious. "'Stuff'? What kind of 'stuff'?"

I looked around the basement. Dad had built every inch of it. "This" I said. "Everything. How to make walls and furniture and, and... *everything*."

Dad made some marks on the ends of the wood. "Do you remember when I made little Marie's puzzle box?"

"Yessir."

"I made parts for two boxes."

"Oh" I said, "That's when you made Billy's, too."

"No" he said. "The second box was to be for you. I had thought you would ask for one when you saw hers, and I would surprise you, but you asked how I had learned to make it."

I remembered. "Mother told me to be quiet and stop asking stupid, annoying questions."

"Mmm" he said. "Yes. She did." He looked away for a moment and leaned against the workbench. "When I was 15, my Papa took me from school and apprenticed me to Herr Feltzer— *Mr.* Feltzer, I mean. Mr. Feltzer was a carpenter. A Woodwright. He built barns, houses,... oh, all kinds of buildings. When there was a raising, he was the one in charge, as well as the hardest worker. He worked me just as hard."

"He also made furniture, and that is what he did best of all."

"Apprenticeships usually last seven years. After four years, Herr Feltzer handed me a box. A puzzle box. 'Open it' he said. I did much faster than Billy did with his. Then Herr Feltzer took it from me and said, 'Make one.'" Dad smiled. "I made one. Then Herr Feltzer— Mr. Feltzer— said 'You have learned all I can teach you. The rest comes from experience. From now, you will work *with* me, not for me.'" Dad looked at me. "You will get splinters."

I hated splinters. "Okay."

"Cuts and scrapes, and mashed fingernails too."

I didn't like that either. "Alright."

"Your Mother will not like this. She will complain to both of us."

I grinned. "I don't care." But I did, a little. I didn't want her to throw his clothes outside.

Dad looked at me VERY seriously. "I will teach you all that I know. I cannot promise we will build a house— "

I interrupted again. "Maybe Aunt Sally will want another room."

Dad raised his eyebrows. "If so, you will learn how to do it." He held out his hand. I stared at it. "Shake hands" he said, and I did. "You are now my apprentice. I will teach you how to build this table."

I got three splinters and a cut that first day.

By the time we were finished, I lost my left thumbnail (it grew back), had to get stitches twice (four the first time, three the next), and dislocated my right index finger (Dad pulled it, and it popped back to where it should be.)

It rained clothes three times.

But Mrs. Lehmann loved her table.

In April, Mrs. McGonigle told us she couldn't come up with anymore different math stuff for us, but she said she'd talk to the other teachers and see about a "learning plan" for next year. Meanwhile, because we were learning Greek and Roman Mythology, she had us do math problems in Greek and Roman numerals.

Right after Easter, the front left leg of Dad's kitchen chair broke, and he almost pulled the table over when he grabbed it to keep himself from falling. Mother said we'd have to buy a new kitchen set, but I told her that Dad and I could fix it. Mother glared at me, and then hissed at Dad "Go ahead. Ruin her. She'll never be ladylike because of you and that woman next door and that sister of mine." She got up and cleared the table even though we weren't finished. Dad didn't say anything, he just nodded his head towards the basement door.

We didn't fix the old chair; we made a new one. Dad showed me how to use spoke-shaves and his lathe (it works on a treadle like Granny Annie's sewing machine). We went to the B&O engine yards on a Saturday so that we could use steam to bend the "bow-back" for the chair. It took a while because Dad said he didn't want me to get scalded. I didn't. Mr. O'Kelly, the foreman at the engine yards, said he'd heard about steam-bending, but had never seen it done before. He told Dad that he was pretty handy for a Boss, and Dad laughed.

CHAPTER FOURTEEN

Sick Again

When we finished the chair, we sanded and painted the other chairs and the table too. Mother got mad because she couldn't tell which was the new chair, and Dad and I ate all our meals out until she got over it.

I started getting a sore throat all the time and Mother said it was from breathing sawdust and paint and all those germs in the pool. Dr. Dobihal said it was tonsilitis, and that I should have had them taken out when I was three, like other kids did. He and Mother talked about when I'd get operated on. Dr. Dobihal said it could wait until school was over. I said that's when I had to go to the ocean.

Mother looked at me and told me to go out to the waiting room and be still. When she came out, she pulled me off the chair and out the door and wouldn't say anything until we got home. She finally told me I'd still go down to Aunt Sally's the day after school closed. Then she went into the kitchen and started making that— noise— she made when she was laughing.

It was almost summer, and Mother still wouldn't tell me when I'd get my tonsils taken out. "If you knew, you would only be more frightened" she told me. I wasn't scared, I just knew she was up to something. Dad only said I'd be fine. When I tried to write a letter to Aunt Sally, Mother tore it up.

The day before school stopped, Mother and Dad took me to the hospital early in the morning. When we got there, I had to put on a nightgown that was open in the back and it was COLD, and then I had to lay on a skinny bed with wheels and got pushed down the hall and on an elevator and more halls and finally a room with a BIG light and people in robes and masks and gloves and NOW I was getting scared and then one of the people leaned over me and said "Hi Sally" and it was Dr. Dobihal and I grabbed his arm and asked if I was still going to be able to go Downeyoshun and he said "Sure Honey and you'll eat ice cream all day for a couple days and you'll be fine and it's time to go to sleep" and they put this thing on my face and told me to take deep breaths...

I woke up in another room. My throat hurt, and my mouth tasted like blood and metal, and I was dizzy. It hurt to swallow. Mother and Dad were there. Dad looked worried, but he was smiling. He was holding my hand and patting it. Mother just looked at me. Dad said I would feel better later, and that he had to go to work, but Mother would stay with me and that he'd see me later. When he left, Mother pulled out underwear and a pair of shorts and a blouse that she had crammed into her purse and told me to get dressed because we had to leave right now. When I was dressed, she pulled me out of the room and down the hall. One of the other mothers called her a name. When we got to the elevator, one of the nurses came running after us and yelled "Hold it! You're not going anywhere!" Mother pushed the button and the door closed. When we got downstairs, another nurse came running too, and kept saying "Excuse me. Excuse me! EXCUSE ME!" But Mother ignored her and dragged me outside into a taxicab.

When we got back to our house, Aunt Sally and Miss Carmella were sitting on the porch.

Aunt Sally yelled at Mother "You told me that the Doctor changed his mind, and she wasn't getting her tonsils out until the end of Summer!"

"Yeah, and you told me your sister called and said she wouldn't be here till Saturday!" Miss Carmella yelled.

Mother ignored them, went in, threw my shoes, socks, and suitcase out, and locked the door. Aunt Sally yelled "Jesus, Susan, what is WRONG with you?"

Mother said through the door "Don't use the Lord's name in vain. You want to pretend to be her mother in the Summer? Try it when she's sick, as I have done all this year."

Aunt Sally stood there with her mouth open, and then she raised her fists above her head and screamed the same name the lady in the hospital said. She turned around and still had fists, and I flinched away and held my hands in front of my face. Aunt Sally dropped her hands and stepped back and said, "Oh my God, Honey, I'm sorry, never be scared of me, too." Then she hugged me and started to cry. I hugged her back and patted her and whispered, "It's okay, I'm just used to ducking." I think that made her cry a little bit more.

Miss Carmella said, "Don't go anywheres, give me a few minutes." Aunt Sally took me to the car, and put my suitcase in the trunk, and put my shoes and socks on. Miss Carmella came out with a big aluminum Thermos jug, a coffee cup, and a box of Sucrets. "It's ice water" she told Aunt Sally. She looked at me. "Here, kid, suck on these things. They'll make your throat feel better." She hugged, kissed me, and said she'd explain it all to Marie when she came home from school. Aunt Sally hugged Miss Carmella and said "God bless you, Carmella. Thanks." And we went home to Ocean City.

When we got there, we picked Billy up from his school (we were only a little late), and then we went to see their Doctor, Dr. Flanaghan. Aunt Sally talked to the lady in the office, and they went in to see the Doctor, and then Billy and I went in. Dr. Flanaghan was old, bald, and squinty-eyed, and had a thin, wide mouth that frowned. He looked at Billy. "You again! Well, this time you're in for it. It's the 'Square Needle', and I've been sharpening this one up just for you," and he pulled this HUGE needle out of his pocket, and it looked like—

"That's a cut-steel masonry nail on the end" I whispered.

The Doctor looked at me and frowned even more. Billy was laughing. "Masonry nail, huh? Well, Miss Smarty-Pants, let's see what I can do to YOU. Open up and say 'ow.'"

He shined a light inside my mouth. "Tonsils and adenoids. Nice job." He sat down in his chair and looked at Aunt Sally. Neither of them said anything, then he looked at me. "Alright Miss Smarty-Pants, just for ruining my fun with the needle, I'm going to prescribe something yucky for you to drink, and I'm going to make you drink it every time your throat hurts. How do you like that?" He wrote it on a piece of paper and gave it to me. It said vanilla milkshakes. "Now this part you're really going to hate. No swimming in the ocean for two whole weeks."

I told him we swam in a pool. "Doesn't matter. No swimming. How long are you down for?"

"All summer" I told him.

"Darn it! I thought I was going to ruin your whole vacation. Go on, get outta here, and get that prescription filled. Beat it!"

We went down to the boardwalk and Dumser's Dairyland. I drank my milkshake slowly and took deep breaths through my nose. There was the milky smell from Dumser's, the electrical smell from Trimper's Rides, French Fries from Thrasher's, Sea & Ski suntan lotion from two ladies that walked by us, and further away, the smell of burnt sugar and butter from Fisher's Caramel Popcorn. And above everything, the smell of the ocean. I was so glad to be home, I didn't care how much my throat hurt.

CHAPTER FIFTEEN

Wood and Water

Two weeks without swimming turned into three. Aunt Sally was teaching summer school again, and the third week there were a bunch of all-day meetings. She would take us to Granny Annie's in the morning on her way to school. Granny Annie couldn't come up to us because her car was "in the shop", and the bus only went up to about a block past her house. When Granny Annie went to work in the afternoon, we'd stay there and wait for Aunt Sally and kept out of trouble.

Mostly.

Granny Annie's rocking chair had a flat spot on one of the runners, and her table wobbled. I talked Billy into helping me fix them.

The table was easy. One leg was short, but you never make the other legs shorter to match, you make the short leg longer. And you don't make it longer on the bottom end, you make it longer at the top where it's bolted to the table. The hole in the leg that the bolt went through had gotten worn out from the bolt being loose. I took a popsicle stick and hammered it into the bottom of the hole around the bolt and had to add a little piece on the top of the hole to make the leg even and stop rocking. I tightened the nut with pliers.

The rocking chair was harder.

I cut open a big paper bag and Billy held the rocking chair sideways on the table so I could trace around both runners. Then I took scissors and cut out both drawings, scotch-taped them together, and I cut out the difference between the two until they looked the same. Now I had a pattern to use to make the chair runners the same.

Next was the scary part.

We got Billy's Grampy's tools from the garage, and I took the plane out. Dad had used all these tools, so I knew they were all taken care of. I took the blade out of the plane, wiped the grease off Dad had put on it to keep it from rusting, and set the blade to shave so thin you could see through the shavings.

Dad had taught me that you can always take more off, but you can't put it back on, so it took a long time to make the runners' match. But I did it! The rocking chair didn't bump anymore!

We cleaned up and I put the grease back on the blade so it wouldn't rust, and when Aunt Sally came to take us home, we showed her what we did. Aunt Sally said we probably should have asked Granny Annie first.

The next morning when Aunt Sally dropped us off, Granny Annie had her hands on her hips and a big frown.

"I came home from work last night, and my rocking chair rocked, and my table didn't. I had to go back outside and look at my mailbox to make sure I was in the right house." She looked at us. "Well?"

"I told her she shouldn't, but she wouldn't listen to me!" Billy yelled.

"YOU helped!" I said.

Granny Annie looked at him. "So: 'The woman tempted me, and I did eat.' "

Billy said "Huh?" but I knew it was a Bible verse.

Granny Annie looked at me now. "Well?"

I felt my face go all red. "I just wanted to fix things for you" I whispered. "I'm sorry."

Granny Annie said, "Hold your hands out." I thought she was going to hit them like Mother did, but she didn't. She turned them over and looked at them. "No cuts or splinters." She pressed my fingertips and the heel of my palm. "Got some calluses, though."

"Yes ma'am" I said. "I worked hard to get them."

She grinned at me and said, "That's your father talking." She let go of my hands. "Thank you for fixing my table and chair." She kissed me. "But next time, *ask* first, okay?" She turned back to Billy and swatted his behind. "And next time, YOU stand up for your cousin."

Billy looked at her and then me. "I'm sorry" he whispered.

"Okay" I said, "But remember you helped."

"Water under the bridge" Granny Annie said. "Now, who wants breakfast? Oh, and my bedroom door sticks."

We fixed it.

We finally got to go swimming in the last week of June. Boy, was I out of shape! I was running out of breath after just a few laps. But I was doing better by the end of the week. I wished that Aunt Viv was there to train us. But mostly I wished Marie was there. I missed her. So did Billy.

The Friday before the 4th of July, Billy and I were at the pool, swimming back and forth, not racing or anything, just waiting for Aunt Sally to get out of school and take us home. All of a sudden, Miss Jenny the lifeguard started blowing her whistle and yelling "Hey! HEY!" Another kid had jumped into the pool with all her clothes on, and when she came up, it was Marie! We were all laughing and hugging, and Miss Jenny was trying not to laugh too, and told Marie to look at the sign that said, "proper swimwear required." Marie's Aunt Rose was yelling at Marie for running across the parking lot without looking and for not asking if she could go over and see us. One of her cousins brought Marie's shoes and socks and her suitcase over and asked if Marie was leaving with us now. Aunt Sally had just gotten there and was snorting and laughing, and Marie's Aunt Rose went to her and said, "You sure you want her?" Aunt Sally said she couldn't send her back, so we'd have to keep her. Marie's Aunt gave Aunt Sally an envelope and said, "Carmella says she don't want to hear nothing about this, and I ain't getting in the middle, so you'll just have to take it."

Aunt Sally took the envelope and shook her head. "Thanks, Rose. I'll deal with Carmella."

Marie's Aunt Rose said "Yeah, and good luck with that. *Marie*! You behave yourself better than you just did, you hear?"

"Yes ma'am. I'm sorry."

"No, you ain't. Behave." She kissed Marie and shook hands with Aunt Sally and walked back to her family. Aunt Sally looked at us. "Well, they say trouble comes in threes, and this was my idea, so out you all come and dry off as best you can, and we'll go home." She tapped the envelope with her fingers and put it in her purse.

I asked Marie how long she was staying. "Until school starts. Your Pop's going to bring me home with you." Billy yelled "YAY!" and hugged her and turned red, and Marie giggled and hugged him back.

On the way home, Marie told us what happened when Dad got back from work and found out that Mother had sent me home with Aunt Sally. "Boy, was he mad! He YELLED at her, and we never heard him do that before. He told her she was terrible for sending you away when you were sick, and that she didn't care about anyone but herself, and she thought she was perfect, but she wasn't, and that's when she went upstairs and started throwing his clothes out the window. She hit Mrs. Tuttle with a shoe, and Mrs. Tuttle yelled she was going to call the nuthouse in Spring Grove and ask if they were missing her. Your Ma stopped throwing stuff and came outside and picked everything up and went inside again, and then it was quiet the rest of the night."

It was quiet the rest of our ride home, too.

Aunt Viv came down in the middle of July, but not to swim. She was in town for a convention of Avon Ladies. Uncle Bill said that's when a bunch of middle-aged women sneak around, and ring people's doorbells and paint clown faces on whoever opens the door. Aunt Viv laughed and called him a name, and Granny Annie got mad at her for saying it.

It was a long summer, the best we'd ever had. We didn't do a lot of different things, but we did them together, and it was fun.

One extra thing Marie and I did was go to the High School with Aunt Sally after swimming one day. A Math teacher gave us a long test, and then he wrote a bunch of problems on the blackboard with letters and numbers and told us we had to figure out what numbers the letters could be. He kept making the problems harder and harder, until we couldn't do them even when we worked on them together. After that, he drew triangles and pentagons and hexagons and things called "trapezoids" on the board, and we had to figure out degrees for the angles. Mrs. McGonigle had taught us some geometry for fun that year, but this was harder because none of the sides were equal like you'd want them to be.

Billy had been in the library the whole time, and he came looking for us and said he was hungry. The teacher said he was finished and sat back and looked at us and told Aunt Sally we had "an intuitive grasp of higher mathematics." Billy told us intuitive meant that we could figure things out without learning a lot first. The teacher looked at him and asked Aunt Sally what his reading level was. She told him that Billy tests at 12th grade now. The teacher said he'd trade all his students in summer school for the three of us. We told him we were on vacation, and he laughed.

A few weeks later when we came home from swimming, Mother and Dad were sitting on the porch. Mother got up and said, "Come here," but I just looked at her and said "Why?" and didn't move. She came down, grabbed and squeezed me in a hug before I could squirm away and mashed her mouth on my head. Then she let go and wiped her mouth and turned to Dad and said, "Don't you ever say I don't love my child."

Dad had brought down a "Mechanix Illustrated" magazine with plans for a porch glider, all the bolts and bearings and things for it that weren't wood, and a box of his tools. For the next four afternoons, I picked out the wood, measured, cut, and drilled, Billy and Marie painted, and when everything was dry, we put it together, and swung in it after supper. Aunt Sally and Uncle Bill said thanks, and that dad and I should open a furniture factory.

I bet Dad would like that.

It rained the last two days there. Mother wouldn't let me run around outside in my bathing suit like we usually did, even though there wasn't any lightning, because she didn't want me to get wet. So, we stayed inside and played boardgames (too noisy, she said), read books (we took up too much space inside the house), and sat on our glider on the porch. When she came outside and said we were swinging too hard, Aunt Sally growled "That's enough, Susan. Leave them alone. They're not bothering you." Mother got angry and went back inside and slammed the door. We heard Aunt Sally growl "That's MY door, Susan. If you want to have a hissy fit, go out back and stand in the rain until you calm down."

We heard the backdoor slam, and Dad started coughing.

When we left Ocean City, Marie asked if she could come down next summer, and Aunt Sally said it was okay with her, and she'd talk to Miss Carmella and Mr. Vince. Everybody hugged and kissed goodbye, except for Mother (she went out to the car and started blowing the horn).

When we got back to Baltimore, Miss Carmella and Mr. Vince were waiting for us, and they both hugged and kissed Marie, and Miss Carmella cried a little. Marie asked if somebody died, and Miss Carmella said no, they just missed her because she was gone for two whole months. Marie said she missed them too, and Mr. Vince said "Nah, you were having too much fun to miss us" and Marie said she missed them now, and they all laughed. I left the Thermos jug and coffee cup on their porch. I'd thank Miss Carmella later.

CHAPTER SIXTEEN

Math and Monsters

Our new teacher for the 4th grade was Mr. Zeiler. He was our first man teacher. He sat all of us in alphabetical order like Miss Ritter did in 1st grade. Miss Carmella came with us the first day and gave him all the tests and things from Aunt Sally. He said he knew all about it from Mrs. McGonigle and he'd work on it after everybody settled in.

A couple of weeks later, he had us stay after school for "daydreaming" during Math. We told him we weren't; we just already knew it. Marie asked him if he read all the stuff from Mrs. McGonigle and her mother.

He frowned and opened one of his desk drawers and pulled out all the papers and read them. Then he got up and wrote two problems on the board. "Marie, you will do this one and Sally— "

Marie interrupted him. "'A' is 5, 'B' is 27, and 'C' is 40."

"And 'X' is 9, 'Y' is 19, and 'Z' is 51," I said.

Mr. Zeiler stared at us with his mouth open, then he started laughing. "The smart ones are the most trouble."

So, he let us sit together again, and when he gave the other kids tests, he'd show us how to do more complicated problems. He said he hadn't had any tough problems for years and was having trouble keeping ahead of us.

But he got even with us in History and Geography. Honestly, does anyone *really* care about the War of 1812 and Fort McHenry and Spaniards and Aztecs and Hungary and Vietnam and Lebanon? I don't even know where any of them are (except for Fort McHenry: that's here in Baltimore). But Mr. Zeiler said it's ALL important, and if I learn about it, I'll know why.

I suppose.

On Hallowe'en, Mother and Dad went to a masquerade ball for B&O

people like Dad at the Lord Baltimore Hotel. Mother made a ballgown and made Dad rent a tuxedo and top hat and said they were going as Fred Astaire and Ginger Rogers. Dad's tall and skinny, but he doesn't dance, so I don't think anyone will believe them.

Since they were going out, I was going to spend the night with Marie, and I got to go trick-or-treating for the first time. I didn't have a costume, so Miss Carmella said she'd make me look like a little old lady. She drew lines on my face and put powder in my hair to make it look white, and then put a hairnet over it. Mr. Vince took a coat hanger, bent it with pliers, made glasses and told me to wear them at the end of my nose. When I hunched over, I looked like Mrs. Tuttle.

Marie dressed like a gypsy lady. She looked like Chico Marx in that one scene in "A Night at the Opera."

Mr. Vince walked around the block with us, and when we came back, we both had a shopping bag full of candy. I gave mine to Marie because I knew Mother wouldn't let me keep any.

Since it was Halloween, Marie wanted to stay up late and watch a monster movie on TV. Miss Carmella said okay, but if we got scared, the TV would go off and we would go to bed.

We watched a really old movie called "Dracula."

It started out with a man traveling to another country to sell Count Dracula a house. The one he lived in was dirty, dusty and full of spiderwebs. The Real Estate man was named Renfield, and when he cut himself slicing bread, Count Dracula looked hungry. Then Count Dracula and some creepy-looking women surrounded Renfield, and I guess they drank his blood.

The next scene was about a ship that came into the harbor and everybody on board was dead except for one guy. It was Renfield. When they found him, he started laughing.

That's when I screamed.

Miss Carmella jumped up and turned the TV off. I was crying and shaking, and Marie was on one side of me, and Miss Carmella was on the other and they were both holding me and saying it was all pretend, and I knew that, but...

"That man" I said. "Renfield. He laughs like Mother."

I felt Miss Carmella shiver.

When I calmed down, we all went upstairs to bed. I lay there very quietly and didn't move. I was afraid to go to sleep and have a nightmare.

Marie must have guessed because she hugged me and said, "Don't worry, Sorella, I'm right here."

I'd never heard that word before. "What's Sorella?"

Marie hugged me a little closer. "It means 'sister.' "

I relaxed, and I snuggled into Marie's arms. Sorella. Sister. I liked that. "Okay. Goodnight, Sorella."

"Goodnight. No bad dreams."

I fell right to sleep, and I didn't dream.

CHAPTER SEVENTEEN

Cooking the Numbers

On the Saturday before Thanksgiving, I was helping Mother do the dishes when she said, "On Thanksgiving, I will begin to teach you to cook."

I heard myself snort and laugh like Aunt Sally, and then to make it worse, I said "YOU?"

I ducked her slap and ran out the backdoor and up the alley, still laughing, even though she was chasing me. By the time I got around the block to our front door, Mother was about half a block behind, and leaning on someone's car trying to get her breath back. Mr. Vince was on his porch smoking his cigar. "These walls are like paper, kid. Watch yourself when she catches up."

When I went inside, Dad was waiting for me. He only looked at me and said "You should never have said it, Sally. She *is* your mother." He shook his head. "Take your bath and go to bed. I will talk to her." I could hear Mr. Vince talking to Mother. "Hey, Susie, you sound like Carmella when she watches that Jack LaLanne* guy on the TV. You okay?" (*Note: Jack Lalanne was the first TV fitness star.)

Dad and I couldn't eat at our house for two weeks.

But I started to think about cooking. Dad spent a LOT of money at restaurants for us: $38 just for suppers— I counted. So, a couple of Sundays before Christmas I asked Miss Carmella if *she* would teach me to cook.

She looked over her shoulder at the wall between our two houses, and Mr. Vince looked at both of us over the top of his newspaper.

"Nah," she said. "When you grow up and get married, your mother-in-law can teach you how. That way, your Husband'll say 'Oh, it's just like Mama used to make.'" Mr. Vince laughed and said "Yeah, you don't do too bad, Carmella," and Miss Carmella laughed.

"But... what if I DON'T get married? What if... what if I grow up and get a job and buy a house and a car and I don't have enough money to eat out every night? I'd... I'd *STARVE*!"

They both laughed. "You don't want to burden your soul with that, Carmella" Mr. Vince said.

Miss Carmella looked back at our wall again. "Okay, kid" she said quietly. "I'll teach you to cook."

"Me too!" Marie said. "I want to learn how."

Miss Carmella started to say "Your mother-in-law— "

Marie interrupted her. "What if my mother-in-law cooks like Aunt Gina?"

"She's got you there" Mr. Vince agreed.

"Or..." Marie chewed her lip. "Or... how about I married a boy who wasn't a paisan?" Marie was blushing.

Miss Carmella's eyebrows went up and she crossed her arms, and Mr. Vince put his paper down. "Like who, for instance?" she asked.

Marie got even redder. "Maybe somebody like Billy" she whispered.

"But Aunt Sally's a good cook," I told her. "You know that."

"Yeah," Marie nodded. "But she only knows how to cook American." She hesitated. "It's good American. But she doesn't know how to... ". I could barely hear her. "Billy likes the way you cook on Christmas."

Miss Carmella and Mr. Vince looked at each other and burst out laughing. Miss Carmella said, "I'll order the wedding cake from Vaccaro's" and Mr. Vince said "Yeah, and I'll talk to this Billy and see if he can support her." When they stopped laughing, Miss Carmella leaned over and kissed Marie.

"Okay, so I guess I'll teach you, too." She rolled her eyes. "Oh, Jeez," she said. "Puppy love." Then she shivered and got a funny look on her face.

I remembered that happened last Christmas, and Mother came over for supper. I wondered what it meant.

Aunt Sally, Uncle Bill and Billy all came on Christmas Eve, but this time they didn't bring a fish because Miss Carmella told them she had two chefs cooking for her this year (guess who!) We made a big salad, a platter of antipasto things, and a HUGE lasagna. Mother didn't come over for supper, but Dad did, and everybody said it was all delicious. Billy kept telling Marie she was as good a cook as her mom, and Aunt Sally and Miss Carmella were trying not to laugh.

Aunt Sally brought us a letter from Aunt Viv about the Olympics next year. Her daughter Adrienne was competing again and was trying to get on the U.S. Olympic team and go to Rome.

Over Christmas vacation, Miss Carmella helped us find out about where the races were going to be held, which colleges had the fastest swimmers, and who could give us the race results. She said she felt like she was "making book." I don't always get the jokes grown-ups make.

Marie and I made a big chart with all the things we learned and kept adding to it every week. We brought it to school one day and showed it to Mr. Zeiler because we were trying to use math to figure out who might win the races. He looked at us kind of strangely and asked us to stay after school again. Louie Seitch said we always had to stay after school because we were stupid and couldn't do the same math as everybody else. Mac MacTavish hit Louie and said we didn't do the same math because we were smarter.

After school, we spread out our chart and all our notes and explained what, how, and why we were doing it. He sat on top of his desk and frowned and didn't say anything for a long time. Then he gave a big sigh and told us what we were doing was called "statistical mathematics" and that the stock market and insurance companies use it to try and figure out what to invest money in, or how many people are going to die, and things like that. Then he was quiet again.

He finally grinned at us and said we'd make a good "sike experiment," because we were inventing a whole kind of math without knowing it was already there. He said we really needed a better teacher than he was and the sooner the better before we died of boredom.

I raised my hand and asked "Mr. Zeiler? How smart are we?"

He looked at us and said he didn't know, but there were tests to find out, and he'd write us a note to take home for our parents.

I don't think Mother is going to like any of this.

CHAPTER EIGHTEEN

A Gift

Mr. Zeiler wrote two notes for us to take home. I gave mine to Dad after supper. When he read it, he went back into the dining room to show Mother before I could stop him.

"Sally's teacher says that she should be tested for her math talent. He says that she and little Marie are far beyond all the other children in their class. They are doing high school work. *High School*, Susan. Can you believe it?"

Mother stood there with the supper dishes in her hands and didn't even look at Dad. "No" she said. "I don't believe it. Her teacher has made a mistake."

Dad didn't pay attention to the way Mother was talking. "It is not a mistake, Susan. I have seen what she does for homework. She is doing algebra, she has been doing algebra for over a year, now."

Mother still hadn't moved. "Then her teacher has been giving her the wrong homework. She can't possibly understand it. I will go to school tomorrow and straighten this out once and for all." She looked and saw me listening. "Get out" she hissed. "Go upstairs and do your homework."

"Marie and I did our homework during math." I knew it was the wrong thing to say as soon as the words were out of my mouth.

"Did you hear that? She is not doing the math in class, so she can't be doing anything different than anyone else." She looked at me again. "Get out. Now."

I started to go upstairs. I couldn't hear Dad, but I did hear her.

"I will not tolerate this anymore, do you understand?"

"She understands no more math than any other child her age."

"She is not different. We do not have a child who is different."

"I will not have you or anyone else claim that she is smarter than her peers."

"Don't you understand? No decent man will marry a woman smarter than he is. I am trying to guide her into a normal life."

I ran down the steps and out the front door—

And I didn't know where to go.

I heard a whistle. Mr. Vince was smoking his cigar and waved to me to come inside. I could still hear Mother's cold, quiet voice.

"I don't care what that child next door does. I said from the start that I didn't want them associating, and now look what's become of it."

When I went inside, Mr. Vince said softly, "Marie. Your sister needs you." Marie came and hugged me and whispered, "It's okay, Sorella. It's okay." I could see Miss Carmella in the kitchen shaking her fists in front of the wall. She stopped and came over and hugged both of us. Mother was still talking, but now I couldn't hear her anymore.

An hour later, Marie and I were sitting on her sofa watching TV. At the end of the news, a puppet show called "Sam and Friends" * came on. Marie and Mr. Vince always watched it and thought it was funny. It was okay. (*note: Jim Henson's 1st TV Muppet show.)

The doorbell rang and I knew it was Mother. Miss Carmella opened it. "Whaddya want, Susie?" She was mad.

Mother ignored her and pointed at me. "You. Home. Now." She turned away and walked down the steps.

"Hold it up, Susie, I got words I wanna say to you."

Mother ignored her and started to walk up our steps. Miss Carmella went out the door, jumped over the porch wall and stood in front of her.

Mother looked scared.

"I don't give a damn what you think of me and my family, Susie, but all that crap you were saying is a SIN! Our kids got a gift from GOD, and that means it's for GOOD things in their lives, and don't you say otherwise!"

Miss Carmella leaned over Mother on the steps. "Everybody has a gift, Susie, EVERYBODY! Look at you: you can sew anything. You sew everything you wear: dresses, coats, even that fancy gown you wore Hallowe'en. I bet you even made your own wedding gown."

Mother took one step down and looked up and down the street like she wanted someone to save her.

"I never saw anyone that could sew like you, Susie. You always look like you came out of one of them fashion magazines." Miss Carmella shrugged her shoulders. "I was never good at that. All those measurements, all those different shapes to sew together—"

Miss Carmella stopped and looked at Mother. "Ah. Yeah. I bet..." Her voice was soft now. "*You* were good at math and geometry and all that too, weren't you?"

Mother's face... she looked hurt... embarrassed... maybe a little ashamed. She ran up the steps, ducked around Miss Carmella, went inside, and pushed the door closed.

I climbed over to our porch. Miss Carmella shook her head and looked sad. She stroked my cheek, and kissed me and said "Goodnight, kid." Marie blew me a kiss, and I went inside. Mother stood there, but she wouldn't look at me.

Her voice shook. "I don't know why you are so bound and determined to ruin your life... "

I walked past her and went up to my room.

CHAPTER NINETEEN

Pollys and Nightingales

Two weeks later, Miss Carmella took Marie and I out of school (Dad gave her a permission note), and we rode on a bus, a streetcar, and another bus to a high school called Baltimore Polytechnic Institute. She said it was called "Poly" for short and was a school that taught engineering (but not the train kind). When we got there, she talked to a lady in the office named Mrs. Wolfe, and she sent us up to the third floor to see Mr. Hippoe. Marie and I giggled and said this must be a "zoo" school with pollys and wolves and hippos.

But Mr. Hippoe didn't look like a hippo. He had big thick glasses and sloppy-looking lips that stayed open. Miss Carmella handed him an envelope from Mr. Zeiler and started to tell him about us, but he didn't pay attention. He just kept saying "Yes yes yes, remedial arithmetic." Miss Carmella kept saying it wasn't remedial, it was tutoring, and we were already doing high school algebra, but he said, "Oh no no no, they won't have to worry about doing that for years." Miss Carmella was getting mad, and told him we were doing it *now*, and we wanted to learn more. He said, "Yes yes yes, but don't worry Mrs. Blasetti— ""It's Giametti !" "Yes yes yes, but perhaps you should let them learn basic arithmetic first. After all, girls won't need to learn algebra, will they?"

By now, Miss Carmella looked like she wanted to sock Mr. Hippoe, but then another man walked into the room. He was tall and skinny, had a crewcut, and looked like Johnny Unitas, one of the football players Mr. Vince yells at on TV.

Mr. Hippoe looked up at him and said "Ah, John, yes yes yes, this is perfect for you to take care of. This is Mrs. Gino Marchetti*— ""GIAMETTI!"

"– and her children need remedial tutoring. You do that sort of thing, don't you?" He made shooing motions with his hands towards all of us. Miss Carmella grabbed the envelope from Mr. Hippoe's desk and slapped it into the other man's hands and pushed him and us out the door and slammed it behind her. The other man started to say something, but Miss Carmella said "Shut it. Read what's in the envelope. THEN we'll talk." (*note: Baltimore Colts player of that era.)

He looked at Miss Carmella and took us to another classroom. We sat down, and he started to read. Mr. Zeiler had stuffed a bunch of paper in the envelope, like all the tests we did, and some of the statistics about Aunt Viv's daughter and her races that we were trying to figure out. Every time he finished a page, the new teacher looked at us, and went on reading. When he read the last page, he looked at us again, then he stood up and held his hand out to Miss Carmella. "I'm John Nightingale, Mrs. -?"

"Giametti. Carmella Giametti." She shook his hand and pointed to us. "My Marie, and her sis-... her best friend Sally Osterhoff."

John Nightingale, I thought. It really *is* a zoo high school.

Mr. Nightingale looked at his watch. "How long can you stay?"

Miss Carmella said, "As long as it takes" and took off her coat. We took off our coats too.

Mr. Nightingale pulled a drawer open on his desk and took out some papers. "How about taking a test for me? Algebra, geometry, and some surprises. Your teacher says you like to do it all in your head. I want to see it on paper."

Mr. Nightingale didn't look like a bird; he looked like a cat that was going to catch it. He handed us the tests upside down and looked at his watch again and said "Go."

We turned the tests over. They were all BIG problems. Marie and I looked at each other and grinned. This was going to be fun!

All the problems were hard, but when I got to #13, I thought there was something wrong with it. I had to figure out the volume of two cylinders shaped like a "tee," but the dimensions didn't work out right with the formula. I looked over at Marie and she was stuck too. I raised my hand.

Mr. Nightingale pointed at me. "Yes?"

"I think the numbers are wrong for number thirteen."

Now he looked like the cat who caught the bird and was getting ready to eat it. "Well, if you can't do it, just go on to the next problem."

Marie waved her hand. "Hey, we can do it, but you got the wrong numbers here."

He looked scary now. "You think they're the wrong numbers?"

Then I understood. "No" I grinned back. "We KNOW they're wrong."

He grinned and said, "Write your proof and continue."

After we finished (and we got *everything* right), he said "I like to throw in something that can't be solved. It lets me find the ones like you two that won't just plod along." He laughed and said "Boy, if you two can do this now, I can't wait to see what you'll be able to do when you start classes here!"

Miss Carmella crossed her arms and looked at him. "So, when does Poly go from being a boy's school to co-ed?"

Mr. Nightingale stopped laughing, and I remembered that I hadn't seen any girls here. He looked at all of us and said, "Now I understand." Miss Carmella nodded at him.

"I do private tutoring on Saturdays" he said. "I charge $3 an hour per student. I know it's a lot— "

"We can pay it," Miss Carmella interrupted.

"Thank you" he said. "I'm putting my two girls through Hopkins Pre-Med right now." He pulled out a little book from his jacket pocket and looked at it. "Ten o'clock on Saturdays, starting tomorrow?"

"That's when we go swimming" Marie told him.

"We're training for the Olympics" I explained. He laughed and said for us to send him a postcard from Rome.

Marie frowned. "Not *this* year" she told him.

"We're going to be in the 1968 Olympics," I said.

"And 1972," Marie added.

Miss Carmella frowned at him. "They're not kidding."

He looked at us. "No, you aren't kidding, are you?" He looked in his book again. "How about nine o'clock? I'll make you the first of the day."

Miss Carmella told him where we lived, and he shook hands with all of us, and we left. But on the ride home, I kept thinking: what kind of school *will* we go to?

Mr. Nightingale came every Saturday and made us work HARD. But we didn't care, because we kept learning more and more. One Saturday just a couple of weeks before summer vacation, he brought us something TERRIFIC! It looked like three rulers that were stuck together with a magnifying glass on them.

"This" he said, "is a slide-rule. Engineers use them to make quick calculations instead of having to write them down, just like you'd rather do. You can multiply, divide, figure a logarithm, have sword fights— ", and he waved it in the air like Errol Flynn. We started laughing. "Some engineers call it a 'slip-stick.'"

Marie giggled. "A lipstick?"

"No, a slip-stick" he said.

"No!" I was laughing too. "It's a slapstick!"

"Wrong!" he said. "It's a stick-shift!" and he moved his hands like he was driving and said "Vroom! Vroom!"

"Alright" Miss Carmella called from the kitchen. "Enough silliness." She brought Mr. Nightingale a cup of coffee and a biscotti. "And you're as bad as they are. I bet your girls got spoiled rotten."

Mr. Nightingale nodded. "I tried to make-up for the years I missed."

I knew he was talking about the war. "I don't get it" I said. "Why do they have wars? Nobody likes it and people get hurt and killed. What's it for?"

"Good question" Mr. Nightingale said. "Wish I had an answer."

Miss Carmella looked at me. "You want an answer? Learn your history and all that like Mr. Zeiler keeps telling you. And read more in the newspaper besides the funnies and the college sports. What you don't know in this world is going to turn around and bite both of you one of these days." She crossed her arms. "I want to see some better grades from you two than I've been seeing when school is over next month."

Mr. Nightingale nodded. "Your mother's right. There's more to life than just numbers. You need to— ". He stopped and looked at Miss Carmella. "Sorry, Carmella. I keep thinking they're sisters."

"We are. Mostly." Marie said.

"Yeah, almost all the time" I added.

Miss Carmella looked a little sad. "Sometimes I forget and think so, too." She went back to the kitchen. "I'll make a sandwich to take with you for lunch, Johnny."

"Thank you, Carmella. I appreciate it." He turned back to us. "Okay, back to work," and he showed us how to use the slide-rule.

When the lesson was over, Marie ran upstairs for her towel and bathing suit. I went into the kitchen. Miss Carmella was drinking coffee. I stood next to her. She smiled a little. "What's up, kid?"

I hesitated for a second, and then I hugged her. She hugged back. "What's this for?" she whispered.

"Just because I wanted to" I told her.

She stood up, touched my cheek, and looked like she wanted to say something, but she hugged me again instead. We heard Marie running down the steps. "I'll see you two when you get home. Go on, beat it." She kissed us.

Marie and I walked down the street, holding each other's hand. "I don't know how" she said. "But I *know* you and I were really supposed to be sisters."

I held Marie's hand a little tighter. "We are" I said.

CHAPTER TWENTY

Fire and Water

Marie and I came home from school the day after Memorial Day, and Miss Carmella was waiting for us. She wasn't smiling, she looked worried. She held her arms out to us.

"What's the matter? Did something bad happen?" we asked.

She held us and said "Your Uncle Bill is in the hospital. He got hurt at work."

My stomach did flip-flops. "Is he going to be alright?"

"He'll be fine— no, wait." She took a deep breath. "Okay, you're not babies anymore. He— wait." She closed her eyes, and I started to shake. She held me a little closer. "I'm upset, too, bambino. Your Aunt Sally says there was a fire in one of those cheap motels, and a wall fell on him. He— his right hip and arm and shoulder all got broken, and—" I was crying now. Marie was too. "There's still more. He got burnt. Not all over, just... your aunt says the right side of his head, neck and ear got burnt the worst, and he's going to need skin grafts, and he'll be in the hospital a long time, but he's NOT going to die, and he WILL get better. It's just going to take a while, okay? And she says nobody else got hurt, thank God, and... well, it'll just be a while before he's all better."

I made myself stop crying. "Is Aunt Sally okay?"

Marie asked, "Is Billy okay?"

"They're fine. They've been at the hospital all day and last night. She called me Long Distance on a payphone in the waiting room. She tried calling your ma, but I don't think she's been home." I felt her arms twitch around me. "Speak of the devil and up she comes." She patted me. "You didn't hear that, okay?" she whispered.

I heard Mother's voice. "What are you doing?"

"Your sister called. She says Bill got hurt in a fire— "

"She calls you, but not me?" Mother hissed.

"You were out, so she asked me to tell you what happened— "

Mother leaned over the porch wall, yanked me over to our house, shoved me inside, and slammed the door. I heard Miss Carmella spitting something in Italian.

Mother leaned over me and grabbed my face. "You. Tell me everything that woman told you."

I repeated everything I'd been told. She stared at me and ground her teeth. Then she got this nasty look on her face.

"You can't fool me, you selfish little brat, so wipe off those crocodile tears. All you care about is that you won't be able to go down there and wrap your aunt around your little finger all summer."

I hadn't thought about it, but now I guessed that I wouldn't be going, and I felt my face getting red because that meant I'd be here with HER all summer.

She pushed her face into mine. "I knew it." She sneered at me. "Go up to your room. You disgust me."

I went upstairs and listened to her laughing that— laugh— of hers.

Marie and I had been waiting and waiting to find out who's going to the Olympics. We figured Adrienne had to be going because she had some of the best times in the Nationals. They named the men's team a month ago. What's taking so long?

More bad news (for Marie and I). Mr. Nightingale is going on a vacation trip for the whole summer, so we won't have any interesting math stuff to do. But the WORST thing is that Patterson Park High School is moving! Hampstead Hill Junior High is taking over the building and closing the pool, and there won't be any place for the YWCA to swim in the Fall! And where are we going to swim NOW? This summer?

Maybe Mother is right. Maybe I am selfish.

Marie doesn't want to be here, either. She says it gets really, really hot in the summer, and NO breezes.

But at least there's one good thing. Marie's grandmother, Mama Loretta, gave her an old sewing machine. It works on a treadle like Granny Annie's. She had some trouble keeping it going, but it's like swimming: you just have to find the rhythm. I taught her how to make her first blouse in three days.

There was a public pool at the park, but there was a problem with Mother. Colored people swim there too, and she said "No, absolutely not" but Dad said that I COULD go and that I WOULD go. Mother threw his clothes out the window for the first time since Thanksgiving.

The first time we went, we had to show the lifeguards that we knew how to swim good enough for the deep pool. It wasn't as crowded as the other pool. We saw Doris Johnson at the pool, and she watched us doing laps. She said she didn't know how to swim, and we said we'd teach her, but a bigger colored girl came over and told her not to talk to the white kids. Doris went back to the other pool.

We saw her again the next day, and we waved to each other, but the big girl smacked her hand.

Marie and I swam in the deep pool for a while, and then Marie said, "How about we go in the other pool near Doris, and you pretend you're teaching me how to swim?"

We didn't get too close, and we didn't look at her, and she didn't look at us, but then she started doing the things we were doing. The big girl watched all of us. She didn't say anything, and neither did the lifeguards, but they all looked at us like we were doing something wrong.

Every day, we'd teach something else, the same way Aunt Viv taught us. We all started swimming in the deep pool, and we showed her how to dive in from the side of the pool. Finally, I said to Marie real loud, "Well, that's it, that's everything I know. You're doing good. Now all you have to do is practice."

Doris smiled down at the water, and we heard her say "Thanks."

Aunt Sally wrote to Miss Carmella about Uncle Bill. She said he was getting better faster than the doctors thought he would, and that they took off the cast around his behind. She said he was happy that he could poop in a toilet again instead of a bedpan, but his arm and shoulder were still in a big cast, and he was getting skin grafts for all the burns. She said he still wouldn't be better for a long time yet.

She also told us that Aunt Viv had written her, and that Adrienne got picked for the Olympic team the same time the men were. Miss Carmella called the sportswriters in the newspapers about that, but they said it didn't matter because they were just the girls' team. After she hung up, she said something in Italian that must have been nasty because Mr. Vince yelled at her for saying it in front of us. At least now we know Adrienne will be in the Olympics. YAY!

Summer was better than we thought it would be, but the heat would sort of make it easier to get mad about things. One day we were sewing clothes for school, and Marie was having problems stitching the edge of a pleat on her sewing machine. I kept showing her how, but no matter how slow she went, it would come out all wavey. After she tried five times on one pleat, she threw the dress across the room and yelled "This isn't any fun!"

I heard Mother's voice hiss out of my mouth "It's not supposed to be fun. It's supposed to be useful."

She looked at me and yelled back, "You're just like your mother!"

I yelled back at her "That's a rotten thing to say to me!" and my eyes started to burn, and I was crying. Miss Carmella came in the room and said "That's it. Put the sewing stuff away. Look at each other. Apologize. And say what you're apologizing for." We did. "I know it's hot, and there's no boardwalk and no breeze. And no Billy. But that just means you two gotta take care of each other a little more to make up for it. So, no more yelling or fighting." Marie and I looked at each other and apologized again. "Okay, then" Miss Carmella said. "How about we walk down to Mamie's Luncheonette and get snowballs?"

BOOM! We all jumped. BOOM! again, and this time we knew it was thunder. Then it started to pour outside in *buckets*! We went into the kitchen and watched. The sky had turned a greenish-black and lightning was going everywhere, and the rain was hitting the ground and turning into steam and making it feel even hotter than it already was. Mother had laundry hanging outside, and now it was wetter than when she hung it.

The rain started to slow down, and then stopped. The clouds got lighter and broke up. The sun came out again, and it felt like we couldn't breathe.

"Snowballs" Miss Carmella said. "We'll get one big as a bathtub and take turns sitting in it."

I could see Mother in the backyard now, looking at the laundry. Miss Carmella saw her too. "Shh" she said. "Out the front door. Quietly."

I had pineapple.

CHAPTER TWENTY-ONE

The Roof

All through supper, Mother complained about the rain and the laundry.

"Mrs. Boardmann down the alleyway has an aluminum awning that she hangs her clothes under, and they never get wet from the rain" Mother said.

Dad didn't look up. "That is the house that you say looks like a circus tent." His eyes looked at me and I saw his eyelid sort of wink. "Didn't they just replace it because the snow buckled the old one?"

Mother was grinding her teeth. "They have shade in their backyard in the afternoon."

Dad sat back in his chair. "So do we. Their yard faces west. Ours faces east. And their awning is attached under their sleeping porch. All the houses on their side have sleeping porches. Our side does not. Our houses were probably built by another builder. Wasn't this house built back in 1910 or 1915? Sometime then?"

Mother stood up with her hands in fists, and then opened them and started clearing the table. I was almost finished anyway.

Dad looked at her like he didn't know what she was talking about. "Susan? Do you want something hanging from the back of the house?"

Mother stopped picking up the dishes. "I would like something to keep the laundry dry in a storm. I would like you to find out who does that sort of thing, how much it would cost, and when it could be done."

Dad still played dumb. "What about a clothes dryer machine? And a new washing machine?"

It was like watching someone tease a wild animal. I stayed quiet and still.

Mother finally hissed “I want you to get a roof or something over part of the backyard. Now do you understand me?”

Dad said “Ah. You should have said so in the first place.”

“I did say so.” Mother’s teeth were showing.

Dad smiled. “I go on vacation next week. Since we will not be visiting your sister this year, I am sure that Sally and I can build something before school starts.” He turned to me. “Go downstairs and bring up my folding rule, and my yellow pad and pencil. We will measure and plan before you go to bed tonight.”

I walked past them and went downstairs. Mother knew she’d been tricked but didn’t know how.

Dad gave Miss Carmella some money to buy me boy clothes to work in. Marie helped me alter them to fit better, but still be loose and comfortable. I held the pants up with suspenders. Dad bought me a straw hat, and when I put it on, he laughed and said something to me in that funny German he speaks. Miss Carmella laughed when she saw me too and said with my “Prince Val” haircut I looked like one of those Pennsylvania Dutch Amish boys.

Dad got me safety goggles and small work gloves, and I was ready.

We bought lumber, Sakrete, shingles, nails, gutter pipe, flashing metal and all sorts of stuff. This was going to be the biggest thing I’d worked on. I learned how to use a “star chisel” to drill holes in the concrete in the yard for the footers, and into the brick mortar on the wall where we’d mount anchor bolts. I learned how to use a “drawing knife,” and that was scary. It’s like a knife with a handle at each end, and you push it down the length of a board to shape an edge. Even Dad got a little worried while I was doing it.

I learned how to work on a ladder and even walk across the bare beams of the roof. Dad told me not to show off.

It was hot, and Dad would pour water on our shirt collars and cuffs to help keep us cool. I sweat so much that Marie said I smelled like her father does when he comes home from work sometimes. Dad laughed and told her “Hard work the wickedness sweats out.” Marie told him I wasn’t wicked, and Dad laughed again.

The day we did the flashing and the shingles, some people a block away were getting their roof tarred. Dad got a coffee can, and we ran down to where the roofers were and bought some hot pitch from them to seal the flashing. We both laid down across the roof, and Dad had a soaking wet towel in one hand and the can in the other. I painted pitch on the whole edge of the roof where it meets the wall, and then nailed the flashing in place and gave it another coat. Then we nailed the shingles to the roof and ran and got another can of pitch to seal the top run of the shingles at the flashing. When I stuck the brush in the fresh pitch, there must have been a bubble inside, because it popped, and I got some on my cheek. Dad put the towel on it right away, but it BURNT, and I yelled "*Schiess*!"

Mother was in the kitchen, and she hissed up to Dad, "Are you teaching her to swear, too?"

Dad winked at me and asked Mother if she thought it was something I should learn. We heard her go upstairs and throw something through the window screen in her bedroom. I looked at Dad and said, "I'm sorry I cussed." Dad shook his head and said it was worth it. Miss Carmella said from her kitchen door that sometimes Dad really surprised her, and that she would put his clothes in a basket on her porch.

When we finished work for the day, Dad got Vaseline jelly out of the medicine cabinet and very gently dabbed and rubbed the spot of pitch on my cheek. He'd rub for a while, and wipe, rub and wipe, rub and wipe, and the spot got softer and smaller. Mother was watching, and her fingers kept twitching and I knew she wanted to grab it and rip it off my face.

Finally, with an "ouch," it came off, along with a little skin because there had been a blister under it. Dad painted Merthiolate on it and said it looked like a big orange freckle. After I took a bath, he put a band-aid on it. "Tomorrow" he said, "we will mount the gutter and the rain spout. After that, we will paint."

The next day, Marie watched us paint. "Ma says she was scared every time you were up on the ladder or walking on the roof. She says she was afraid you'd fall."

I was going to tell her I knew what I was doing, but Dad stopped me.

"Don't boast" he said, "Next time you must be *more* careful— or you will not finish your apprenticeship. Vershtanden?"

"Yessir."

"Next time?" Marie asked.

"Dad's teaching me everything he knows about carpentry and making furniture and... and... barn-raising, and all that."

Dad coughed a little. "Not too many barns to build in Baltimore."

Marie looked at Dad. "Will she know how to build a house?"

"Yes" he told her. "Other hands to help, but yes, she will know how."

"Good" Marie told him. "When we grow up, I want her to build houses for us, so we'll always live next door to each other."

Dad coughed.

The day we finished, Dad and I had just screwed in the hooks for the clothesline when the sky got dark. Dad looked up at the sky and stood there waiting for the storm. I stood next to him and held his hand. There was a breeze that smelled like electricity and hot water, then the wind started blowing so hard we could hear garbage cans being knocked over and see trash bouncing down the alley. The thunder and lightning started next, and I grabbed Dad with both arms, and the rain came, and it POURED, and it was so much it overflowed the gutter and made it look like a waterfall, but *we* were still dry!

Dad was looking all over the underside of the roof, and NOTHING was leaking through ANYWHERE! Dad patted me across the shoulders a couple of times, and he said "You have built a fine roof, Sally! A fine roof!" Then he started laughing and squeezed me close to him, and I was laughing too.

It rained almost an hour, and the temperature cooled down and the air smelled clean. Dad and I went up to my room, and we looked out my windows at the shingles. They were *all* there. We went back outside and waited for the rest of the storm to pass. Dad and I slouched on the back step with our legs stretched out in front of us. Dad looked happy and relaxed.

He jumped up and called in to Mother. "No cooking tonight. We go out for dinner." Then he jumped over the fence and knocked on Marie's back door. "Carmella! You do not cook tonight! We ALL go out! What time does Vince home come?" I could hear Miss Carmella laughing. Dad pointed at me. "A bath you get! Fast! And a pretty dress put on!"

We all drove in our station wagon to a restaurant called "Maria's 301" that Mr. Vince said was good, and we all had a delicious dinner and a lot of fun. Except for Mother. She only sat and didn't eat much or say anything. After dinner Dad and Mr. Vince drank tiny glasses of something yellow. When Dad finished his, I leaned over and sniffed the empty glass. It made my nose burn and my eyes water. Mother kicked me under the table, but she was the one who said "ow." Miss Carmella said, "Sorry, Susie. I musta had a leg cramp" and winked at me.

When we got home, we got chairs from our kitchens and sat out under our roof. Mr. Vince smoked his cigar, and he and Dad talked about who was going to be President that year. It was nighttime then, and the only light was from the telephone pole in the alley. Marie and I were leaning against each other trying to stay awake. Miss Carmella looked at us and said "Alright, you two kids go to bed." She looked at Dad and Mr. Vince and laughed "And you two go to bed." We took our chairs inside, and Mr. Vince called out to Dad "Hey, Freddie. Nice job." Dad smiled and said, "My apprentice did more than I did" and I smiled. Then Mr. Vince said "Freddie... do you *like* what you do at the railroad?"

Dad sighed and started to say, "I make a good salary for my family— ", but he stopped, and looked up at what we had built, and said "No, Vince." He looked sad.

Mr. Vince nodded and said "Yeah. Me neither, Freddie."

Mother bought a clothes dryer and never hung clothes under our roof.

CHAPTER TWENTY-TWO

Adrienne and the Olympics

The week before the Olympics started, Miss Carmella took us to the movies. The newsreel showed the U.S. Men's Teams practicing in the stadiums and the pools. The men were jumping and running and throwing things, but the only thing that they showed the women doing was standing there in short-shorts and bathing suits. The narrator said "Watch out, fellows! These are fast women!" Miss Carmella said he was a smart-ass, and for us not to say that.

The news on channel 13 said the Olympics will be filmed in Rome in the daytime, and the film will be flown and shown here on TV that night. Neat o!

We finally got to see Adrienne racing. She was in the 400-meter freestyle, and she was winning all her races by a LOT, but then she wasn't there anymore. Miss Carmella called the newspapers and one of the reporters told her that Adrienne had been disqualified and taken off the team because somebody said she was a professional swimmer. Miss Carmella got mad and said the only people that were professional swimmers were Tarzan and Esther Williams, and nobody else gets paid to swim. The reporter told her that since Adrienne got paid to be a mermaid in Florida, she wasn't an amateur, and couldn't race in the Olympics. Miss Carmella said she was sorry for yelling and hung up.

Marie and I felt so sad for Adrienne. Aunt Viv had said she'd been in all the Nationals since 1956, and this was the year she won medals and got picked to go to the Olympics, and was sure she would win medals there, too. We still didn't really understand why. Being a mermaid in a show isn't racing.

I bet she was crying. So were we.

CHAPTER TWENTY-THREE

Family Matters

Summer was finally over, and we were back in school. 5th graders! Our new teacher was Mrs. Schmidt. She said she knew all about us and our math, but she wasn't even going to try to keep up with us. This year we were going to "open our eyes and learn about the rest of the world." She said we had gotten away with not learning what we should've about history, geography, science, and all that other stuff. This year, if we don't pay attention and learn, WE. WILL. FAIL! She says she's not being mean; she's being the teacher we need most.

We didn't like her much the first week, but she got better at teaching, and by the end of the month, we thought she was really smart. Did you know that no matter whether Vice President Nixon or Senator Kennedy win, they'll be the first President born in THIS century? And that almost a hundred years ago, Alaska was part of the Russian Empire? And that Hawaii was part of the British Empire? She knew all sorts of interesting stuff like that. We liked her.

Mr. Nightingale started tutoring us again (we missed him!), and the best thing was that Mrs. Thune called us and got us permission to swim at the new high school when the team practices on Saturday. She says she's going to use us to make the team swim faster. That means we'll be racing almost for real. We'll have to take a bus to the new school, but Miss Carmella said she'd come with us the first couple of times till we learn where to get on and off.

Miss Carmella got a l-o-o-o-ng letter from Aunt Sally about Uncle Bill. He was home from the hospital and his casts were off, and the exercise that he had needed to build his muscles back up again was over, and he only needed a few more skin grafts. But she said that when he got out of the hospital, they went to the grocery store to buy him a steak, and some little kid saw him and started screaming. Now he doesn't want to go out anymore.

Marie wanted to know if that meant they wouldn't be up for Christmas that year. Mr. Vince told her that if he had to, he'd go down and bring her boyfriend back to see her. Marie went really red, and Miss Carmella and I pretended we didn't see.

On Hallowe'en, Marie and I went trick-or-treating again. This year we made a costume out of two dresses and said we were going to be Siamese Twins. Miss Carmella went to Woolworth's and bought two costume wigs with red hair and pigtails. Mr. Vince kidded us and said no one would be able to tell us apart. We practiced going up and down the stairs together, and when we went out, she carried one handle on the bag, and I carried the other. Every house we went to thought it was funny and gave us extra candy.

Marie and I watched another scary movie that night called "The Invisible Man." He had a bunch of bandages around his face, and I thought about Uncle Bill. When he started taking his bandages and clothes off and there wasn't anything there, I went into the kitchen with Miss Carmella. I wasn't scared, I just thought I'd keep her company.

We sat there and ate anisette cookies (they taste like licorice), and I remembered something I wanted to ask her. I told her about how Marie and I called Aunt Viv "Aunt" even though she wasn't, and Miss Carmella smiled and said lots of people do that. I had a hard time talking, and Miss Carmella cuddled me and said "Okay, kid, whatcha got?" and I asked if I could call her "Aunt" Carmella. She said she'd like that a lot, but then she frowned and said that Mother would probably "blow her mind" the first time she heard it. Then she held my face in her hands and looked in my eyes and said "Bambino, if you call me Aunt Carmella in your heart, I promise I'll always hear it." I smiled so big my eyes watered, and she said "Yep, I heard it" and we both laughed. But I'm going to say it out loud anyway.

Why can't Mother be like Aunt Carmella and Aunt Sally?

Christmas Eve came and so did Aunt Sally and Uncle Bill and Billy. I was at Marie's, and we heard them come to my house, and Mother saying

"Just drop your suitcases off, just treat me like a hotel. Go next door, that's where you'd rather be." Aunt Sally said "Thanks, Susan, we'll be back tonight, then." Aunt Carmella slapped her hand over her mouth to keep from laughing out loud, and Marie opened the door. We all yelled Bueno Natale and took turns hugging each other. Uncle Bill and Mr. Vince shook hands for a long time. Uncle Bill didn't smile. He had a knit cap pulled down over the right side of his head covering where he got burned. I went over and gave him a kiss on the cheek where the skin wasn't shiny and told him I was glad he was better. He just patted me, and he still didn't smile. Marie and Billy finally let go of each other, and Marie said "Hi, Mr. Bill! I'm glad you're here!" and gave him a hug and kiss. Aunt Carmella said "Yeah, I bet you're glad Billy's here, too, huh?" Aunt Sally snorted. "Yeah, I think Billy might be happy as well." I laughed when they both turned red.

Uncle Bill asked Mr. Vince to help him with the ice chest. "Blue Fin again, Carmella. Okay?" We all went into the kitchen. Everybody was talking, and Uncle Bill cupped his hand against his head, and I remembered that his ear had gotten burnt. Mr. Vince kept talking louder and louder to Uncle Bill. He finally said "Jeez, Bill, take your hat off, you look like you're going to run out the door any second."

Everybody stopped talking. Uncle Bill slowly rolled the hat off and bunched it up in his hand, then leaned over and stuck it in his back pocket. The right side of his head was all red and pink squares like a checkerboard, and the ear was just a hole. Mr. Vince nodded his head and said "Good. Can you hear me better, now?"

Uncle Bill slowly put his hand back up to his ear. "Yeah. But it helps if I..." He stopped talking and shrugged his shoulders. I stood next to him and looked a little closer. He turned around and said "What?" almost like he was mad. Aunt Sally said "Bill." His shoulders relaxed and he said "What?" a little softer. I was still looking and thinking hard. "Would it help if you could wear something shaped like an ear?"

"Yeah" he said, really nasty. "Maybe you can make me one out of wood. With a knothole I can plug with a cork!"

"Bill!" Aunt Sally yelled.

I was getting scared because Uncle Bill had never talked like that before. I knew I had a good idea, almost. "I was thinking about something made out of leather."

Mr. Vince slapped the table and yelled "Pirate John!"

Everybody looked at him. "Pirate John" he said. "Down at the VFW. He's got an eyepatch. Thinks it makes him look like the Hathaway Shirt guy*. It don't." (*Note: The Hathaway Co. used a male model who wore an eyepatch.)

"*That's* what I wanted to say." I had it now. "Only instead of an *eye* patch like him, it would be an *ear* patch."

Uncle Bill looked at me. I could tell he was thinking about it the same way I was. He said "ha" and his mouth smiled just a bit. "Ha. An earpatch. ha." He started to grin and kept saying "earpatch," and then he started laughing while he said it.

Aunt Carmella said 'Mr. Tommy" and we all looked at her.

"Mr. Tommy. The shoe repair man on Bank Street. I bet he could make something that looks like a real ear."

Uncle Bill was laughing hard now. "An earpatch. Made of shoe leather. I could spit-shine it!" Mr. Vince was laughing too, and he grabbed a dish towel and snapped it against his head like he was shining a shoe. Uncle Bill was laughing and coughing at the same time, and I almost couldn't hear him say "If it starts to wear out, I could get cleats put on it!"

Mr. Vince stood up and spread his arms wide and said "Friends!" and then pointed at himself and said "Romans!" And he and Uncle Bill both yelled "Countrymen! Lend me your ears!" Billy jumped up and grabbed Uncle Bill around the neck and cried louder than they were laughing. Uncle Bill looked confused and worried, and held Billy and said "What's the matter? Why're you crying?"

Billy kept crying and holding Uncle Bill and then he said, "You're laughing."

Uncle Bill looked at Aunt Sally. She was crying too. "Bill. You haven't laughed since... since..." She grabbed him and hugged him.

Aunt Carmella pushed me, Marie, and Mr. Vince out of the kitchen, grabbed coats and shoved us outside. "Let's leave them alone for a little while" she said. She looked at me and touched my cheek. "You know what, kid? You're pretty good at fixing things."

CHAPTER TWENTY-FOUR

Life's Surprises

Practicing with Patterson's swim team was a lot of fun. When we first started going, the bigger girls didn't like us, but we got invited to go to a race at Eastern High School and got told to bring our bathing suits. Mrs. Thune told us we could swim while all the girls on the other teams warmed up and said we should swim in the lanes next to Merganthaler Vocational High School's fastest swimmer. We had dived at the same time as she did and raced as fast as we could like we always do. When the Mervo girl saw we were beating her, she sped up and got to the other end first. She must have thought we were finished, because she stopped, but when she saw us turn and go back the other way, she started racing us again. She got there first again, but we kept going. We did that two more times, and I beat her on the last lap. Her coach yelled at her to stop wearing herself out and get out and rest-up for the meet and went over to Mrs. Thune and called her sneaky and conniving and complained to the judges about us. The judges were laughing, but they told Mrs. Thune that we could come to the meets in the future, but we couldn't swim. Patterson won all the races, but the Mervo girl didn't do well at all.

From then on, the girls on the team called us their mascots, and said we were good luck. Well, not all of them. A girl named Leosakos called us Thing 1 and Thing 2. One day in the showers after practice, she started pointing at us and whispering to the other girls. A lot of them started giggling. Marie and I knew what they were laughing about. Our nipples were getting bigger and sticking out. She was embarrassing us, but she was making us mad, too. Then she came over, bent down, squinted at my chest, and poked me. I slapped her hand away, HARD. She laughed and said

"Whatcha growing there, Thing 2? Is that a skeeter bite?"

The other girls were all laughing now. Marie poked HER, and said "Yeah, and next week we'll be as big as you."

All the girls went "WHOAH!!" and laughed harder, because Leosakos was pretty flat-chested. She got mad and swatted a handful of water at Marie and said, "Don't bleed in the pool, brat!" and left. The rest of the girls said, "Good one, Giametti" and said that Leosakos could "dish it out but couldn't take it."

Marie and I whispered back and forth on the bus ride home. We sort of knew a little about what Leosakos meant about bleeding in the pool, but not really, so we guessed we should talk to Aunt Carmella.

Mr. Vince wasn't home, and Mother was out, so we could talk out loud and, well, ask stuff. Older girl stuff.

Marie started first. "Ma, I think we're growing boobs."

Aunt Carmella laughed once, and then tried not to smile. "C'mere." She tugged Marie's blouse collar out and looked down. "Yep." She looked at me. "You too?"

"Yes ma'am."

She sighed and frowned. "Oh, Jeez." She looked over at the wall. "She know?"

"No, ma'am."

"Well, thank God for small mercies" and bit her lip. She looked at me. "Look, kid, it sure ain't my place to... teach anything about... ". She stopped. "Ah, Jeez. If I don't, she... look, all *I* know is what all the old women told me, and most of that was crap." She looked at the clock. "What time's that library close?"

"Five" we told her.

"Right" she said and got our coats. She smiled at us. "My little girls are growing up." She hugged us. "C'mon" she said. "Let's go find out about... things."

Aunt Carmella whispered to the librarian, and she looked at us. "Non-Fiction. In the back" and led us to a shelf. "There" she pointed and left.

It was a book called "Girls Should Know" and Aunt Carmella opened it and turned a couple pages. We could see some drawings. She snapped the book shut, and said something in Italian, and opened it again. She turned more pages, just looking, and closed it and stuck it under her arm. "Right" she said. "We'll take this one home." We started walking towards the front, and she stopped and said, "Hold it" and went back and got another book that said, "Boys Should Know." Her face was red, but she grinned at us. "Might as well learn all of it."

We kept those books for two weeks, and we still had a lot of questions that the books didn't talk about. Aunt Carmella wrote a letter to Aunt Sally to ask if she had any books at her school that had more answers, and she sent them, but they still didn't tell everything.

Aunt Carmella read with us, and sometimes she got red, and sometimes she said she never knew about this or that, and we all wished that someone would write better books than these, like a "how-to" book or something.

Anyway, I remembered Granny Annie saying that life would give me surprises when I got older.

SURPRISE!

I was setting the table for supper a month later when Mother looked at me, grabbed my blouse and pulled it tight against my chest. She let go and stared at me like she was disgusted. She went in the kitchen and turned all the pots "off" and told Dad there wouldn't be supper tonight.

She grabbed me, pulled me out the door and dragged me up to Epstein's Department Store on Eastern Avenue. When we got there, she whipped a tape measure off a saleslady's neck, and pushed me into a changing room. When I took my top off, I was expecting her to be rough, and make me wear something that would feel... well, I don't know what I was expecting, but she took my measurements very carefully, and brought a bunch of boxes of different styles of training bras and made me try them on. She kept going back and forth, and even got some new bathing suits for me to try on.

I thought about all the things I'd learned about growing up, and I was wondering if she would try to tell me things that weren't true. It was like she read my mind, because she looked at me and hissed "That woman next door has been telling you about... Hasn't she?"

I looked her right in the eye and told her no, I'd been reading about it in the library.

I knew she didn't believe me.

When we were finished, everything fit and looked pretty. They were a lot fancier than the ones Aunt Carmella had bought Marie. One thing that everyone says about Mother is that she knows fashion and always looks attractive.

Another thing everybody says about her is that beauty is only skin deep.

CHAPTER TWENTY-FIVE

By the Sea

The last day of school! Half a day! Going down to the ocean as soon as we get home! We had packed our suitcases last night and we were READY!

But Aunt Sally wasn't there.

We ran up Marie's steps. "Ma! Where's Miss Sally? Is she late?"

Aunt Carmella was leaning against the door jamb with her arms crossed. "Not here yet? I guess that means me and your father'll have to take you."

Marie and I looked at her. "Does that mean you're going on vacation, too?"

Mr. Vince came out of the house carrying a big cardboard box. "Maybe" he said. "We'll see. Maybe for the weekend."

"Two weeks, Vince" Aunt Carmella told him. "They asked, and we said yes."

Mr. Vince just grunted and put the box on the sidewalk next to the car.

Aunt Carmella waved us inside. "Lunch on the table. Eat. Change clothes. Go to the bathroom." She looked at me. "She gave me your suitcase before she took off. I think everything's there. I took out shorts and a top for you."

Before we got in the car, there was something I wanted to do.

"Mister Vince?"

"Yeah, kid." He was loading the car.

"Can I call you Uncle?"

He looked at me and frowned. "What's in it for me?"

I grinned and said "This," and I gave him a hug and a kiss. His cheeks were scratchy.

He grinned back and messed up my hair the same way he does to Marie.

"Yeah, that'll work." He leaned over and gave me a quick kiss. "Let's go, in the car" and I could hear Aunt Carmella and Marie laughing.

And off we went.

Aunt Sally and Dad both always drove through Delaware, but Uncle Vince took us over the Chesapeake Bay Bridge. It's HUGE! We were so high up we could see on top of all the big ships that were sailing under it. That was neat!

We got down to the ocean faster that way, too.

When we drove through Ocean City up to Aunt Sally's, we passed a restaurant that had been on fire. Everything was still all wet. Uncle Vince said, "Uh oh" and Aunt Carmella crossed herself. Marie and I looked at each other, but we didn't say anything. But when we parked the car, Aunt Sally, Uncle Bill, and Billy were all sitting on the porch. Uncle Bill's eyes were big, and he had a scary smile. "Hey Vince!" he yelled. "How ya doing, pal?"

Uncle Vince walked up the steps and shook hands with him. "We saw your little barbeque down the road. How're *you* doing?"

Aunt Sally said "Bill, why don't you tell him all about it. Out back, so you can air-out some more." I got closer, and Uncle Bill smelled like smoke and grease. Uncle Bill said "Yeah! Yeah! That's a great idea! C'mon, Vince!" Uncle Bill's hands were shaking. They went through the house to the backyard.

I looked at Marie and Billy. Marie had grown two inches taller than Billy! I almost laughed, but Aunt Carmella pinched my nose shut so I couldn't snort and whispered "Shh. It's not funny for them." I looked at them again. They were both red, and they weren't smiling. They tried hugging, but they didn't fit together right. Billy looked down at the ground and said, "I'm going out back with Dad" and went inside. Marie looked like she was going to cry. Aunt Sally reached for her and hugged her. "Don't worry, Marie, he's not finished growing yet." Marie nodded, but she wasn't happy. "Come on" I told her. "Let's get our suitcases and unpack."

When we got in my room, we could hear Aunt Sally in the kitchen. "-been back three months... BIG grease fire, lots of smoke... one of his men got turned around and couldn't find his way out... went in and brought him out, just like they did with him... says he feels like he's got his nerve back. Carmella, after supper, could you and Vince take the kids down to the boardwalk for a while?"

Aunt Carmella laughed. "Sure, Amico. We'll keep 'em out all night if you want."

We went out to the backyard and listened to Uncle Bill and Uncle Vince talking. Uncle Bill looked a little calmer, and Uncle Vince was nodding. "So, you went and jumped back in and did what you were supposed to do and did it with a cool head, right?"

Uncle Bill blew out a big breath. "Yeah. Didn't even think about it, just went back in." He looked down at his hands. "Didn't get the shakes till I got home." He laughed, and then he saw me looking at the side of his head that had been burnt. He tugged off his earpatch and sang into it: "'My baby whispers in my ear... mm 'mm, sweet nothin's.'" We all laughed because we knew he was only being funny. Aunt Sally and Aunt Carmella had come outside, and Aunt Sally wrapped her arms around him and called him a nut. I told him his skin grafts didn't look all red and shiny anymore, and Marie said it didn't look like a checkerboard, either. There was a tiny buckle on the elastic for his earpatch, and I whispered to Aunt Sally "Is that buckle from a bra strap?" She whispered back "Yeah, he thinks it's there to keep the strap tight, but it's really because he's a boob." I laughed.

Aunt Sally took Aunt Carmella by the arm and said, "Come on, Carmella, I'll teach you how to make fried chicken Eastern Shore style." Billy said to Marie "My mom makes the best fried chicken in the whole world!" Marie looked at him and said "I have to learn too! Please?" I said "Me, too" and we followed them inside.

It's going to be a won-der-ful summer!

CHAPTER TWENTY-SIX

That Girl

We went down to the boardwalk after supper. Aunt Carmella and Uncle Vince never saw much the last time they were here, so we showed them all the neat stuff like the Rescue Museum down at the inlet. Uncle Vince stood there at the inlet for a long time and watched how the waves from the ocean and the water from the bay would fight each other and make whirlpools. They rode the merry-go-round three times, and sat and listened to the Wurlitzer with us, and we all had ice cream. At the fishing pier, there's a building above it that's a ballroom where people dance in the evenings. They looked at the sign for it, and kind of nudged each other back and forth, and started dancing on the boardwalk without any music.

Aunt Carmella went into an Auction House to see what kind of stuff they had, and Uncle Vince saw a sign that said, "Bicycles 4 Rent 7AM—Noon." When he saw the Orange Julius stand, he wanted to know what that was, and he bought everybody one, and after he finished his, he bought another one. He told Aunt Carmella that this was a lot of fun, and maybe they'd stay for more than the weekend after all. Aunt Carmella said "Two weeks, Vince. That's what they invited us for."

Marie and Billy and I were walking ahead of them, and holding hands like we always do, with Billy in the middle. Then this girl stepped right in front of us, and we stopped. She was Billy's height and had long brown hair in a ponytail. I guess she was probably pretty, sometimes, but she had a sneery-looking face, and she looked at Billy and said, "Who are *they*?"

Billy frowned back at her and said, "This is my cousin Sally" and lifted my hand up. "And this is her... ", and he stopped talking and looked at Marie and let go of my hand and took both of hers. "I mean, this is *my* girlfriend,

Marie. Marie Giametti." The girl looked at Marie and said, "You've got a big nose." Billy leaned up on his toes and kissed Marie on her nose and said "No, it isn't. It's perfect." He and Marie were blushing so much you could see it even though it was getting dark! The girl looked at me now like she was mad and said, "You've both got too many muscles." I stared right back, and I remembered something Reverend Lehmann said in a sermon. "Your *soul* is too small." She sneered at me again, turned and flounced away with her ponytail bouncing up and down.

Marie and I said, "Who was *that*?"

Billy looked disgusted. "That's Cynthia Smith. She's in my class at school. She thinks all the boys are in love with her, but we all think she's a pill." He looked at Marie, and I could hardly hear him when he said "I missed you. I'm glad you're here again." He hugged Marie, and this time they fit together just right, and Marie leaned over and kissed him.

That's when we heard Aunt Carmella say "Alright, you two, you're blocking traffic, and there's enough time for that in a few more years. Get moving." Marie and Billy started giggling, and we walked ahead again.

We stayed out until 10 o'clock!

The next morning after breakfast, Aunt Carmella and Uncle Vince took us down to the hotel we were supposed to swim at, but the pool was closed. There were two men working on machinery down in the ground, and told us the pump broke, but it would be fixed tomorrow. Uncle Vince said we'd go bike riding instead. Marie and I didn't know how, but Billy did, and he said he'd teach Marie. Uncle Vince said he could see that one coming a mile away, and that he'd teach me.

It was hard, but I learned faster than I thought I would. Marie probably learned quicker than she let on, but she and Billy were having a lot of fun. We went up all the way to the end of the boardwalk, and then all the way back. My legs hurt and my behind was sore, and I was glad we were finished, but Uncle Vince and Aunt Carmella said they'd like to do this every morning while we went swimming.

Aunt Carmella said she saw another auction house that we rode by, and we walked back to it and went inside. Uncle Vince saw a toy streetcar made of tin in one of the display cases and pointed it out to us. He said it was the "Toonerville Trolley" from the funny pages when he was a kid. He started telling us about the characters in the comic strip.

When we got home, Uncle Vince got some blank notebook pages and a pencil from Billy and started drawing the characters from the Toonerville Trolley comic strip. "The Skipper" drove the streetcar, "Powerful Katrinka" would pick-up the streetcar at the end of the line and turn it around, and there was "Aunt Eppie Hogg, The Fattest Woman in Three Counties" and "Mickey McGuire" and "Terrible-Tempered Truman," and Billy asked him to draw Maggie & Jiggs and Dick Tracy, and then Marie wanted Little Iodine and Blondie, and they all looked like the ones in the funny pages. Aunt Carmella said she didn't know he could do that, and Uncle Vince laughed and said Sister Margarete Theresa used to whack him with a yard-stick every time she caught him drawing in school, and this was the first time he'd drawn anything since he was in the Navy, and *that* was mostly "cheesecake," which I didn't understand, but Uncle Bill sure did from the way he laughed.

CHAPTER TWENTY-SEVEN

But Is It Art?

It was raining when we got up the next morning again, so there was still no swimming. Uncle Bill went to work, Aunt Sally and Aunt Carmella sat on the porch and drank coffee and talked, Uncle Vince read the paper, and Marie and Billy and I sat on my bed and played cards.

Later, Aunt Sally and Aunt Carmella were making lunch and Uncle Vince talked to Aunt Sally, then talked to Billy, and Billy went in his room and gave something to him. Uncle Vince told Marie and I "Out you go, kids. Go eat." Then he closed the door— MY door— and said, "Don't come back till I tell you."

Aunt Carmella rolled her eyes and told me, "Yeah, he can charm the birds out of the trees. C'mon, lunch."

About half an hour later, Uncle Vince stuck his head out of my door just far enough to call "Billy. I need a pencil sharpener." Aunt Carmella said, "Try saying 'please,' Vince." Billy gave him the sharpener, and Uncle Vince said "Please. And thanks" and closed the door.

It was almost suppertime before he came out. He handed Billy the sharpener and a bunch of nubs that were all that was left of a whole pack of colored pencils. He looked at me and stuck his thumb over his shoulder and said, "Okay kid, tell me what you think."

We all went in to look.

On the whole length of the wall alongside the bed, Uncle Vince had drawn Ocean City. At one end was our little grey home, and at the other end was Trimper's Rides. And it wasn't just places, there were people, too. Us! Cartoon us! And they *looked* like us!

Sitting on Aunt Sally's porch, Marie and Billy were holding hands and little pink hearts were floating above them. Aunt Sally was standing outside a little red schoolhouse, and the boy from Pinocchio that turned into a donkey was handing her an apple with a bite out of it, and a worm was sticking out and winking at her. At the Firehouse, Uncle Bill was sitting in Smokey Stover's two-wheeled fire engine. On the beach, Aunt Carmella was wearing a bathing suit and posing with one hand on her hip and one behind her head. Uncle Vince was painting her picture, only what was on the easel was that "Kilroy Was Here" thing that everybody knows how to draw.

And I was sitting in front of the Wurlitzer with little pink hearts over ME!

There were other people there, too. Dagwood and Wimpy were eating at the Alaska Stand, Dick Tracy and Fearless Fosdick were staring at each other nose-to-nose at the Beach Patrol Station, and Superman was losing to the arm-wrestling machine at the penny arcade.

There were a bunch of other people that I didn't recognize, but Aunt Sally, Aunt Carmella and Uncle Bill were all pointing and saying "Look! Moon Mullins! Joe Palooka! Alley Oop! Major Hoople!"

I looked at Uncle Vince. He said "Whatcha think, kid?" I grabbed him and gave him the biggest hug and kiss and told him it was all beautiful and I LOVED it and said "Thank you" about a million times.

We finally got to go swimming on our third day. Miss Jenny, the lifeguard, said she was wondering if we found another free place to swim. When we were finished, Uncle Vince took us home for lunch, and Aunt Carmella was showing Aunt Sally how she made her red gravy for pasta and other things. She had brought down a big box of cans, bottles, and jars to teach Aunt Sally how to cook Italian, and Aunt Sally would teach her how to cook Eastern Shore and Southern. Uncle Vince said it was a good thing he was going to go bike riding every day, otherwise he might not fit in the car to drive home.

Marie and I fixed all the ingredients for meatballs: ground beef, pork, veal, minced onions, peppers, garlic, basil, parmesan cheese, breadcrumbs from the "Sun of Italy Company" (the ONLY breadcrumbs Aunt Carmella will have in her kitchen), and a beaten egg to hold it all together. We shaped them and handed them one at a time to Aunt Carmella, and she swirled them around in a hot frying pan to sear them before she put them in her red gravy.

We were so busy; we didn't notice Uncle Vince drawing until he put down Billy's new colored pencils. I leaned around to see what he'd done. It was a picture of Aunt Carmella cooking at the stove, but she was wearing high heels, short-shorts and a little pinafore apron that barely covered her... well, her top. She looked sort of like a sexy movie star. "Is that the shortcake?" I asked. He winked and said "Cheesecake." Aunt Sally looked over and said, no, she was making a fresh strawberry pie. That's when Aunt Carmella turned around and said "Alright, Vince, what're you up to?" He bounced his eyebrows like Groucho Marx and laughed.

Aunt Carmella came over and looked, and she got all pink and tried not to smile. "That doesn't look like me. I haven't looked that good in years." Aunt Sally came over and looked and laughed and told her, "You look like a 'Petty Girl' pin-up." Then she looked again and said "Vince? This is pretty good. You should go back to school and take art classes. I mean it."

Uncle Vince started to say "Nah," but I saw Aunt Carmella shiver and say "Vince. Go back to school." Uncle Vince laughed and said "What? Your gypsy blood coming out again?" She leaned over and kissed him. "Go back to school, Vince. And put that picture away."

Marie whispered to me "Ma gets feelings sometimes." I remembered Christmas when she put another plate out for Mother, and when Marie talked about cooking for Billy.

Weird.

CHAPTER TWENTY-EIGHT

Adrienne and the Olympics

During the second week of vacation, Aunt Sally asked Aunt Carmella and Uncle Vince to stay another week. Uncle Vince gets six weeks of vacation, but Aunt Carmella said it wouldn't be fair to Aunt Sally, and she and Vince were going to visit family in Philadelphia because they didn't see them last summer.

Aunt Sally said "Carmella, we like having you here. You help me with the cooking and everything else, which is more than Bill and Billy do, so please stay, and enjoy yourselves. God knows you're better company than Susan," then she looked at me and said "Sorry, Honey," but I said she was right.

Uncle Vince said "Ah, Hell, send 'em postcards and tell 'em we'll see 'em Thanksgiving."

They stayed two more weeks. Aunt Carmella liked Granny Annie as much as she liked Aunt Sally (and that's a *lot*). On their last week, Aunt Viv came to visit! This was a terrific summer! The best!

Except for one thing.

We all asked Aunt Viv what had happened to Adrienne, and she looked disgusted and told us what happened.

"Well, kids, you know that Adrienne is a mermaid during the summer." She had a mean look on her face. "Well, the Russians went to a man named Avery Brundage— he's the man that runs the U.S. Teams— and the Russians said they'd file a complaint with the International Committee and call-in reporters unless he took my girl off the team. Well, of course HE caved in to them, did the same thing in '36 when I was there and pulled the Jewish athletes out of the competition so 'it won't offend Herr Hitler'. So, there's my girl, just won her first 'heats', and was probably going to medal, but instead of facing-down the Russians and showing the world how petty and sneaky they were because they were afraid of a girl in show business, he has her yanked off the team right then and there, and has her brought to his office with her hair still wet, and lays into her about the 'EMBARRASSMENT' and 'SHAME' she brought to the team, and he was going to make her pay back all the money that was spent on her for uniforms and travel to Rome and God knows what else."

"Now, I taught my Adrienne that if a man tries to lord it over her behind a desk, GET UP and move your chair around so's there's nothing between you and him, and if HE stands, YOU stand, and if HE leans over you, YOU lean and make HIM back-up. And if he so much as puts ONE finger on you, you give him a knee where it'll do the most good. Well, he tried all of that, and she finally let him have it, and told him that if he wanted his money, THERE'S his down-payment, and he could come around himself for the rest of it, if he had the ba -uh, I mean if he had the guts. On the way out his door, she said 'Who do you *really* work for? Us, or the Russians?' She left the door open behind her so everybody in that office could see. Told me the secretaries were trying not to laugh when she walked out." Aunt Viv looked proud, but sad, too.

"She came to my hotel room, and we went back and got all her things, and took the next flight to Paris, and she didn't cry until we got in our hotel room there." Aunt Viv shook her head. "But we had ourselves a fine time in Paris, and the 'coon-ass French' (whoops, I mean 'Cajun') that my Hubby had taught me either outraged or amused everyone we talked to over there." She laughed and said, "We came home with perfume and clothes, and all of it better than anyplace else in the whole world," but then she looked sad again and said she wished Adrienne could have had her chance to win.

We did too.

Aunt Viv only stayed a few days, and swam with us just once, because she was going to drive down the coast to Florida to see Adrienne, and maybe she'd be a mermaid herself "just for fun" when she got there. "A Big-Momma Mermaid," and if she did, she'd send pictures to all of us, even her little brother with the pork-rind ear. Uncle Bill laughed so hard he fell off his chair.

We asked her to say hi to Adrienne and tell her we were her fan club. Aunt Viv said Adrienne already knew that because she wrote and told her, and that she was going to get on her to write letters to us and the rest of the family. She says Adrienne hates to write letters, and mostly sends postcards "when the spirit moves her."

CHAPTER TWENTY-NINE

A Family

A couple of nights before Aunt Carmella and Uncle Vince went back to Baltimore, the Orioles had a double-header on the TV at the VFW, so all the "menfolk" went there, and all the "womenfolk" stayed home.

We sat on the porch, Aunt Carmella on the glider with Marie's head in her lap, and I sat on the floor in front of Aunt Sally while she combed Alberto VO5 in my hair (it always gets dry in the summer).

We were talking about this and that and having a nice, quiet time, when Marie said "Hey, Ma, you said me and Sally have a gift for math, and Pop can draw, and Mr. Freddie can build things, and Mrs. Osterhoff can sew, right? What's your gift?"

Aunt Carmella laughed and said, "I'll be satisfied if I can be a good Mother for the two of you." Then she made a funny noise in her throat and clapped her hands over her mouth and looked scared. She stood up and ran inside the house. Aunt Sally pointed to us and told us to stay put and don't move an inch, and she went inside.

We could hear Aunt Sally tapping on the bathroom door. "Carmella? Carmella, can I come in? Carmella, please? Carmella, the lock on the door doesn't really work, please let me come in?"

The door opened, and we could hear Aunt Carmella crying really hard, and she was saying she wanted a houseful of kids, but she couldn't, and now she was stealing another woman's child, and it was a sin, and maybe I wouldn't grow up right, and it would be all her fault.

Aunt Sally told her to stop it, because she wasn't stealing anything that Susan ever wanted, and it wasn't a sin, it was a blessing, because if it wasn't for the two of them, I'd grow up like Susan.

That's when *I* went in and said "Oooohhh NO, I'm won't! I'll NEVER be like her! She doesn't love anyone, and she doesn't even want to know how! I'M going to be different! I'm going to LOVE people, and, and... ". My tongue got confused, but Marie took my hand and I got some of the words back. I looked at Aunt Carmella. "I know you're not my real mother, and neither is Aunt Sally, but I know that you're both GOOD mothers, and I know you love me like mothers, 'cause that's the way you are." I stopped and took a breath. "And I love you, too." I couldn't say anything else.

But Marie could. "Ma, be a good mother to my sister. Miss Sally can't do it all by herself."

Nobody said anything. Then Aunt Sally whispered "Marie, Honey, you know that you could call *me* 'Aunt.' "

Marie gave her a hug and a kiss. "I know" she said. "But it'll sound funny when Billy and I grow up and get married."

Aunt Carmella shivered a little and laughed a tiny bit, and Aunt Sally snorted once, and we all just stood there looking at each other. Aunt Sally said it was too hot for four people in the bathroom, and let's go back outside. Aunt Carmella blew her nose and looked at me and held her arms open and said "C'mere, bambino." Aunt Carmella gives the best hugs, and I told her so. There was a lot more I wanted to say, but she shushed me. "Another time, bambino. We'll sit down and we'll have all the right words."

"I know" I said. "But right now, I can hear both of us in our hearts."

She hugged me a little tighter and kissed me. "Me too."

When we got back outside, Marie was sitting on the floor in front of Aunt Sally and pointed to the glider.

Aunt Carmella has a nice lap to lay your head on.

The last day Aunt Carmella and Uncle Vince were here was a Sunday. It was like everybody was doing everything slowly to make the day last longer. We slept late, dawdled over breakfast, and then went out on the porch and we shared the newspaper until lunchtime. Uncle Vince wanted to have an Orange Julius, so we went down to the boardwalk and strolled until everybody gave up and it was time to go.

We went home, and Aunt Carmella packed their suitcases. Uncle Vince said being down the ocean wasn't too bad if it stayed on the other side of the hill. They both thanked Aunt Sally and Uncle Bill for letting them stay so long. Uncle Bill said they should come down for their whole vacation next year. He and Uncle Vince shook hands and pounded on each other's back and walked out to the car.

Aunt Sally and Aunt Carmella looked at each other and Aunt Carmella said she grew up with four brothers and had always wanted a sister, and Aunt Sally snorted and said *she* had always wanted a sister, too. They both laughed.

Aunt Carmella pointed to Marie and I and told us to behave and do what we were told and no backtalk, and hugged and kissed both of us and we walked out to the car.

Everybody stood there looking at each other, then Aunt Sally and Aunt Carmella both said "Adio, Sorella" at the same time and got all weepy-eyed and Uncle Bill and Uncle Vince rolled their eyes.

Then they got in the car, and we waved, and they drove back to Baltimore.

It was quiet the rest of the day.

Aunt Sally came into my room to talk to us that night. She didn't say anything for a long time. Every time she looked like she was going to, she'd change her mind and think some more. She finally put her arms around us and said "Sally, Honey... "

"I know" I said. "She's still my mother, and I have to be respectful, and I will. But's it's hard."

Aunt Sally took a deep breath and sighed slowly. "It's a bit more than that, Honey." She stroked Marie's cheek. "You've got a sister here, and her mom and Dad, and us, and your dad tries his best, I know he does... I can't help what she is, Sally, but I want you to never turn away from her. One day, maybe something will make a difference... Just try to keep your heart open." She rested her cheek against my head.

I got to do a little carpentry before Mother and Dad came down. Aunt Sally and Uncle Bill said our bed in my room was too small for the two of us. We *were* getting cramped, especially on hot nights, and so I bumped out the frame and base almost to the door, and they bought us a new double sized mattress like Marie has at her home, and sheets and a nice blanket. Marie went to Granny Annie's and sewed a new coverlet and pillow shams all by herself, and she was proud of it.

When Mother and Dad came down for the last two weeks of vacation, they didn't get there until almost 5 o'clock. Dad looked tired and hot and not very happy, and Mother went right over to Aunt Sally's chair and sat in it and said it felt good to finally sit down. Aunt Sally snorted and asked if it was a long walk down from Baltimore. Mother ignored her and looked at Marie. "Why is she still here?"

Billy, Marie, and I bunched together and stared back at her. Mother was opening her mouth to say something else, but Aunt Sally turned sideways and said "Oh, Susan, it's so kind of you to visit us in our humble abode." Then she turned the other way and said "Why, Sally, it's always a joy, an absolute joy to visit you at your Palais de Mer." While she went on like that, we went to my room and waved Dad in with us.

I showed him Uncle Vince's "mural" (that's what Billy calls it), but he was more interested in how I rebuilt the bed. He checked that the drawers still slid out easily, and that the trim and paint were neat and smooth. He said it was "fine work" and that he approved and said he would be using me as a "sub-contractor" for a job in Baltimore. He said that someone wanted to get their basement finished so that when friends and family came to visit, they would have a place to stay that wouldn't inconvenience someone else, and then he winked at me.

I knew who he meant, and I nodded back while Marie and Billy tried not to laugh too loud, but I thought it was hard to keep an open heart when it seemed like nobody else was even trying.

CHAPTER THIRTY

Wood and Stone

Two weeks later, we were all back in Baltimore. Marie and I had grown over the summer, so we had to sew a lot of clothes, and FAST! We were in the 6th grade, and our new teacher was Mrs. Kreisler. Mac MacTavish said she was so old that she taught God when He was a boy, and she looked it. We get a lot of homework and tests every day.

Something that I hoped would be fun might not be after all. Dad "contracted" to finish Aunt Carmella and Uncle Vince's basement by Christmas, but he "sub-contracted" me to do most of the work. I'd get paid $100, BUT: out of that money, I had to pay HIM to help me. That means ANY kind of help, like labor (how much an hour?), and advice (how important is it to me?)

All the materials would be paid for by Uncle Vince, BUT: I had to pay him back for all materials NOT used. PLUS (and this is the worst): Uncle Vince was getting a plumber to put in a toilet and sink for a powder room, and an electrician to put in outlets and light fixtures, and I had to figure out how to work with them.

Dad said he was trying to teach me how to plan, boss a job, and make a profit (even though I think it'll only be 5 cents). I almost wanted to say I was only eleven, but I wanted to see if I could do it, PLUS do all my sewing, swimming, and school stuff. I was pretty sure I could, and I guess I'd find out.

Oh, and "All work to commence on the second Saturday of September and completed by December 23rd."

I wouldn't be doing a lot of swimming.

When Mr. Nightingale found out what I had to do, he started teaching us some accounting and business math. Marie loved it.

So, first things first:

One pocket-sized notebook for record-keeping and accounts—$.05

Wages for Dad—$.50 an hour, minimum 1 hour.

Advice from Dad—$.05 per question.

Boy's clothes to work in and cheap work shoes from Sonny's Army—Navy Surplus—$16.83 (that's $5.48 from my coin bank, and $10.35 from that $100).

Aunt Carmella liked the way Dad made our basement with board and battens, but she didn't like the knotty pine. Could I do it like this picture in "House Beautiful" magazine, with the white-washed pine?

Write letter to magazine—$.02 stamp.

Write a second letter to the decorator—$.02 stamp.

Measure basement, draw floor plan, and sketch a "blueprint" (sort of) on a big white paper bag, estimate materials (don't buy all I think I'll need, buy what I KNOW I'll use—$.05 advice from Dad).

Have Dad nail-in the baseplate into 45-year-old concrete and "furring strips" (and why are they called that?) on brick walls—$10.50, and worth every penny. Plus $.05 for a question with no answer.

Pay Uncle Vince $.50 to schedule the electrician and plumber to come and do what they had to do before I started nailing my board and batten.

The electrician was okay. He thought it was funny that a "little girl" was "bossing the job" but after he showed me where he was going to put the outlets and switches, I started doing the front wall (no outlets there). By the time he was through, I had boxed in the two front casement windows and had most of my board up. Before he left, he shook my hand, called me "Miss Osterhoff," and apologized for laughing, and said I did good work. I checked all that *he* had done (very neat) and asked about coming back to do the powder room. He gave me his business card and shook my hand again and left.

The plumber was different. He came the next Saturday, and the first thing he said was "Beat it, brat!" and tried to shove me upstairs. I remembered what Aunt Viv said to Adrienne, but I didn't give him a knee, I only leaned back into his push and said I needed to know what clearances he wanted for the powder room. He looked at me like I was a talking dog or something and yelled upstairs "Carmella! Get her outta here!"

Aunt Carmella called back down, "Sally, deal with him like you did the electrician."

I walked around him and said, "There's a floor clean-out over here (I had just learned what it was called that morning), "and Mrs. Giametti wants a toilet mounted on it." He just stared at me. "She also wants a hand basin."

He turned purple and yelled "CARMELLA!"

"She told you what I want, Mike" Aunt Carmella called back.

He yelled at me. "Who the Hell are YOU?"

I said, "I am MISS Osterhoff, I am apprenticed to a Master Cabinetmaker and Woodwright, and what you see here," I waved my hand around the basement, "is MY work. Now, how much room do you need? I have to frame the walls."

He looked at me and the sawdust on my clothes and shoes. "YOUR work? Show me!"

Well, as it happened, I had just gotten to one of the outlets. I measured and cut a plank, sawed-out where the outlet would be, filed the hole smooth, and nailed it into place. It fit PERFECTLY.

He turned away, measured, and drew lines on the floor with a big yellow crayon, and stomped up the steps. "One of these days your husband'll shut that smart mouth of yours" he called back.

"One of these days she'll marry a good man that'll respect her" I heard Aunt Carmella say to him. "When you get home, tell Ma we're all fine here."

The plumber was one of her brothers. So was the electrician.

About an hour later, the doorbell rang, and I heard somebody outside yell in Italian. Everybody upstairs ran to the door laughing like kids. When they opened the door, the voice and the laughter got louder, and there was just so much HAPPINESS going on up there I had to go see.

He was a HUGE man that looked like he could pick-up the whole house with one hand. He had white hair that went in all directions, big gaps in his teeth, a scar under his right eye, and a laugh even bigger than Aunt

Viv's. He didn't speak English, but his hands swooped around like giant birds, and you could tell what he was saying by watching them and his face.

Uncle Vince saw me first, and almost threw me to the big man, and there was more laughing and yelling, and Marie was saying "sister" and the man looked at me and tugged my blond hair and looked at Aunt Carmella and said something to Uncle Vince. Aunt Carmella blushed and gave him a little push and laughed, and then he looked at me and said that I must be an angel from heaven. I laughed and said "No, I'm not" and Uncle Vince said sometimes I was, and the man grabbed me in a hug and said to call him Papa Julie. He looked at me up and down and said I must be the carpenter, and our Blessed Lord was a carpenter, so maybe I really *was* an angel, and I could understand almost everything he said!

He spread his arms and swept us through the house and down the stairs to the basement, and Aunt Carmella showed him where the powder room would be. He looked at the lines on the floor and frowned. He took a piece of chalk from his pocket, looked again, and drew lines that were in almost the same places, but his were straighter like he used a ruler. He stood there, rubbed his chin, and thought.

I whispered to Marie who he was, and she said he was her Great-Great-Grandfather on Uncle Vince's side of the family, and that he was a hundred years old, and a stonemason, and he could do with stone everything that Dad could do with wood. I believed it. He was going to do the flooring in the bathroom.

Papa Julie clapped his hands and we all jumped. He told Uncle Vince to go outside and unload all the things he needed from his truck and hand them to him through the window and told me to measure and cut the wood I needed for the baseplate in the powder room (and I could still understand him!)

Papa Julie moved around so fast I felt out of breath just watching him. He pointed to the scar under his eye and asked if I had another pair of goggles for Marie, then he took a chisel and cut a herring-bone pattern on the floor. Then he held the wood that I had cut while I nailed it to the floor (45-year-old concrete! Ow!) He filled the laundry sink with water and laid all these little pieces of different shades of marble hexagons on the floor and arranged them in a pattern. We watched him trim some of them underwater with a beer can opener (some of the chips almost came up out of the water), and then he winked at us and took a piece of roof slate and started chipping at that. He made small pieces, put them on the side, held a finger over his lips, and grinned. We didn't know what he was doing.

He picked up the tiles and mixed up some cement till it looked like mud, and smeared it all over the floor, and then put all the tiles back in place. There was a little spot left in a corner. He took the pieces of roof slate and put them there.

It looked like a little grey mouse.

He stood up and pretended to be a lady that went into the bathroom, sat down, and saw the mouse.

We laughed so hard we had headaches.

Aunt Carmella called us for supper, and he covered the floor with damp rags, and we went upstairs and ate. Papa Julie said Aunt Carmella was a good cook even though she was too skinny (she's not, she looks like Sophia Loren). After we finished eating, he went into the living room and sat in Uncle Vince's chair and took a nap for about an hour. When he woke up, we went back downstairs, and he smoothed all this white grout stuff between the tiles and covered it up again. He told me to keep it covered until tomorrow, and he'd come back and clean up. Then he packed up all his things and handed them out the window to Uncle Vince, gave everybody hugs and kisses, and drove away.

Aunt Carmella and Uncle Vince came down and looked under the rags, and she saw the mouse and jumped, and we all laughed. Uncle Vince said he'd take me to Mary Our Queen Cathedral one day and show me the Baptismal Fount that Papa Julie had carved a long time ago. He said there's a secret that only the family knows: down at the bottom of the base in all the fancy carving, there's a tiny imp hiding under an umbrella, so he won't get splashed by the Holy Water.

I have GOT to see that.

CHAPTER THIRTY-ONE

Finishing and Explaining

I had to finish doing the powder room first, which meant having to work with the electrician (Mr. Joe), and the plumber (*MISTER* DiCarlo). Then I had to experiment with the painting. The interior decorator had written that he used VERY thinned flat white wall paint with bluing on unprimed pine to allow the grain to show through. It was supposed to look like a whitewashed wall that hadn't been whitewashed for a while, and "all ready for Tom and Huck to paint." That sounded stupid to me. I got Marie to help, and I paid her $.50 an hour for it. Aunt Carmella said she liked it and that it looked like the pictures in the magazine. Uncle Vince painted an ivy plant on one wall in the powder room, and she liked that too. She didn't see that he had painted a knothole under a leaf with an eye peeking in. I think he gets his sense of humor from Papa Julie.

We painted the rest of the basement the same way, and I paid Dad to staple the ceiling tile squares in place (it was faster than me going up and down a ladder). It took Aunt Carmella a week to decide what she wanted the linoleum to be (Spring Green, no pattern), and two men came and laid it down. I nailed the floor trim in place and did my accounts.

Advice: $1.65

Materials, unused: $5.16 (nails, wood, and paint)

Labor, Marie, painting: $4.50

Labor, Dad, everything else: $24

Plus $10.37 for my clothes equals $45.68

Net profit: $54.32

I got Dad to come over and see if I missed doing anything or should have done something better. He looked over every square inch, and told me it was "fine work" and what he had expected of me, but then he asked me "What troubles you?"

I took a deep breath. "I'm only eleven. It felt like a lot of work for a kid to do."

He nodded. "Tell me what you have learned."

I couldn't stop myself from grinning. "Write my own contracts."

He laughed. "What else?"

I thought. "I think I did pretty good estimating materials. I didn't estimate labor, but I'll know better next time. I worked with other trades, but I'm always going to have trouble even when I grow up because I'm a girl, and I'll have to prove to *them* that I know what I'm doing, even though if I'm the boss it should be the other way around." I looked at him. "Okay, so why? Why now? This is another lesson, right? Why now instead of when I'm older?"

He wouldn't look at me. "There *was* a reason, but there is no need to talk of it."

"No," I said. "That's cheating. You have to tell me."

He took a deep breath. "This summer... your mother and I... we argued... about what does not matter. She said if she got a divorce, I would never see you again."

"Yes, I would. I'd live with you."

He sighed again. "No, kinder. In a divorce, the children nearly always go with the mother." He looked at me. "I suppose I wanted to teach you so much that you would be able to rely on yourself even more than you already do. If a divorce happened."

I started to think some horrible things about Mother, but I stopped myself. I don't want to be like her.

Aunt Carmella called down the stairs. "Hey! When can I see my new basement?"

Dad and I looked at each other. I nodded. Dad smiled a little and called back "Down the stairs come then. The work is done."

The work was done, but my apprenticeship would still go on.

CHAPTER THIRTY-TWO

Christmas

Aunt Carmella and Uncle Vince bought a sofa and an easy chair that both unfolded into beds, and some throw rugs and side tables and stuff for the basement. One thing I liked was a framed drawing Uncle Vince had done of Marie and I painting the walls together. He showed us a mark on the back that said "very mature work" from his Art teacher at Baltimore Junior College. It looked nice, not like a cartoon at all. I guess I'd been so busy I didn't even notice him drawing us.

Aunt Sally and Uncle Bill and Billy came on Christmas Eve, and Aunt Sally opened our door and yelled "Merry Christmas, Susan! You know where we'll be!" They went into Aunt Carmella's home laughing.

As soon as Marie saw Billy, she got all giggly. Billy was wearing glasses. BIG glasses. Old-time glasses, like the kind old people wear. They made him look like the boy in the Felix the Cat cartoons named—

"Poindexter!" Marie was acting really weird now. "You look like Poindexter!"

Billy grinned at her and said in Poindexter's voice "Merry— Christmas—Mister— Felix."

Marie grabbed him in a big hug and yelled "Oh, you look so CUTE!" and they were both acting silly, and Marie started baby-talking to him, and that was enough for me. I went over to hug Aunt Sally and Uncle Bill.

Aunt Sally was telling how Billy had helped Granny Annie clean her garage, and he found an old pair of his Grampy Andy's glasses in a Chase and Sanborn coffee can. He put them on and wouldn't take them off because he said he could see better. They took him to the eye doctor, and he told them Billy needed glasses, and the old glasses he found were the prescription he needed. That's kind of cool. Aunt Sally says the kids at school call him Poindexter, and they just got the cable and a TV, so she knew about the cartoon.

Aunt Carmella yelled at Marie and Billy "Hey! You two! Come up for air!" because Marie and Billy were still hugging and kissing. I think I felt a little left-out. Aunt Carmella stroked my hair, and said "How about you take all of us downstairs and show-off the basement?"

Aunt Carmella showed Aunt Sally the pictures in the magazine, and Aunt Sally said how pretty it all looked, and Billy liked the picture of Marie (and *I* was in it, too), and he liked Papa Julie's mouse when Aunt Sally saw it and jumped. Uncle Bill looked at everything hard and close, and said if they ever need work done at home, they'd call me first. Then he messed up my hair like Uncle Vince does to Marie and I. Why do men do that?

This year instead of fish, Aunt Sally brought a Virginia Ham. It was all wrapped up in cloth, and it smelled like smoke. When she unwrapped it, it was covered in grey ash and looked all shriveled. She wiped off one end and cut some paper-thin slices for us to try.

It was a little salty, but it tasted good! Kind of like prosciutto.

Aunt Carmella started making a shopping list.

Christmas Day was fun. Aunt Sally and Aunt Carmella had come over early in the morning to give us some biscuits and ham they had made for breakfast. Mother ignored Aunt Sally completely.

Aunt Carmella told Dad to come over at noon so he could take us kids to the movies. I asked her "Aren't we cooking this year?"

She said "Nah, me and your aunt are gonna go wild with this ham, so if it don't work out, you and Marie won't get the blame."

Dad said that he'd never been to a movie except training films in the Army. He said the Amish think that they're worldly and sinful. Aunt Sally said, "Don't worry, Freddie, it's Disney, you'll love it."

The movie was called "The Parent Trap." It was about two girls that were twins and their parents had gotten divorced when they were babies and split them up. They met each other in a camp like Girl Scouts and traded places and made their parents get back together and get married again. It was funny, but I don't think Dad liked it very much except for the popcorn with the melted butter on it.

Christmas Dinner was "a gourmet's delight to the senses" according to Billy (Marie poked him). It was a combination of Italian and American, just like us. There was ham in everything: the soup, the antipasto, mixed into the chicken tortellini, in the green beans, slices of ham in "red-eye gravy" and bits of ham in the cornbread. It made a crazy, mixed-up dinner, but it was great!

Mother came to eat again, and she ate everything, but when she was finished, she got up and walked out without saying a word. Aunt Sally lifted the plate up and said "No tip again" but nobody laughed this time. "She only cheated herself out of dessert."

Aunt Sally had brought a Smith Island Cake!

CHAPTER THIRTY-THREE

Pool and Prejudice - 1

Everybody stayed until New Year's Day. Uncle Bill had a bunch of ear-patches made, and Aunt Sally and Aunt Carmella dragged Marie and Billy around to every store in Baltimore (probably so they could keep an eye on them). I guess I was sorry when everybody went home (Marie and Billy were miserable), but I was happy to have Marie back just with me (and, NO, I wasn't jealous.)

We were looking forward to going swimming again when school started, but then Mrs. Thune called Aunt Carmella and told us that the school said we couldn't swim there anymore, and that we shouldn't have been allowed to in the first place.

Since the YWCA never had their own pool, and the public pool in the park doesn't open until summer, we thought we wouldn't be able to swim until we went back to Ocean City.

Marie said that maybe Papa Julie could build an indoor pool in the basement, and Uncle Vince said he could just picture him building something out of the Roman Empire. Aunt Carmella said she didn't want to see him making drawings of it.

Dad came home one night and said he might have a solution, and for Marie and I to be patient. Meanwhile, Marie and I did all those Jack LaLanne exercises that Aunt Carmella does just to keep our "muscle tone," whatever that is.

Dad came over to Marie's after Mother went to the Beauty Parlor on Saturday. He looked kind of embarrassed.

"I've found a way for the girls to go swimming" he told us. Marie and I cheered, but Aunt Carmella and Uncle Vince looked at Dad, and said

"What's the catch?"

Dad told us about the "Founder's Club." It's a club that began with the men who started the B&O Railroad. "Ruling Members" were descendants of those people, and "Executive Members" were the big bosses of the railroad. "Associate Members" were big stockholders, and finally "Special Members" were people that worked for the railroad and were especially invited to join. These were people like Dad and other mid-level executives.

"And that's what you are, huh?" Uncle Vince asked.

Well, no. Dad didn't have all the right "connections," and there was something else: after meeting Mother at the Hallowe'en Balls, none of the women wanted her to be a member.

Aunt Carmella let out one whoop, and then said she was sorry. Dad said it was okay.

Uncle Vince leaned back in his chair and said "Spit it out, Freddie. What else?"

Dad said there was one more membership: "Junior Members." That's when he stopped talking and didn't look at anybody.

Aunt Carmella sighed. "Let me guess: no Jews, Catholics, Colored, Dagos, Polacks, Bohunks, Spics, and so on, right?" She didn't look mad, she just looked like she'd heard all of that before. Dad said Catholics could join because some of the original members were Catholic, like Charles Carroll. He was one of the people that signed the Declaration of Independence, and he "broke ground" for the B&O when he was an old, old man. Uncle Vince didn't say anything. Marie looked hurt.

"I'm not going without Marie" I told Dad.

He shook his head. "Marie can join" and explained how.

There was a member who would sponsor both of us. He had a son that was married to a Greek lady, and she had a niece that joined under her husband's name. His son knew Mother back when she was still Susan Peterson, and he knew Aunt Sally, too. Mother is blond, and so am I, and Aunt Sally is dark— and so is Marie. Marie could get in as Aunt Sally's daughter. I told Dad that if people cheat to get in, and others know it and are helping, why try to keep people out in the first place? Then Uncle Vince said he wasn't ashamed of who he was or where he came from. Aunt Carmella shook her head and told Marie and I that *we* would have to decide. In other words, like Billy would have said, if we join, we're "complicit in the hypocrisy of maintaining the status quo."

It was easy. We said we'd rather be real sisters than lie and be fake cousins.

But we still wanted to go swimming. Dad said if we didn't stop whining about it, he'd build a big horse trough in the backyard, fill it with ice water, and make us swim in it.

Mr. Nightingale found out what was going on, and the next Saturday he came in with that "cat eats the canary" look on his face. He sat down and told us how we could swim. It was sort of like a mathematical progression, but it all added up:

Mr. Nightingale has a friend at Poly named Mr. Goldman.

His sister is Mrs. Betty Persky.

She's the swimming coach at Western High.

She's also a Red Cross Swimming Instructor on the weekends at the Jewish Community Center over in Pikesville.

Uncle Vince said to hold it, and do we have to be Jewish, now?

Mr. Nightingale laughed and said no, the courses were open to everybody.

I said we already knew how to swim.

He said we could take the *Instructor's* Course and teach other kids how to swim. He told us that Mrs. Persky already knew who we were from seeing us at swim meets.

Uncle Vince said so long as we don't have to lie about who we are, it was fine with him.

Dad had come over earlier to pay Mr. Nightingale, and he said he didn't know any Jewish people, but so long as Mother didn't know about it, it was okay with him, too.

I didn't know anything about Jewish people either, except that they don't believe in Jesus, and the Nazis tried to kill all of them during the war, and that Einstein was Jewish, but none of that had anything to do with me, so I was ready to go swimming.

But when I looked at Marie, she looked kind of... scared? Aunt Carmella was looking at her like she was mad. Marie started to say "Ma- "

Aunt Carmella *was* mad. "Shut it, Marie. I told you those were all lies. Not one more word out of you." She was growling like Aunt Sally does with Mother.

Marie started to say "Ma" again.

Aunt Carmella yelled "NO!" Then she said a lot quieter, "Go upstairs. Now. I'll talk to you in a minute." Marie went upstairs and didn't look back.

Aunt Carmella turned back to Mr. Nightingale. "Just crap she heard from kids. Not this one" she said and touched my cheek. "Some rotten kids in her Catechism Class a few years ago. Ask your friends when they can start. And thanks, Johnny, I mean it. Thanks." She looked up the stairs. "I think she'll skip the lesson today. I gotta talk to her about something else" and she went upstairs.

Mr. Nightingale started our lesson, but he kept looking upstairs and at Dad and Uncle Vince every time that we could almost hear what they were saying.

All of a sudden, we didn't have to *try* to hear, WE HEARD!

It was Aunt Carmella. "I don't care WHO told you, or HOW MANY told you, it's a GODDAM LIE, Marie! Think! THINK! That's what God gave you brains for!" I thought I heard Marie say something, and then Aunt Carmella yelled, "That's it! Back downstairs! There's more brains down there than there is up here!"

They came downstairs and Aunt Carmella looked around at everyone. Dad and Mr. Nightingale both looked like they didn't want to be there, but Mr. Vince sat and watched like he was seeing something funny on TV and was waiting for the punchline. I guess that left me.

Aunt Carmella said "Here, I bet your sister can figure it out. Would you believe *her*?" Then she said "Sally. Marie thinks Jewish people eat bread made outta the blood of Catholic babies."

I never heard anything so crazy in my life! All I could say was "WHHAAAATT?"

Aunt Carmella leaned over me. "If it was true, how would you prove it?"

This was too crazy even to think about, but I tried. I knew that in Baltimore, there's Italian bakeries, German bakeries, Polish bakeries, and Greek bakeries, and I guessed there were Jewish bakeries, too, and Aunt Carmella said there were, so I said the first thing I'd do would be to check the trash cans behind their store for dead babies. That's when Uncle Vince started laughing, and then Mr. Nightingale was laughing, and Dad stood there with his mouth hanging open.

Aunt Carmella nodded. "What else?"

I thought some more. "I'd ask the police if anybody was missing their babies." I remembered something. "Is it the bread that says Jewish Rye in the A&P?" Uncle Vince was pounding the table, now.

Aunt Carmella laughed a little, too. "No. It's called Matzoh. It's unleavened bread, like in the Bible. It looks like crackers."

NOW I knew what it was! I'd seen whole boxes of it at the A&P, and that would be a LOT of babies, and EVERYBODY would have noticed! I told Aunt Carmella that, too, and she nodded and turned to Marie and said "Well?"

Marie looked at us and nodded. I didn't think I had changed her mind, but I thought that maybe she'd wait and see what happens at this community place. I hoped.

But we're going swimming!

CHAPTER THIRTY-FOUR

Pool and Prejudice—2

Mr. Nightingale called Aunt Carmella during the week and said that Mrs. Persky wanted us at the Jewish Community Center at 9AM on Saturday, and that we'd skip our math lesson just this once. Uncle Vince drove us there, dropped us off, and told Marie to be polite, not nasty, and enjoy our swim.

Marie had been quiet all morning, and after Uncle Vince left, she looked scared to death and just stood there.

I had to tug her along the sidewalk, and said "Honestly, Marie, what's the matter with you? Nobody's going to do anything to you."

She was dragging her feet, and whispering (Marie— whispering!) about these kids at Church telling her all these crazy things, and I said "That's ENOUGH, Marie! You sound like Mother talking about Colored people!"

THAT made her mad. "Oh, yeah? Well, I'm not like HER! And Pop says all the stuff people say about Colored people isn't true, 'cause he works with them every day on the docks, and he says they're the hardest workers there, and I like Doris, and she's Colored, and— "

"So how come you want to believe all this stupid stuff about Jewish people?" I didn't like this. She wasn't acting like my Marie. I felt mad at her for the first time since I taught her how to sew, and I didn't want to be mad, but I was, and I hissed "Just stop it. You're embarrassing both of us."

She yelled back "Stop talking like your mother!"

She was right: I was. We both stood there and stared at each other. I felt like I wanted to cry a little, and I think she did, too, but all I did was grab her hand and pull her into the building.

There was a lady sitting at a desk inside the lobby. She looked at our towels we had under our arms and said, "Sally Osterhoff and Marie Giametti, right?"

"Yes, ma'am" I said. "Are you Mrs. Persky?"

"Oh, no" she smiled. "Mrs. Persky is waiting for you at the pool. Go down this hall, and it's the last set of doors on your left." I pulled Marie down the hall, and pushed her through the doors, and shoved her into another one that said "Women," found an empty locker, changed, showered, went through one more door, and right into Heaven!

Well, it felt that way to me. Warm, damp, and smelling like chlorine.

There was a lady in the pool, and another lady doing sit-ups on a towel. They looked at us, and Marie tried to hide behind me. I moved to the side and said "Hi, we're looking for Mrs. Persky. We're—"

"The 'Mascots' ", the lady in the pool laughed. "Your Mrs. Thune always wanted you two for Patterson, but *I* want you for Western." She pulled herself out of the pool. She was tall, and had shoulders like Aunt Viv, but smoother muscles. If cats could swim, they'd look like her. She shook my hand, and reached out to Marie, but Marie was still trying to hide behind me. I wanted to scream!

Mrs. Persky looked at Marie and shrugged. "Okay, so here's what we'll do this morning. First, get in the pool and warm-up and show me your best; and second, I'm going to push you through the Instructor's Course. If you pass, you'll be teaching this afternoon. We've got a new group coming in, and you'll take the youngest. Miss Bertha, here, will be watching over you. After the group swim, you'll be staying for Lifeguard training, but you're NOT getting pushed through that, you'll work hard." She nodded. "In the pool, two laps to warm up, and then a four-lap race."

It felt wonderful! I was gliding through the water like an eel or a dolphin, maybe. When we finished, I lay there in the water with my eyes closed and a big silly grin on my face. A whistle blew and I looked up. Mrs. Persky was squatting down at the edge of the pool.

"Yeah" she said. "I'll work on you two and get rid of that old-fashioned style you were taught."

What? Old-fashioned? "Excuse me" I said, "WE were taught by our Aunt Viv, and SHE was an Olympian."

"Is that a fact?" she grinned. "Well, I was faster than Viv Palkin back in '36, and I'm still faster than 'Madame Vivienne Marchelle' today." She laughed at us and told us to close our mouths before we swallowed the pool.

I snorted and started to laugh. "You were in the Olympics, too!" Then I remembered something. "They didn't let you swim when you got there because you were Jewish."

She nodded. "Mmhmm. And I think that lost the U.S. a medal or two. And the fastest girls in Germany back then were Jewish, so Hitler lost medals, too."

"That was stupid."

She nodded again. "Mmhmm. Stupid people do stupid things."

"The same guy wouldn't let Adrienne swim."

"Nope." She twirled her whistle on its lanyard. "Some stupid people never learn."

We were all quiet for a while.

"Do you think you could teach us to swim faster?" I asked.

She looked at me. "You can bet on it."

We got our Instructor's Certificates before lunchtime. Mrs. Persky said we should really be 16 and have our Lifeguard Certificates first. She told us how she and Aunt Viv met on the ship to Germany, and that they both had boyfriends and covered for each other when they were supposed to be in their rooms at night, and they just stayed friends and wrote to each other all the time, just like Aunt Sally and Aunt Carmella. Mrs. Persky told us she knew who we were even before she saw us swim with the Patterson girls.

To me it felt like making a new friend that had always known you, so I liked her right away. Marie was still scared of her and didn't say a lot. Finally, Mrs. Persky told her to go sit on the bench, and told me to help Miss Bertha, and she talked to Marie, and I couldn't hear what she said. After a while, she got up and walked away from Marie. I was afraid we'd both have to leave, but Marie got up and went over to her and they talked some more, and Marie slowly held her hand out, and Mrs. Persky shook it. I was going to go over and ask Marie what had happened, but Miss Bertha said it was time for our students to show up and for me to come with her to the locker room.

Two groups of girls came in. Some were white, and some were Colored, and some were older than us, and some were younger, but they all came in and looked at us and each other, and they all sort of separated into white girls and Colored girls and nobody said anything.

Miss Bertha called out "Alright, girls, everybody listen, please." She opened one of the lockers. "You'll all get undressed, put your bathing suits on, take a shower, and then you'll go through that door into the pool area, and wait to be told what to do next. Okay?"

The youngest girls started to hide behind the bigger ones. "Yeah, a new experience for you little ones. Just think of it as practice for Junior High and High School. The older girls can tell you."

A little girl said, "In front of the ofay girls?"

Miss Bertha sighed. "And you can leave words like that in your lockers, too. You're all here to go swimming. Change and shower."

The bigger girls started poking and pushing the younger ones, and everybody changed and went out to the pool.

Mrs. Persky said "Okay, eleven years and younger, right here, and twelve and up on the other side of the pool with me." She looked at Marie. "They're all yours. Get to work."

Marie stepped forward and said, "I'm Marie, and this is Sally, and we're going to teach you how to swim, and yeah, we're not much bigger than you are, so that'll make it easier." She whispered to me: "Mrs. Persky said to keep everything moving and not give them time to think of reasons not to do something."

We taught them the same way we taught Doris, and the way I taught Marie, and the way Aunt Viv taught me: dry practice on the floor, then float, then swim, and we had all ten of our students qualified on the backstroke before two o'clock (which was better than Mrs. Persky did— she had two girls that still couldn't float by *three* o'clock).

When all the girls left at three, Mrs. Persky started our lifesaving instruction. We were getting hungry by then because we didn't have lunch (no swimming for an hour after eating— is that true?) Mrs. Persky had the lady at the receptionist's desk call Uncle Vince, and she started teaching us.

It was hard, and it was scary. Mrs. Persky and Miss Bertha showed us how people that are drowning will grab the people trying to save them, and they'd drown too, so you've got to be careful and get behind them and grab them in a way that they can't grab you. I asked why can't we wait until they're going down for the third time and then save them?

Everybody gave me a funny look and Miss Bertha said that the third time thing wasn't true, and we were supposed to save them as soon as we could, so that they'd have a better chance of surviving.

I wanted to ask what about ME surviving, but I didn't. Anyway, we learned different holds and practiced towing each other to the side of the pool.

It was 5 o'clock then, and Mrs. Persky said we were finished for the day, and would come back in two weeks, because they have classes for boys every other week, and different people to teach them.

CHAPTER THIRTY-FIVE

Looks and Life

Uncle Vince was waiting in the lobby. He and the lady behind the desk were laughing. She showed us a picture he had drawn of her while he was waiting for us. He made her look sort of like Ann Southern in her "Private Secretary" TV show.

When we got out to the car, Uncle Vince looked at Marie and said "Well?" Marie wouldn't look at him. "I didn't talk to her when we got there, but I apologized" she said. "Honest. I meant it too. She's— well, she's a friend of Aunt Viv's, and she's not like what the kids said, and I'm *really* sorry, Pop." She looked up.

Uncle Vince said, "Told ya," and looked at me. "Knows Viv, huh? She another bruiser?" and he hunched up like Charles Atlas the strongman bodybuilder in the back of the comic books.

I laughed. "No, sir" I told him. "She's real slender, except her shoulders."

He laughed, and said "Like you two, huh?"

I laughed again, but on the way home, I thought about what he said, and I thought about that Cynthia Smith saying we had too many muscles, and Mother saying that I've ruined myself from swimming, and I wished that Aunt Carmella was in the car with us, and maybe Aunt Sally too, because I wanted to ask questions about the way we looked. I'd never thought about it much before. Do we look okay?

When we got home, I had to go to our house because Mother was complaining again that I spent too much time with Marie. Mother was the LAST person in the whole world I would EVER talk to about the way I look, and I mean EVER*EVER*! I didn't want to ask Dad because I knew he wouldn't understand.

I didn't get to talk to Aunt Carmella on Sunday.

Or Monday.

Or the rest of the week until after our math lesson on Saturday, and by then I almost didn't want to say anything about it. But I finally did when Marie said she was tired and went upstairs to take a nap (at our age!) She said her stomach felt funny, but she wasn't sick, she only wanted to sleep.

I sat in the kitchen with Aunt Carmella and ate a biscotti. Aunt Carmella kept looking up at the ceiling and tapping her fingernails on the table. She shook her head, looked at me and smiled. "You're quieter than usual, kid. What's up?"

I bit my lip, and I tried to talk, and it finally came out. "Do I... and Marie, too... do we look... okay?"

She reached over and felt my forehead. "You feel sick, too, bambino?"

"No" I said. "That's not it. I wanted to know... do we look like... this?" and I posed like a wrestler on TV.

She frowned. "No, you DON'T look like that. Who said you looked like that?" She tipped her head toward our house and whispered "Her?"

"No ma'am. Not this time."

She frowned some more, and reached over and stroked my hair and cheek. "Ah, wait, is this about your Aunt Viv?"

I nodded my head so hard my neck popped.

She leaned over the table and kissed me. "Forget it, kid. For starters, you're not really related to her, and your Granny Annie says she looked like that the day she was born."

I tried to picture that, and I snorted and laughed.

Aunt Carmella was smiling now. "Okay, kid— now think: does Adrienne look like her?"

"No ma'am."

"And all those girls on those swim teams— do they look like that?"

I thought. "One of them did."

She crossed her arms. "One. Just one. Now, from what I can see, you, Marie, and all those other girls, you all look the same: you're all pretty and healthy, right?"

"Are we really?" I was chewing my lips again. "Are we... pretty?"

She hugged me. "Yeah, kid. You and Marie are going to be real heart-breakers in a few more years. Vince and your father'll be sitting out on the porch with baseball bats to keep the boys away. You're gonna to be a knock-out." She kissed me and let go. "Okay, kid, I'm going to have to kick you out of here for a while." She looked at the ceiling again. "I think I know what ails your sister." She rolled her eyes, sighed, and kissed me again. "Go on, beat it. Go build something with your father."

I went to see Marie after we came back from Church on Sunday. Uncle Vince let me in and messed-up my hair and whispered, "Big goings-on today."

Marie and Aunt Carmella were in the kitchen. Marie looked mean and grumpy. Aunt Carmella looked at her and said "Well? Go on and tell her."

Marie clenched her teeth and said, "I'm having a period."

I almost said "cool," but I didn't think she'd agree with me, so I just asked what it was like.

She frowned even more. "I heard when you left yesterday, and I got up and went to the bathroom, and when I wiped, there was some blood on the paper and I yelled for Ma and asked her if it was a period and she said it probably was and she had things I needed that she'd put-away for me and she showed me how to put it on and it was just a little bit the rest of the day but this morning it was—". She stopped and growled in the back of her throat. "Ma put a rubber sheet over my mattress last night and it's a good thing, 'cause it LEAKED 'cause the pad came undone and they feel rough and the snaps on the elastic bands that hold it on keep yanking my hair out and there's not a lot coming out right now but it feels like I gotta wipe all the time—", and she said something in Italian, and Aunt Carmella yelled at her, and Uncle Vince was out in the living room coughing like Dad does.

I wasn't sure what to say to Marie, so I thought about what we read in all the books. I couldn't remember something, and I asked Aunt Carmella "How long does it last?," and I heard Uncle Vince say, "About forty years," and Aunt Carmella yelled "Shut up, Vince!," but she was trying not to laugh. Marie yelled "It's not funny!"

Then I remembered it was about three to five days, and I said so. Aunt Carmella said I was right, and I told Marie we'd be able to go swimming on Saturday, but she stood up and looked like she was going to scream at me, but she started to cry, instead.

I came around the table and tried to hug her, but she pulled away, but then she grabbed me in a too-tight hug and cried louder. I just hung on to Marie until she stopped crying.

I finally got some air and whispered to Marie "Don't worry, When I start getting mine, we can have them the same time and be miserable together."

Aunt Carmella sounded like she was choking, and then she laughed. "It don't work that way, kid. You won't know when until they start, and you don't get to pick the days, either."

Marie whispered "Well, I hope it's not for a long time, because it's not any fun. But thanks anyway" and tried to smile.

I'm going to have to re-read all those books again, so I don't say anything else dumb.

CHAPTER THIRTY-SIX

Austin

Marie was okay by Saturday, and we went swimming again. This time, Marie... well, it was like she was forcing herself to talk to Mrs. Persky at first, but then she started asking Mrs. Persky about being Jewish and how that works, and what was different from being Catholic and all that. Mrs. Persky started to roll her eyes with every question. She finally got Marie to shut up when she started teaching us artificial respiration. When I had to breathe into Marie's mouth, she laughed so hard into mine that my ears popped. Mrs. Persky says she's taught Boy Scouts that ran around going "Eeww! Eeww!" after they did it, and one of them even threw up afterwards. That's when *we* said "Eeww!"

We had brought extra clothes to learn how to take them off in the water and use them to float on, and by May, we had passed the course. She said she'd get us patches to sew on our bathing suits like she and Miss Bertha have. That will look SO cool!

I wonder if Marie and I could get summer jobs being lifeguards at some hotel pool down at Ocean City. Maybe we could teach people how to swim, too. When we get older, I mean. And *after* the Olympics.

Oh, and Uncle Vince has EIGHT weeks of vacation now. That's two weeks for every five years he's worked, starting from the time when he was in the war. He and Aunt Carmella are going to stay longer this summer. Marie said she heard them saying that they were going to do ALL the grocery shopping down there to pay-back for staying with Aunt Sally for free. I wondered if Mother and Dad did something like that for me. I bet Mother wouldn't even think about it.

A couple of days before school stopped, Mrs. Kreisler gave Marie and

I our report cards before anyone else got theirs. Marie had A's and A+ in everything, and I had A+ in Math, Science, and English, but I only had B's and C's in History, Geography and Social Studies. Mrs. Kreisler told us that because we have that much difference in our grades, we might not be in the same class in Hampstead Junior High in the Fall, and I might not get into the College Prep course at Western High School unless I started to get better grades (but it's hard to learn stuff that doesn't have anything to do with me). I hope Mrs. Kreisler is wrong, because I wouldn't want to be in a class without Marie. We've been together since kindergarten! Would they really put us in different classes?

School stopped, we packed up, and I think Aunt Carmella bought everything that was in DiPasquale's and Stella Mara grocery stores. Dad said he and Mother would miss me like they always do. I think Dad misses me.

We got to Aunt Sally's about 11 o'clock in the morning. Nobody was home, so Aunt Carmella got the door key out from under the glider, and we brought everything in. She packed every inch of the pantry and refrigerator with all the food she brought.

Marie heard Aunt Sally drive up, and she ran outside to see Billy. He hadn't grown at all since Christmas, and now Marie was almost a head taller than he was. He and Marie got the giggles, and Marie hugged him and bent him over backwards in her arms like they were in one of those old movies on TV that Aunt Carmella cries over. Marie said "Oh, my darling! I've waited so many lonely days and nights for this moment!," and Billy said "Your passion has overwhelmed me! Do with me as you will!" and they both fell down in the front yard and just laid there and laughed.

Aunt Carmella told Aunt Sally that this time she means it and she was going to get a bucket of cold water to dump on them, but they got up and only kissed once (but it was a long one), and they started calling each other Felix and Poindexter again.

I hope I don't act like that when *I* have a boyfriend.

After lunch, Uncle Vince said he was thirsty for an Orange Julius because he hadn't had one since last year, and that he'd treat everyone. Aunt

Sally and Aunt Carmella laughed and told him to take Uncle Bill, and that they'd stay home and get everything settled in without us being in the way.

When we got to the boardwalk, Billy said he'd take Marie and I on the rides while Uncle Bill and Uncle Vince got the drinks. I said I'd rather sit and listen to the Wurlitzer, so Marie and Billy went on the Spook House ride (I knew that it was so they could kiss, and nobody would stop them).

While I was listening to the music, a boy that was sitting there kept looking at me. When the people sitting next to me left, he came over and asked if he could sit next to me. I said yeah, sure, go ahead. He said his name was Austin Terrance, and that he lived in Ocean City and that he was going into the 7th grade when school starts again. I told him my name and that I was going into the 7th grade, too, but just then, that Cynthia Smith girl shows up and says "Hello, Gargantua." She stood there and sneered and said "You don't know who Gargantua was, do you? He was a big gorilla in the circus, and he had arms like yours."

That hurt a little, but I only said, "Your soul's gotten smaller since last year."

Austin told her to bug-off and told me she didn't have any friends because she was so nasty to everybody.

Cynthia Smith ignored him and said "Where's the other ape girl? Babysitting her little boyfriend?"

She didn't know Marie and Billy were right behind her. Marie pinched her bra strap through her blouse and snapped it.

Cynthia Smith spun around with her hand up to slap, but she stopped when she saw Billy. She smiled and said "Hi, Billy" like she was trying to be sweet or something.

Billy didn't even look at her. He said "Hi, Austin, this is my girlfriend Marie, and this is my cousin Sally."

Austin started laughing, and said "You're the one that stays here all summer, right?" I nodded, and he said he hoped he'd get to see me some more. I said I hoped so, too.

He was cute!

That's when Uncle Vince and Uncle Bill came back with our drinks.

Cynthia Smith left, but she rubbed by Billy like she didn't have any room and said "Bye, Billy" in that fake voice and smiled nasty at Marie again.

Somebody whistled and yelled "Austin!" Austin turned and waved, saying it was his brother and that he had to go. He told Billy to call him and maybe we could all get together sometime, and he smiled at me.

I hope we can.

The next day, Marie woke up grumpy and had cramps, so we didn't go swimming. Billy didn't ask or say anything, but he went next door to the rental house, stole a rose off one of the bushes and gave it to Marie. She got mad and told him she wasn't dying; she just wasn't feeling good. Billy smiled and said, "Just in case." She stomped back to our room and slammed the door, and Aunt Carmella yelled "HEY!" But when I went in later, Marie was lying on the bed holding the rose and smiling a little. Later, Granny Annie showed her how to press it in a book, so she'd always have it. I guess it's supposed to be romantic or something.

After lunch, Uncle Vince said he wanted to go down to the boardwalk and draw stuff. Aunt Carmella told him to take us with him, so he'd draw something besides girls in bikinis. He patted her behind and asked if she'd brought one with her. She laughed and told him supper would be at 6 o'clock and don't be late. Uncle Bill drove us down and we'd take the bus back home (he was working "the shift" that week).

Uncle Vince got an Orange Julius for everyone, and then he started drawing the stores, and people walking by, and the rides at Trimper's, and the boats at the docks. We ended up at the inlet, and he watched the water fighting itself. He started trying to draw the waves and the whirlpools, but he couldn't get it right. He'd draw and stop and tear off the page and throw it at the trash barrel (and we'd have to pick it up) and tried again and again.

He leaned over the rail and drew faster and faster and threw more sheets away, and he started swearing in Italian— softly at first, but then he got louder (and it's probably a good thing nobody could understand him, because people were starting to look).

All of a sudden, he stopped and yelled "I got it! I got it!" There was a policeman there, and he tapped Uncle Vince on the shoulder and told him to calm down. Uncle Vince laughed and said he was sorry, and he showed him what he had drawn. The policeman nodded and turned away, then he turned back and took another look, but Uncle Vince was already drawing new ones even faster. Now the policeman was catching the drawings too. When Uncle Vince stopped, he took the drawings we'd been catching and looked at them and laughed again.

He shook the policeman's hand and said "Thanks, Buddy" and started to walk away. The policeman asked if he could have one of the drawings. Uncle Vince peeled the last picture he'd drawn off the pad and gave it to him, then he took it back and signed it. Then he said, "C'mon kids, ice cream!" and we walked away. But I looked back and saw the policeman rolling-up the drawing very carefully instead of folding it.

We got our ice cream and sat in front of the Wurlitzer. Austin was there! He waved at me, and I sat next to him. We listened for a while, and when the song stopped, he leaned over and said "You know what I like about this thing? Whatever it plays, it always sounds like it's having a good time." Then he turned red, and looked away like he was embarrassed. I knew what he meant, because I felt the same way, and I told him so. He smiled at me, and I felt *my* face turn red.

Austin said that he and his brother Thomas come down to the docks with their mother every morning when it's still dark. They wash the boats off that the tourists fish from, and their mother cleans, fillets, and packs the fish they catch (unless they want a trophy, then somebody else takes care of that.)

Austin says that he and his brother only get a dollar or two per boat, but they clean a LOT of boats. Their mother makes them save most of it for college. He says he's going to be a mechanic and fix boat engines for a living when he grows up.

Austin knows a lot about me. He knows I'm going to the Olympics, and that I like math and carpentry and I can cook, and I sew my own clothes.

Marie and Billy were sitting somewhere behind us and giggling over something stupid.

We'd been sitting there a long time, and Austin's brother came over and said they had to go. Austin and I said we'd see each other again soon.

Uncle Vince said we should be heading home, too. When we got on the bus, Marie and Billy were still giggling. I turned around and said, "What's so funny?" They looked at each other and started talking.

"Oh, Austin, I agree! The Wurlitzer sounds like it wants to get up and dance around!"

"Oh, Austin, you get up so early and work so hard!"

"Oh, Austin, saving for college! That is *so* smart of you!"

"Oh, Austin, you know so much about me, I hope I can get to know you, too!"

Now Uncle Vince was trying not to laugh, and he told them to stop teasing me, and that they were a lot worse. Billy laughed and said, "Yeah, but *we* know we're being like that."

I felt my face get redder and hotter, and my ears were ringing. "Oh, this is ridiculous!" I told them. "I'm not in love with Austin. I just like him. And that's that!"

And it's not one bit funny!

We finally got to go swimming by the end of the week, and Miss Jenny told us this would be the last summer we could swim there. I guess we can't complain. We only got to swim there because Uncle Bill fixed it. He told us not to worry, he'd find someplace for next summer.

Aunt Sally said she would still pick us up when she gets out of summer school classes after 12 o'clock, but she said she wants us to stay at the hotel, and NOT at Trimper's. She told me "If that boy wants to see you, let *him* figure out how." I told her I only wanted to listen to the Wurlitzer, not to see Austin, and Aunt Carmella started singing a song that went "I got it bad, and that ain't good." Everybody started laughing, but I still didn't think it was funny. I got a book from Billy, sat in my room, and read it till suppertime.

Nobody makes fun of Marie and Billy.

Well, maybe not as much.

On Saturday it POURED down rain, and we were all inside. It was hot and sticky, and then Uncle Vince said we'd all go to the movies, his treat.

He had checked the paper and found a movie called "Hatari" that had John Wayne in it. When we got there, it was like a cowboy movie with John Wayne catching wild animals in Africa. I didn't pay much attention to it because Austin was there! He asked if he could sit with us, and he sat next to me, and while some lady in the movie was getting a baby elephant for a pet, HE HELD MY HAND.

It felt funny. I mean, Marie and I hold hands sometimes, and Marie and Billy and I hold hands when we walk on the boardwalk together, and Marie and Billy are ALWAYS holding hands— but this was different.

I could feel our hands getting sweaty, and I didn't know if I should let go and wipe my hand or what, but then *he* let go and got up and said he'd be back in a minute. When he came back, he had a box of Milk Duds, and we shared them. After we ate them, he put his arm over the back of my seat, and I leaned over closer to him, and he put his hand on my shoulder and I kind of put my head on *his* shoulder. It was a little bit scary, but it was nice, too. When I relaxed, it felt even nicer.

I'm not going to think Marie and Billy are silly anymore.

After the movie, Austin told me he'd try to come around to the hotel to see me swim sometime if he finished cleaning the boats soon enough, and he asked if he could come up to our home on a Sunday sometime if it was okay with Aunt Sally and Uncle Bill. They said yes.

On the way home, Aunt Sally asked me how many elephants did Dallas have? I didn't understand and asked if she meant Texas? That must have been a stupid answer because they all started laughing. Then I remembered that the lady in the movie was named Dallas, and I think she got a couple more elephants than just the one she had before Austin held me in his arms— well, one arm. I felt myself turn red, but then I thought it was funny, too, and I started laughing.

Uh oh. I snort when I laugh. I wonder what Austin thinks?

CHAPTER THIRTY-SEVEN

A Doctor Thing

The weather stayed hot and sticky, and there was no breeze at all. Even the waves rolled in slowly and didn't crest much. Uncle Vince kept going to the icehouse near the docks and bringing back blocks of ice to chop up and put in bowls in front of the window fans at night. It was miserable, but at least Marie and Billy and I got to go swimming in the morning.

One day when we were swimming, it was just so hot that it gave me a headache, and even the pool couldn't cool me off. I pulled myself out of the water and sat on the edge, and wondered if there was a movie we could go see, just so we could sit in the air conditioning. Even a bad movie would be okay so long as it wasn't a scary one. I stood up and walked over to the little water fountain by the restrooms to get a drink of water, and Miss Jenny came up behind me and whispered "Sally, Honey, is it your time of the month?"

For a second, I didn't know what she meant, but then I did. I had left a spot of blood on the tiles where I'd been sitting. Miss Jenny told Marie and I to go into the Ladies Room, and she came in a minute later and gave us a nickel for the machine in there. I got cleaned up and Marie helped me, and she and I went home on the bus. Billy stayed and waited for Aunt Sally. When we got home, Aunt Carmella took charge and got me... well, "all fixed up." She made me feel a lot less embarrassed when she said "It coulda been worse, kid. Your mother coulda been here." Boy, I didn't even want to think about that!

That evening, Uncle Bill, Uncle Vince, and Billy all went to the VFW to watch baseball (and why couldn't WE go, too? It was HOT!)

We sat on the porch with a couple of fans and tried to keep cool. I remembered something from a long time ago that I wanted to ask Aunt Sally. I started saying, "Now that I'm a woman— "

Aunt Sally and Aunt Carmella both busted out laughing and snorting and coughing and choking. When they slowed down, Aunt Sally said "Alright, Honey, 'woman-to-woman,' what's on your mind?"

I said, "A long time ago, I asked why you didn't have any more kids, and you said it was a 'Doctor thing', and you'd explain when I got older."

Neither one of them were laughing or smiling now, they just looked sad, and I wished I hadn't asked. Aunt Carmella asked Aunt Sally if we wanted to be alone, but she shook her head no.

Aunt Sally sighed and started to talk. "It's like this, Honey. Sometimes things go wrong when you're pregnant or when you're delivering. With me, it was delivering." She was quiet again and was touching her tummy and looking so sad that I wanted to say never mind, don't tell me, but she started talking again. "Billy was a breech birth. That's when the baby wants to come out backwards. Well, Billy tried to come out *bottom* first, and..." She stopped again. "I should've had a Caesarian, but that... that so-called doctor didn't 'believe' in them." She looked at me. "A Caesarian is when— ""I know what that is," I told her, and I REALLY wished I hadn't asked. "Billy finally came out, but my... my... Another doctor came in and took over, and I wished he had come sooner..."

I saw tears coming down her face, and I hugged her and said I didn't need to know any more and I was sorry, but she shook her head and hugged me back. "Anyway, Honey, my... it had to come out, and I didn't have any place to grow any more babies, so that's why..."

I started to cry— just tears, no noise, because I didn't want to make Aunt Sally feel worse than I'd already made her. Then I heard Marie say "Ma? What about you?" I wanted to say *no*! don't ask! But Aunt Carmella made one little "ha" and said we sound like all the old women that tell horror stories about giving birth, and I felt Aunt Sally snort a little.

Aunt Carmella hugged Marie. "I just couldn't keep a baby inside long enough. A couple of months, and I'd lose them. You were number four, and I stayed in bed on my back for most of my time, and you were still a month early and we almost lost you anyway, but you made it." She smiled kind of crookedly. "We tried one more time, and I lost again, and... and don't EVER say this in front of your father's family... I had my tubes tied. Your father said that me and you was all he wanted, and he wouldn't risk losing me anymore." She laughed. "He'll get his son the day you get married."

Marie asked, "Does he like Billy?"

Aunt Carmella shivered and smiled. "Yeah, he likes your boyfriend—as long as he behaves himself."

We were starting to relax again, but Marie asked, "Are *we* going to have trouble having babies?" Aunt Sally said that things like they went through didn't happen all the time and that we'd be fine, but I saw Aunt Carmella shiver again and I felt scared, but she saw me and laughed and told me "Don't you worry, Bambino, you'll BOTH be fine." That made me feel better, but I don't know why. I still wasn't sure if I wanted to have kids.

CHAPTER THIRTY-EIGHT

Austin

The next day, I still couldn't go swimming, so after Uncle Vince dropped Marie and Billy off at the pool, he and Aunt Carmella and I went down to the boardwalk. Uncle Vince walked around drawing things and people, and "us girls" window shopped. We'd all meet up for lunch.

Aunt Carmella looked GORGEOUS! She was wearing a big white hat, a yellow polka-dot sundress, and white tennis shoes. Sometimes when she dresses pretty like that, she really does look like Sophia Loren. When Uncle Vince tells her that, she says "no" but then she smiles.

I wonder if Austin thinks I'm pretty.

Marie and Billy caught up with us and we had rib-eye sandwiches at the Alaska Stand, and (you guessed it) Orange Julius to drink. When we finished, we went down to Trimper's. Austin was sitting in front of the Wurlitzer and scooted over so I could sit down next to him. Marie and Billy got in line for the Spook House ride, and Aunt Carmella and Uncle Vince went on the Ferris Wheel. Uncle Vince said he wanted to draw from way-up at the top. Aunt Carmella poked him in the ribs and said it wasn't that many years ago that they would have gone on it so they could cuddle.

Austin and I sat and listened to the music, and we started to feel a breeze— a COOL breeze, so we sat a little closer, and it got a little breezier, and then a little windy, and it started getting dark. We got up and looked out at the sky, and all these big black clouds were coming in from the ocean. The people at Trimper's were stopping the rides that were outside, and closing the places that faced the boardwalk that played games. It got so dark it looked like night, and then the storm started! Lightning started shooting across the sky, and everybody was trying to get away from the big doors, but the wind blew the rain in anyway.

Aunt Carmella and Uncle Vince came over and asked where Marie and Billy were, and I said the Spook House, and that's when all the lights went out and everything stopped, even the music. Uncle Vince said, "Stay put, kid" and they went over to the ride to wait for the power to come back and let Marie and Billy out. I knew Marie and Billy wouldn't care how long they were stuck inside, and Austin was holding me in his arms, and *I* was hoping the storm would last a long time. I turned around a little so I could hold him, and we looked at each other and our faces were close and...

And I felt so STUPID because I puckered-up like a stupid little kid when he kissed me... but then I *didn't* feel so stupid, because he had done the same thing. We were both embarrassed and...

And we tried it again without puckering, and that was a lot better, and we tried it a few more times and it felt nicer each time. We looked at each other and started to laugh, and he hugged me tighter. I had my head on his shoulder and my face was against his neck. His shirt smelled a little bit like fish from cleaning the boats, but I didn't care.

HE KISSED ME!

CHAPTER THIRTY-NINE

Missteps and Dance Steps

Aunt Sally said it was okay if I invited Austin over for supper sometime, so I got Aunt Carmella to help me plan it. We'd have a salad with a vinaigrette, linguini with fresh tomatoes, garlic and herbs, and chicken thighs in a garlic, lemon, and butter sauce. The bread was just supermarket bread, but apricots were in season and Aunt Sally said she'd make a cobbler.

The evening Austin came over, he watched me in the kitchen for a few minutes, and then went outside with Billy and Marie. When everything was done, I had a last taste—PERFECT! Aunt Carmella told me to go wash off the sweat and spatter and put on a nice blouse while she put everything on the table.

When we started eating, Austin just picked at it, and mostly just ate bread. I asked if everything was okay, and he said he wasn't very hungry (but he ate TWO servings of cobbler). I had to know, so when we were sitting on the porch after we ate, I asked if he liked it. He squirmed around and wouldn't look at me and finally said he didn't like Italian food because of all the garlic and spices and "stinky cheese," and he was sorry because he knew I worked hard to make all of it.

I didn't know whether to be mad or hurt, and I felt it both ways. He stayed a little longer, and then said he had to go home (probably to get something to eat.) I bet he'd LOVE Mother's cooking.

After he left, Aunt Sally and Aunt Carmella came out and sat with me. We didn't say anything. I got up and said I was tired and that I'd take an early bath. When I went inside, Uncle Bill and Uncle Vince said, "Good supper, Sally" and I said thanks, and then I thought a little. Seven of us liked it. Only one didn't.

Well, then, that's his loss. I'm a good cook!

So why do I want to cry?

Anyway, the next morning when we got to the pool, Austin was waiting for me. He had a milk carton full of flowers that he said came from his mother's garden— pink, white, and red Carnations, two yellow roses and a big blue Iris. He said he was sorry again about yesterday and that he hoped I still liked him, and he wanted to take me to a movie if I wanted to go with him.

I guess I can't stay mad at him, but I wish I had known what kind of food he liked. I kissed him anyway, and told him I liked the flowers, and that I'd go to the movies with him on Saturday. I asked him why he wasn't working today, and he said making-up with me was more important.

That is SO romantic!

I'm going to get Granny Annie to press my Iris like she did with Marie's Rose.

When I told Aunt Sally about going to the movies, she said we'd ALL go, just like last time. Uncle Vince checked the paper and said that "The Music Man" would start playing on Thursday, and that Buddy Hackett was in it, and Uncle Bill said Buddy Hackett was on Jack Paar a lot, and he'd like to see it. Aunt Carmella and Aunt Sally looked at the paper and said Shirley Jones was in it, and they liked her in "Oklahoma" and "Carrousel." Billy said instead of a single date, it was going to be a quadruple date.

At least when we got there, we couldn't all sit in the same row, so Austin and I and Marie and Billy sat by ourselves. Aunt Carmella told all of us to take it easy with kissing and cuddling and watch the movie this time.

It was a good movie, too. It was long enough that it had an Intermission. I'd heard some of the songs on the radio, like "Seventy-Six Trombones." Austin and I both liked the barbershop quartet songs the best because they reminded us of the songs our Wurlitzer plays.

But what I really liked best was the dancing. I wished that I could dance.

After the movie, we all waited for Austin's bus to come. Marie and Billy were trying to dance, and Billy was singing "Shipoopie, Shipoopie, The Girl Who's Hard to Get." I heard a choking sound, and Aunt Sally and

Aunt Carmella were trying not to laugh.

Uncle Vince was watching too. He said "Hey, Carmella, we never did go dancing at that ballroom. You want to go this time?" Aunt Carmella laughed and said, "You think you still got the moves?" Uncle Vince said "One way to find out. Bill, you know what time that ballroom opens?"

"It opens at six, and the music starts at 6:30." We all turned around because it was Austin who answered. He turned pink, and added "It's $.75 for singles, and $1.25 for couples. They have a couple of rock and roll bands and another band that plays old music."

He started telling us how his brother's girlfriend had the cable at her house, and she watched the Buddy Dean Show and Dick Clark and The Arthur Murray Dance Studio, and that she taught him and that they'd go to the ballroom on Saturday nights.

I looked at him and he was blood-red by then, and Aunt Carmella said, "You're dating your brother's girlfriend?" and he said NO, and Thomas was there, but he didn't like to dance, and Linda was four years older than he was, and they weren't even friends. Then he looked at me and said, "But I'd like to go dancing with you."

Aunt Sally and Aunt Carmella were standing there with their arms crossed, and I was thinking that this girlfriend/boyfriend thing was getting complicated. Then Aunt Sally and Aunt Carmella looked at each other and rolled their eyes, and said we'd ALL go, and how about we go tonight, and we did.

Austin taught me how to do all kinds of dances. It was fun and I liked it, and we'd all do it again next Saturday.

But, yeah, it feels... complicated. It's not like Marie and Billy are.

CHAPTER FORTY

Summer's End

I did a little carpentry for Uncle Vince, and he sort of got in trouble for it.

He asked if I could make him an easel to draw on, like the other artists on the boardwalk have. I said sure, and I made mine so that it folds up smaller than theirs, and the case for his pencils and crayons and chalks and stuff are all part of it.

What got him into trouble was that he put up a sign that said, "Caricatures $3, Portraits $5." He made $28 the first day, but then he got told by the same policeman that liked his drawings of the inlet that he needed to get a permit, and it cost $85, plus you have to keep records and pay taxes. Aunt Carmella yelled at him when he told her, but later I heard her say "Vincent Van Giametti" and laugh.

You know what? Uncle Vince bought the permit. I guess that makes him like a professional artist.

Cool.

This was probably the best summer of my life. I was down at the ocean, I was with all the people I loved (except Dad wasn't there), I had a *boyfriend* (and I had never even thought about that before— honest!). It felt like we were all just one HUGE family, and I guess we were.

Then August started, and I started to worry. Well, not worry, I just felt kind of nervous. Well, not that either.

The problem was that Mother would be showing up eventually, and I wasn't looking forward to it. I'd had my period twice, now, and I knew she would go crazy when she found out. Plus, I wasn't going to hide Austin (and I bet Dad would like him because he works and saves his money for college and he's respectful to everybody), but I know Mother.

There's going to be trouble.

And *I'M* going to be in it.

It was finally time for Aunt Carmella and Uncle Vince to go back to Baltimore. Uncle Vince had even thought about calling in sick. Aunt Sally and Uncle Bill said they should think about moving down here when he retires, and maybe start looking for a place that they can rent out in the summer like the house next door. Marie and Billy were all for that, and Marie wanted to move down now. She said Uncle Vince could make a living selling pictures. Aunt Carmella asked who's going to buy them in the wintertime, seagulls?

Then she said Aunt Sally wants her close by so that they could share babysitting when they became Grandmas and she shivered and got one of those weird looks after she said it. Marie looked at her and said "Ma, we're only twelve. We're not even going to get married until we graduate from college." Aunt Carmella shivered again, and then said "Alright, enough of this, we gotta go get your father his Orange Julius before we hit the road." Uncle Vince shook his head and said "Gypsy Blood" to Uncle Bill.

Marie was supposed to go back with them this time, but Aunt Sally had already asked if she could stay here until I went home. Aunt Carmella said it was better than having her mope around the house, so we packed their car, and went down to the boardwalk.

We all finally said goodbye after Uncle Vince had two Orange Julius. He and Uncle Bill shook hands and beat each other on the back again, and Aunt Sally and Aunt Carmella hugged and kissed and got all weepy-eyed. Before they drove away, Uncle Vince said "Maybe the bayside. Not too close to the water. Me and Carmella'll talk about it."

When we got home, Dad's station wagon was there. Aunt Sally yelled "Oh, Hellfire and Damnation! She's a day early!" I'd only ever heard her swear a couple times before. Come to think of it, it was because of Mother then, too.

She turned around in the front seat and said "Sally. Say 'hi' to your father, and then all three of you run to the beach and stay there until one of us comes for you."

I thought I knew what she was trying to do— for me— and I said, "Maybe I should stay and—" "No," she said. "I'll see to it." She smiled and touched my cheek and said "Don't worry, Honey. Remember: you're always mine until school starts."

We all walked along the surf, just feeling the sand wash out from under our feet with each wave. We heard a whistle, looked back, and saw Dad coming toward us. He had taken his shoes and socks off and waded along with us. I asked if we had to go back now, and he said no, and that Aunt Sally was still talking to Mother. He looked red and embarrassed and didn't look at me.

"I guess Aunt Sally told you— "

"We do not speak of such things, especially in front of your cousin." He was looking out at the ocean now.

Billy leaned up under his face and looked at him and said it was a perfectly normal function, and he had books, but Dad said "No" and turned away from us. It hurt when he did that. I expected Mother to go crazy, not Dad.

Marie and Billy looked at him and split apart and they each took one of my hands, and in a way that hurt a little more.

We stood there, not talking, and finally Uncle Bill called across the beach to us, and we went home. When I walked into the room, Mother gave me one of her looks and walked out. Aunt Sally looked at Dad and said, "I could've used some help, Freddie."

Dad sat down and looked at the floor. "I know my failings, Sally. I was embarrassed."

Aunt Sally sighed. "You might have thought a bit more for your daughter."

"I know" he told her. "I know."

The rest of the summer stank. Mother followed me everywhere: swimming, on the boardwalk, and down at Trimper's. She really embarrassed me when Austin sat next to me. She got so nasty that an old lady that was sitting there poked Mother with her cane and told her to shut up, or she'd whack her a good one.

With all the running around in the sun, Mother got a nasty sunburn—with blisters. I wanted to think that she deserved it, but that would only make me just like her.

On Saturday night, Mother and Dad both said I couldn't go dancing because I was "too young," but Aunt Sally and Uncle Bill took Marie and Billy. Mother sat on the sofa with her arms crossed and stared a hole through the wall, and Dad sat out on the porch. I went into my room and read.

I bet Austin was dancing with his brother's girlfriend.

On our last day there, Austin came up early in the morning (he missed work for me!) We stood out on the porch and talked while Aunt Sally kept Mother away from us. I asked Austin if he'd write to me if I wrote to him. He tried to say something, but nothing came out. I told him it was okay, and that I had a wonderful summer, and I was glad we met, and I kissed him. He smiled then and said "Me, too" and hugged me and we kissed again.

We could both hear Aunt Sally growl "Sit down, Susan" and we both shrugged our shoulders at the same time and kind of laughed, and then he said "Bye" and kissed me one last time, and he walked across the street and down to the bus stop.

And summer was over.

CHAPTER FORTY-ONE

I Hate Junior High School!

Everything in my life is ruined! I'm not in the same class as Marie anymore! She's in the "Advanced Placement" classes because she got better grades in Social Studies and History and all that other stuff that doesn't mean anything, and Aunt Carmella said she tried to tell me last year, and so did my teacher, and so, alright I DIDN'T listen and I DIDN'T do as well as I should have, and I know it's MY fault, and Mother just looks at me and does that disgusting monster movie laugh of hers, and –

sigh

Well, at least Marie and I can still walk back and forth to school together, and Mr. Nightingale is still tutoring us, and we'll still swim with Mrs. Persky, and—

But I miss Marie all day at school.

So, now I've got to get a LOT better at all the stupid stuff so I can get into those Prep courses at Western High School in the 9th grade and get on the swim team.

And I'm still going to be in the Olympics one day, no matter what.

There's one good thing: the girl who sits next to me in all my classes is Karen Olejnik. She kind of reminds me of Marie, except she isn't like her.

Well, THAT didn't make any sense.

Okay, Karen is short, has honey blond hair (like Dad), and she's a bit… well, pudgy, because her family owns Olejnik's Bakery on Foster Avenue. She's got three brothers and two sisters and she's the "baby" of the family. She's sort of loud like Marie, and she says she's got to be or nobody in the family would know she was there.

She sews her own clothes like I do, but she uses BIZARRE prints— one dress has jet planes flying, and another is women's eyes all made up with mascara and eye shadow. She buys remnants from Shockett's for 3 cents a yard.

She likes to cook, too, and she knows everything about baking. She got into a big argument with our Home Economics teacher about spices and seasonings. Mrs. Holmes is trying to teach us to cook like Mother— GAG!

I got into an argument with Mrs. Holmes about budgeting. I don't think the class has changed the prices they use for food in a hundred years! Eggs don't cost 10 cents a dozen, bread isn't a nickel a loaf, a quart of milk isn't 7 cents with a 1-cent deposit on the bottle, and NOBODY sells beef roasts for TWELVE CENTS A POUND!

Anyway, Karen and I like each other. She's going to teach me Slavic recipes and baking, and I'm going to teach her math— and boy, does she need help! Everybody in our class does, except me. Miss Hussey is teaching "New Math." It's all "bases" and "powers," and I have to help Miss Hussey explain it, like base eight is like counting to ten and you only have eight fingers.

But I've still got History, Geography and Social Studies.

And I really miss Marie.

I think I'm really, really, REALLY in trouble this time.

The newspapers and TV have all this stuff about the Russians putting missiles in Cuba that they could shoot at us. There were drawings about where the missiles could hit and how long it would take them to get there. Washington D.C. is only about an hour away from Baltimore, and the papers say that Sparrow's Point steel mill would be a good target.

Anyway, we keep having these drills in school— "Duck & Cover!" and we're all supposed to find a fallout shelter if the sirens go off or if a bomb goes off. HA! If one goes off at Sparrow's Point, it'll blow up everything in Baltimore no matter where you hide.

Okay, what happened was that we had a drill, and Mrs. Stacey, our Social Studies teacher had taken us down to the school basement and had us kneel on the floor (and I ruined another pair of nylons and got dirt all over the skirt I had just made), and I made her mad when I said nobody was dumb enough to bring the world to an end on purpose, and then she really got mad when I told something Uncle Vince had said about President Kennedy and Premier Khruschev having a "pissing contest."

Everybody stopped making noise, and one boy in the back said, "Dumb Blonde." Mrs. Stacey just looked at me and told me to get down on the floor with everyone else, and that she and I were going to have a talk about my "crudity and abysmal ignorance" after school.

Yeah, I'm in trouble.

So, there I was, her room, 2:30, and Mrs. Stacey stood in the doorway until the hall was empty. She closed the door, pulled a file out of her desk, dragged her chair over to mine, pushed another chair in front of it, kicked off her shoes, put her feet up and slouched. I guess teachers relax too, but I'd never seen it before.

She ignored me, opened the file, and started reading. It was almost 3 o'clock before she finished. She finally looked at me and said "I'm going to ignore the crudity. I really don't expect much else from this part of town." I started to say something, but she stared at me, and I stayed quiet.

"I can't do anything about the way you were raised, but I AM going to do something about the obliviousness you cocoon yourself in, vis-à-vis your relationship with world events." She sounded like Billy when he was showing off his vocabulary.

She tapped the file. "I brought this up from the office. It says you have an IQ well into the genius range. Your math ability is not a mere 'idiot savant' talent. You have the ability to excel in ANY curriculum."

She leaned over, and I could tell that she smoked. "Here's what's going to happen, little genius: I am going to talk with your teachers in History, Geography, and English, and from now on, you are going to produce college-level work. No more lackadaisical attitude on your part ever again. There is a dangerous world outside, and it's time you woke up to that. 'Nobody's dumb enough to end the world' hmm? Humanity has been trying for a very long time to do just that. The difference now is that we are finally capable of it." She dropped her feet on the floor, stood and turned away from me. "Go home."

Yep, I'm in it right up to my neck, and there's no one to blame but me.

After supper I went over to Marie's and watched Huntley and Brinkley on channel 11, and Walter Cronkite on channel 2, and read the newspapers— and this time I *really* read them, not just the funnies and skimming through the rest like I usually do. Uncle Vince watched me and asked why the sudden interest in the world? I started to tell him about Mrs. Stacey, and that I was going to have to do some big homework assignment, but I stopped in the middle and asked, "Is there going to be a war?"

Uncle Vince got a funny look on his face and said, "Everybody's wondering about that one, kid." He sighed and rubbed his eyes with both hands. "Y'see, Kennedy and Khruschev gotta look tough for their countries— especially Khruschev. Otherwise, they won't get re-elected here or whatever they do in Russia. The trouble with that is maybe one of them will dare the other one too hard and something might start that they can't stop. I don't *think* that'll happen, but all you need is just one hothead, or some little accident..."

He looked at me then and reached over to mess up my hair. "Don't worry about it, kid. I told your aunt and your sister the same thing: don't worry about it."

But HE looked worried. I gave him a hug and a kiss, and said goodnight, and went back to my house.

The next day in English class, Mrs. Reed gave me some old, mimeographed papers that she said was a guide to writing essays and term papers. She said I was showing "good initiative" in wanting to do extra-credit work, and that she would help grade the written part. Mr. Donahue in Geography gave me a HUGE old map of Europe and Russia and China and said I could draw new borders on it since it was outdated. He said he wished other students showed the same interest as me. After class in History, Mrs. Swenson handed me a list of books to get from the library.

I didn't say that this wasn't my idea.

I went to Mrs. Stacey's room after school, and she gave me some books that she said were hers and told me not to damage them or mark them (as if I would!)

My assignment is the famine in the Ukraine in the 1930's. She says I'll see how Russia runs things.

I got some big help two days later. Karen asked me what I'd been doing since Mrs. Stacey got mad at me. When I told her, she got a funny look on her face and said I should talk to her grandmother, because she was there.

I did ask, but wished I hadn't. I'd been reading all the books I had gotten, and they talked about 7-year plans, and going from agriculture to industry overnight, but the books also talked about the Ukraine wanting to be its own country instead of part of Russia— I mean the USSR. Anyway, the Russians came in and took ALL the crops so they could be "redistributed fairly and not kept by greedy farmers." So, if you didn't have food, you starved. To DEATH!

That's where Karen's Baba Anya came in. Her family had run a bakery in the Ukraine, too, and so they had some money to help them escape to Poland. But before they could leave, her father and her husband got denounced by their neighbors and taken away. Baba Anya took her kids and ran away from the town and walked to Poland. It was a long walk, and she saw a lot of horrible things that people did to each other. Like cannibalism. She said some people even ate their own dead children.

I wanted to throw up because I could see she was telling the truth, and it was the way she told it that made it worse. It was like she was telling about another Baba Anya that was there, but not being part of there— no, I can't explain it, and I'm not going to. NOBODY should have to live through things like that and remember them.

Her story had a happy— no, not happy. A good ending. Maybe. I guess. When they got to Poland, she met a man that also escaped, and he was a baker, too, and they got married and came to America. That's a good ending, isn't it?

I thanked her for telling me about what the Communists did, and I was sorry about all the horrible things that happened to her, but she said it didn't matter whether it was Communists or Czarists, Stalin or Nicholas, they were all the same: if you rule, you have to rule EVERYTHING. And anything you DON'T rule is a threat you've got to get rid of. She said she wasn't even mad anymore about her neighbors telling lies about her husband and father, because it had always been that way since forever.

I thought about that part all night.

That weekend, the Russians said they'd take their missiles out of Cuba, and everybody said that President Kennedy won, and everything was okay again. On Monday, Mrs. Stacey said I didn't have to finish the term paper, and that she had only been mad at me because I didn't care what went on in the world. So, stupid me, *I* got mad and said I wanted to finish the paper, and I wanted a good grade on it, too.

She sat there and stared at me like I was something that fell out of the sky, and then she said "Alright. It's still due the day before Thanksgiving."

I've got to learn to keep my mouth shut.

I kept thinking about what Karen's grandmother had said about people always turning each other in to the police or whoever was in charge. I went to the library and got more History books about Russia that went *all* the way back to Ancient Greece and Rome and Vikings and Mongols and Czars that all had run Russia.

They all worked the same way: come in, steal everything, get people to turn against each other so that the ones doing the stealing could steal more and get rid of all the troublemakers at the same time.

I wrote this up, did the notes and sources, drew different borders and trade routes on the map and handed everything in on time.

Mrs. Reed, Mr. Donahue, and Mrs. Swenson all gave me A+'s.

Mrs. Stacey gave me a B, and said it was too simplistic, but a fair effort, and the good part was that I had found an eyewitness. She said if I wanted a better grade, I could try again, and since I liked going into the past (NO), I could do this: China. Water Kingdoms. Mao. By St. Valentine's Day.

"B."

I'll show her.

CHAPTER FORTY-TWO

Papa Julie

Christmas time came, and so did Aunt Sally, Uncle Bill, and Billy. I heard Marie yell "He's here!" and Aunt Carmella said "Oh, *he's* here? I wonder when Sally and Bill are coming?" I don't think Marie heard her because she flew out the door and down the street to where they were parking. I ran out of our house.

Billy jumped out as soon as the engine got turned off, and Marie grabbed him and stopped. "Poindexter! You grew!" He had! He was up to her eyes instead of below her nose. They were laughing, hugging, and kissing, and even though I hadn't thought about Austin (okay, not much), I felt lonely and maybe a little bit jealous of Marie. NOT for Billy, he's my cousin, but because... well, I wished I had someone that loved me like they do.

Aunt Sally hugged me from behind and said "Don't worry, Honey, you're still only twelve. Plenty of time to come yet."

Uncle Bill nudged Billy. "Come on, Romeo. Grab a suitcase." I tried to act "non-sha-lont" and asked how Austin was.

Billy laughed and said he was fine, and that he had asked Billy to say "Hi" and "Merry Christmas" to me, but he laughed more when I asked if he was "going with" anyone. Last week at the High School Christmas Dance, his brother's girlfriend Linda took *Austin* to the dance. There was a lot of talking going on about that, he said, and Thomas wasn't too happy about it.

When we got up on the porch, Mother poked her head out the door and looked at me and nobody else and said really snotty, "I wonder why you don't move in with them, you're never here with your real family except to sleep."

Aunt Carmella was holding the door open for everyone, and she looked like she wanted to say something back, but instead she only said, "We eat at six, Susie."

Christmas Vacation came and went quickly this year. Too quick for Marie and Billy. Aunt Carmella and Aunt Sally sent all of us to the movies twice. They said I was supposed to be a chaperone.

I missed Austin.

I worked on that China paper for Mrs. Stacey.

I didn't have a lot of fun.

A week after they all went home Uncle Vince took us to St. Leo's Cathedral after swimming.

Papa Julie was there, and he had made something for the Church that would be mounted into the wall behind the Altar.

When we got there, it was like every Giametti in the world was there. There were so many, Aunt Carmella said it looked like High Mass on Easter.

Papa Julie and a bunch of men with ropes and block and tackle and a wooden scaffold and stuff were lifting whatever it was into place. It was in three slabs, about a square yard each, and covered with brown paper. All I knew was that it couldn't be a mouse like in Aunt Carmella's powder room. When it was all in place, the men took all the ropes and stuff away, and Papa Julie peeled away the paper.

It was the Last Supper, like the one Leonardo Da Vinci painted, only carved in marble. Everybody started pushing around to see it and we waited on the side. Papa Julie went over to where the Priest was and said something that didn't quite sound like Italian. The Priest looked surprised, and Aunt Carmella heard it too, and shivered a little and crossed herself.

Papa Julie knelt and said something else, and the Priest made the sign of the cross over him and said a bunch of words I didn't understand, and when Papa Julie stood up, the Priest hugged him and kept saying "Grazia, grazia." Papa Julie nodded, and I knew he was saying "Oh, it's nothing, just a decoration" and he walked down the aisle and sat in the back of the Church.

Marie and I went back to see him and got in the pew in front of his. He was holding his Rosary, and he looked tired but happy. He looked at us and said "Ah, Marie and her sister the angel." I understood him and laughed and said I wasn't an angel, and he said, "Then you must be Sally the carpenter," and held his arms open and hugged us over the back of the pew. Then he grinned and made a "shushing" sound with his finger over his lips and told us to go look at Judas' feet and winked.

We went up and squeezed in. Judas was the one with the money bag, and we looked under the table and there it was: a tiny imp with a stonecutter's mallet, and he was getting ready to smash Judas' toes.

We held our laughter in and ran back down to Papa Julie.

But something had happened.

I could see Papa Julie, but I knew he wasn't there anymore.

Marie screamed and ran back to Aunt Carmella, but I just stood there, and I couldn't leave, and I couldn't stop looking.

I felt Uncle Vince wrap his arms around me and turn me away, and whispered "Don't be scared, Sal. It's okay, just come away now."

Everybody else was crowding around now, and they were all crying and praying. Uncle Vince and Aunt Carmella were holding Marie and I and walked us out the doors and into the car. Marie was crying so much she could hardly walk.

We all just sat there in the car, Marie and Aunt Carmella in the back, and Uncle Vince and I in the front. Nobody said anything.

I finally had to ask. "What did Papa Julie say to the Priest?" Aunt Carmella didn't answer right away. "I saw you shiver."

She held Marie a little tighter and whispered those words. Uncle Vince jumped this time. He looked at me and said "It's the Latin, kid. He said, 'It is finished'" and started to cry.

Then I remembered that was the last thing Jesus said when He died.

I didn't think we would ever stop crying.

How can you fall so much in love with someone you only saw twice in your whole life?

When we got home, I went over to our house. Dad was in his workshop. We had been building something fancy called a "Bombe" chest. It was a big fat chest of drawers. Dad had seen a picture of one and thought it would be fun for us to make.

I told him what had happened to Papa Julie. Dad said I should go to the funeral to show respect. I told him I'd already decided to. That's when Mother came in. She must've snuck down to listen.

She started hissing that I wasn't going to the funeral, and that "those people" weren't my family, and they were loud and crude and that little slut of theirs was always pawing at Billy, and when she said that I felt something ugly coming up my throat, and then WHAM!— Dad had slammed his fist on the workbench and yelled "ENOUGH! Our neighbors are good, honest, hardworking, and God-loving people, and I will hear NOTHING against them ANYMORE— ESPECIALLY little Marie!"

Mother had jumped backwards out of the workshop and looked shocked that Dad said anything back to her. She ran upstairs to the bedroom, and we heard BOTH windows break, and we knew she was throwing Dad's clothes out again.

Dad sat down on top of the workbench and looked at his watch and nodded. He said he wouldn't bother the glazier on the weekend, and it could wait until Monday or even later, and that he would be warm and comfortable in his basement again. He grinned at me and told me to get the laundry basket and come outside.

Uncle Vince was already there, catching clothes, and Marie was folding them up after Aunt Carmella checked them for broken bits of glass. Aunt Carmella and Marie leaned over the porch wall and gave Dad a hug, and Uncle Vince did too. Dad had a funny look on his face, because he doesn't always dig hugs, especially from another man. He told them he was sorry about Papa Julie, and to let him know when the funeral was, and pointed to me and said it might be better if I stayed with my sister that night, and maybe Sunday night, too, and that I'd need a black dress, and he got his wallet out, but Aunt Carmella said put it away, because Marie would need one, too, and she hugged him again.

The funeral was on Thursday, and it was at St. Leo's again. Besides Latin, it was in Italian too, because the Pope said it was okay to say everything "in the vernacular." Uncle Vince whispered in my ear everything that was said. My knees hurt from all the kneeling we did.

The Priest was talking about Papa Julie (it's called a eulogy), and the Bible said that after King David had done all that God had wanted him to do, he died, and that was how Papa Julie lived. Later he said something about Papa Julie's "impish" sense of humor, and people laughed. The Priest was one of Papa Julie's great-nephews, so he was "in the know" Uncle Vince said.

That's when Marie and I remembered the imp getting ready to hit Judas' toes in the Last Supper carving, and we hadn't told Uncle Vince yet. We whispered in his ear after the service was over, and he laughed and told Aunt Carmella to take us out to the car. He tapped another man on the shoulder, and said "Hey, Tommy, guess what our girls just told me."

I didn't hear the rest, but I heard Uncle Vince say, "OUR girls."

Mother was wrong again. They *are* family.

Uncle Vince took Marie and I back to the cemetery a week later after swimming. He wanted us to see Papa Julie's headstone that he'd carved for himself. I was surprised it looked so small and plain, especially since his wife's was all decorated with flowers and vines on it, and it said "Barbara Elizabeth Giametti, beloved Wife and Mother" and the dates when she was born and died. The only thing his said was Julius Pietro Giametti. But Uncle Vince knelt and pushed back the new grass, and we saw it: at the base of the stone, there were a bunch of imps, arm-in-arm, dancing. Uncle Vince said they were doing a Tarantella.

We're all going to miss Papa Julie.

CHAPTER FORTY-THREE

Term Papers

Happy St. Valentine's Day!

Ha-ha-ha.

I turned in my term paper (and do the kids in the Advanced Placement classes have to do these? I bet not!) I got A+'s again from everybody else, but I still only got a B from Mrs. Stacey. We argued about that, and she said alright, B+, but I said it was good enough for an A. She said she didn't want "good enough" and dropped it down to a B again. ARRRGH! God, I hate her!

Then I made the same stupid mistake of opening my big mouth and asked why do people get rid of one kind of bad government and then turn around and get a new one just as bad? She leaned back and said "YOU tell ME."

I didn't want to write another term paper, so I thought really fast and started talking and said that maybe it was ignorance, because most of the people in China and Russia back then were peasants, and maybe a lot of them still are, maybe, but that's not right, either, and maybe it was a "cultural" ignorance, because they didn't know the ways other countries do things. I think I was right, maybe not completely, but I think that's a lot of it, because the Russians had the Czars, and they ruled by "Divine Right," and the Chinese had Emperors, and they *were* divine, and now they all had the Communist Party, and the *Party* was always right, and the people had all gotten used to being treated the way they always had been, but that wasn't it, either. Then I started talking about how Germany had the Kaiser and "militantariamenism" (and I hoped that was a real word, but it wasn't), and then they got a democracy, but they threw it away and ended up with

Hitler and more war and more killing, all because the people wanted to believe what he was saying that everything wrong was somebody else's fault.

That's when I noticed that Marie and Karen were in the room, and Marie said come on, let's go home, it's late; but I still wanted to keep going, and I told them that Mrs. Stacey and I were having a— what? A dielectric? A diatribe? I kept fumbling for the word, and Karen said, "A Socratic Dialogue."

We all looked at her, and she shrugged and said "Hey, I'm only stupid with numbers."

Mrs. Stacey flipped back a page in her notebook and wrote something down.

I told Karen she wasn't stupid; she just never had a teacher that explained things the right way like I did.

Mrs. Stacey flipped the page back and wrote something else down. Then she stood up and looked at the clock on the wall and said that while it was mildly entertaining to watch me think for a change, it was late, and she had better things to do and got up and walked out the door.

I yelled "Hey! What about my A?"

She turned around and looked at me. "Well, 'Plato,' if you write up your little 'dialogue' for me by tomorrow, I'll think about it." She started out the door again, but turned around and said, "French Colonialism under Louis Napoleon the Third, specifically Indochina" and left.

ARRRGH! She got me again! I said "I hate her! She's such a rotten teacher!" I calmed down and thought and asked Karen: "Plato's from Greek Mythology, right? And what's 'Socratic' mean?"

She and Marie looked at each other, and I knew they were trying not to laugh, then they each grabbed my arms and Karen said she'd explain it on the walk home. She did, and I said that *I'm* the one who was stupid, but she said, "Nah. You just never had a teacher explain things the right way," and she and Marie started laughing.

I didn't want to, but I laughed, too.

I did my next paper and found out Louis Napoleon the Third was an idiot, and not even close to being as smart as his uncle Napoleon Bonaparte (who made plenty of mistakes, too). Louis wanted to have an empire like the British had, but all he ended up with were mostly places nobody else was interested in, and he lost a lot of them, too. And when he tried to be a General, he got captured by the Germans and had to abdicate. Like I said, not smart.

But France managed to hang on to Indochina (which is really Vietnam) for about a hundred years until they got kicked out when I was still almost a baby. Now America is over there in a war, and I didn't understand why.

I guess I'll *have* to study about Communism one day. Mrs. Stacey said I'll have to study Capitalism, Socialism, Marxism, Leninism, Stalinism, and Maoism first, and good luck trying to figure it all out, because nobody else has.

She finally gave me an A, and said it was the last one I'd have to do this year. I was hoping that I'd never have her as a teacher again, but it was like she read my mind, and she said I'd be in her class next year.

But she also told me I'd be in the Advanced Placement classes next year, but not to spread it around.

I asked if Karen would be there, too, and she said that would depend: the only thing that had ever held Karen back were her "abysmal" math grades, but she'd heard that they're better this year because she'd been working with a very good teacher that explains things to her "the right way." Then she looked at me and didn't say anything else.

I thought maybe she meant that *I'm* the good teacher.

CHAPTER FORTY-FOUR

Austin

School was over at last, and we were all going down to the ocean, BUT: Mrs. Stacey gave me a list of stuff to research, AND she sent a copy of it to Aunt Sally. Marie had told her that Aunt Sally taught English and gave her our address. I'll get even with Marie as soon as I figure out how.

But when we got to Aunt Sally's, I forgot all about that, because Austin was there! Waiting for me! I almost tackled him the way Marie did Billy, and it felt wonderful when he held me and kissed me. Maybe it didn't feel the same as it did last summer, but that's just because we hadn't seen each other for almost a year. I figured we'd feel the same way soon, especially since he asked me to go dancing with him that Saturday.

I couldn't wait.

Austin didn't stay long (he was probably afraid I'd cook something for him), but that was okay, I'd see him all summer long, and maybe I'd bake some of the cakes and stuff that Karen taught me to make. He'd *better* like those.

We all went down to the boardwalk that evening, and Uncle Vince drank about a gallon of Orange Julius, and Marie and Billy went on the Spook House ride about a dozen times, and I listened to the Wurlitzer.

I'm home again!

On Saturday night, we all went dancing at the Ballroom. Everybody was having fun like we always did last summer, except there was this one older girl that kept cutting-in on us. I didn't mind too much at first, because Austin is such a good dancer, and other girls had cut-in a few times last year, but this girl kept doing it, and I thought she was being rude, and I was getting annoyed with Austin for letting her keep doing it. I sat down next to Aunt Carmella, and we watched them, and I heard a voice behind me say "That's his new girlfriend."

I turned around, and it was that Cynthia Smith.

I ignored her, but she kept talking about how Austin broke-up her and his brother, and that he goes out with her all the time now, and that they were secretly going steady, and on and on, and each word hurt, but I wouldn't show it no matter what, and she finally left.

When Marie and Billy took a rest, she and I went to the Ladies' Room, and I told her what Cynthia Smith said. When we came out, she told Billy, and he told me it was all bull crap, and that Cynthia Smith was just being nasty, as usual.

I looked around for Austin, and I saw him and that girl in a corner of the ballroom with Aunt Sally and Aunt Carmella talking to them. I wished they weren't, but then Austin and the girl started acting strange. They kept trying to stand in front of one another like they were guarding or protecting each other. While I was watching, Aunt Sally and Aunt Carmella both crossed their arms, and I recognized the look they gave them. Marie saw it too and whispered, "Maybe it's true."

I told Marie and Billy I didn't feel like dancing anymore tonight, and I left and sat in front of the Wurlitzer. Last summer, Austin said that the Wurlitzer always sounded like it was having a good time.

I wished I was.

Austin sat down next to me a few minutes later. I moved away from him, and he started to move over, but he stopped.

"I'm sorry" he said. "I'm sorry I hurt your feelings."

I turned around and looked at him. "It's all true, isn't it? You're dating her?"

"No." It was that girl. "We just like dancing together. That's all."

I looked at her. She looked...

Okay, so I'm not as pretty as she is, and I know I'm not some delicate little girl, either. I try not to notice it so much, but sometimes I feel... well, *stronger* than most girls, sort of.

She looked absolutely beautiful.

That made me mad, and I felt mean and nasty like Mother, and I hissed "Isn't he kind of young for you?"

They both said "We're NOT dating" but they reached for each other's hand without looking. I stood up and stared down at their hands and they looked down, too, and then looked at each other like they were surprised or... or *something*, and I thought... well, I don't know what I thought, but it hurt some more, and it was like back in the ballroom when they were trying to protect each other, and I felt sorry for myself, but I felt sorry for them, too, and I didn't know why.

Aunt Carmella came out of the ballroom and looked around for me. She took my hand, and we walked up the boardwalk.

Her voice was soft, like a hug. "So, bambino, you just had your first broken heart, huh?"

I think I wanted to cry, but I didn't. We went on walking until the end of the boardwalk. I hadn't even noticed. How long had we been walking?

We were pretty lucky, because the boardwalk train thing was right there, and the man driving it said, "Last trip tonight."

My feet hurt, and so did Aunt Carmella's. I apologized, but she just laughed and hugged me, and we rode back down to the ballroom, and everybody was outside waiting for us, and we went home and took baths and went to bed.

Marie held me until I fell asleep.

CHAPTER FORTY-FIVE

"The name's Bond, James Bond"

I didn't have time to sit around and feel sorry for myself, because the next day, Aunt Sally brought home a big stack of books Mrs. Stacey wanted me to study. I was SO mad! "I'm on vacation, and all she wants me to do is think!" As soon as I yelled that, Aunt Sally just about died from laughing.

Most of the books were about India and Australia and countries in Africa, and even islands in the Caribbean. When he saw what I had, Billy went into his room and brought me a bunch of books by Rudyard Kipling and H. Rider Haggard and others, and when I got mad at him, he said they'd help me understand the others. It turned out he was right, but I'd never tell him that.

But it wasn't all studying that summer. We still swam in the mornings, and hung out on the boardwalk sometimes, and went dancing. When I was with Austin last summer, I hadn't noticed that there were boys my age there, but now they would ask me to dance (not as good as Austin), but when one of them tried to "cop a feel," I punched him. Nobody wanted to dance with me the rest of that night.

Anyway, summer was turning out to be pretty dull that year, except that Aunt Carmella and Uncle Vince looked at houses for sale. They didn't buy one, but they were looking.

I just don't want Marie to move away from me until after we graduate college, and she gets married.

It rained one day, and Uncle Vince can't draw people on the boardwalk when it rains, and we can't go swimming either, because the pool is closed (I don't know why, you get wet anyway).

It was too hot and sticky to stay home, so Aunt Carmella looked in the paper to see if there was a good movie anywhere. A movie called "Dr. No" was playing, and she grinned and said that the Catholic Review condemned it, but President Kennedy liked it, so we'd see it. Uncle Vince said she'd get burned at the stake one day for heresy, and she laughed and said if the people that condemned it saw it and didn't go blind, then it was okay for them to see.

When we got there, the poster had a guy with a gun and a bunch of women posing like they were sexy, and the words said "The 007 means he has a license to kill. Anyone. Anywhere. Anytime."

Uncle Vince said he didn't think it was something for us kids to see. Marie and Billy said they wanted to see it, but I didn't want to watch a bunch of people getting killed, and Uncle Vince looked at me and said if I didn't want to go, he and I would find something else to do. Aunt Carmella said he just wanted to get an Orange Julius.

We split up, and said we'd meet outside the theatre in two hours. And, yeah, we had Orange Julius to drink, and listened to the Wurlitzer, and then it stopped raining, so we went down to the inlet so Uncle Vince could watch the water again until it was time to go.

They were waiting for us just inside the lobby and got in the car all giggling and acting strange. Aunt Carmella scooted across the seat up against Uncle Vince and kissed him and said "It was good. Billy says there's a whole bunch of books, so maybe they'll make more movies." She leaned her head against his shoulder and said, "If they do, I just might trade you in for a Limey."

Marie and Billy were snuggled up in the back seat next to me. Billy whispered "The name's Palkin. Billy Palkin." Marie whispered back "No, it's Dexter. Poin Dexter."

I hate it when they act stupid.

For me, summer was swimming in the morning, studying in the afternoon, and reading Billy's stories before I went to bed. Boy, all the countries in Europe did horrible things to people in other countries. Uncle Bill never talks a lot, but he says America did a lot of things just as bad to the Indians right here, and to Filipinos, and to the Columbians when we wanted to build the Panama Canal right through their country. He said I should study all that, too. I think I'll never get finished with all this stuff. But I liked some of the books that Billy had. I loved "Kim," but I didn't like the way the English looked down on everybody.

It was finally time for Aunt Carmella and Uncle Vince to go back to Baltimore. We went down to the boardwalk and Uncle Vince drank gallons of Orange Julius as usual. The next day, Mother and Dad came down, and things were quiet (Mother wasn't talking to anyone, who cares why) for the last two weeks of summer. For the first time ever, I hadn't had a lot of fun, and I told Aunt Sally I wasn't going to spend another summer studying like that ever again, and she told me I needed to do better in school from now on, and don't look at her that way, because I look like Mother when I do. At least I got to swim almost every day.

CHAPTER FORTY-SIX

The Teacher

School started again, and I'm sitting with Marie! YAY US! And Karen's in class with us, too. Unfortunately, Mrs. Stacey isn't just one of our teachers, she's also Homeroom. That means I have to see her first thing in the morning, then class, then last thing before we leave.

Now, the worst thing of all: the rest of the class didn't know all the things I'd been studying, and when somebody asked a question, she'd point to me and make *me* answer it. Well, we'd only been back two weeks and she kept doing that, and when she started talking about the tea trade and the effect it had on the British economy, I raised my hand (stupid me!) because I thought I'd beat her to it this time and get it over with.

Oh, I got it, alright.

She sat down and said, "Go ahead, explain."

I started talking about how much everybody in England loved tea, and China was the only place you could get it, and China only sold it for gold or silver— no other trade— and how that was ruining the English economy because the money was only going ONE way— out. But then, the English found something the Chinese *would* trade for.

Opium.

And the money started going back to England.

The English also sent spies into China and had them steal tea seeds, and they planted them in India so they could grow their own tea and not pay China anything.

Meanwhile, everybody in class kept asking me more questions, and then Marie (*MY* Marie!) raises her hand and said "Oh, *Miss* Osterhoff, could you explain -?" and then *Karen* says 'Miss Osterhoff' and then the other kids started doing it, but THEY weren't kidding, and Mrs. Stacey just sat there writing in her little notebook.

Then Doris asked me a question (and at least she didn't say 'Miss'.)

She wanted to know why the English did this? Why did they think it was okay to go in and take over other countries, or do anything they wanted to people that weren't like them?

I sat on the corner of Mrs. Stacey's desk like she does (I was already standing at the front of the class) and thought as hard as I could. I figured I knew some of the answers, but I wanted to try to put it the right way.

"The main answer is always money" I started, "but that's only for the Government and businesses like the East India Company. What you're really asking is how they got all the other people in England to go along with it, because they were the ones who had to go there and do all the work."

The bell rang for the end of class. Nobody moved, they just watched me and waited.

I took a deep breath. "I don't know" I said, "but I read something this summer that might be part of the answer. It's a poem by Rudyard Kipling. You can find it in his 'Barrack Room Ballads' and other books that have his poems. It's called 'The White Man's Burden'." I looked at Doris. "I think he was being sarcastic like some of his other poems." I turned around and looked at Mrs. Stacey. She wasn't writing any more, she was watching me. I could hear people in the hall outside and some from the next class were looking through the door window. Everybody in class was still watching me and waiting.

"Okay, homework!" I said it louder than I wanted to. "Go down to the library, I don't care if you all go at one time, but go, find the poem, read it, and write what you think about it. I don't care how much you write, a page or a paragraph or one word, just do it." I looked at Mrs. Stacey. "It's to make you think." She coughed like Dad does.

Everybody left, and the next class came in. I was still sitting on Mrs. Stacey's desk. She looked at me. "Well, little genius, it looks like you can teach something other than math." I almost said something back, but then she asked me "Did you like it?"

Did I? "I don't know" I answered.

"Write what you think about it. I don't care how much you write, a page or a paragraph or one word, just do it." She smirked at me. "You're late for your next class. Don't forget your books."

CHAPTER FORTY-SEVEN

The President

The week before Thanksgiving, President Kennedy got killed.

It happened during gym class. We were playing volleyball, and Marie and I were on opposite teams, and the score was tied 3— 3. The PA speaker said "Attention. Attention. All students will IMMEADIATELY return to their homerooms. There will be a special announcement. All students please return to their homerooms." The phone was ringing in Mrs. Talley's office. We couldn't hear what the other person was saying, but Mrs. Talley yelled "He what? HE'S WHAT? Oh, my God. Oh, my God." She hung up and came out of her office and said "Go change. Skip the shower. Change. Go back to your homeroom. Go." She was starting to cry. "Go. And hurry."

We started hearing about it in the hallways: The President got shot. President Kennedy is dead. It was the Russians. It was the Cubans. It was the Mafia and the Ku Klux Klan.

I kept thinking: it's not true. It didn't happen. We're all going to get to homeroom and they're going to tell us it's all rumors and a mistake and don't believe it, because it didn't happen, and somebody on the radio or TV got confused and said the wrong thing but everything is alright and it didn't happen and President Kennedy is okay and so is Jackie and Caroline and John-John and nothing's wrong and I started bumping into people because I couldn't see because I was crying and I stopped walking and leaned against the wall just for a second and slid and sat down on the floor just for a second and Mac MacTavish helped me up and said he'd walk me back to my homeroom if I'd tell him where it was and I got snot all over his shoulder while I held onto him and cried just for a second and he patted my back and the PA said that the President had been assassinated while driving through Dallas on his way to make a speech and that's all we know at this time and school will be letting out early and we should go home and watch TV and it's not certain if there would be school on Monday, so just go home quietly please.

I stood there with Mac holding me and patting me on the back, and I felt so sad. Marie found us and put her arms around us and said "Hey, Sorella, you got lost. C'mon, we'll go home, okay?" Her face looked like she'd been crying, too.

I nodded and let go of Mac and started to turn away, but then I looked back at Mac and said it was nice to see him again. He picked up my books and handed them to me, and then he pulled one of those little cellophane packs of Kleenex out of his pocket and gave it to me. I said thanks, and he said it was nice to see me again, too.

When we got home, I watched the TV with Marie and Aunt Carmella until Uncle Vince came home. I went back to our house for supper. No one said anything all through the meal. When we finished, I said I was going back to Marie's, but Mother said no, I should go upstairs and do whatever homework I had and take a bath and go to bed. Dad said he wanted to go and watch the news, too, but Mother said no again.

Dad said "Susan. The President was assassinated today."

Mother said "Yes. I couldn't help hearing it on that woman's television. She keeps it much too loud."

Dad looked at her. "Susan. This is the President of our country that has been murdered."

She looked back. "That is none of our concern. It has nothing whatsoever to do with us."

My stomach did a flip-flop. Is that what *I* sounded like? My face got hot, and I felt ashamed of all the times I had said those words.

I took a deep breath. "It has everything to do with us. It has everything to do with the whole world." I walked out the front door. Dad got up and followed me, and Mother followed him.

When we stepped out onto the porch, Mother slammed the door behind us and we heard the lock snap, and Mother's footsteps going up the stairs.

Dad sighed. "Ask your aunt for her laundry basket, please."

Dad and I stayed at Marie's all weekend because Dad didn't have his keys. He had all his clothes, of course, and Marie and I are pretty much the same size. He slept in their basement, and I slept with Marie— or at least we all tried to.

It was crazy. They knew that Lee Harvey Oswald did it almost right away, and they caught him so fast, too. How did they know? Maybe they could have arrested him before he did it.

He used to be a Marine ("Bill's gonna love that," Uncle Vince said), and he lived in Russia after that and married a Russian girl ("I bet this is Khruschev paying us back for that missile thing," Aunt Carmella said), and he had something to do with Cuba and Castro ("There, you see?" Aunt Carmella said.)

But nobody was saying anything about war, not like last year with the missiles, and the Russians weren't saying anything at all. Now, THAT was really strange.

On Sunday, Lee Harvey Oswald got killed right on TV while we watched. Dad got SO mad he stood up and shouted "Why have they let all those people in? Didn't they know this could happen? Where are the guards?" We were all surprised because Dad doesn't ever act like that.

They buried the President on Monday. We all cried when little John-John saluted. We went back to our house that night after Mother went outside when Uncle Vince took the garbage out and she asked if we were moving in with them.

I wished we would.

CHAPTER FORTY-EIGHT

It's The Holiday Season

After school on Tuesday, I stayed behind. I wanted to talk to Mrs. Stacey about everything that happened.

She looked at me and before I could say anything, she said "I don't have any answers for you. I don't have any for myself."

I told her I wasn't going to ask anything about that (which we both knew wasn't true), but she just sighed and pulled her chair over and propped her feet up on a student's chair. She gave me a funny look when I did the same thing. "My feet hurt" I told her. "Mr. Ainsley pulled me from English, History, and Gym and had me explain math stuff to two 7th grade classes and one 8th grade class." I frowned. "I wish he'd take notes. The way I teach is easier to understand than his way."

Mrs. Stacey laughed. "So, you're a better teacher than he is, hmm?"

She always irritates me. "And that reminds me: why are you trying to teach me to be a teacher?" I asked.

She laughed a little louder. "Is that what I'm doing, little genius?"

Now I was getting mad. "Stop calling me that." I was starting to hiss like Mother, and I hate when I do that.

She stopped laughing and smiled at me a little bit nicer. "I'm sorry, Sally. Truly. I promise I won't call you that again." She looked serious now. "But you are, you know. A genius, I mean. You *and* your sister." She frowned. "Now, *I* have a question. Just what *are* you two to each other? Everyone seems to automatically think that you two are sisters."

"We are" I said. "Well, *we* think we are. And our families think we are. Except Mother." Mrs. Stacey looked even more confused. I took a deep breath. "Marie and I think we were supposed to be sisters, but the Angels had to take our souls to different mothers instead of just her mother because she had problems staying pregnant long enough just with Marie, and STOP LAUGHING!"

Mrs. Stacey "whooped" when she laughed, and she kept on doing it, but then she got this weird look on her face and stopped. She looked at me and her mouth moved, but nothing came out. She sat up straight. "I was going to say that your theology is a bit suspect, but I just remembered something I read or heard a long time ago. I think it's Buddhist. 'We are born into one family, and as we travel through life, we find our true family.'" She was quiet for a moment, then she shrugged her shoulders. "Well, whatever the two of you believe is all that matters." She frowned at me again. "Do you think I'm trying to teach you to be a teacher?"

"Well, aren't you?"

"No. What I've tried to do is teach you to think and engage with the world around you. There's more to knowledge than numbers, Sally. I must admit it's been interesting watching you explain things. You're able to simplify a lot of information without losing what's important. I'll also admit that I pushed you very hard last year and this year as well, because I knew you could handle it. You need to keep that brain of yours in 'high gear,' so to speak, not spinning and doing nothing." She paused. "I think you might be— well, never mind for now. It's late, and I've got grocery shopping to do, or we'll be eating meatloaf instead of turkey for Thanksgiving." She grinned and pointed to the door. "Your 'sister' is waiting for you."

At supper, Mother said she would make Thanksgiving Dinner for us. I couldn't remember how many years it had been since she last did it. I remembered Grandmother and Grandfather leaving in a huff because of "those people next door" and they've never been back since. I also remembered the way Thanksgiving Dinner tasted (or DIDN'T taste) back then. Dad did too, and we looked at each other. We didn't say anything, but Mother started grinding her teeth, and hissed "If you don't want good, healthy *American* food, you can just go eat at that filthy restaurant as you've been doing or get that woman next door to feed you."

She grabbed our plates and took them into the kitchen. Dad looked at me, sighed and shrugged his shoulders. We heard Mother drag the garbage can inside and heard her tossing plates and glasses into it. Dad sighed again and told me to go upstairs and take a bath and go to bed.

I guessed we'd be eating out again for a while.

When Dad came home the next day, Uncle Vince was waiting on the porch for him. He told Dad "That woman next door" had it all fixed, and that we'd eat with them at her brother's place for Thanksgiving.

We did, and boy, was it good!

And Marie has a really cute cousin named Joey.

Things were better by Christmas. Mother had bought new china and crystal from Hutzler's and was cooking again. Well, *that* part wasn't better, but Dad and I never said a word or even looked at each other during meals.

Aunt Sally and Uncle Bill and Billy came up on Christmas Eve as usual and stayed at Marie's home instead of our house as usual, and Marie and Billy acted like they usually did: silly and stupid and pretending they were being "romantic." They were on the sofa, and Billy had his head in her lap, and she was feeding him pieces of tangerine. The last piece Marie held between her teeth and kissed him. Aunt Carmella was bringing a pitcher of water for the Christmas tree and saw them.

"Alright, Anthony and Cleopatra, that's enough! Sit up!"

Marie said "Ma! We're not doing anything!"

Aunt Sally called from the dining room "You've got that right."

Billy said "Mom! We're not doing anything!"

Aunt Carmella said, "Do I put your sister in between you?'

"Hey!" I said. "How did I get into this?"

Billy said "We're not getting married until after Marie gets out of college— "

"And Billy gets out of the Marines" Marie continued.

"Plus, she and Sally will be going to the Olympics that year— "

"And he'll be going to firefighter's school while we're there— "

"Basta! Enough!" Aunt Carmella yelled. She was shivering so hard she was spilling the pitcher. Aunt Sally came in and took it away from her. They both looked at Marie and Billy, and each other. "Nine years" Aunt Sally said. "We'll have white hair by then" Aunt Carmella finished.

The Saturday after Christmas, Uncle Vince drove Marie, Billy and I to the Community Center to go swimming. When we came out of the locker room, Aunt Viv was there. She hugged and kissed all of us, and pushed Marie and Billy back-to-back to see how tall they were, and said "Throw him back, Marie. He's too small to keep."

Marie wrapped herself up in her towel and ran out to the lobby and asked Uncle Vince if it was okay to invite Aunt Viv and Mrs. Persky home with us, and he said sure, and he called Aunt Carmella.

We had supper, and Aunt Viv talked loudly and laughed big. I could hear Mother through the wall hissing about uncouth people, and Aunt Viv laughed louder. She dropped her fork once, and when she leaned over to pick it up, something fell out of her neckline. It was a gold chain and a ring with something yellow on it. I asked what it was, and Uncle Bill said, "Here we go!" and Aunt Viv stuck her tongue out and crossed her eyes at him. She held the ring up and smiled at it.

"Why, this is my engagement ring, Honey. Back when my dear Hubby graduated from LSU, he started driving up to Maryland the day after. When he came through Arkansas, he saw a sign that said, 'Mine for Diamonds at Crater of Diamonds State Park' and he turned and drove there. When he got to the field where you could find them, he told me he didn't walk but two steps, and looked down and saw it, and he picked it up and brought it back to the Park people, and they told him 'Yep, that's a real one, and that's the color they are here, and it's a big one, too, and congratulations!' So, he got back in the car, and drove up to Maryland and Ocean City (and he stopped at some jewelry store on the way, and had it mounted), and he asked me to marry him and said he'd get it cut one day, but we never did because I kind of liked it the way it was. How many men give their wives a diamond that they found just for her?"

Marie and I said, "How romantic!" and everybody laughed.

CHAPTER FORTY-NINE

That Guy

The rest of 8th grade went by quickly. Mrs. Stacey didn't try to make me teach as often, and sometimes she would only ask me to explain something (and she would take notes that she used for her other classes). By the last day of school, I had finally figured out that she was the best teacher I had ever had, and I told her so. She laughed and said, "But you still don't like me, do you, 'little genius?'"

I started to get mad, but I only said, "Thank you" and started to walk out. She called me back. "Sally. Good luck in High School. And College. And the Olympics when you get there." I could tell she meant it, and I thanked her again, and this time *I* meant it.

We stayed in Baltimore until I got Confirmed in the Lutheran Church the next Sunday. I was now an Adult Member, and able to take Communion like Marie does at her Church. The classes at Church had been interesting, especially the ones back when we started in the Fall that Father Dunne from St. Bridget's across the street came to, and helped Reverend Lehmann explain some of the Reformation. Aunt Carmella said Churches don't always get along, even if they're the same kind, so it's good that some do, because it's all the same God anyway. I had read enough history to know that some of the worst things people do to each other is because they think that only THEIR way of believing in God is the right way. Stupid. And crazy. And horrible, too.

Anyway, right after Church, we packed Uncle Vince's car and drove to Ocean City. When we got there, Marie and Billy started to act goofy again, but then they got quieter and more serious. Aunt Sally and Aunt Carmella watched them for a while, and looked at each other and said, "Should we be more worried?" Billy and Marie said they wanted to go dancing that night, and so after supper, we all went.

I saw Austin there, and his girlfriend Linda, and she told him to go dance with me. He taught me some new steps, and even slow danced with me once. I went over to Linda afterwards and said thanks. It must be strange having a boyfriend four years younger than you are, and Aunt Sally and Aunt Carmella said it WAS strange, and that Linda had better watch herself because she was eighteen.

We were some of the last people to leave, and the Ladies Room was crowded, and I had to go so bad that I was going to the one on the boardwalk. I ran down the stairs, and Marie yelled "Wait up!" but I REALLY had to go.

When I got inside, there was a guy there, and he punched me in the stomach, and pushed me against a sink. His thing was sticking out of his pants, and he was pulling on it, and it was HUGE, and it was purple and ugly, and he said "You see this? Look at it, bitch, 'cause I'm going to shove every inch of it— "

That's when Marie came in and screamed so loud my ears hurt, and the guy turned around and punched her in the mouth and said, "You're next." Billy must have heard Marie scream, because he came in and ROARED and jumped on the guy, but Officer Charlie from the Beach Patrol was right behind him, and pulled Billy off the guy, and Officer Charlie started to swing his nightstick, but the guy had already raised his hands and laughed and said he was too soon and nothing had happened yet.

Officer Charlie looked like he wanted to kill the guy, but he put his nightstick down, and put handcuffs on the guy's hands behind his back and took him outside with his thing still sticking out. We heard Aunt Sally and Aunt Carmella scream, and they came running inside and asked were we alright and did he do anything, and Aunt Carmella saw Marie's bloody mouth and grabbed Marie from Billy, and hugged her so hard I heard all the breath come out of her, and Aunt Sally was doing the same thing to me, and I was still trying to get MY breath back from getting punched. Uncle Bill and Uncle Vince yelled in if we were okay, and we could hear them telling Officer Charlie that he should let *them* take care of him, and Officer Charlie said that the guy's father was the richest man in town and if he let them do anything, we'd ALL go to prison. Aunt Carmella heard that, and she gave Marie back to Billy and went outside, and Officer Charlie yelled "Don't, Carmella! Jesus, Vince, get ahold of her!" and Uncle Vince said "Fuck him! Let her kick his cock off."

I could hear other people out there, and I was starting to breathe better. Billy had grabbed a handful of paper towels and soaked it in water and was holding it against Marie's lips. I heard him tell her that he would never let anyone hurt her again, ever, and that he'd always be there to protect her. Aunt Sally asked me if I was alright, and that's when I knew I had peed myself and I told her and started crying.

Aunt Carmella came back in and hugged Marie and Billy and I, and Aunt Sally washed my panties and held them in front of the hand dryer. She helped me wash off with wet toilet paper, and I had to take my nylons and shoes off and she wiped out my shoes, too.

Uncle Bill called in "Sally? We gotta file a complaint. For all the good that'll do."

Aunt Sally snarled "Hunter's little bastard." That was only the fourth time I'd heard her swear.

We came out and Marie and I screamed because he was still there, but he was face down on the boardwalk. A Paddy Wagon pulled up next to the Ladies Room, and two other officers came over and looked at each other and picked him up and dropped him and dragged him across the boardwalk to the concrete and then picked him up. His thing was still sticking out and I hoped he'd got a million splinters in it. He was screaming that his father would have them all locked up for hurting him. The two officers looked at each other again and tripped him when he climbed into the Paddy Wagon.

Officer Charlie took us to the Beach Patrol Station just a little walk away. Another officer there told him that Atkinson was out-of-town, and the Assistant Prosecutor would be coming over. Officer Charlie said that was HALF a good thing, anyway, and took us into an office to wait.

About fifteen minutes later, Officer Charlie came back in with another man who looked like *he* wanted to kill someone, too. I knew then that this wasn't the first time this had happened. He asked Marie and I what had happened, and what the guy said to us, and he wrote it all down. Aunt Sally was growling, and Aunt Carmella was swearing in Italian, and Uncle Bill and Uncle Vince and Billy didn't say anything, but I watched their hands keep clenching up.

About 3 o'clock in the morning, we were getting ready to go home, but the other officer came into the room and said that he'd just got word that Judge Clement had already set the trial for 8AM this morning and didn't have any subpoenas sent out to us. The Assistant Prosecutor (I still didn't know his name) slammed both his fists on the table and then kicked it across the room and yelled "By Christ, I'll get ALL those crooked bastards one day! Atkinson, Clement, and that piece of shit Deltonham, AND Hunter, AND his kid!" He sat and tried to calm down. "Eight o'clock. Berlin Courthouse. Better get there earlier."

We went home, and everybody had a bath (I needed one the most). Aunt Carmella made coffee and cinnamon toast and made Marie and I eat some, and then we got dressed and left.

We got to the Courthouse at a quarter till seven, and Officer Charlie was waiting for us, and said the staff wasn't even in yet, but that Hunter was there already with his kid and his lawyer, and they were all set to go as soon as the Judge showed up.

We went into Courtroom #1 and sat down. That guy was there, and he grinned at me and made a humping move in his chair, but he stopped and made a face. I remembered him getting dragged across the boardwalk, and I hope it gets infected and rots off from all the splinters he probably got.

At seven, the Bailiff and the Court Recorder came in (they looked like the people on Perry Mason), and then the Judge came in through a door behind where he sits. He almost fell off the chair when he sat down. "Drunk already" Officer Charlie whispered. The Assistant Prosecutor came rushing in and sat down. "I got waylaid by Clement's secretary, tried to keep me from coming in" he whispered to Officer Charlie.

The Judge waved a hand at the Bailiff. "Alright, let's get this over with."

The Bailiff made everybody stand and said all the stuff just like they do on TV (and that's when I found out the Assistant Prosecutor was named Tolliver), and we sat back down. Mr. Tolliver said the charges were indecent exposure, lewd behavior, and physical assault, and that the prosecution was ready to proceed, and the defense lawyer said he was ready to proceed and that his client waived a jury trial. The Judge nodded and pointed at Mr. Tolliver and told him to get started and be quick about it.

That's when the Judge fell off his chair.

The Bailiff ran up behind the Bench, and we heard him saying "Judge? Judge? Wake up, Judge." Then he stood up and said, "He's passed out."

Mr. Tolliver grabbed Officer Charlie by the arm and whispered "Find Judge Feinman. Tell him what's happened and get him in here, NOW."

The Defense lawyer came over and said we can do this tomorrow, but Mr. Tolliver said not a chance in Hell. The Defense lawyer said "How about no contest and a fine and no record?" That's when this other Judge came in with Officer Charlie and looked at the Judge on the floor. He said to Officer Charlie "Help Keith carry him back to his office. Keith, get somebody to give him a blood test. We'll start up again when you get back."

The Defense lawyer yelled "Your Honor, the defense asks for— "

"*Sit*, Mr. Deltonham. We'll start again when they get back." The Judge tapped the gavel. "SIT."

The Bailiff and Officer Charlie came back in a few minutes. The Judge said "Now, let's see what I've missed" and he had the Court Recorder read everything back to him. When the Recorder finished, the Defense lawyer jumped up again, and the Judge told him to sit down, NOW, and told the Recorder that the trial would continue, Judge Feinman presiding.

The Defense lawyer was up again and asked for a continuance, but the Judge had the Recorder read back the parts where he had said "ready to proceed" and "no jury."

Mr. Tolliver stood up and started talking about what had happened and what Marie and I were going to testify and then I had to get up and sit in the witness chair and swear on the Bible and then Mr. Tolliver started asking what happened and I was telling everybody and that guy kept looking at me and grinning and I got to the part where he was pulling on his penis and saying look at it...

And I threw up.

The Bailiff brought a spittoon over (I'd only ever seen one on TV) and held it in front of me, and the Judge said something about suspending something, and we'd get started again in a few minutes and Charlie go get Queenie in here and mop up. I kept saying I was sorry, and an old colored lady came in with a mop and bucket and a Coca-Cola. She handed the soda to me and said "Here, Sugar, you take a mouthful and swish it round in your mouth and spit it out." I did, and she said, "Now do it again" and I did. "Mouth a little better?" I said yes ma'am, and she told me to take little sips and let my stomach settle. She started mopping the floor. I drank it like she said, and I leaned over and told her I was sorry, but she said, "Don't you worry, Sugar, it's okay, you just take them small sips."

We both finished at the same time, and I handed the bottle back to her and said thank you, and she told the Judge she'd come back later and mop the whole floor. The Judge nodded and asked if I was ready, and tapped his gavel and said Court was in session again, and I finished talking about how Marie came in, and the guy hit her, and Officer Charlie came in and arrested him.

Then the Defense lawyer started asking me questions and didn't I make a mistake and go into the wrong restroom, and maybe I did it deliberately because I wanted to see what a man looked like, and Mr. Tolliver objected, and the Judge sustained, and told the Defense lawyer that questions like that violated something, and that I'd already testified that it was the Ladies Room, and the guy kept grinning at me and the lawyer said maybe I invited him in with me, and Mr. Tolliver objected again, and the Judge sustained and said "So, your client *was* in the Ladies Room, then?," and the lawyer said he'd withdraw the question.

The older man that I guess was the Mr. Hunter that everyone talked about started whispering and jabbing the lawyer. The Judge told him to stop or be held in contempt of court. He sat back and gave the Judge a dirty look. His son kept grinning, but the lawyer was starting to look worried. I got down, and Marie went up, and she told what happened, and the lawyer said that she and I conspired to falsely accuse his client, and the Judge said he'd warned him about that, and the lawyer said no more questions.

Officer Charlie went up and testified, and the lawyer said he had it in for his client, and was always harassing him, and the Judge said enough of that, too.

Mr. Tolliver said he had no more witnesses, and that the Prosecution rests, and the Defense lawyer said it was all a big misunderstanding, and was all blown out of proportion, and not to embarrass anyone any further. Mr. Hunter started jabbing him again and talking about how much he pays him and to start earning his money, and the Judge tapped his gavel again and told him the next time he interrupts, he'll be found in contempt. Then the Judge said the Defendant will rise. Mr. Hunter took a checkbook out of his pocket.

The Judge looked at the guy and smiled, and the guy grinned back. I thought this is what Mr. Tolliver meant about everybody being crooked, and I felt sick again.

The Judge started talking. "The Court finds the Defendant, Michael Hunter, GUILTY of indecent exposure, lewd behavior, and physical assault of two MINOR children." The Judge was grinning now. "The Court takes note that the defendant turned eighteen a week ago and will therefore be sentenced as an adult."

The guy's father started poking the lawyer again and saying what the Hell goes?

"Sentencing guidelines in such cases are quite— ", and the Judge was laughing now, "quite— STIFF, shall we say?" He looked at the guy's father. "So, you can put that checkbook away, Hunter." He turned toward the guy again, and now the guy was looking scared— REAL scared.

"The Court sentences you to the *maximum* for each count allowed— to be served *consecutively*—and that comes to *fifteen* years, Michael Hunter, and you'll be spending them in the Maryland State Penitentiary in Baltimore City."

Mr. Hunter stood up and started screaming at the Judge, Mr. Tolliver,

Officer Charlie, and Marie and I, and how WE were all going to jail, not his boy, and the Judge smiled and started tapping his gavel and saying thirty days contempt of court, sixty days, ninety, one hundred and twenty, one-fifty, and SLAMMED the gavel down and broke it and yelled "Six months, Hunter! You're not buying your way out of this one! Court adjourned! Bailiff, get them both out of here!"

Mr. Hunter started screaming at his lawyer, now, and punched him right in the face, and then punched the Bailiff, and started walking toward the Judge, and Officer Charlie picked up the Bailiff's nightstick and whacked Mr. Hunter across the shins, rammed him in the stomach, knocked him in the head and down on the floor, and put handcuffs on him. The guy— his son— was starting to cry.

The Judge looked at him and smiled like he was giving him a present. "Now, don't you worry, Michael, you'll be fine. You'll make a LOT of new friends there. For what you're going up for, there'll be plenty of men that will want to show you what THEY have."

Aunt Sally and Aunt Carmella grabbed Marie and I and said "C'mon, girls, it's all over, let's go home." Mr. Tolliver was telling Uncle Bill and Uncle Vince that there were three rape cases he felt better about today.

Out in the hallway, there were a bunch of people watching and listening. I saw Miss Queenie, and I went over and apologized and thanked her for the Coke again. She smiled and said "Don't you worry none about that, Sugar. People saying you done a good job today."

I said that Mr. Tolliver said that the guy had done it to three other girls. Miss Queenie stopped smiling and her face turned cold. "White girls. He done *seven* colored girls, all younger than you. But they don't arrest white boys for that around here." She put a smile on her face again, and this time I could see it wasn't real. "But you go on, now, Sugar. All *you* got was a little bitty scared. You go on with your folks and have a nice vacation." She walked away.

We all went home to Aunt Sally's.

I didn't say anything about Miss Queenie.

I didn't know how to say it.

I wished I could talk to Doris.

By the end of the next week, Marie and I weren't as scared, except that we wouldn't go into the Ladies Room by ourselves. Aunt Sally and Aunt Carmella wouldn't have let us anyway. One evening we were all on the boardwalk together, and there was a Ladies Room on the boardwalk across from the Orange Julius place. We had to go, so "us women" went in. We were all in the stalls when we heard someone whisper "I've escaped, and I've come back to get you." Marie and I screamed, and we heard the doors slamming and we thought he was looking for us, but then we heard Aunt Sally yelling "YOU! I might have known it would be YOU!"

Marie and I looked out, and Billy had come in when he heard us scream, and Marie grabbed him and started crying while he held her and he told her it was okay, and that he had her, and she was safe. Aunt Carmella held all of us while Aunt Sally yelled at someone. It was that Cynthia Smith. She stood there and smirked while Aunt Sally yelled "I know this is a small town, and word gets around, but what you just did— ". Aunt Sally stopped yelling and growled the way she talks to Mother when she's really mad. "Cynthia, you are the nastiest, most vicious, ill-raised, conceited, self-centered, shameless— ", and Cynthia Smith turned away from her and went over to Marie and Billy and told him "Little boys shouldn't be in the Ladies Room." Billy held Marie a little tighter and he SNARLED at her from deep in his throat, "FUCK YOU, Cynthia." She just turned around and pushed through Uncle Vince and Uncle Bill, and walked out, still smirking.

We finished and washed up while Billy stood in the doorway, and Uncle Bill and Uncle Vince stood out on the boardwalk. Aunt Sally said how about we go down to Trimper's, and we did, but Marie didn't want to go on the Spook House ride as usual, she just wanted to sit with Billy. All the lights and the music from the Wurlitzer made me feel better, and Marie had curled up on Billy's lap, and her eyes were closed like she was asleep. Sometimes it looks funny that Billy is shorter than Marie, but right then, he looked bigger and stronger than he was if that makes any sense, just like he did when he tried to get that guy that night. Maybe Aunt Carmella was thinking the same thing, because she went behind Billy and stroked his hair and kissed him and smiled at Aunt Sally.

Things slowly got back to normal after that. We all decided not to say anything about what had happened to Mother or Dad. Aunt Sally said she'd just use it as an excuse to be even nastier to me, and then told me she was sorry for saying it, but we all knew that it was true. I felt bad about not telling Dad, and I knew he would be hurt if he knew, but none of us thought he could keep it a secret from Mother.

We all had a very quiet... and very gentle... and very loving... rest of the summer.

CHAPTER FIFTY

Someone

Western High School was old and run-down, but Marie and I didn't care. We knew we'd have special math tutoring (thanks to Mr. Nightingale), along with all our other college prep courses. Our Math teacher, Mr. Reid, said he'd start us out at a college Sophomore level and see if we got bored— HA!

But there's always something we didn't expect. This time it was swimming. We found out there weren't any Girl's Junior Varsity swim teams—yet. Mrs. Persky and other coaches were trying to change that, especially since there are BOY'S Junior Varsity teams. Meanwhile, she said we could practice with the Varsity and see how we measure up.

We had been doing practice laps with them, and Mrs. Persky was right, we weren't ready to compete by a LONG shot. She'd already told us we'd have to smooth out our strokes instead of attacking the water like Aunt Viv. She also coached the diving team, so when swim practice was over, she asked Marie and I to stay and "spot" as lifeguards while she had try-outs for the diving team, so we tread water on either side of the low and high boards. We saw Doris in the group, and wondered where she learned to dive, and she looked at us and grinned.

When it was her turn, Mrs. Persky said "Johnson. I've heard that you're someone to watch for. Show me what you've got." Doris walked out onto the board just as cool as can be, and bounced once and did something called a "jack-knife." WOW! It was perfect, and not much of a splash, either.

"Nice" Mrs. Persky told her. "Show us the rest."

She did flips, twists, jumped backwards, did one standing on her hands, and she was great! Mrs. Persky told her that she wanted Doris to come and practice with the Varsity, and wished Doris was older so she could compete *now*.

After the try-outs, we were talking in the showers, and she told us that one of the lifeguards at the public pool dove for the University of Maryland and had been teaching her how. We told her how cool she looked, and she said, "I am *SO* cool, I'll be going to the Olympics with you two!"

While we were getting dressed, she told us she loves chemistry the same way we love math. Her brother had gotten a Gilbert Chemistry set for Christmas a couple of years ago, and got tired of it, so she took it and started doing experiments with it. She buys chemicals from Gelfmann's Hobbies and works on things in college textbooks. Cool!

It was Thanksgiving before we knew it, and Mother said she would cook this year, rather than see us eating "that kind of food" from "that woman." I was tempted to say or do something to stop her from cooking, but Dad said, "That will be nice, Susan." I just sat quietly.

We ate leftovers for a week. Well, not quite. Aunt Carmella made a BIG lunch for Marie to take to school and share, and I'd eat a roll of Peppermint Lifesavers so that Mother couldn't tell.

Christmas came, and Uncle Bill worked again for another guy whose kid was having her 1st Christmas. Aunt Sally and Billy came up, and she went to see Mr. Tommy the shoe repair man about more ears for Uncle Bill.

Marie and Billy still acted stupid, and called each other Felix and Poindexter, and held on to each other as much as they could get away with, but they talked more about the future. Billy said he would take some special medical courses that they give ambulance drivers after he got out of the Marines and did Firefighter's training, and Marie said she wanted to get at *least* a Batchelor's degree in Math, but she didn't want to teach or do research or something like me, so maybe she'd think about being an accountant. Aunt Carmella just shivered whenever she heard them talk. I had thought a little about what *I* wanted to do after college, and maybe teaching would be a good choice. Elementary School? High School? College? HA! *Professor* Osterhoff!

Well, I'd think about it. But I was going to the Olympics first.

Marie got a record player for Christmas, and an album by the Beatles. I don't care much for them. Their hair is as long as mine and Marie's, and the lyrics are stupid, like "She loves you, yeah, yeah, yeah." Aunt Carmella listens to WBAL on the radio, and she likes Frank Sinatra and Tony Bennett and Dean Martin and Al Martino and Perry Como and Mel Torme. Come to think of it, I do too.

We went to a swim meet with Eastern High School, and something strange happened there. Marie and I were watching the racing, and Doris was waiting for the diving after, but there was this one girl on the Eastern team that looked sort of familiar, like I should've known who she was. She was tall, about as tall as Aunt Sally, and kind of built like her, too, except her shoulders. When she took off her bathing cap, she had white-blonde hair. I couldn't figure out why she looked so like someone I thought knew, and then Marie said "Hey, that girl looks like your mother, only she smiles."

Oh my God! She was right! And that's when that girl turned and looked at me, and I could see her thinking that *I* looked familiar, and all of a sudden, her face froze up like Mother's.

Marie said "WOW! See? Just like her." Then she pulled me up and said "C'mon! I bet she's a lost relative or something!" I didn't want to go over, but Marie dragged me over in front of her, and started talking to her, and her name was Lina Pedersen, and my stomach was doing flip-flops, and I mumbled that my name was Sally Osterhoff, and she relaxed, but when I said that Mother's maiden name was Peterson, she stood up and said she was a *Pedersen*, spelled p-e-*D*-e-r-s-*E*-n, and that's NORWEGIAN, not p-e-*T*-e-r-s-*O*-n, like SWEDES spelled it, and Marie said "Hey, you've both got that same look on your faces just like your mother!" That's when the girl said, "GOD FORBID!" and went to the other end of the bench.

Marie just kept talking. "Yeah, I bet when your mother's people came off the boat, somebody changed the way their name was spelled, like when they changed Papa Julie from a Giamatti to a Giametti, and there was probably a big fight in the family a long time ago, and nobody talks to each other, just like some of Pop's family won't even LOOK at each other, not even at weddings!"

Marie kept talking and talking, and the girls on Eastern's team looked at me, at Lina, at Marie, and back again. I started to walk away, but I thought that would be rude and something that Mother would do, so I turned around and walked over to where she was sitting and I said I was sorry, and I hoped I hadn't embarrassed her. She looked at me, turned pink and said she was sorry, and what was my last name again, Osterman? I said no, it's Osterhoff, and she said oh well, it's probably just a random thing that we look a little bit alike, and I agreed, and we both laughed a little, and then stared at each other again, because we both snorted when we laughed. I grabbed Marie and told Lina good luck with her races, and she said good luck with mine, even though I wasn't racing, or even in a bathing suit.

We went back to our team, and Marie and Doris talked about family feuds, and sometimes Lina and I would look over at each other. Lina won all her races that day.

When I got back to our house that evening, we could hear Marie telling Aunt Carmella what had happened. Mother was listening and told me "There is nothing in common gossip that is ever true. We have no relations outside of this family, which does not include those people next door. As to my family name, we are Swedish, and we have always been American."

Well, I laughed at that because I could just picture Swedish Indians meeting Columbus. That's when she slapped me the first time. Dad said, "Susan! There was no cause for that." She looked at him, then slapped me again, and told me to bathe and go to bed. Dad looked angry, but he didn't say anything else. I turned away from both of them and went upstairs.

The next morning when I left the house, Marie was waiting, but so was Aunt Carmella. She could see I had a bruise on my cheek, and she gave a dirty look to our front door and said, "One of these days, Susie, me and you are going to have a long— no, we're going to have a SHORT talk about how to raise kids." I could hear Mother through the door. "How you raise your child is no concern of mine. My daughter will be raised correctly, as I was."

I looked at Aunt Carmella and whispered, "Too late" and grinned. She grinned back and gave me a kiss on my other cheek and said, "Go on, you two, you'll miss your bus."

I started writing a long letter to Aunt Sally on the bus and during lunch and on the way home; and I gave it to Marie to have Aunt Carmella mail it for me. A few days later, I got her letter back. It read:

"Hi Honey!

I'm sorry she hit you, and I hope it's looking better. Your Grandmother often did the same to me, which I know doesn't help you, but at least you'll know I understand.

As for the rest, I'm sorry to tell you I don't know anything about that, either. Although I suppose I shouldn't say it, I heard things growing up that the older people in the neighborhood would say about a Will that was broken and inheritances reassigned, and deeds forged for properties. I also don't know about any name changes. I *can* say that Mother and Father were not well-liked. Your Grandfather owned at least a dozen properties in Highlandtown and Canton, and how he managed to acquire so many was a mystery. I think I should also say that Landlords were not popular during the Depression.

But I hope that if you see this young girl again, that you will be polite and friendly toward her. If there is any possibility of being related, then bad blood shouldn't continue through later generations. Just be the sweet girl that I know you are.

Count your blessings, too, because you have a family there that loves you just as much as I. It was my friends and their families that kept me from becoming someone cold and bitter, and your Uncle Bill was the best part of the cure!

That's pretty much all I have to say, Honey, so I'll just say God Bless."

I did get to see and talk to Lina a few more times before she graduated in the Spring, and at the last meet she said she was sorry she never had a chance to see me swim, and I wished her a happy life whatever she does. She snorted and grinned and said yeah, you too, and she started to turn away to leave, but she stopped and looked back and whispered "Bye, cousin."

I guess I'll never know for sure.

CHAPTER FIFTY-ONE

Their Own Place

It was almost time to go back to Aunt Sally's for the summer. Marie couldn't wait to see Billy again, and I couldn't wait to get away from Mother. But it looked like we would have to wait because Uncle Vince's Union was out on strike, and he had to walk on the picket line. Aunt Carmella wouldn't go because she said Uncle Vince didn't know how to cook or do his laundry. Uncle Vince said, "Susie'll take care of me" and I could hear Dad trying to cough loud enough so he wouldn't laugh, but it didn't work. We heard Mother go upstairs and start throwing his clothes out. Aunt Carmella told Marie to go downstairs and get the laundry basket, and she told Uncle Vince it was his fault. He just grinned and said, "What's she gonna do, come over here and throw MY clothes out the window?" Dad didn't even try to cough that time. Marie and I folded Dad's clothes, and I took them into our house and brought the basket back home to Aunt Carmella.

I wished I was home in Ocean City. I know the Ten Commandments say, "Honor thy Father and Mother," but it doesn't say anything about this.

Aunt Carmella sent a letter to Aunt Sally, and she sent letters back to Aunt Carmella and Mother that she would come and pick us up the day after school stops and BE READY.

We were waiting on Marie's porch that morning, when a bright-red car double-parked in front of us. It was one of those brand-new Mustangs with the convertible top down. A lady got out, and she was wearing white slacks and an aquamarine blouse, an aquamarine and white headscarf, and big sunglasses. She took the scarf off, shook her hair out, took off the sunglasses and posed with one hand on the windshield frame.

It was Aunt Sally!

Marie yelled "Ma! C'mere, you gotta see this!" Aunt Carmella came out, looked, and yelled for Uncle Vince. She ran down the steps and hugged Aunt Sally and said she looked like a million bucks in that outfit, and she should be on TV doing the commercials for that car, and where did you get it?

Marie was looking in the back seat for Billy, but he wasn't there. She looked a little upset, and then she looked a LOT upset when he came up behind her. Aunt Sally had dropped him off at the other end of the block because she wanted to make her "Grand Entrance." I could've told Billy to never sneak up behind Marie because neither of us like surprises, especially since that guy.

Aunt Sally told us that the car had been Aunt Viv's for only a week last month, but she didn't like it, so she sold it to Aunt Sally. Uncle Vince asked about Aunt Viv's Thunderbird, and Aunt Sally said that Aunt Viv would NEVER get rid of that, she had only wanted something newer to drive around in when she was doing all her Avon work. Then Aunt Sally looked over at our house and called "Oh, hello, Susan!" but we didn't see Mother there. Then we heard her say "I see you remembered you have a sister" but Aunt Sally said no, it was just a lucky guess that she'd be eavesdropping. Mother didn't say anything back.

Billy put our suitcases in the trunk (it was pretty small), and we all went in to go to the bathroom. Uncle Vince told me to keep an eye on Marie and Billy, and I heard Mother hiss something that made Aunt Carmella give our house a look that almost burned a hole through it. Aunt Sally looked disgusted and said "Yes, Susan, I can hardly wait to see you in August." We hugged and kissed, and off we went.

I sat in the front with Aunt Sally (bucket seats!). At about the third or fourth stop light, Aunt Sally leaned over and kissed me and said don't grow up like Mother, but not to grow up like her, either, and try to be forgiving even when it's hard. I think I understand, but I'd rather be like her than Mother, and I said so.

That summer, Uncle Bill found another place for us to swim for free, just be out and gone by 10AM. It was a new motel and only a ten-minute walk down the road. Aunt Sally says the hotels and motels are going to take over everything one day, and the people that always lived here would probably sell-out for a lot of money and move to Florida. I hope that I'll be able to afford to live here when I grow up. I wouldn't want to be anyplace else.

Marie and Billy got into a little trouble. One morning after swimming, we came home and took our showers outside and hung our bathing suits up to dry like we always do, but Aunt Sally was inside waiting for us with her arms crossed. She told Marie and Billy that there was "an excessive amount of peek-a-booing going on while they were drying off" (she could see us from the kitchen window), and that if Aunt Carmella were here, she'd kill Marie, and if Uncle Vince were here, he'd kill Billy. She said that to prevent bloodstains on her new linoleum that had just been put down in May, we would start wearing bathrobes instead of wrapping a towel around ourselves like we always had, because we were getting older than she thought.

I told Aunt Sally that Marie and I could sew bathrobes cheaper than buying them, so that's what we did.

I wanted to get cheap beach towels that had the girl from the Coppertone bottle on them (the girl with her behind showing) to use for Marie's robe, but Aunt Sally said no, and that she didn't know where I got my sense of humor from, but it certainly wasn't from Mother. When we finished, Aunt Sally said the robes looked nice, but then she had to yell at Marie and Billy for hugging when that was all that they had on.

Aunt Carmella and Uncle Vince finally came down the last week of June. It had been a long strike, and Uncle Vince said that the shipping companies and big companies like McCormick were all "pissed-off" at the Union, and that the next time the contract came up, the workers could all march straight to Hell before they'd get so much as one penny. Uncle Vince said it would probably come to that one day, and the companies would figure out ways to do things without the Longshoremen, but hopefully it wouldn't happen until AFTER he retires. He said the bosses always want more, and the people that do the work want more, but the bosses always win out in the end. Aunt Sally told me to read some books about the labor movement sometime.

Not on *my* summer vacation.

Aunt Carmella and Uncle Vince did a lot of looking for a house that they could buy and rent-out until Uncle Vince retires, but nothing seemed right. Everywhere here is expensive, but a lot were crummy, like beat-up trailers, and places full of termites, too small, too far from the beach, or not close enough to the highways. Aunt Carmella said she'd like a little place like Aunt Sally's, but Uncle Vince doesn't want to live that close to the beach. She says he's afraid sharks will break in at night.

The first week of August, the Drive-In Movie Theatre had a triple feature on Friday of all those James Bond movies that Aunt Sally and Aunt Carmella and Marie and Billy liked, and they were all going to go. Why would anybody want to spend a whole night watching people get killed? Uncle Bill was working the shift, and Uncle Vince didn't want to see James Bond either, so *they* went to the movies, and *we* went down to the boardwalk and had Orange Julius, and I listened to the Wurlitzer while we drank them, and we both went on the new roller coaster ride called "The Wild Mouse." It doesn't look like much because it's small, but it really is WILD! We went on it four times and laughed and screamed the whole time. Uncle Vince says he's going to take Aunt Carmella on it just so he could hear *her* scream.

They came home about 4 o'clock in the morning and woke us up saying dumb stuff from the movies and told us not to wake them up tomorrow. I said it was already tomorrow.

Uncle Vince and I never got back to sleep, so we got up when it started getting light, and went over the hill to watch the sunrise, and had toast and jam for breakfast. We finished just in time to answer the phone on the first ring. It was the real estate guy, and he wanted to show Uncle Vince "the perfect place." Uncle Vince said "At 7 o'clock in the morning?," and the real estate guy said it was right off Route 50, and the vacation traffic would be picking up soon. I made Aunt Carmella some coffee in her little expresso pot while Uncle Vince woke her up. She was in a bad mood the whole drive there. "The perfect place" was on the other side of the Route 50 drawbridge, and about three miles out and turn left at the Gulf station, and a quarter mile farther down that road and look for a white Cadillac on the left.

There were four little houses made of cinder blocks and they were painted pink, sky blue, pastel green, and yellow. All the paint was flaking off, and the roofs were rusty tin. Aunt Carmella took one look and told me to walk all around them and look for cracks in the walls and whatever I could see of the foundation. When she got out of the car, she yelled "You got us out here for this? We don't want some crummy motel; we just want one house." The guy said it had just been sub-divided yesterday, and Aunt Carmella said, "So you couldn't sell them together, huh?" He said that meant that they would sell faster now, and she said she could see the mob lining up for them.

They went into the first one while I walked around all of them. There were cracks in the walls you could see through on three of them, and the one they were in had a HUGE crack in the foundation. I heard her say "Vince. Stand here and jump" and the whole house shifted. She yelled "What are you trying to pull here? You're wasting our time." He said the other houses would be better.

When they came outside, I could see Aunt Carmella's eyes all squinted-up like they do at the auction places. I went into the next one with them. The floorplan was like Aunt Sally's, but without the kids' rooms. She said "Vince. Jump" but this house didn't rock. She started complaining about the bare cinder block walls and the cracks in them, and no interior walls, just partitions that didn't even go all the way up, and I pointed out the water stains inside the roof (there wasn't a ceiling), and we went into the next one.

There weren't any wall cracks, and the roof looked dry. She started in again about the bare walls and no ceiling, and the wiring was exposed, and the bathroom and kitchen waterpipes were exposed and rusty and probably leaked, and that was why the water was turned off, and where was the heat, and the concrete floor made her back ache just standing there. The real estate guy told her it just needed a little paint, and it would be ready to rent. She told him it would be a cold day in Hell before *she'd* stay in a place like this and walked out. He followed her and said it was a steal at forty thousand, but maybe he could take thirty-five. I said that the doors and windows were rotten, and he gave me a dirty look and said there was nothing wrong with them and poked one to show us, and his finger went in up to the first knuckle.

He took us into the last house, and it was almost as bad as the second. Aunt Carmella said it would cost too much to fix everything that was wrong, and it probably wouldn't meet the code even if it was fixed, and she knew it because her brothers were in the building trades. He said that meant she could get it fixed up cheap because they could do the work for her, and she yelled "You think they're going to come all the way down here from Baltimore?" He said thirty-two thousand, and she said he was nuts. Uncle Vince took me outside and nodded at the third one and said, "I think your aunt found her dream house."

I asked him for his pocketknife, and he held me up so I could check the wood under the eaves. I was pretty sure it was solid, and we stood there and listened to her asking how big the lots were and he said that she'd be able to park two cars and she said is *that* all they are? and her backyard in Baltimore was bigger than that, and the more she argued, the more the price came down, until he got down to thirty thousand and said that was ABSOLUTELY the lowest he'd go.

We heard her talking about water and sewage, and the electric, and the meters had to be moved to the house, not the big one on the street for all four houses, and how much were the real estate taxes, and Uncle Vince said it was all over but the paperwork now. She finally settled on twenty-nine thousand, and she wanted the third house, not the one they were in, and he said she was cutting his heart out.

When they came outside, he looked at Uncle Vince like he wanted to say something, and Uncle Vince grinned at him and said "I just hand her the paycheck on Fridays, and you saw it: when she says 'jump'..."

We went to his office and they wrote out a "provisional intent-to-buy agreement" and then we all went to the 1st National Bank Branch, and we waited while they called the one in Baltimore to check the accounts, and they printed a check for five thousand dollars for the real estate guy and told him that someone from the bank would go out to look at the property, and everybody would be back on Monday to figure out the mortgage.

On the way home, Aunt Carmella was quiet and didn't say much except to ask Uncle Vince if it was okay. Did he like it? Would he be happy there when he retired? He laughed and told her "Sure, Doll, whatever makes you happy makes me happy. You know that." He tugged her over next to him, put his arm around her, kissed her cheek, and I saw her shoulders relax.

All of a sudden, she sat up straight and shivered and said "oh, shit." He looked at me in the mirror and winked and said "Carmella, Queen of the Gypsies; knows all, sees all, tells all." She looked worried and said "Vince, don't. Just speed up a little."

When we got home, we saw Dad's station wagon. "She's a week early" we all said and went inside.

Aunt Sally was standing there with her arms crossed, and Mother was giving her one of her icy looks. Mother said "They're here. Tell them."

Aunt Carmella put a smile on her face and said "Hey Sally, guess what? We just bought a house."

Mother looked at us and told Aunt Sally "There. They have their own place. They can leave and stop sponging off you."

Aunt Sally looked at Mother and growled "My friends— and *I* at least HAVE friends— do NOT 'sponge off' me. They buy groceries, help clean and do laundry, and DON'T come down a week early without notice and tell me how to conduct my life."

Mother opened her mouth, but Dad spoke first. "I'm sorry, Sally. When Susan said... I should have called to be sure. I think there was some confusion about the dates." He looked away when Mother gave him one of her looks.

Mother looked at me. "You. Pack. Get in the car."

Aunt Sally growled back "She's mine until school starts, Susan. She stays."

Mother walked past Dad and went out to the car and started blowing the horn. "We'll stay somewhere else, this year" he said. Mother wasn't beeping any more, she was holding the horn down. "Perhaps separate rooms." He tried to smile at Aunt Carmella. "Congratulations on your new house."

"It needs work, Dad. Maybe you and I could come down on weekends?"

Dad nodded. "That sounds like a good idea" he said. "We could get away from...." He waved his hand and left.

Aunt Carmella looked upset. "Sally, I'm sorry, we should be the ones leaving."

Aunt Sally took a deep breath and uncrossed her arms and smiled. "Don't be silly, Carmella. I owe you a big favor, now. I won't have to put up with—"She looked at me. "I'm sorry, Honey." I gave her a big hug and said it was okay.

Marie came out of our room yawning. "What's going on?"

"We bought a house" Uncle Vince said, and Marie woke up all the way, and ran into Billy's room and yelled "Wake up, Poindexter! We got a house!"

Dad called about an hour later and asked if he could come up and see me. He said Mother was at the Best Western and he was at the French Quarter. Aunt Sally told him that he could've stayed here because HE was ALWAYS welcome. He got there at the same time as Uncle Bill, and we all went to see the "Second Honeymoon Cottage" (that's what Aunt Carmella said she'd call it). She had gotten a key when they signed the papers this morning. When we went inside, Marie asked where our room was, and Aunt Carmella said that's why it's a SECOND Honeymoon.

Dad looked at the roof inside and checked the eaves and windows like I did, and said the tin roof would have to go, but the wood under it was probably sound. I thought it would be. He paced off measurements and drew on the back of his hotel bill. Aunt Carmella said her brothers would come down and do the plumbing and electric, and the plastering and painting too, and their wives and her mother would be glad to have them do something besides drink beer on the weekends and make some money "on the side" they wouldn't have to pay taxes on. Dad said we could all get together and figure out who does what and when. Uncle Bill said he'd ask around about a roofer.

This was going to be fun!

We went out to a restaurant for supper to celebrate, and then Uncle Bill and Uncle Vince went to the VFW to watch the ballgame. Everybody was too tired to do anything else (except me: *I* didn't stay up all night watching James Bond). We took baths and went to bed.

I woke up around 10 o'clock when I heard Aunt Carmella laughing in our doorway but trying not to. She went out on the porch and Aunt Sally asked what was funny. "The girls" she told her. "They roll-over in unison like an old married couple."

Aunt Sally snorted a little, and then sighed. "I worry about her."

"She'll turn out okay. She's got us in Baltimore, and you down here."

Aunt Sally sighed again. "I know. And thank God for that. But she'll still have scars."

I heard that, and thought no, I only have the one on my forehead, but inside I knew what she meant. And I knew I would never, EVER be like Mother, no matter what.

Now they started talking about Mother, and Aunt Carmella was wondering how she ever got Dad to marry her. "I bet she gave him her cherry and told him he HAD to marry her."

Aunt Sally said Mother had never given away anything in her life, and she probably looked at Dad and decided she could make him dance to whatever tune she played, and then just "steam-rollered" him into marriage.

I didn't think I should be listening to any of this.

"It's just like today, Carmella. She comes in here and starts telling me how to run my life, and to get you and Vince out— "

"We should've gone" Aunt Carmella interrupted her.

"No, Carmella. You either stop Susan right from the start, or you can't stop her at all, and the next time it would be worse. SHE'S the one who decided she'd come here for a vacation every year, and I didn't stop her then. It was probably a good thing in the long run, otherwise I wouldn't have Sally here in the summer."

I heard Uncle Vince's car drive up, and they stopped talking and went to bed.

It took me a long time to get back to sleep.

CHAPTER FIFTY-TWO

Buildings and Birthdays

It was a crazy week. Aunt Carmella and Uncle Vince got the mortgage money settled, but they weren't signing the final contract until the water and electric meters were moved and the doors and windows were replaced, and the Bank agreed and told the real estate guy that he wouldn't get the money until that was done. Uncle Vince said that when she was born, Aunt Carmella wouldn't let her mother sign the Birth Certificate until the Doctor lowered his fee.

Aunt Carmella made some phone calls, and you know what? Her brothers all came down right away. Mr. Mike the plumber (the one who doesn't like me), was already here in Ocean City deep-sea fishing, and he made the city dig-up and replace ALL the pipe from the main water line out at the street up to the new meter on the side of the house AND one foot to the INSIDE of the house. And all in just FOUR days! Wow, I thought he was just a big fat jerk, but he got the job DONE! Mr. Joe the electrician (the one that calls me Miss Osterhoff), had the electric company hang new wire from the telephone pole to the new meter on the side of the house and put a "main breaker box" inside. Aunt Carmella says her brothers all know the right people that know all the other right people *everywhere* that'll do the things they need when they need it done in a hurry.

Her other two brothers I had only seen at Thanksgiving. They were George and Vic, "DiCarlo Brothers Painting and Plastering." And there was one more brother, but he was Uncle Vince's: "Sal Giametti Heating and Air Conditioning."

Want to guess who the carpenters are?

Everybody came to Aunt Sally's to figure out what Aunt Carmella wanted for her new house. Electric, propane, or oil for heating and hot water? Electric or hot water baseboard, or forced-air heating and air conditioning? Shower or tub? Water, electricity, or propane to hook up a washer and dryer now, or after Uncle Vince retires and they move in for good? Wood floor, carpet, or linoleum? (Uncle Vince said dirt. Aunt Carmella told him to shut up.)

I was like the secretary writing all this down, and it all went on and on. Then the roofer showed up, and it was just too much!

Dad was watching me and grinning. "More to house building than four walls and a roof, Sally?"

I said yeah, and how did they do it when he was building them? Everybody listened.

"Not like the English" he said. "My people would have a hand pump for water (and he moved his hand up and down to show me), a stove to cook and the water make hot, and vents in the ceiling for heat to up-go for bedrooms in winter." Dad always starts to talk funny when he talks about when he was younger.

The other men laughed and said it sounded like the Old Country, and they were glad they were Americans. Dad looked like he wished he was back in Ohio instead of working in an office. I thought of the word "wistful" and now I really understood it. I asked him if he could go back, would he?

We were all quiet. Dad looked at me and touched my cheek. "No, Sally. I would not have you."

I gave him a big hug.

The next day, Dad and I went to the lumberyard and bought five windows and two doors, and dropped the bill off at the real estate office and told him we would bill him later for our labor when we hung them. He looked like he wished he'd never even *heard* of Aunt Carmella.

We got to the house and started bringing the doors and windows in, and Mr. Mike showed up and *told* us (he didn't *ask* us) to start tearing out the partition between the kitchen and the bathroom so he could see the old plumbing better. We tore the whole thing down in about five minutes (it was only ¼ inch plywood and a few 2x4's— is that any way to build? I ask you!) He stood watching us work and complained the whole time about me doing "*men's* work." Dad grinned at him and said I was doing "women's work"— I was doing the mending. We both laughed at him, and he got mad and said the only things women are supposed to do is cook, clean, and screw, and Dad yelled "Sally! Raus mitten zie!" and I took off!

I was all the way out by the street, and I could still hear Dad and Mr. Mike yelling, but then it stopped. Dad came outside and waved me back, and we carried another window in. Mr. Mike didn't look at us. When we stood the window against the wall, it slipped and I dislocated my index finger again, and I yelled "Schiess!" Dad reached for it, but I said I could get it, and I pulled up and out and it snapped back in place, and I said "Schiess" again, and shook my hand a couple of times. Mr. Mike made a noise, and I turned around and he looked a little green, and he ran outside and threw up in the parking lot and got in his car and drove away. Dad and I looked at each other and started laughing while he massaged my hand.

It took the rest of the day to hang everything. We didn't stop for lunch, and we had to start the car and turn the headlights on so we could see to put the knob and lock on the front door. Dad looked at his watch and marked our time on a piece of paper and said he'd charge Union wages for both of us— Master and Apprentice.

The real estate guy isn't going to like *us*, either.

I know I'd rather be a Mathematician when I graduate from college, and maybe teach, but I love doing this too. Maybe because it's more than just numbers on paper. Maybe I'll do both, like Dad does office work and cabinetry. We'll see.

Aunt Carmella and Uncle Vince and Mother and Dad went home at the end of the next week. Aunt Sally told all of them that she'd bring us home Labor Day weekend, so we could have one more week of summer.

When I woke up on the last day of August, Marie was lying next to me with her head propped up on her elbow. She leaned over and kissed me and said, "Happy Birthday."

I frowned and said "Yeah, we go back to Baltimore on Sunday."

She said "Happy Birthday, Sal" a little louder.

I said "Shh," and she said, "She's not here, so don't say 'shh'. You can have a happy birthday this year, okay?"

I sighed. "Okay, I'll have a happy birthday."

Now Marie was frowning, and she started to sing, and sang loud!

"Happy Birthday to you.
Happy Birthday to you.
Happy Birthday dear Sally,
Happy Birthday to you!"

"God, Marie, alright! Jeez, what's the matter with you? It's just my birthday."

Aunt Sally was standing in the doorway. "I tried to tell you, Honey" she said to Marie. "She's never had a birthday party. Neither did her mother, nor me." She bent down and kissed both of us. "It's hard to miss what you never had."

"Well, she should have had parties, or at least a birthday cake." Granny Annie was there, too. "I swear, that woman could take the joy out of Resurrection Day in Heaven."

Aunt Sally snorted, but Marie looked hurt. I said "Well, you don't do any of that, either" and she turned red, and I knew: "You don't have a birthday party because I don't."

Marie shrugged her shoulders and wouldn't look at me. "I didn't want you to feel bad" she said.

"Oh, Marie." I hugged her. "Tell you what: how about I have my birthday when you have yours? June 14th? Next year we'll both be sixteen together, okay?"

"In the meantime, get up and have some birthday cake before we go swimming." Billy had poked his head in the door, too.

"BILLY!" Marie yelled at him. "It was supposed to be a surprise, Poindexter!"

Oh God, I thought. Let's just get it over with. I put on a smile, got up, went outside in my pajamas, grabbed my bathing suit and robe off the clothesline and got dressed in the bathroom, and waited while Billy and Marie did the same. On the kitchen table, there was a big peach shortcake that I knew Granny Annie had made with white peaches (my favorite kind), and there was a candle on it. Uncle Bill was watching me and smiling. "You make a wish and blow the candle out." I told him I'd seen it on TV, so I got a kitchen match and lit it and blew it out while Uncle bill laughed. "You're supposed to wait until everybody sings." Marie told him she'd already taken care of that and come on and open your present.

When I picked it up, I knew it was record albums, and I hoped it wasn't the Beatles.

It was "Merry-Go-Round Melodies" "Merry-Go-Round Memories" "Carrousel Music from the Mighty Wurlitzer" and "Calliope! Steam-Powered Music." Marie hugged me and told me which one came from who, and I could keep them at her home so Mother couldn't throw them out.

Then she gave me a card. It was homemade, and Uncle Vince had drawn a picture of Marie and I looking at each other. It said, "Happy Birthday, Twin Sister" and there was a verse inside and one of the lines was "When I look into the mirror, the face I see is yours." She told me she stole the verse from a real card. I said thank you to everyone, and I said that this was really my FIRST birthday instead of my fifteenth, and I thought I was going to laugh, but I started to cry instead, even though I was happy, and everybody said "Aww" and hugged and kissed me.

We all had shortcake for breakfast.

CHAPTER FIFTY-THREE

Osterhoff Remodelers

We were Sophomores and Mrs. Persky had us try out for the Varsity. Doris breezed right through and made the diving team, but we barely made the cut. Mrs. Persky keeps telling us to smooth out our strokes. "You're not Johnny Weissmuller or Viv Marchelle, so stop attacking the water!" A couple of the girls said we swim like boys, and Marie laughed and said, "Boys don't have these" and patted her boobs. But Mrs. Persky's right: we have to change how we swim; it's just hard to relearn everything.

Dad and I go down to Ocean City most weekends. We go down to Aunt Sally's Friday evening, get up at 5AM on Saturday, work till it's dark, and go home Sunday morning after Church (Dad doesn't work on Sunday.) When we get home, Aunt Carmella has Dad's clothes cleaned and folded, he goes inside to hear Mother hiss, and I sleep at Marie's.

Oh, and when I say "we" I mean Marie comes down too. Aunt Carmella had told her she'd stay home instead of going down and smooching Billy, but when she heard Mother making that sick noise of hers that she calls a laugh, Aunt Carmella sent Marie down anyway.

The worst of it is that sneer on Mother's face, and her nasty cracks about Dad taking his "little boy" to play "Handyman" and that "he" (me) will turn into a "morfodike lizbonian" and I *KNOW* that she knows the real words.

Does it sound like I'm getting fed up?

Aunt Sally and Aunt Carmella say that one day they'll *both* play football, with Mother as the ball. I haven't gotten to that point, yet (and inside, I know I never will), but I might be a Cheerleader, and that isn't good at all.

There was one weekend that was kind of funny in a way. When Mr.

Mike came down to "rough-in" the plumbing, he kept watching Dad and I work. After we had lunch, he said "Hey, tough girl. Get over here." Dad and I looked at each other, and he nodded, so I went over. Mr. Mike said "Watch and learn" and I watched him measure and cut and clean and fit the copper pipe and put the grease called flux in all the joints, and watched him heat them with a blowtorch (like the kind in cartoons), and poke solder sticks into them to melt, and then wipe them with more flux while they were still hot, "because that's the way I got taught, that's why." When he was finished, he said "Alright. You: from here to here."

I did everything he had done, and when I was finished, he squatted down and looked at every inch, and told me nobody would ever hire me, but he didn't think it would leak, so he'd let it stay, and maybe I'd figure it out better if I practiced. Then he told me to beat it and stop bothering him.

Somewhere in all of that, I think I got a compliment.

When we came home the last Sunday of October, the front bedroom windows were broken, and MY bedroom windows were broken, too. Marie said if Mother was throwing my clothes out too, then maybe I could move in with them. We didn't know why she did it until we went downstairs to the workshop to put our tools away and saw where she'd been hacking away around the padlock hasp with a butcher's knife (the blade had broken and was still stuck in the wood). I said that at least she didn't get in, but Dad frowned at me and said that at least she didn't hurt herself. I didn't say anything else.

I slept with Marie that night, Dad slept in the basement, and Mother slept in her cold bedroom. Dad called the glaziers again in the morning.

Dad and I finished all the carpentry on Thanksgiving weekend, and Mr. Joe finished the electric at the same time. Mr. Sal did the heating and air conditioning the next weekend, and we went down with Mr. George and Mr. Vic after that to watch them insulate and do "gypsum board." Dad had only ever seen plastering done. He said this looked a lot easier. We did the trim and mounted the kitchen cabinets Dad and I had made, and Mr. Mike came on Sunday and put in the sinks and tub and toilet, and Mr. George and Mr. Vic painted, and the heavy work was all done. Finally,

Aunt Carmella and Uncle Vince came down and bought some cheap but solid furniture, Aunt Sally and Uncle Bill gave them plates and bowls and stainless flatware, and Granny Annie gave them some cooking pots, and the Second Honeymoon Cottage was finished, except for painting the outside in Spring. Uncle Vince said the Bank Account was finished too. A lady that Aunt Sally knows that does rentals said there'd be no problem getting $20 a night from May through September.

We all went to Ocean City Christmas week instead of them coming up to Baltimore this year. Well, I went. Mother wouldn't go, and Dad figured he should stay with her and save money on window glass. I thought Christmas was happier.

And I don't feel bad about it, either.

CHAPTER FIFTY-FOUR

Growing Up

Marie and I did a lot better at our swim meets in the Spring. We're finally ranked "on the board", at least with the city schools, and Doris has won every competition she's been in, and is sure to at least "place" in the State competitions.

I've been coasting through classes again. I'm not the only one being bored to death, though. You would think that since this is the college prep program, it would be harder. Our teachers are having some of us teach other classes, like I did in Junior High, but it's still not enough. Classes need to be harder. Wait, what?

We were told that we could pick extra courses next year. Marie is going to do Economics and Business Math and Accounting, and I'll probably do Political Science and Theory, and maybe double-up on my French Classes. Yeah, I know, I don't like any of them, but at least I'll be forced to pay attention.

The last weekend in April, Uncle Vince and Mr. George and Mr. Vic went to Ocean City to paint the outside of the cottage. Uncle Vince was going to paint a rose trellis and vines on the front wall to make it look fancy from the street. He says they'll never have to worry about weeds. Marie went down with him, SUPPOSEDLY to check the want-ads in the local paper. Aunt Carmella said she could just as easily do that at home, and that's what I was doing by calling the newspapers about summer job listings. Marie and I will be sixteen, and able to earn money for college (only two years away!) Aunt Sally told me to call her Long Distance if we get any offers, so she can tell us if the job would be worth taking.

Dad said it was okay with him for me to find a job, but not to mention it to Mother. As if I would. I'm sick and tired of listening to her complain about what's "proper" for me as "*her* daughter." (I thought I was Dad's "son" back in the Fall.)

School ended, we got "A" s in everything, and we packed up and left Baltimore for the summer. We had found jobs waitressing at restaurants at two different hotels doing breakfast and lunch (for 65 cents an hour, plus tips— usually 25 or 50 cents). Aunt Sally had told us the tips would be smaller, but it won't be as hectic as dinner, and the customers are usually friendlier. She told us to watch out for kids spilling stuff and ignore the parents if they smack their kids for not behaving. I won't like that part of it.

Billy got a job at a pool-cleaning company (for $1.25 an hour), and he got his boss to find us a place to swim. It'll be the Coastal View Motor Home, and we can swim there for free in the evenings between 8 until 10.

I remember Austin telling me they got $2 for each boat he and his brother cleaned. That seemed like a lot of money then. It still does.

Marie and I came home on "our" birthday ("sweet sixteen and never been kissed" HA HA!), and we saw Billy and Uncle Vince sitting on the bus stop bench across the street. Aunt Carmella was standing on the porch shivering. Aunt Sally and Granny Annie were inside sitting at the table. Aunt Sally looked worried. She asked Marie "Is there something going on with Billy that you want to tell me about?" Marie and I looked at each other, shrugged our shoulders and sat down. We could see out the window, and Uncle Vince didn't look mad or anything. Uncle Bill came home and looked at Aunt Sally. "We don't know either, Bill."

Billy and Uncle Vince stood up and shook hands, and then Uncle Vince gave Billy a big hug. They came back to us, and Uncle Vince said, "Put a sweater on, Carmella, you're getting frostbite." Billy went into his room, came back out and took Marie outside and up to the beach.

Aunt Sally and Aunt Carmella looked at Uncle Vince. "What's going on?" He grinned and didn't say anything. Granny Annie said "You two would know if you'd think. Lord knows you talk about it enough."

Aunt Carmella yelled "Vince! Is he proposing?" Aunt Sally yelled "They're only sixteen!" Granny Annie laughed and said, "Andy married me when I was fifteen, and I had Viv when I was sixteen."

Aunt Sally was yelling louder now. "MOM! It's not the same today! They can't get married— wait— Vince! What happened? Is she...? Are they...?"

Uncle Bill was laughing. "Sally. If she was, Vince would have killed him."

Aunt Sally and Aunt Carmella went over to the kitchen sink and they both tried to look out the window at the same time. I went over to the back door with Granny Annie.

Billy and Marie came over the dune with their arms around each other and smiling and kissing, and Marie kept looking at her left hand. They came inside. "Billy asked me to marry him. I said yes. He already asked Pop." She held out her hand. There was a ring with two pearls on it.

Aunt Carmella was looking at Billy. "Oh, Jeez. Those earrings at the auction. You said it was her birthday present."

I started laughing. "You got her ring size when you had her try on those Friendship rings at the 5&10."

"And I got the pearls mounted on the ring for him" Granny Annie laughed.

Aunt Carmella flopped on a kitchen chair. "Oh, Jeez. Sixteen."

Uncle Vince stroked her cheek. "You were seventeen when *I* proposed, Carmella."

"It was the war! Everybody was getting married!"

"Hey, wait a minute!" Marie yelled now. "We're still not getting married until we're 22!"

"We're only making it formal, that's all" Billy said.

Aunt Carmella looked at Uncle Vince. "I said they could get engaged, Carmella" he told her. "Not married. Yet. And it's not permission for any... you know." He turned to Aunt Sally and Uncle Bill. "I know you two didn't raise a bum. He's a good kid. He's got respect for Marie." He looked at Billy. "Or else. Got it?"

Billy nodded. "Yessir. I promised."

Aunt Carmella and Aunt Sally looked at each other and rolled their eyes and said "Oh, Jeez. Engaged." They went over to Marie and Billy, and the hugging started, and the kissing, and the laughing, and the birthday party turned into an engagement party.

A couple of days later, I lost my job.

During the break between breakfast and lunch, I took all the cigarette butts in the big can that we dumped them in and poured water on them and then poured all of that into the big trash dumpster thing behind the kitchen. One of the maids from the hotel was there. It was Doris Johnson.

I said "Hi." She jumped and looked around and didn't say anything, and I heard the restaurant Hostess Mrs. Norvel say "You. Beat it. Get back to work." Doris grabbed the little cart she had for trash and took off. I looked behind me and Mrs. Norvel was frowning at me. "It don't do no good," she said.

I didn't know what she meant. "What doesn't?"

"Trying to be friendly with these coons. You're a city girl, you got them ideas about them being equal and all that, but it's not good for them, and you're not doing them any favors. It just gives them ideas. The wrong kind. And all you get is trouble." She was looking mad, now. "You probably go to school with them. We know better down here. Get inside."

About an hour later, I was refilling some guy's coffee cup, and he stuck his hand all the way up my skirt. I jumped back and I tried to hit him with the coffee pot, but Mrs. Norvel was there, and she grabbed my arm and took the pot away from me. "What the Hell do you think you're doing?" She hissed like Mother. "Get in the kitchen. Now."

"But he stuck his hand— "

"Shut up, damn you, people are looking" she hissed. "Oh, I am SO sorry" she said to the guy that grabbed me. "She's new. Don't worry, I'll take care of you myself. *I said* GET." I went back to the kitchen.

She came storming back right behind me. I yelled before she could. "He stuck his hand up between my legs and grabbed me!"

"I don't give a good goddam what he did! HE'S the customer. This sort of thing happens. You gotta be quick and smart enough not to *let* it happen!"

I was madder than she was. "I'm not letting some jerk grab me– "

"Shut up! You're fired! Get the Hell out of here! Goddammit, first you start with stirring up the niggers, then you get fresh with the customers! OUT! NOW!"

All the colored people doing the cooking and washing in the kitchen didn't look at us at all.

I looked at her and I hissed "You owe me my pay."

"You can go to Hell for it! Get out!"

I left.

I went across the street to the bus stop. I saw Doris and some older colored ladies standing there, and I started to say Hi again, but she whispered without moving her lips "Don't look at me, don't talk to me, just sit on the bench and look down the street for the bus."

I sat and looked down the street like she said. "Doris— ".

"Shh!" she said. "Look, girl, I NEED this job. This is MY college money. I won't be getting some scholarship like you." She looked down the street and moved further away from me. "That white bitch is— ". She stopped and started over. "That woman is over there watching us, so DON'T look at me or talk." I could see Mrs. Norvel out of the corner of my eye. "We're not in school, we're not on the bus, we're not ANYPLACE but HERE, and this is the Eastern Shore, and that means this is the SOUTH, and that means DEEP SOUTH. I NEED this job. I DON'T need the kind of trouble that still happens down here." A car full of colored ladies in the front seat pulled up to the curb, and the back door opened. Doris s-l-o-w-l-y got into the car after the other ladies did. "I know you were just being friendly, but NOT down here."

"I don't understand" I whispered.

She pulled the car door closed. "Oh, girl. You're about the smartest person I know, but right now you got a bad case of the dumbs." They drove off.

Mrs. Norvel watched me until the bus came.

I rode the bus towards home and tried to think. I stared out the window, and when we stopped across the street from the Sea Star Diner, I saw a sign that said, "Waitress Wanted" and I called for the driver to open the door and got out and went over and inside. There was a girl a few years older than me behind the counter. "Hi" I said. "I saw your sign, and— oh." I recognized her. It was Linda, Austin's girlfriend. She looked at me and then she recognized me too. "Oh" she said, "It's Sally, right?" Then she laughed and said "Well, of course it is! It's there on your name tag." I looked down and there it still was, complete with the Hotel's name on it.

"Hang on" she said. "Back in a second." She went to the cash register and rang up the bill and told the people thanks and come again, and went over to the table and scooped up the plates, cups and flatware, and her tip— a whole dollar—, came back, put the plates on the open shelf where the food comes through, took full plates to a booth, came back again, got a wet, soapy rag from the sink under the counter and squeezed it out, wiped off the first table, took some people who had just walked in to it, gave them menus, got them some water, and came back to me.

"You got fired, huh? What happened?"

I told her about the guy that grabbed me, and then about talking to a colored girl (I didn't say who.) She shook her head. "That guy. That crap doesn't go here. Somebody tries it gets hot coffee dumped in his lap, then Dad comes out from the kitchen and gives them the 'bum's rush' out the door. And usually a boot, too." She looked over to another table. "Right back." She was SO fast, and made it look so easy. "The colored thing. I got raised better than that. My mom taught me it's sinful to hate."

She took off again and came back and said "You're hired. Start tomorrow at 5AM, work till 1, we got a big breakfast trade here, scrape that hotel name off the tag. It's 90 cents an hour." She called through the pass-through. "Dad! Got a girl. Tomorrow." She grinned and said, "See ya!" and took off again.

I hoped I could keep up!

I told everybody what happened when I got home. They all got mad, and Uncle Vince wanted to go down there and look for the guy, and Aunt Carmella wanted to go and "slap the crap" out of Mrs. Norvel, but Aunt Sally said she'd take care of it, and she'd make sure I got my pay "to the penny," or everyone in town would know that Lucy Norvel let some animal paw a sixteen-year-old girl.

I just hoped nothing would happen to Doris.

There was one thing that happened that summer that I was embarrassed about, or maybe ashamed of.

We were on the boardwalk one evening when we saw that Cynthia Smith. There were a bunch of other girls with her, and they were all smirking at us. Cynthia Smith was wearing a micro-mini beach skirt, and a purple bikini top with a purple plastic ring between the cups, and you're supposed to wear a blouse or something, because there's signs that say, "No swimwear permitted on the boardwalk." Anyway, she walks right up to us and says "Aww, isn't that sweet! They're taking their little boy out for ice cream."

Marie just smiled and held her hand up in front of Cynthia Smith's face. "No, my *FIANCE* and I are taking a stroll."

Cynthia Smith grabbed Marie's hand and looked at her ring. "That's not a diamond. They're pearls. And one's smaller than the other." Billy laughed right in her face and said, "So are we!" and they both walked away laughing. I tried to follow, but she stepped in front of me and squeezed my arm and said, "Did you make the wrestling team this year?" I slapped her hand away, and told her "Yeah, and I guess they made YOU Captain of the Bitch Squad."

They all stopped smirking and laughing, and then she slapped me in the face. BIG mistake. I might have to put up with that from Mother, but NOT from her.

So, I made a bigger mistake.

I grabbed that purple ring on her bikini top, and I swear to God all I was going to do was pull and let it snap back, and...

and the ring broke, and...

her top popped open...

and two falsies fell out and bounced on the boardwalk.

Some boy grabbed them and started... okay, boys can be really gross sometimes.

Cynthia Smith didn't scream, or cover herself, or anything. She just looked at me, and if I were the Wicked Witch and she were Dorothy, I'd have been a puddle. *Then* she held her top over herself, and one of the other girls said "C'mon, Cindy, I've got some safety pins in my coin purse" and they walked away towards one of the boardwalk Ladies Rooms.

But the girl with the safety pins looked back at the other girls and had a nasty grin on her face, and the other girls were grinning back and trying not to laugh.

My stomach did flip-flops, and I ran to catch up with Marie and Billy.

Some friends. I think I felt sorry for Cynthia Smith.

The rest of the summer was busy, but nice. I got to be just as fast at the diner as Linda, and one of us could take a day off during the week while the other worked. I took Tuesdays and she took Thursdays.

Aunt Carmella and Uncle Vince spent the last week of their vacation at the Second Honeymoon Cottage, and Aunt Sally and Uncle Bill hung out down there that week. I was told to keep an eye on Marie and Billy, but they pretty much behaved. Marie says she's a "Good Catholic Italian Girl," and she'll stay that way.

Mother and Dad came down for the last two weeks of August like they were supposed to, and Mother blew her mind at Aunt Sally, then Dad, and then me about being a "common waitress" and that I'd end up like Aunt Sally. I said, "Sounds good to me," ducked her slap, and walked out.

CHAPTER FIFTY-FIVE

Junior Year

School started, and Marie and I began our extra courses along with our regular classes. Marie loved all the economics and business stuff, and she says she'll be a millionaire one day. I believe it, especially if Aunt Carmella lends a hand. I found out all the political science stuff was more interesting than I thought it would be. I tried explaining some of it to Aunt Carmella, but she laughs and says she handles politics like this: never vote "FOR," always vote "AGAINST." She says it's less wear and tear on the nerves.

Doris Johnson isn't in our classes this year. She's taking all sorts of extra science classes. I finally got to talk to her alone in a stairwell our second week back. She said she'd heard I'd been fired, and I asked if anything had happened to her. She said no, people like Mrs. Norvel think that all colored people look alike. When I asked her if we were still friends, she looked surprised, and got all these different expressions on her face, and said she didn't know that I liked her like a friend. We both stood there and didn't say anything, and I asked if I was having "the dumbs" again. She laughed, but then said that maybe this is what Dr. King meant when he talked about different kinds of kids playing together. Then she said she guesses that means that I'm her first white girlfriend. We noticed it was quiet, and everybody else was in class, so we just laughed and kind of shook hands and we both went to class. I'm glad she didn't get in trouble. And I'm glad that she and I are friends.

Aunt Carmella had Thanksgiving at her home again this year, and she invited us. Mother of course refused, but Dad and I went over, and I helped the men on the porch catch his clothes. When we went inside, we got a big surprise: Aunt Sally and Uncle Bill and Billy and Granny Annie were there.

All the women were looking at Marie's ring, and the men were looking and poking at Billy and pretending they were measuring him. Uncle Vince told them he was going to be proud to have Billy for a son-in-law in a few years, and by the time dinner was over, the men were saying he'd do.

Granny Annie said she had the best time of her life, and all the women liked her, and tried to teach her some Italian, and they asked her for the recipe for the hot milk walnut cakes she'd brought.

When we tried to go back to our house, Mother had chained the door, so we stayed at Marie's. Dad said it was very considerate of Mother to send a change of clothes over, but we all stopped laughing when we heard her smash her bedroom window with his shoes.

I don't think he cared.

At Christmastime, Aunt Sally and everyone came up for the week. Granny Annie kept saying thank you to Aunt Carmella for inviting her, and she told her to knock it off because she's family. The coolest thing was how they got here this year. Uncle Bill had a brand-new car, and BILLY drove it all the way from home! He said he took Driver's Ed at school and got his license the week after Thanksgiving.

Billy had been hoping that he'd get the old car, and he might have, except that the car salesman bought it himself because it was in such good shape with no rust, and had a big motor, and was from 1951. He said he wanted to sell it to somebody he knew that would make a hot rod out of it, so Uncle Bill only had to pay $600 for his new car.

I wanted to go to Driver's Ed in the Spring. Mother, of course, forbade me to go because men drive, ladies are driven, and even that woman next door didn't drive, and that was that. Dad told me to let him know when, where, and how much. She didn't say anything, but I know she'll do something rotten to him eventually.

Marie and I are winning all our races, and Mrs. Persky says with luck, she'll have a WHOLE team in the State Finals this year. I don't think we'll make it to the 1968 Olympics unless a miracle happens and everybody drowns at the Nationals, but I bet we'll be there in 1972.

We started Driver's Ed in April, and the first lessons were pretty scary.

We'd take the bus after school to the Mondawmin Shopping Center and go over to the Social Security building next door and use their parking lot.

Polytechnic did theirs the same days we did. The boys went first, and all of them tried to do everything fast, and kept knocking over all the traffic cones that showed where to go. When they were finished, one of the instructors told them that now that they had shown all the girls what brainless idiots they were, none of us would ever get in a car with them.

When it was our turn, the instructor kept telling me to relax and drop my shoulders, loosen my death grip on the wheel, and GENTLY let up on the clutch, and GENTLY press down on the gas pedal, and when I stopped or slowed to be careful not to stall the engine when I braked. When I drove through the course for the third time that evening, I was getting better, but not as good as some of the other girls. I'm afraid of running someone over or crashing the car.

Dad picked Marie and I up after class, and he and I had a cold dried-up supper at our house. I know she cooked early deliberately.

We got our licenses the third week of May. Uncle Vince told us that when we went down to the ocean this year, we would each drive halfway, and that he would turn around and go over the Bay Bridge twice so we could both do it. We're nervous about that because the lanes are so close.

Marie and I made it to the State Finals, but we weren't good enough to make the Nationals. Doris did, though, and she placed 17th in the 3-meter board. Mrs. Persky said that was excellent for her first time, and that it meant she was the 17th best diver in the country.

School was finally out, and we were where we were supposed to be: Ocean City. I was working at the Sea Star again doing breakfast and lunch, and Marie got hired by Phillip's Crab House for dinners, so we didn't see each other very much. Billy was still cleaning pools, and he found two places for us to swim when we weren't working.

When Aunt Carmella and Uncle Vince went to check on the cottage, they found out that the real estate guy had torn down the other three houses and was trying to sell the lots. Aunt Carmella got her brothers to buy them, and they bargained the price so low that the real estate guy said he never wants to see anyone in her family again in this life or the next. The rental lady said that now that those other houses were gone, she could get an even better clientele and charge more money per night.

Summer just flew by, and Mother and Dad came down the last two weeks of August. Mother wasn't talking to anyone again. Dad said she'd been trying to get into his workshop again, and had hired a locksmith to pick the padlock, but he wouldn't do it because it was a railroad lock, and those were only supposed to be for railroad use only, and for fun years ago Dad had hung a sign on the door that said "This equipment belongs to the B&O Railroad. Trespassers will be prosecuted to the fullest extent of the law." Dad found out that the locksmith had reported Mother to the railroad, and the people he works with thought it was funny. When we get back to Baltimore, Dad said he's going to ask Uncle Vince if he can store some things in their basement, because next time, she might find someone smarter.

CHAPTER FIFTY-SIX

Seniors

The brand-new "Polytechnic / Western Complex" was finished (on time!), and classes started the day after Labor Day. Marie and I found out that Seniors and teachers were supposed to have been at school a week earlier so that we could learn where everything was and show the all the other students where to go on the first days of classes.

We never knew about that, but it didn't matter anyway, because NOBODY knew where they were supposed to be. The guys at Poly had it worse: besides the academic building, they had another building for all their shop classes, drafting and surveying. Both schools share the cafeteria and gym buildings (there were big folding partitions that divided both into Western's side and Poly's.)

Poly had something that no other school had: a computer. A BIG computer, in a special room with dust-free air and temperature and humidity controls, and people from IBM who taught students how to make punch-cards to program the computer. All paid for by IBM and some big companies in Baltimore.

So, what was the first thing the geniuses at Poly did with it?

They got it to print a picture from Playboy magazine out of dots and zeroes.

We found out about it when Marie and I and some other girls got invited to take Computer Science classes with them and they had it taped to the wall. Marie said that she bet none of them had ever "done it" or even seen it. They all looked embarrassed, and I bet she was right.

But the guys that did the programing got scholarships to M.I.T.

Mr. Nightingale said our Saturday morning tutoring was over, and we could join Poly's Math Club and the new Computer Club instead. He said he'd miss Aunt Carmella's lunches, and maybe miss us, too. He told us he'd do his best to help us get scholarships, but he said they're harder for girls to get, even when they're smarter than the boys, like us. Mrs. Persky said it's the same with Athletic scholarships, but she'd help us with those as well.

Dad and Aunt Carmella and Uncle Vince said for us not to worry about it, and that we'd get to college with or without scholarships. Marie and I had already estimated how much it would cost: even if we just go to the University of Maryland, it'll still cost a couple of thousand dollars for each of us, and that's only for our Batchelor's degree. The reason it would cost so much is because we would have to live on campus, and College Park is too far to drive every day, even if we had a car. We didn't even think about going to Hopkins, and I didn't want to go to Goucher, and Marie didn't want to go to College of Notre Dame of Maryland, and M.I.T. didn't take girls, and neither did most of the other colleges that had the courses we wanted to take.

One of these days, things like that are going to have to change.

Sharing facilities at school meant that scheduling had to be exact. That's how we found out that the boys swim in the nude. Guess who ran around going "Eek?"

It wasn't the girls of Western, HA HA HA!

Marie and I had lost some speed over the summer, but we picked it back up in a couple of weeks. Doris practiced every day until Mrs. Persky went home. She didn't have a pool to practice in down at Ocean City because she's colored.

That's got to change, too.

The swim and diving meets had all started earlier this year because the Nationals would be starting earlier because: The 1968 Olympics in Mexico City were coming!

Mrs. Persky told the team not to get our hopes up too much, but not to give up trying, either. "Two girls from Maryland made the Olympic Team in 1936. Their Aunt" she said, pointing to us, "and me. So bust your tails and win!"

Marie's cousin Joey goes to Poly, and we'd hang out in the Courtyard in the mornings before class, and for lunch when we matched. Marie would sit with us and grin the whole time, and then teased me the rest of the day that it was about time I started getting interested in boys. She knew that the real reason I'd never gone out on dates was Mother. Well, Dad too. Mother wanted someone "suitable," and Dad worried about how "the English" behaved with girls, not like "his people" did. He finally said it was okay after Aunt Carmella told him that she'd "trim" Joey if he tried anything.

I like Joey. He's good-looking, polite, and dances almost as well as Austin.

I'm thinking more and more about the war in Vietnam. It just keeps going on and on, and nobody's winning. I still don't think Senator Goldwater should have won four years ago, but I don't believe ANYTHING that President Johnson says about the war. I'm worried about Billy going into the Marines, and Austin going into the Navy, and Joey going into the Air Force, and all the boys that are getting drafted.

And THAT has to change most of all.

The State competitions were held, and Western won, and we were invited to compete in the collegiate championships (the next step to the Nationals!). We didn't win, and we pretty much didn't expect to, but Marie and I nearly equaled the best times of the freestyle and backstroke winners, and Doris DID win, and she'll go with the divers from Hopkins and University of Maryland to the Nationals again in May. Super cool!

Joey and I bring our lunches with us instead of buying so we can eat outside in the Courtyard together, and we started going out on dates every Friday, Saturday, and Sunday. Marie keeps saying "My little girl is growing up" and Joey and I both laugh. I really like Joey. I don't know if I'm in love with him, at least not like Marie and Billy, but I know there's something there. He makes me feel all— well, a lot like what Marie and Billy feel when they're fooling around.

I like it.

He asked me to go to the Prom with him. Mother had a fit, and said I wasn't going to the Prom because all sorts of animal behavior goes on there, and gave me all this crap in that voice of hers about how he's not acceptable, and that he's Catholic and not Lutheran, and that he's not "pure-blooded," and Dad said what kind of Nazi filth was that? Anyway, Dad said I was going to the Prom, and I was going to keep seeing Joey, and that he trusts both of us, and Mother went upstairs and did her usual throwing his clothes out the window. Aunt Carmella and Marie and some of the other women in the neighborhood that were outside made a game out of catching them.

I didn't think it was a damned bit funny, and I never had. Summer and college can't get here soon enough.

Marie is going down to Ocean City to go to Billy's Prom, and it's the same night as Joey's. Aunt Carmella told Marie again and again that it's a dance, NOT a honeymoon, and to watch herself. Marie keeps telling her 1972, and Aunt Carmella says that's fine, but Marie better not have a daughter for a flower girl, or a son for a ring bearer. Uncle Vince goes out on the porch to laugh.

Marie and I made our gowns. We had to: our shoulders are too wide for anything off the rack. Maybe not as big as Aunt Viv's, but still bigger than other girls except our teammates. Our gowns are mainly like a de Givenchy sheath, but we added very loose short sleeves instead of spaghetti straps, and they're not bad at all. Marie's is Emerald Green, and mine is Electric Blue. Both Satin, of course. Aunt Carmella says they look more grown-up and formal than a prom gown, and we'll really turn heads. I bet Billy and Joey will go wild— well, probably not. Uncle Vince says guys don't care how it's wrapped.

Dr. Martin Luther King got killed, and there were riots all over the country. In Baltimore, the Mayor went off on vacation when one started here, and the Governor sent in the National Guard. School was closed until it was over. People on the bus acted funny with each other. Not funny ha ha, but funny strange. Nobody talked a lot, especially between white and colored— I mean Black, I keep forgetting that. Doris rides the bus with us. She lives on Baylis Street in Canton a few stops before we get on, and nothing bad or wrong ever happens in her neighborhood, so I guess things were okay? I don't know how to say it. Nobody does, really. I know she had her "nothing" face on like she used to do in Elementary school when some kids said things to her, and nobody else sat next to her or talked to her until we got on. We'd sit and talk about swimming and diving meets and classes. After a couple of weeks, everybody started talking again, but something had changed, and nobody wanted to talk about what had happened. One thing that changed that everybody noticed and DID talk about was that WCAO radio wasn't playing as much Soul music anymore.

Why?

Doris went to the Nationals in May, and came in 8th, and Mrs. Persky told her she'd definitely be getting an Athletic scholarship now. Doris hopes she'll get an Academic scholarship, too.

CHAPTER FIFTY-SEVEN

The Prom

Prom weekend finally came. Marie got picked-up by Billy in Aunt Sally's Mustang on Friday afternoon at school. He hooked school with Aunt Sally's permission, just so Marie could show him off. I don't think the other girls were all that impressed (he's 4" shorter than Marie.) The only thing I cared about was that they forgot to take me home with them, and I had to ride the bus.

On Saturday afternoon, I went to the shoe repair shop to pick up my shoes. I had bought white pumps and had them dyed to match my dress. They looked perfect! I went home, took a long bath, did my hair and make-up, and went into my room to get dressed.

I couldn't find my bra or pantyhose.

I couldn't find my slip.

I couldn't find *any* of my clothes or shoes.

And then I looked at my dress.

Every seam had been opened.

I could hear that sick, disgusting laugh coming from her bedroom.

I wrapped my bathrobe tight, and went downstairs, out the front door, and into Aunt Carmella's.

She and Uncle Vince looked at me. She stood up, and I made shushing motions, and she stopped and whispered "What. Did. She. Do?"

I told her, and I said please be quiet because I didn't want to give her any satisfaction by even acknowledging what she did, and I absolutely refused to cry, either.

That's when Joey came in. He'd gone over to my house, and Dad said he'd heard me leave, and that he was disappointed that he didn't see me in my dress. So, there I was in my bathrobe. He looked at me funny, and then grinned and said I looked beautiful, and was I ready to go?

I ran upstairs to Marie's room. I'd be damned if I would cry in front of him.

I still heard Mother laughing. I heard Dad go upstairs, and then I heard him start yelling at her, and calling her evil, and a horrible and vicious woman, and how could she even bear to see her own reflection in a mirror, and I lay on Marie's bed, and held her pillow over my ears, and I was never going to cry or even anything, except that I was.

Aunt Carmella came in and lay down next to me and hugged me and said Joey was waiting and wanted to take me to the Prom no matter what I wore, and that he thought I was the most beautiful girl in the world, and that he'd be the proudest guy at the Prom, and she said he meant every word, and let's go wash your face, and we'll look for something in Marie's closet to wear.

Marie's bras were loose on me, and Aunt Carmella safety-pinned one tighter. She found a "Granny Dress" in Cranberry, and she had a shawl of hers that almost matched, and Uncle Vince had a long white silk "Opera" scarf that she tied around my waist like a sash. We found out that she and I wore the same size shoes, so she gave me her black pumps. I put on some of Marie's lip gloss, and I guessed I looked about as good as I could get.

When we came downstairs, Joey kissed me and said every guy there was going to be jealous of him, and all the girls would hide in the ladies' room so that no one would see how plain they all looked compared to me. I told him he was full of crap, and I kissed him as hard as I could.

We left then and walked around all the broken glass and Dad's clothes on the sidewalk. We got in Joey's car and went to the ballroom at the Lord Baltimore Hotel. By the time we got there, I didn't want to go in. Joey said if I really and truly didn't want to stay, that was okay, but I had to go in and dance with him at least once.

We went in, and people stared at me, and I started feeling more ashamed than embarrassed, and I went into the ladies' room, and almost died from all the girls staring at me, and came back out and told Joey I wanted to go, but he said I promised one dance, and of course it had to be a slow one that started playing.

I knew everybody was watching us, and whispering, and pointing. Then the whole place heard one girl yell "What? She WHAT? Her MOTHER? *HER OWN MOTHER*?" I knew that Joey had told what happened, and now everybody knew, and I wanted to leave and never see Joey again.

Somebody poked me on the shoulder. I turned around and had to look down at this girl who was a foot shorter than I was. She was the one with the loud voice.

"Hey! Is that true? Your own mother cut-up your dress? What the Hell she do that for? She nuts or something?"

I don't know why, but I started explaining to her that Mother didn't want me to go out with Joey because he was Italian and Catholic, and the girl yelled "WHAT A BITCH! Boy, if MY mother tried to pull that kind of shit with me, I'd KILL her!"

She turned to Joey. "You brung her anyways, huh?" Then she started giggling like a little girl. "Jeez, all you Poly guys say that you're supposed to be 'Gentlemen'. Well, you're the first one I met that is!"

She gave me a punch in the arm. "Blondie, you got more balls than a football team! I like you! My friends call me Peanut! Screw your mother! Dance your asses off!"

Other girls were laughing at her, and I heard one of them saying "Oh, Peanut, you're so classy and ladylike. So refined and well-mannered." I heard a chaperone sigh "Margaret Rose Delany. The Pride of Dundalk." Some of the girls were smiling at me. NICE smiles. Joey gave my hands a tug. "Hey, we're supposed to be dancing."

We did, and it was fun, and it was wonderful, and we stayed and danced and danced.

At midnight, the band stopped playing, and one of the chaperones called out "Last dance!" and he sat down at the grand piano and played "I Could Have Danced All Night." Joey held me close, and I started humming, and then singing a little. Peanut was dancing near us and yelled "Hey, Blondie! Sing louder!" and I did, and I sang the rest of the song as clearly as

I could, and went for the big finish, and my voice cracked, and we all started laughing and couldn't stop.

We left the Prom and went to Maria's 301 restaurant in Little Italy and had their "After the Ball" special menu (I was STARVING!) They threw everybody out at two-thirty in the morning, and Joey drove us home, and we parked a block away and made-out for a while. Then Joey drove down to right in front of Aunt Carmella's, and walked me to the door, and we started kissing some more until Aunt Carmella came out and said "Okay, Romeo, smooch her one more time, and hit the road."

We went upstairs, and she helped me get undressed, and I fell into bed and that was it for me until noon.

It was the happiest night of my entire whole life!

When I got up, I took a bath, and when I got back to Marie's bedroom, Aunt Carmella had all my clothes that Mother had thrown out last night washed and folded on the bed, and she had laid hangers on top of them. I didn't hang things up right then, but I would. This was pretty much the last straw with Mother.

I BOUNCED down the steps and went into the kitchen twirling around like a ballerina and singing "I Could Have Danced All Night" again. Dad was sitting at the table with Uncle Vince, so I gave him a big hug and kiss, and did the same to Uncle Vince, and looked for Aunt Carmella.

She was out in the backyard laughing at Mother. "HOOK it, Susie, don't beat on it!" Mother had a clothesline pole in her hands and was beating at something caught on the gutter on our yard's roof overhang.

It was one of my bras.

I couldn't help myself. I laughed and called out "Oh, the scandal! The shame! Whatever will the neighbors think of all the wild goings-on in that house?"

Mother tried to look over to see me but couldn't. She whacked at my bra a few more times and threw the pole down and went inside. We could hear her smash something, and I laughed even harder.

Dad said "Sally" very quietly, and I apologized to him. He shook his head and asked me about the Prom, and I told everybody EVERYTHING (except me and Joey in the car), and what a wonderful night it was and how happy I was, and I asked Aunt Carmella if I had said thank you last night when I came home. She said only about umpteen times, and I hugged her and kissed her and said "Thankyouthankyouthankyou, and now it's an even zillion!"

We heard something else smash next door.

Aunt Carmella said, "Your Aunt called and said your sister should be here probably around one or two o'clock" and we heard more smashes, and then a hiss. "She is not her sister. I have tried for years to protect my child from all of you."

Aunt Carmella screamed at the wall "VAH FUNGOOL!" Uncle Vince held her and said to ignore Mother. Dad had brought all my schoolbooks over and said it would probably be best if I stayed a day or so here instead of there. I thought so too. He got up and said "Carmella, you are a good mother to your children" and gave me a quick hug and left. Probably to catch his clothes again.

In bed that night, Marie and I whispered ALL the things we had done at our Proms. We both had the best night of our lives, but she thought that maybe mine was better, because it was like Cinderella, with the rotten stepmother and TWO Fairy Godmothers (Aunt Carmella and Peanut). I guess that made Joey Prince Charming, but I told her I preferred Joey as Joey. He's a lot sexier!

Marie went to sleep, but I lay there awake for a long time, and did a lot of thinking. I couldn't stay at Marie's forever, even though I wanted to, but I wanted to have to deal with Mother as little as possible, and I do mean little.

Then I remembered the puzzle boxes Dad had made, and how he finished his apprenticeship. Okay, I thought. I don't know how to build a house yet, but I *do* know how to build furniture, and building my puzzle box would keep me busy in Dad's workshop all evening, every evening, until exams were over, and I went to Ocean City. I wouldn't have to be around Mother at all, except perhaps for suppertime, and *that* only if I didn't eat at Aunt Carmella's.

I made my decision and went to sleep.

CHAPTER FIFTY-EIGHT

Puzzle Box

I had already thought about what I would build when it came time to complete my apprenticeship, and I had some things stored away for it. A ½" by 6" by 3-foot piece of what is called "Bird's-Eye" Maple, some scraps of Mahogany from a buffet we'd built, a 5" square of ¼" thick Rosewood (VERY expensive), and a piece of Ebony as long and thick as my pinky. I also had some shell from a whelk, a razor clam, and an oyster.

Dad knew I was making something, but he only said, "Do not neglect your studies."

I tried not to neglect Joey, either.

I finished the puzzle box the same day as my last exams. I had a reason for that. I brought Dad downstairs after Mother went off to Choir practice, and handed him an octagonal-shaped box, with inlay work on the top. He laughed at the inlay pattern and tried to put on a serious face.

"So, my apprentice, you are finished learning your trade?"

"Yessir. All except building a house."

He nodded. "That you will learn. 'When' is the question, and that will happen in its own time."

He picked up the box and took out his magnifying glass and went over every inch of it, and then began all the pushing and sliding of all the pieces holding the box closed. I had made it as intricate as I could, and he stopped a couple of times, smiled and nodded, and started again. He finally got to the last step but couldn't figure out what to do next. He slowly pushed the box toward me and held his hands up. "I am confounded, kinder. How much more?"

I took the box and turned it upside-down, and tugged one of the

Ebony feet up, and twisted to the left, and the bottom slid out. He clapped his hands, laughed, and laughed even harder when he saw what was inside.

It was a toy cow, wrapped in a piece of paper.

"You knew!" he said. "Ah, Sally, you are so clever! But how did you know?"

I flattened out the paper. It was a newspaper picture of an Amish barn with a Hex sign. The caption said the sign kept witches away from the dairy cows inside. That was my inlay on the box.

Dad said that witches come at night and suckle the cows and dry their udders. I told him it sounded gross, and did the Amish believe in things like that? He said no, it was all superstition and old stories. He put the box back together (with the cow inside) and smiled at me and shook my hand.

"You are no longer my apprentice. Until we build a house, you are now my partner."

I felt happy— and relieved! I had wanted this to go right. Dad spoke softly now. "What troubles your soul, Sally?"

I told him I wanted to skip the graduation ceremony and just go down to the ocean and work to earn my money for college. I told him that I knew I had passed my exams, and that any scholarship offers would be mailed to Aunt Sally's. I said Mother didn't really care about my graduation, only how it appeared to other people, and nobody cared except him and Marie and Aunt Carmella and Uncle Vince and Aunt Sally and—

"Shh, Liebchen." He held up his hand, and looked at me almost as closely as he did the puzzle box. "The travel? How would you get there?"

I took a deep breath. "There's a Greyhound Bus that leaves tomorrow morning at seven. My suitcase is over at Marie's." I was whispering now. "I know she'll take it out on you, but after what she did to my gown..."

He nodded. "I would like you to stay until nine o'clock. I will drive. You will understand."

"Okay." I didn't ask why.

"Good." He looked at me and asked "Your Joey. What will you tell him?"

I felt myself blush. I admitted that I already told him.

Dad sighed. "When you find the boy you marry, you will promise to have him ask for my blessing. Do you promise this?"

I stood up and hugged him. "Yes, Dad. I promise."

"Then to bed. I will get your suitcase and put it in the car tonight, and she will not see."

"Thanks, Dad." I hesitated. "Dad? I love you."

"I know, Liebchen. For all my lacks, I love you also."

The next morning, I stayed in bed until 8:30, got dressed quickly, gulped down a bowl of shredded wheat biscuit, walked out the door, and down the street to where Dad was waiting (he hadn't gone to work), and we drove away. We stopped at Wolfmann's Garage. I thought he was going to get gas, but he parked and got out. "Come, Sally. We have business."

We went into the office, and Dad and Mr. Wolfmann talked quietly for a minute, and then they went to the back door of the garage, and held it open for me. Dad had an ear-to-ear grin.

Everybody says I've got a head full of numbers and not much else sometimes, but occasionally I notice what's going on.

There was a car.

MY car!

Mr. Wolfmann said it was a 1960 Volkswagen Karmann-Ghia. He had rebuilt the engine and transmission, and replaced the front seats with newer ones from another car, and the battery compartment under the backseat had been cut-out and patched over and the battery put on a new shelf with the engine because in Volkswagens the batteries always eat away the metal under the seat; painted it bright red, and there was a whole bunch of other stuff he had done, and that it would last another ten years at least, and it was MY CAR!

Mr. Wolfmann showed me how to check the belt and oil and tire pressures and battery water, and how the jack worked, and made me change a tire like I did in Driver's Ed. He told me about when to bring the car in for maintenance, and how the car will handle in the rain and on the highway, and how far it takes to stop, and you'd better believe I paid attention to every word he said. He said it had been ready for me for a week, so sign these papers, and here ya go, kitten, and handed me the keys.

Dad had called his insurance agent, and I would owe Dad the first quarterly payment. I put my suitcase in the backseat (the trunk was in front and even smaller than Aunt Sally's Mustang.)

It was time to go.

Dad said to be calm, careful, drive safely, and that he would see me in August. I hugged Dad and wouldn't let go, and thanked him, and he patted me on my shoulder and said to go before the summer ends.

I waved as I drove away. I felt like Aunt Sally and her Mustang.

No. I felt like Aunt Viv and her Thunderbird!

CHAPTER FIFTY-NINE

Grown-Up

I stopped by the Sea Star on the way home to Aunt Sally's, and Linda said their regular girl that did dinners got married and wasn't coming this summer, and could I start today (YES! Bigger tips!), so I got a uniform out of my suitcase, and called the High School and left a message for Aunt Sally to let her know where I was (she already knew I was coming), and to let her know I probably wouldn't be home till ten.

Linda left right after, then came right back in and told me that she and Austin had gotten married on his 18th birthday, and that she would tell me all about it tomorrow, and I said congratulations. Whew! Full speed ahead! I barely saw the family until my day off (on Thursdays this year.)

That's the way things were until the 6th of June.

I woke up and everyone had gone to work, so I turned the "Today Show" on, just to see the news and weather report.

Bobby Kennedy had been killed.

I didn't think about him, I didn't think about his family, I didn't think about anything except that he wouldn't be the next President, and Vietnam would just go on and on and on and never end, and Billy and Joey and Austin and every boy I knew would all have to go there.

I had to get out of the house. I had to walk and not think about it, or about other people getting killed or assassinated or...

I walked north up the beach, walking in the surf for about an hour, when I met someone coming the other way. We nodded to each other, and then I recognized him. It was Mac MacTavish from Elementary and Junior High schools.

We said hi, and how are you, and what are you doing down here, and he told me he was with some friends, and they had rented a house for the week as a sort of graduation celebration. He asked me if I had heard about Bobby Kennedy, and I started crying. He held me, and I remembered that he had held me when President Kennedy had been killed, and I told him. He said he remembered it too, and I realized I was getting snot all over him again, and he said he didn't carry Kleenex anymore, and he held my nose between his fingers and said blow, and I didn't even think, I just did it, and I said "Oh, God, I'm sorry, that is just so gross, I'm really sorry" He laughed and washed his hand in the surf.

It's funny. He was such a whiny little boy in kindergarten, and always complained about everything in all the other grades we were in, so it was funny that it was him that I cried on both times.

We talked a little more. He'd enlisted in the Marines and was waiting to hear when he would go to Boot Camp. That made me sad again, because he was someone else I knew that might go to Vietnam. We stood there for a while, watching the waves and the sandpipers running back and forth and not saying anything else. I noticed the sun was getting high, and I told him I had to go to work soon. I kissed him on his cheek and told him I hoped he'd be okay in the Marines, and he said he hoped I'd win the Olympics one day. It was nice that he remembered that about me. We said goodbye and I walked home, changed clothes, and went to work.

Marie came down a week later. She was working at Phillip's again, so we had our mornings together, and Billy got permission for us to swim at another pool. Billy had joined the Marines on his birthday last month, and he was waiting for Boot Camp too. Austin had joined the Navy, and he left the first week of July. Linda said it would be okay, and he'd come back and open his repair shop for boat engines, and they'd have kids and all that. God, I hoped so.

Marie and I got our scholarships to the University of Maryland—Academic *and* Athletic. We had to go to College Park the first week of August to pay the rest of our tuition and dorm expenses, and schedule classes. Billy got a letter that told him he would go to Boot Camp the next week, and Marie quit her job so she could spend all her time with him.

Aunt Carmella and Uncle Vince went back to Baltimore, and we would all go to their home the day before Billy reported for induction and transport to Parris Island from Fort Holabird in Dundalk.

On our last Thursday together, we swam in the morning, and played Frisbee on the beach that afternoon, and just hung out together the way we always had every summer since we were little. We went home to take showers and wash the sand off.

I finished first and put my robe on and bent over to pick up my bathing suit, and Billy flicked me on the back of my thigh with his towel. He took off running into the house, and I was right behind him and grabbed his towel off him, spun it and snapped it, and I got him just *perfect*: right between and right under his butt cheeks! I raised him about two feet off the ground, and he let out a yell, and I laughed and threw his towel to him and said, "It serves you right!" Uncle Bill was there and pointed to the front door.

Mother.

I yelled "Oh, Goddammit to Hell, you snuck down here early again!"

Mother looked at me, at Billy, and Aunt Sally.

"Incest" she hissed. "Incest. I always knew— "

Aunt Sally slapped her in her mouth so hard she knocked her down.

"Get out, Susan." Aunt Sally's voice scared me. "Take your filthy mind and your disgusting insinuations and get out of my home and don't you *EVER* come back."

Mother got up and opened her mouth (it was bleeding), and Aunt Sally said, "Not another word, Susan." I could feel my hair trying to stand up.

Mother stepped back from her and looked at me and hissed "You. Pack."

And I said "no."

Mother looked almost as crazy as Aunt Sally. "What did you say to me?"

"*I SAID 'NO.'* I belong to Aunt Sally until school starts." Then it was like a light went on inside my head. I looked Mother in the eye and said

"When school starts, I'll be eighteen. And I'll NEVER have to go back."

I turned to Dad. He looked sad but not surprised. "I'm sorry, Dad." He nodded and tried to smile. I turned back to Mother and gave her back her own icy stare.

She spun around, bent over to pick up her make-up case, and hissed "Degenerate Hillbillies."

Aunt Sally KICKED her, and Mother went through the screen door, cleared the porch completely, and almost cleared the steps.

I had never heard Mother scream before.

She got up, limped to the car, got in, and started blowing the horn.

I looked at Dad, and now he was smiling, and then he took me in his arms and gave me a hug— a real, gentle, tender hug, and kissed me on my cheek. He let go and pulled out his business card case. "You can always reach me here during the weekdays, Liebchen. I will let your aunts know where and how to reach me as soon as I can." He kissed me again and grinned.

Aunt Sally was holding her right hand and standing on her left leg. "YOU are always welcome here, Freddie." Dad very carefully kissed her. Uncle Bill said, "Dump her at the Greyhound, Freddie" and Dad laughed and said "No, I would come back to a hole in the ground." He was laughing so hard that his face was bright red. Uncle Bill shook his hand, and Dad carried the suitcases out to the station wagon. He opened the hood and pulled a wire loose from the horn, looked through the windshield at Mother, and bent over laughing. He tossed the suitcases in the back, got in, started the car, looked at her again, and ROARED! He backed the car out, waved, and drove off, still laughing.

I was standing next to Aunt Sally. "He's leaving her."

"Yep" she said. Her teeth were clenched. Uncle Bill said "I heard the leg crack. Hand, too?"

"Yep. Get me over to the phone, Bill."

He picked her up very gently. "Carmella?" he asked.

"Yep. Have to let her know what happened."

"Then the hospital" he said, and I realized that Aunt Sally's leg had broken when she kicked Mother.

I dialed the phone and held it for her. Marie came in from the shower and looked at the four of us. "Did I miss something?"

CHAPTER SIXTY

On Our Own

We went to Aunt Carmella's the day before Billy went away. When I walked up the steps, I couldn't help myself, and looked at her window.

"She's not there, Sal" Aunt Carmella said. "She's gone."

I relaxed. The last thing I wanted was to see her, but... "'Gone'? Gone where? Not just out, 'gone'?"

"Gone. Packed up and left. Drove off with some old man with the same snotty look as hers."

"Father." Aunt Sally said. Uncle Bill carried her up the steps and set her down. "I haven't seen him or Mother since before the kids were born. Just as well, no love lost there, either."

Aunt Carmella held the door for her while she tried to balance on her crutches. Uncle Bill scooped her up again and carried her in. He grinned and kissed her. "Just like our Honeymoon." Aunt Sally snorted. We went in, and Uncle Bill helped her sit down. "Doesn't want a wheelchair" he told Aunt Carmella. "Thinks she can get around fine on one leg and one hand."

"Alright, Bill, enough for now." She looked at Aunt Carmella. "Let's hear it."

Aunt Carmella grinned. "Okay. So, they drive up, and Susie gets out. Half the women in the neighborhood are standing there waiting for her. I yell 'Hiya, Susie! So, your sister finally had enough of your nasty mouth and popped you in it, huh?' She SLAMS the car door and tries to charge right up the steps, and almost falls over. 'Oh, and she put her foot up your behind too?' Freddie's out of the car, and takes her suitcases up on the porch, and she opens the front door, goes in, slams it shut and puts the chain on. Then the women start. 'Oh, my goodness, she's locked her husband out of the house.' Freddie's not saying a word. Everybody backs away, and the next thing, she's throwing his shoes and clothes through BOTH windows upstairs, and they start up again. 'Oh, my goodness, she's "tossing his shoes," and they're all laughing. 'Oh, poor Mr. Osterhoff, poor Freddie, his wife's throwing him out and getting rid of him, and he's such a nice man, a good provider, so quiet and polite, and he was always too good for her, and she never cared. Such a shame!' and they're all in hysterics, now."

Aunt Sally had a nasty grin on her face. I should've felt bad for hearing this, but I knew I had the same grin.

"Everybody's catching and picking up his clothes, and old Mrs. Tuttle is helping him put them in the car."

"Then we hear a big crash out in the back, and they all start running, and they're saying 'Oh, she's throwing her daughter out, too. Such a sweet girl, Honor Roll at school, never any trouble, and the way that woman would beat her, the BRUISES that poor child had all her growing up, it's a sin to beat a child like that.'"

I felt funny. I didn't think anybody else in the neighborhood knew about that. Aunt Carmella touched my cheek. "Everybody always saw the bruises."

"Anyway, she throws out all the rest of your clothes that weren't already over here, and she throws out your sewing machine and your dress dummy, too. I think they probably went out first. Your Dad said to tell you don't worry; he'll buy you the best ones made to replace them. Did you have anything else there, Sal? Pictures or letters or books or something?"

"Nothing she hadn't already thrown out whenever she found it. What happened then?"

"Well, they all came back around front, and they're still going on. 'How terrible, how horrible, to throw you and your daughter out like the garbage.' They all coulda got the Oscar. Then Freddie comes up on the porch, gives me a kiss (and you coulda knocked me over with a feather!), shakes Vince's hand, hops in the car, waves, and drives off. Next morning, Susie gets herself down to Dr. Dobihal's, and Bonnie Nardone is there and hears every word. Dr. Dobihal's calling her a liar, and Freddie never did that to her, the bruises are too small, and he'd be damned if he'd say otherwise, and he'd tell every doctor he knew to watch out for her if she came to them. Bonnie says Susie looked like a crazy woman when she left. She tried to go to the Police, but I guess someone must've called and told them too, 'cause they wouldn't even write a report. I bet it was Geraldine, her husband's on the Force." Aunt Carmella shook her head. "It's a damned shame when you think about it. There wasn't one single person that would stick-up for her." She shrugged. "Bright and early Monday morning, this old man—her father?—shows up and they drive off, and the only person I've seen there since was the guy that always fixes the windows. Oh, and a locksmith."

There was nothing more to say.

Dad showed up around then, and said we had to go to the DMV and change my address to Aunt Carmella's "if it was alright with her." Aunt Carmella said she should smack him for even asking, but she was smiling. He asked if I had my Bank Account book with me and said that going there would be the first stop.

We got there, and the Teller sent us to the Head Teller, who sent us to the Manager, who sent us to a man in an office in the back.

On Friday, Mother had withdrawn all the money that I had saved for YEARS and closed my account.

I started yelling, and Dad told me to calm down, and that she had done it to him, too, and then I *really* got mad, and the bank guy got all huffy and told me to be quiet or he'd have me thrown out, but that just made me get even louder, and I told him he had no right to do it, but he said he did because her name was on the account because I was a minor child, and I yelled "YOU SONOFABITCH, YOU HELPED HER STEAL OUR MONEY!," and that's when he had the Bank Guard throw us out.

Dad said he was disappointed in me for calling that jerk what I did, but I wasn't one bit sorry, even though what they did was probably legal. Dad told me to calm down, and he'd tell me things that would make me feel better.

He had a bank account at work for railroad employees. He said he'd had it for a long time, ever since Mother had tried to put a "hold" on a check he'd written years ago when he tried to buy a set of antique tools. That reminded me about his tools in his workshop, but he said he'd gotten almost everything including *all* the hardest to replace tools into Aunt Carmella's basement not long after I went to the ocean. Anyway, he had this bank account at work and said he'd give me whatever she stole. I told him that I'd manage without it, but he said no, I needed to concentrate on my classes at college. I told him that any money he gave me would only be a loan. He said no again, and that he'd get my money back somehow, and that was an end to it, and no more argument.

I looked at Dad, and I think he was even more mad about her stealing *my* money than his, and it wasn't the same kind of mad he'd ever been before. I knew he would get my money back somehow, so I calmed myself down.

I think that's when I decided to stop feeling anything about Mother. I just sort of "closed the door" on that part of my life for good. When I did, something inside of me said "whew!"

When we came home later (and now Marie's home was MY home, too: it says so on my license!), Aunt Carmella and Aunt Sally started to say something about Mother, but I held up my hands and told them "What's done is past, and nothing more needs to be said, and who cares anyway, when's supper?" Uncle Vince and Uncle Bill and even Dad laughed and said, "good for me" and that was it.

Whew!

Supper was,... well, good on the one hand, because we were all there as a family, but sad on the other hand because Billy would be leaving tomorrow morning. He and Marie kept looking at each other, touching, hugging and kissing. After we ate, Aunt Sally and Aunt Carmella sat in the kitchen, Uncle Bill and Uncle Vince and Dad sat in the dining room, and I got told to go to the living room to "keep an eye" on Marie and Billy. I said for everyone to leave them alone, they're not kids anymore, and Aunt Carmella said that was why she wanted me with them. Marie said maybe they should do it on the porch so everybody in the neighborhood could watch. I went upstairs.

Breakfast was quiet. I don't think anybody really slept much. I know Billy had always wanted to be a Marine, but now that he was going, Marie and Billy knew they weren't going to see each other even as often as they had growing up.

We drove down to the Induction Center at Fort Holabird and parked on Dundalk Avenue right outside the fence in front of Building Eleven. There was a small gate, and an Army Soldier was there checking off names as guys went inside.

Everybody hugged and kissed Billy, and he and Marie looked at each other. Billy said he'd try to write every day, and Marie said only if he wasn't too tired, and if he doesn't write, not to worry about it, and she'd understand. Then she kissed him one more time, and said "Okay, Poindexter, get moving," and Billy said in that cartoon voice: "I-Love-You-Mister-Felix" and went in the gate and into the building, and that was it.

Aunt Sally, Uncle Bill and I drove back to Ocean City right after. We had to stop once when Uncle Bill started crying. I made it back to the diner in time for my shift, and I told Linda and her father I'd finish the week like I promised, and I'd see them next summer.

For the first time ever, I was glad to leave Ocean City.

I saw Joey for a few hours the day before we left for college. Things had cooled off a little while I was away, and I guess that couldn't be helped. He was going into the Air Force like he said, and he'd be leaving at the end of the month, and would I write to him? I said sure, and I'd even send a photo of me in my bathing suit to hang in his locker. I hoped he'd be okay.

Aunt Carmella was running around the house before Marie and I left, asking if we packed everything, and worrying if we'd eat the right food, and get enough sleep, and to stay away from all those dope addicts and protestors she sees on the TV, and above all, BEHAVE, because "I raised you two right!" We told her we'd try to come home on weekends unless we had swim practice or meets, and then it was time to go.

Marie and I loaded up the trunk, back seat, and Marie's lap, and we drove off to college, feeling all grown up and on our own— at least for a couple of miles.

CHAPTER SIXTY-ONE

Fall Semester

We got to College Park and carried our things all the way to the third floor of our dorm. And there she was: Cynthia Smith. She didn't say anything to us, but I knew that if she ever got a chance to do me a bad turn, she would.

The rest of the day, Marie and I ran all around the campus figuring out where our classes were, and the best way to get there. At the end of the day, we had supper at the cafeteria (the food was LOUSY!)

There was a common room at the dorm where the residents could hang out and watch TV, but there weren't a lot of chairs, and they were pretty much staked out by the Upperclassmen (and why aren't they called UpperclassWOMEN?)

Classes started the next day, and we found out that we were WAY ahead of everyone with our math courses, so we had to change and reschedule, and Marie was ahead with Economics and business stuff, so that had to be changed. The women that worked in the offices were getting annoyed, and one of them said at this rate, we'd be Seniors and graduating in June, and that Western High School does this to them every year, and it makes their job harder. "You girls Prepped, so you should only be Sophomores— NO HIGHER!"

Marie and I talked about it, and we thought that if we got our Batchelor's early, maybe we could stretch our scholarships and get our Master's by '72. Well, "don't count your chickens" and all that, but we'll try.

By the end of the second week, we had settled in and figured out who's who and what's what, and mostly found out which instructors were good, and which ones to avoid.

Psych 101 had never brushed her teeth in her entire life. You could see the tartar on her teeth and smell her breath all the way to the back row.

Music 101 had grabby hands. At least Marie and I had experience dodging jerks like him.

Pol Sci told everyone he was a Maoist. Karen Olejnik told him he was an Assholist, and we transferred out of his class too.

Finally, I annoyed my new Math Instructor so much by correcting *his* mistakes, that HE wanted me out. I ended up with the most boring Professor on campus, but at least if I had a question, he'd say "That's a very good point," explain, and everybody else would go back to sleep.

I've been getting so mad lately that Marie says I'm swearing too much, and I sound like her Uncle Mike. She's probably right. I can swear in English, Italian, some of that Low German from Dad, and even a little Ukrainian that I learned from Karen. But I don't think that Dad or the rest of the family would think that was much of an accomplishment.

Marie and I get letters from Billy and Joey, and we send twice as many back (and I sent a photo of me in my bathing suit to Joey— God, all those muscles!)

Billy mailed his glasses to Marie from Boot Camp. The Marines made him get a pair of glasses with black plastic frames and a strap to hold them on. They told him that if it wasn't wartime, he'd be tossed out because he's blind (he's 20/30 for God's sake!), and because he's a midget (okay, he's only 5'5.") He says that Uncle Bill had told him that the Drill Instructors always look for someone who can't take it, but just ignore it and they'll find someone else to pick-on.

Marie says that on the one hand, she wishes he would get thrown out, but on the other hand, he'd probably get sent to the Army, and she doesn't want that, either.

I just want the damned war to be over. I keep wondering what's going to happen if Nixon gets in?

Probably nothing.

Oh, and all those protestors that Aunt Carmella was worried about? They're mostly Legacies, Frat Boys and Sorority Girls— in other words, the ones who aren't going to be expelled no matter what.

The swim team was a lot tougher than high school, and the diving team coach complained to Doris that she wasn't what he expected after seeing her in the Nationals. She tried to tell him she didn't have a chance to practice over the summer because there weren't any pools she could go to in Ocean City. He just ignored her and told her she'd better shape up quick, or she'd be back in the city before she knew it.

Marie and I didn't like the way he said, "in the city," and started to walk over to them, but Doris saw us and shook her head once, and didn't look at us again.

By the time competitions started, she was back in form, and won her first meet of the season. She even managed to flip the finger to that coach on her last dive, and the judges never saw it. Now, of course, she's his "Fair-Haired Girl," and he'll "ride her all the way to the Nationals."

"Fair-Haired Girl."

Marie's right, I swear too much.

CHAPTER SIXTY-TWO

Not The Best Time

Thanksgiving was at Marie's Aunt Rose's this year. Dad, Aunt Sally, Uncle Bill and Granny Annie came, and all the women made a big fuss over Granny Annie again. This time, she brought up two ENORMOUS apple pies (I didn't know they made pie pans that big!) that had sage, pearl onions, and bacon in them. She said the recipe came from England over 200 years ago with her family, the Brownes. Nobody makes anything like it in Italy, that's for sure. The more everybody nibbled, the more they liked it. They said it tasted "American" and was perfect with the turkey, and they all wanted the recipe.

When we got home to Aunt Carmella's, Dad told us what had been happening with him and Mother.

It was pretty ugly.

After she cleaned out our bank accounts, she got some lawyer to put Dad's name on papers that said that the house was all hers and then she sold it. The lawyer put Dad's name on more paperwork, and she went out to Nevada and got a divorce.

I guess she thought Dad would just go along with it, but he didn't. His lawyer told her lawyer that she could keep the money from selling the house, and that Dad wouldn't challenge the divorce, but only on two conditions: she had to give back our bank account money, and she had to renounce any and all claim to his pension money from the railroad, and that THAT would be IRREVOCABLE.

So, we got our money back, and I paid Dad the loan back *with* interest. When he said no, I said well, I'll have to pay my share of what the lawyer charged him, because what's right is right, and what's fair is fair. Dad raised his hands and said alright, just the interest and nothing more, and he said I was an honest woman.

You're damned right I am.

Billy didn't come home after Boot Camp. The same week he finished; his infantry training began. He didn't come home for Thanksgiving, either. Marie was pretty upset.

He didn't make it home for Christmas. They don't take a break in the middle of training. Marie was doing a lot of crying.

Joey came home for three days on the 2nd of January. The classes for his job were starting right away too. When Joey went to Poly, he was in the "A" course, and he took electronics. His hobby at home was building things called "Heathkits:" radios that used different frequencies, something called an "oh-silla-scope" and even a color TV.

So, what's his job going to be in the Air Force?

An Aircraft Ordinanceman.

The guy that loads the bombs on a plane.

I told Dad about it, and he laughed and said when he went into the Army, they took a farm boy and made him an officer.

Very funny, Dad.

Billy came home on the 16th of February for two weeks leave. Aunt Sally, Uncle Bill and Granny Annie all took two weeks from their jobs to come and stay in Baltimore. Marie made all sorts of arrangements with the classes we don't share so she could spend every second with Billy.

Billy's going to Vietnam.

Everybody's terrified, and nobody's showing it, but you can feel it.

He's so small! He shouldn't be running around in a war! Somebody could hurt him!

I wanted to go to Washington and yell that to President Nixon and Congress and everybody at the Pentagon, and I was going to...

Until we got to the airport.

Some guy spit on Billy.

Billy knocked him down first, then Marie, then Uncle Bill and Uncle Vince; and then Aunt Sally, Aunt Carmella, Granny Annie and I tried, but the airport rent-a-cop said he couldn't ignore us forever, and for us to leave something for the janitors to clean up. Older people were grinning, and some came over and said good luck to Billy, and most of the people my age looked embarrassed, but there were a few others that looked like they wanted to say something but decided not to.

When we got to the airplane, there were some other guys in uniform with their families all bunched together. Billy was going to San Francisco first and then get on a Military flight to Saigon. I know a lot of people want to stop Communism, and a lot of others just want us to get out of somebody else's war, but shouldn't there be people there to cheer or something? None of these guys started the war, and I don't think most of them really wanted to go there.

They started boarding the plane, and Marie was crying and trying not to, and so was everybody else. I had a crazy thought that maybe someone would hijack the plane to Canada, and they'd keep all the soldiers from going to Vietnam.

Oh, God, PLEASE let him come back okay!

Spring 1969 was not the best time of our lives. UM didn't make the WNCAA finals, and Marie and I didn't make it on our own. Doris did, and this year she placed 5th, and she says she would have gone higher if that jerk of a coach hadn't made her mad by "rubbing her head for luck."

Marie and I had a fight. The BIGGEST one we've had since we were little and got mad at each other over sewing. She'd been playing the same songs on her record player over and over and over. One was "Which Way You Going, Billy?" and the other one was "Peggy Dear," both stupid and sad, especially the "Peggy Dear" one with the girl grieving herself to death because her new husband got killed. When she got another one about some girl telling her husband or boyfriend "Billy, Don't Be A Hero," I took all three and snapped them in half and threw them in the trash, and then I yelled at her (and I DID yell, not hiss like Mother like she said I did), and I told her she was making herself sick, and to stop it, and no more crying over nothing and driving me nuts from her listening to those stupid songs, and if she didn't cut it out, I'd tell Billy in my next letter to him. She yelled at me that I didn't know what love was, and I never would because I'm just like Mother, and we yelled some more, and the girls on our floor yelled for us to shut up, and we didn't say anything to each other until the next evening.

I told her I was sorry for breaking her records, and then she said no, I was right, and she apologized, and we both started crying, and the other girls started banging on our door and told us to shut up again.

Joey got sent to Germany, thank God. He sent me a letter and said that the beer in Germany is bitter, but the girls were sweet. I'll smack him for that when he comes home. He said they have a big asparagus festival in the Spring, and everybody eats asparagus and drinks beer, and so NEVER go into a public restroom during the festival. Gross.

CHAPTER SIXTY-THREE

Summertime

We aced our exams, packed up everything and took it home, got our waitress uniforms out of the closet, and drove off for the ocean! Aunt Sally found an older motel with a shorter pool that we could swim in. We'd probably lose a little speed, but it was better than nothing.

Linda at the Sea Star told me that Austin was in Vietnam on a riverboat. It's not what it sounds like, with paddlewheels and gamblers, it's sort of a big speedboat with machine guns, maybe like "McHale's Navy." Austin takes care of the engines, just like he wanted to when he was a kid. He told Linda it was safe, and she says that's bull crap so that she doesn't worry, but she says at least he's down with the engines where he won't get shot at. THAT sounded like bull crap to me, but she wants to believe it.

Marie just kind of mopes around when we're not working or swimming. At night she sleeps in Billy's room, and I can hear her crying. Billy doesn't say much in his letters about what he's doing, just that he's fine, and that he loves her and misses her, and that he's got a buddy named Steve, and they hang out together all the time. The other Marines call them "Mutt and Jeff" because Steve is 6 foot tall, and Billy is... well, Billy.

Billy wants photos of Marie and everybody. Marie bought a cheap, TINY bikini for the photos. Aunt Carmella and Aunt Sally warned her that Billy would be showing them to all the guys there, but I took the picture anyway, with Marie turned a little bit sideways so her wide shoulders wouldn't show so much (but everything else sure did!) Marie took the picture of me, and it was blurry, and I was squinting in the sun, but Billy's not going to care what *I* look like. We mailed him some Fisher's Popcorn and Dolle's Taffy, and I wish we could have sent Thrasher's French Fries, too

(and Marie wishes she could have mailed herself.)

In July, everybody in the world watched the Moon landing on TV. Some of our older regulars at the diner said they never thought that they'd live to see it happen, and other ones said that we'd see people living on the Moon and Mars and Venus, just like in the movies, and a few said it was all a waste of taxes. I think that once we learn how to do something, we'll keep on doing it. Maybe I wouldn't want to live on the Moon, but I bet a lot of other people would. They'd be pioneers, like "Wagon Train" on TV.

That would be cool.

The next month, there was a bunch of stuff on the news about an outdoor rock and roll show that had half a million people show up for it. The TV and newspapers said it was all rain and mud, no place to stay, no food, and no bathrooms, but they had a LOT of drugs. People are stupid.

Right about then, Billy sent a letter saying that he and Steve went on R&R (that's rest and relaxation or recuperation or something), and they were in Yokosuka, Japan for two weeks. Marie's mad because she thought she could have flown out there to be with him, but he wrote back and said they didn't know when or where they were going until two days before they left.

I wish the war was over.

CHAPTER SIXTY-FOUR

WHAT?

Back at UM, we're Juniors now, and almost done with our Humanities, and by January we'll be doubling-up on our majors: higher math courses for me, and more business courses for Marie. She's serious about getting her CPA and starting her own accounting firm, and maybe being an investment broker.

I've finally decided I want to teach. I'm tutoring some jocks "Remedial Math" so they can count their under-the-table money. I'm charging them *$15 an hour*, and they don't even blink. But they're passing their tests with honest grades.

If I can teach them, I can teach anyone.

Doris got into it again with that jerk of a diving coach. He told her she should have found a bridge or a pier to jump off in the summer, instead of "slacking off." She told *him* to dive off the Empire State Building, and now he won't let her practice more than the rest of the team does. All he's doing is cutting his nose off to spite his face, since she's the best diver on the team. Marie and I take turns helping her sneak into the pool at night to practice.

I hadn't been getting letters as often from Joey, and he finally told me why. He's getting married to some German girl that works in the Enlisted Men's Club on the Base. He says he fell in love with her because she reminded him of me.

I SHOULD HAVE REMINDED HIM OF ME!

I got mad and stomped and swore, and Marie laughed and said "Aww, did your little heart get broken? Are you going to cry yourself to sleep every night? Are you going to join a Convent?"

I calmed down and laughed because she was right: it was just my pride that got hurt. How *dare* he dump wonderful me!

Well, I know I'll always remember that he took me to the Prom, and I'll always be grateful for that.

The very next day, one of my jock students asked me for a date. Funny how things work, isn't it?

No, not really.

Dave was the first-string catcher for the UM baseball team. He was good-looking, clean and neat, smelled nice and was always polite. Not what you'd expect from a jock.

He took me dancing, dinner in nice restaurants, tried to teach me how to ice skate, and we "attended" a very proper, well-catered, exclusive "affair" at his Fraternity, and he didn't get upset when I told him I thought it was boring as Hell, and can we leave and go to a movie or something instead?

After eight dates, I thought that *he* was boring as Hell. No kissing, and no handholding except for the ice-skating lesson. I was beginning to wonder what was going on? Did I have bad breath? I knew I smelled like chlorine a lot, was that it? I *do* have Mother's fashion sense, so I know I don't look like a skag.

I finally said, "After eight dates, you can kiss me."

He looked around and asked if someone I knew was watching us. I laughed and asked him if he was feeling shy.

He just stood there.

I know some jocks have IQs in the low single digits, but not like this. I leaned up against him and kissed him.

He stepped back and made a face and said, "I didn't know you were bi."

Sometimes I feel like I've been raised in a cave far away from the rest of the world. I asked "What's 'bi'?"

I could have sworn he said "bicycle."

We went back and forth like that, and it finally sunk in that he thought I was a lesbian (and Marie, too, which made me mad), and now he thought I "swung both ways" and he had to explain that. Then he said *he* was "gay" and had to explain again. Then there was all this "beard" stuff, and I got fed-up with all these cute little code words, and told him so, and he told me

I must really be "deep in the closet" but he didn't mind so long as I would still beard for him, and that's when I slugged him and went back to my dorm.

Marie was asleep when I came in, so I figured it would all keep until the morning.

Yeah.

Saturday morning at 7AM, the Dormitory Residential Advisor sent Cynthia Smith to tell us to report to her office "with all possible speed." Cynthia Smith had a smirk I wanted to slap off.

Miss Eagers started in about "permissive behaviors" and "experimentation" and "unhealthy relationships," and "Now, girls, there's no use denying it, it's common knowledge" and we would have to be split-up "for your own good, and you'll be grateful one day."

That's when Aunt Carmella came charging in, slammed the door, and yelled "What the Hell's going on here?"

Miss Eagers tried to say who are you and how dare you and leave my office at once, and Aunt Carmella told her to shut up, and what's she trying to do with her kids?

Marie told Aunt Carmella that Miss Eagers thought we were lesbians, and Aunt Carmella yelled even louder "Who the Hell says that? This lying little sneak?" and she whipped the door open so fast that Cynthia Smith almost fell into the room. Aunt Carmella yelled at her "Get out of here or I'll rip that lying tongue of yours out by its black root!" and slammed the door in her face.

Miss Eagers tried to get back control, but Aunt Carmella was going full blast now. She said Miss Eagers was disgusting to accuse her daughters of doing that, and yes, they're BOTH my daughters, and don't you even mention that Osterhoff woman's name to me, and all this was probably all *her* fault to begin with, and I don't give a damn they don't look alike, do you want me to find a medical student to explain the birds and the bees to you?

Then Aunt Carmella got quiet and told Miss Eagers that if anyone was going to be moving out, it would be *her*: out of the dorm, off the campus, and into the poor house once her lawyers got through with her.

By now, Miss Eagers was apologizing and saying it was all just a *minor* misunderstanding, and *of course* your daughters wouldn't be separated.

Aunt Carmella ignored her and told us to grab our coats and meet her out in the parking lot, because "Me and your Pop are taking you out for breakfast."

She swung the door open again, and yelled "Beat it, sneak!" at Cynthia Smith, and we all walked out in a "stately procession" as Billy would have said and didn't laugh until we got in the car and drove off campus.

Uncle Vince told us Aunt Carmella had woken him at 5AM, shivering so hard he thought it was an earthquake.

After breakfast, I tried to explain what had happened last night, and that it was probably part of what happened that morning, and that I knew Cynthia Smith had something to do with it, but they all said just stick to dating nice Italian boys that they knew.

Or maybe I'll just say to Hell with it and be an old maid. With cats.

Nah. I don't like cats.

CHAPTER SIXTY-FIVE

Billy

Thanksgiving came and went without us this year. We had a meet with Georgetown and the University of Virginia, and we had to drive ourselves there, because the football team needed the bus to drive them ONE HALF HOUR to the airport.

Why couldn't they drive *themselves* to the airport?

Anyway, I managed to get three of the other girls on the team in the backseat with little bags for their swimsuits and a change of clothes. All they did was complain the whole trip. Next time, they can walk.

Aunt Sally and Uncle Bill and Granny Annie and Dad all came for Christmas. It started off sad, like last year, but right on the dot at noon, the phone rang, and Marie was closest, and she picked it up and screamed.

It was Billy, and it was collect from Saigon, and would you accept the charges?

She yelled YES! and Billy started talking, and she started crying, and I mean WAILING, and telling Billy to keep on talking, and don't stop, and she stuffed a dishtowel in her mouth and lay curled on the floor listening to his voice, and held the phone away from her ear just far enough that we could hear him too.

It was 1AM tomorrow there, and there were about a hundred guys lined up for the phones, and they were limited to 15 minutes. Marie made herself stop crying, and handed the phone around long enough that we could all say Merry Christmas. Aunt Sally jumped up and yelled "Oh, shoot!" and ran outside to the car, and brought in a big package that she said came in her mail back in September, addressed to Marie, with "Don't open 'til Xmas" written on it.

It was a beautiful silk kimono. Billy told her it was a real one, not some cheap tourist thing. It had sashes, stockings, sandals, and ivory hairpins, and a folding fan made of ivory and painted paper with this little knob on a loop of string hanging from the end. There was a drawing to show how to wear everything.

Marie was still crying, and managed to say I love you and I miss you and when are you coming home? He told her probably in March, but he wouldn't know until then, but at least he was short. She said "WHAT?" and he had to explain that "short" over there meant "short timer" and it wouldn't be long till he was home with her.

Then it was time to say goodbye, and we all leaned over and said it, and Marie and Billy kept on repeating "I love you" until they got disconnected.

Marie took the box with the kimono upstairs, and said she wanted to lie down until suppertime, and asked me to come up with her for a little while.

She was still crying but starting to laugh a little. When I asked her what was funny, she showed me the thing that was attached to the fan.

The drawing said it was called a Netsuke, and they're carved in all sorts of designs, and you tucked it under the sash around your waist to keep whatever its string was attached to from getting lost since there's no pockets on a kimono. Marie was blushing a little. "Take a close look at it. I saw it downstairs, and I hope Ma didn't."

The note said it was a "pillow" netsuke. It was ivory, the size of a walnut, and looked old. The carving was incredible. It was a girl taking a bath in a wooden wash tub, and she was— well, the detail was *amazing*, and I hadn't blushed about things like that for *years* since I figured out that everybody does it.

Marie says she's going to write him a letter and tell him it's a good thing nobody else got a good look at it, and that she— well, never mind about that.

She's going to buy a calendar tomorrow and start counting down the days till March.

And she's smiling again, and I'm so happy for her. It was a Merry

Christmas after all.

UM is finally advancing in the rankings, and we're pretty much guaranteed that we'll make it to the Nationals. All I've got to do (besides speed up a little), is keep Marie focused on the meets, and stop worrying about Billy.

Or at least *try* to stop worrying. It's hard. We've both tried to stop reading the papers and watching the news at night, but then we'll hear something from the guys in ROTC (who *just can't wait* to get over there before it ends— not that that is happening soon), or sometimes the Vets on campus will start acting funny and talk about what's going down, and worrying about buddies that are still there, and that's when we start watching the news again.

On St. Valentine's Day, Marie cried because she and Billy had never spent it together, and I hugged her and pulled her out of bed and told her I'd buy her a Whitman's Sampler all for her if she would smile just one time for me.

She laughed then, and said even though I wasn't Billy, I was still the world's best sister.

Three mornings later, we were leaving for class, when the PA system said "Giametti. Visitors."

We looked at each other.

Marie dropped her books and ran downstairs, crashing into the walls, tripping and almost falling. I grabbed her books and tried to run to catch up with her.

When I heard her scream, I dropped everything and ran down the stairs, and when I got to the lobby, I saw the whole family.

Marie was lying on the floor crying.

And underneath Marie was Billy.

Uncle Vince and Uncle Bill were staring at the light fixtures, the walls, the doors, out the window, ANYPLACE except Marie and Billy. Aunt Sally, Aunt Carmella, and Granny Annie couldn't look away from them. I stood at the foot of the stairs and felt so happy and relieved I didn't know whether to laugh or cry.

Then that Cynthia Smith was there, and she said, "I guess your dyke girlfriend got her baby-killer back."

That did it forever! I picked her up, slammed her into the wall, drew back my fist to swing—

And she tried to cover her face with her arms and started crying "Oh God please don't hit me I'm sorry I'm sorry sorry sorry sorry sorry I promise I'll never ever *ever* say anything mean or nasty you ever ever again cross my heart and hope to dieeeee!"

I looked at her, and I was so disgusted. I couldn't hit her. I couldn't hit her because Granny Annie was hanging onto my arm and saying, "Put her down, Honey, just put her down, you'll get in trouble and get thrown out of college or thrown in jail, just put her down *please*, Sally."

I looked at Cynthia Smith. She was still holding her arms over her face and peeking through them at Granny Annie.

I dropped her.

She looked a little shaky, but I could see that smirk starting—

Until Granny Annie grabbed her by the hair and growled "That's *my* Grandson, Cynthia. *I'll* knock your teeth down your throat."

Cynthia Smith's eyes looked like they were going to pop out, and I didn't know if it was from Granny Annie's grip on her hair or being scared to death again. She pulled away and ran up the steps howling.

Granny Annie brushed the hair from her fingers and gave me a quick hug and kiss. We both turned to look at Marie and Billy on the floor. She was starting to calm down, but then she sat up and grabbed him by his ears and shook him and yelled "Why didn't you let me know when you were coming home? *DAMN* you, you know I HATE surprises. You're SUCH an idiot!" She fell on top of him again, crying "I don't want a surprise, I just want youuu."

Billy was stroking her behind (and don't think Aunt Carmella didn't see that!) "I'm sorry, Felix" he said. "I promise I'll never do it again. But this time I couldn't resist. Forgive me?"

Marie pushed herself up and straddled his lap. "Alright, Poindexter" she said. "I'll let you live this time." She flinched at what she had said, and almost cried again, but Billy laughed at her. "It's okay, Felix. I'm home now.

It's okay."

They helped each other up, and Marie looked at him, and then grabbed his arms, chest, back, waist, butt, between his legs (he giggled), ran her hands down his legs, until he took her hands and told her "Everything's still there. Including the toes." *He* made a face then, like maybe *he* wanted to cry, but stopped himself. He and Marie hugged again and swayed back and forth. They were both smiling.

"Hey, Felix" he started stroking her again. "I haven't eaten anything for two days. Military standbys and night flights, and I'm famished. You hungry?"

Marie was about as close to him as she could get. She was leering at him. "What are you in the mood for?"

Aunt Carmella interrupted them. "Okay, that's enough. Don't you two get carried away— "

I said "Marie" and tossed her my car keys. Aunt Carmella and Aunt Sally both yelled "SALLY!" but Uncle Vince said quietly, "Leave 'em alone, Carmella." He looked at them. "Ah, go on, go... get something to eat." Uncle Bill and Billy looked at each other, and Uncle Bill said just as softly, "You ever hurt her, *I'll* kill you." Billy nodded and he and Marie took off. Aunt Carmella said "Vince— ", but then stopped. Aunt Sally said she hoped she'd see him again before his leave ended.

Nobody said anything else, but they all looked at me. Uncle Vince sighed and asked, "Breakfast sound good?" and they all left. I picked up our books and went to class, and I wondered when *I* would see them again.

Marie woke me up when she came in the next morning at six and lay down next to me. She had circles under her eyes, her hair was a mess, her breath stank, and she had the happiest smile I'd ever seen. I grinned back. "You going to tell me about it?"

She giggled. "We didn't make it to a restaurant until nine last night. God, we were STARVED!"

I looked at her. "Uh huh. You know what I mean."

She giggled some more. "Oh, you'll find out about such things when you grow up."

"Oh, c'mon, Marie!"

"'Waal, Pardner, Ah guess Ah been rode hard, and put away wet. An' Ah'm a mite saddle-sore.'"

"That's gross, Marie!" but I was laughing too.

"Okay, it's, well... it's... Okay, it *worked*, you know? But I think it'll take practice to make it work the best. So, we will be 'practicing assiduously.'"

I laughed. "Does he still talk like that?"

"Yeah" she said and rolled off the bed. "Look it up for me, okay? I've got to get going." She grabbed some clothes, toothbrush and toothpaste, comb and hairbrush, and stuffed it all in her overnight bag, and gave me a big kiss, and was gone.

They came back on Friday afternoon and picked me up, and we went home to Aunt Carmella's. Nobody said anything about... anything, but nobody was upset anymore, either. We had a BIG meal; Aunt Carmella, Aunt Sally, and Granny Annie kept pulling more and more out of the refrigerator and pantry, and hugging and kissing Billy, and telling him to eat eat eat, and that when he got home, Granny Annie had a big blow-out planned, and he could put some *real* weight back on.

Billy did look skinnier than when he went away, and there were lines around his eyes, and he didn't smile the same way anymore. Uncle Bill and Uncle Vince both kept watching him, and then they'd look at each other and shake their heads. I was wondering why.

We found out at four in the morning.

Marie and I were asleep in bed when we woke up hearing him scream "STEVE! DON'T MOVE! DON'T MOVE! *DON'T MOVE*!"

Marie made it down to the living room sofa where Billy was sleeping before anyone else in the house. Billy was sitting up and shaking and holding his face in his hands, and Marie was holding him and whispering, "I'm here, I've got you, it's okay now, it's just another bad dream, I'm not going to leave you alone, I'll take care of you."

She looked up at us and wrapped her arms around him tighter. "I've got him. You can all go back to bed." She looked at Uncle Vince. "He's got sharks of his own, Pop."

Aunt Carmella shivered. Aunt Sally tried to sit down next to Billy, but Marie looked at her and said, "I've got him." Aunt Sally looked like *she* wanted to cry then, but she nodded and went back downstairs with Uncle Bill and Granny Annie.

I stood there, watching Marie. In all our life, I'd never seen her like this: so protective, so... so... I didn't know. She looked at me. "I said go back to bed." It wasn't a growl. But it was close.

I went back to bed. Nobody went back to sleep. Around six, I could hear people moving around, upstairs, downstairs; toilets flushing and sinks running— but nobody talking. Marie came into our room and got dressed. She looked at me. "Maybe later" she said. "I'll let you know."

We went downstairs to the kitchen. Marie walked over to the table. "Miss Sally? I'm sorry about... last night. I didn't mean to be..."

Aunt Sally shook her head. "It's alright, Honey" she said quietly. "He's yours, now. He's not my little boy anymore."

"Where is he?" I asked.

Aunt Carmella answered. "Out with your uncles, walking around in the dark." She looked at Marie. "How about you two get married? Maybe it's not the way I wanted, but you can."

Marie shook her head. "No, Ma. 1972 like we planned. We've got a lot to finish before then. College. Marines. Olympics. Fire and Ambulance. You know all that, Ma." She smiled a little. "Relax, Ma, we were careful. Hey, I'm a good Catholic Italian girl, right?"

Aunt Carmella rolled her eyes and said "Oh, Jesus" and Aunt Sally shook her head and snorted. Granny Annie was laughing.

Billy, Uncle Bill and Uncle Vince came home at 7:30, and said that since the bars open at six, they went out for some "eye-openers." We all yelled at them, but we knew they were kidding. They had brought home fresh hot bread from John's Italian Bakery, Chocolate Bismarcks from Hahn's Bakery, and sliced pancetta and peppers and Fontina cheese from DiPasquali's for omelets.

Breakfast lasted a long time. On purpose. The coffees were finished, and chocolate icing licked off fingers, and we all sat and waited. Billy took a deep breath, sighed, and started talking.

His friend Steve was dead.

They were out on patrol, just a month before their "tour of duty" ended, and Steve stepped into a booby trap. Billy said that some booby traps have "pungi sticks" (they're bamboo spikes with shit smeared on them), and some have Russian landmines, and some booby traps have both because the mines don't always work, so at least they'll get somebody when they step in it. And the mines don't go off when you step ON them, they go off when you step OFF of them. So, when Steve stepped into the trap, everybody ran away from him.

Except Billy.

Billy got down on the ground and dug in sideways with his hands, and kept the mine from going off, and got Steve's foot out and took the spikes out. They called for a helicopter to take Steve away.

A couple of days before Billy left Vietnam, some people came and got all Steve's personal stuff, like letters and photos, but they left his uniforms and his gun. Billy said when they do that...

They all thought it was from a bad infection from the pungi sticks because that had happened before. We all tried to tell Billy how brave he was, but he screamed at us that HE wasn't brave, STEVE was, and do you think YOU could stand still with fucking pungi sticks through YOUR feet?

He started crying again, and we all went outside in the cold until Marie said to come back in.

The rest of the day was quiet. Marie took over the kitchen at suppertime. Billy came into the kitchen, snuggled up behind her, kissed her on the neck, and said it smelled good, and he was getting hungry again. Aunt Carmella said they were going to eat their meals with the rest of us from now on. Granny Annie said that was locking the barn door after the horse was gone, and Marie and Billy both started giggling, and Billy whispered, "Hi Yo, Silver" and Marie reached back between them and tickled him and whispered "Up, Scout." (*) Aunt Carmella swatted Marie and Aunt Sally got Billy. (*note: Tonto's command to *his* horse.)

That night in bed, Marie told me that Billy had gotten a medal he wouldn't wear, and a promotion to Sergeant, and that his next duty was to be part of some Admiral's "Praetorian Guard." Marie got up and said she would be downstairs with Billy in case he had a dream.

I woke up and heard him crying later, and Marie telling him she'd always be there.

Sunday afternoon, Billy and everyone went home to Ocean City, and he and Marie would get together next weekend, if I would lend her my car. Yeah, like I'd say no.

Aunt Carmella's not too happy with me.

Marie and I drove back to college after they left, and Marie was up half the night reading and studying all the notes and assignments I had gotten for her during her "week of lustful abandon." Where does Billy get all these?

On Tuesday, she remembered that she still didn't know what the Praetorian Guard was, so she ran off to the library before it closed. It wasn't too long after that that I heard, or barely heard, someone tapping on our door.

When I opened it, Cynthia Smith jumped back all the way to the wall, and held a piece of paper out towards me like it was a Crucifix, and I was a vampire. She was shaking, and I almost couldn't hear what she was saying.

"I'm not being mean or nasty, I promise." She inched toward me. "I got this in the mail. I thought you should know about it."

I took the letter, and she jumped back to the other side of the hall. "Second paragraph" she said. I read it.

"Mommie has some sad news for her baby girl. Do you remember Austin Terrance? He had *such* a crush on you in school, just like all the boys did. On Sunday, Pastor Donaldson said that Austin had been killed over there in that Vietnam war. Mrs. Carpenter said she'd heard he'd just gone back there again for the second time, and I said that was pushing his luck. He probably did it so he could keep that older girl he married in luxury."

I stopped reading it. I wanted to throw up, half because of Austin dying, and half because of the way her mother had written it. I looked at Cynthia Smith. She was holding another piece of paper.

"This is Austin's mother's address. I got it out of our church directory. I thought maybe you would want to send a card or something. I don't know Linda's address."

I took a deep breath so that my stomach would settle. I gave Cynthia Smith her letter back and took the address from her.

"Thank you" I said. "Thanks for telling me." I looked at her. She was starting to relax. "I can probably send a letter to the diner. They're open all year. I work there in the summer." I leaned against the door frame. I felt so tired and so sad for Linda and his mother.

Cynthia Smith said "I forgot about the diner. Could you give me the address? I know it's on Ocean Highway, but I don't know the number. Maybe if I just write "Sea Star" on it..."

"Hang on" I said. I got a piece of paper, wrote the address and gave it to her. We stood there and looked at each other.

"I wasn't being mean" she said. "I just thought... since you and Austin... "

"Yeah" I said. "I'm glad you did. I know you weren't... "

We looked at each other some more, and she started walking away, and I was closing the door when she said "Sally."

I stopped. "Cynthia."

She took a breath. "I've never liked you. But I don't know why."

I tried to smile. "That's okay. I never liked you, either."

She sort of wiggled her fingers to say goodbye, and I did too. I closed the door, turned the lights out, got into bed and cried until Marie came back. I told her what had happened, and she helped me cry some more.

Then I got up and wrote my letters.

CHAPTER SIXTY-SIX

Busy

Spring came, and the Collegiates and the Nationals. We did great. 6th place for me in the 400-meter, and 5th for Marie in the relay. Doris got Bronze for the 3-meter board. Two more years till the Olympics!

The semester ended, and we have enough credits for our Batchelor's. Dad and Uncle Vince told us to go for the higher degrees, and they'll help pay when the scholarships run out. Meanwhile, it's back to waiting tables.

When I got to the Sea Star, Linda was behind the cash register. She looked at me and said she didn't want to hear one more "expression of sorrow at this difficult time," but she was smiling a little when she said it and asked if I wanted to start right now. I said yeah, and she came out from behind the counter to greet and seat new customers.

She was pregnant.

When she came back, she said she didn't want to hear anything about that, either, but a hug from a friend would be nice.

I gave her my best one.

Work was very busy this summer. We hired a new waitress— age 16 and she made me feel old at 20! I taught her the way Linda taught me. She had to dump hot coffee on one jerk with grabby hands, and Linda's Dad came out of the kitchen when he heard the yelling and took care of him out in the parking lot while our regulars cheered. Linda stopped working on the 5th of July, a week before the baby came. It was a boy, 7 ½ pounds, and she named him James. She gets Widow's benefits, and she said James would get Dependent benefits till he turns 17 once she proves he's Austin's with a blood test. It's not much, she says, but anything would help.

Dad came down for the whole month of August. Aunt Carmella's brothers all came down for a weekend to plan their vacation cabins on the lots they bought. Dad told me he might not be working at the railroad too much longer because they merged again. I worried if he would be okay, but he said if he went, he'd get a big severance deal, plus he had about a year's worth of vacation time on the books because he only ever took two weeks when he really had more. Mother never knew. He said if they got rid of him, he'd start a furniture shop somewhere, and maybe build houses, too, like he was going to do for Marie's uncles. When I asked if I would be working with him, he said I was still his apprentice where house building was concerned, and I still had plenty to learn.

Good. I've never forgotten that I promised to build houses for Marie and I.

Marie hasn't moped around this summer like last year. Billy's safe, and she hopes he'll never go back to the war. He's on an aircraft carrier: Admiral Stone's Flagship. "Emperor Stone" Billy calls him. He got into an argument with the Admiral the first day he got on board and got a "60-day reduction in rank," which meant he went back to being a Corporal for two months. He didn't say what the argument was about.

Marie's been getting up early every morning and watching the sunrise. She says she's planning her wedding without Aunt Carmella interfering, and sunrise is her best time to imagine.

The news has been saying that the college students that got shot at Kent State and Jackson State this Spring didn't have any guns, and that the soldiers were ordered to shoot, so they weren't accidents.

I've got to stop trying to ignore things.

Linda came back to the Sea Star Labor Day weekend, just in time to say goodbye and let me hold— well, *insist* I hold— James. He squirmed and cried, and Linda laughed and said get used to it, you'll have your own one day.

Not me, uh uh, no way, don't need one, don't want one.

I wouldn't want to be a mother like... well, Mother.

I'm afraid I would be.

CHAPTER SIXTY-SEVEN

Mentors

Back to UM, and a fair start on our Master's. Or should I say a "false" start. I had the great misfortune to end up with the same incompetent instructor I had for a week when I first got here. No change, I was still correcting *his* mistakes.

In October, he gave us a test, a sort of mid-semester exam. On the fourth problem, I found three transposed numbers, and two negative notations that should have been positive. How can he miss things like that?

I raised my hand, and he ignored me as usual, and when I went down to his tiny little desk, he said (and loud enough for everyone to hear), "Miss Osterhoff, if you are unable to do the problems, perhaps you should consider returning to the 1st grade and learn to count past ten without taking your shoes off."

I kept my temper and tried to explain that the problem was *his* problem, and right in the middle of it, some guy in the front row says "Gee whiz, Dr. Collins, she's right. You DID screw up again."

Alright, he said it differently, but the result was the same. "Miss Osterhoff, I have had quite enough of your blah blah blah, and you've *failed*, blah blah blah, and give me that paper and remoooove yourself from my magnificent presence" and made a grab for my test. I stuffed it in my bag, grabbed my books, and walked out while he shouted that he'd have me thrown off campus.

I went right to the Head of the Math Department. I was going to show him just what Collins had *supposedly* been teaching.

At the department, there was a pretty, middle-aged black lady sitting at the reception desk outside of the other offices. The name plate on her desk said "Miss Clementine." When I started to explain why I was there, she rolled her eyes and said, "Him again?" A man's voice with a kind of a twang to it called out "My Darlin' Clementine, please send the young lady thisaways." She rolled her eyes again, and said, "Dr. Wheeler will see you, now" and grinned and pointed to a door that was open.

A middle-aged man, bald and a bit pudgy, sat behind a desk covered in books and paper. I showed him the test, and started to explain, but he held up his hand and frowned at it. I looked around his office while he read. There were framed diplomas all over the walls: a BS from the University of West Virginia, an MS from Virginia Tech, PhD from Georgia Tech, Post-doctorate from Columbia, and two photographs: one was an *autographed* copy of that picture of Albert Einstein sticking his tongue out, and another, smaller one of a grubby little boy with bare feet and raggedy bib overalls, with a paper label that read "Don't forget where you came from and don't get too big for your britches." When I looked back at him, he held up the test and said, "He also misplaced this integral sign."

I looked, and yeah, Collins had messed that up, too. "I didn't look that far" I said. "After all the other— "

He held up his hand again, stood up, came to the door, waved me through, and into a bigger room with a conference table and a blackboard with a huge equation on it that someone had been working on. He tossed me a piece of chalk and sat down.

"Great" I thought. "'Here, little girl, go on and prove you know what you're doing, and I'll just sit here and watch.'"

I gave a little huff and dove in. After a few minutes, I was grinning so wide that my jaw ached. THIS was the most intricate and complex problem I'd been hit with since Mr. Nightingale taught Marie and I. THIS is what I'd wanted for the past two years! THIS is what I expected college to be! I could just hear that idiot Collins trying to explain this! Take my shoes off to count, huh? I'll bet *he's* always overdrawn at the bank! I could just hear him shouting that he wanted me out! That POMPOUS, PEDANTIC, PATRONISING, PONTIFICATING... PRICK!

When I solved the equation, I sat down on top of the conference table and admired it for a few seconds, then I started snorting and giggling, and drumming my hands on the table. There! That'll show the bald-headed old fart!

I heard someone clear their throat, and remembered I wasn't alone.

"Miss Osterhoff. I can't help but note that in your moments of... hmm... frenzy, let's call it, you seem to have a tendency to— My Darlin' Clementine," he called. "Is it 'verbalize' or 'vocalize'?"

"Do you want me to call the English Department?"

"Um... no." He turned back to me. "What I mean is, when you get yourself all het-up, you talk out loud."

Uh oh.

"Now, while *I* might ignore being called a bald-headed old fart— "

"Because you are" came the voice outside.

"Hmm... Dr. Collins, who dropped by, took great exception to being called a 'pompous, pedantic, patronizing, pontificating— ' well, a lady shouldn't never say that last word. Anywho, after standing right there hearing it, he wants you thrown out of his class, and off this campus completely. I agree. At least insofar as getting you out of that so-called class of his."

"Stop teasing her, John."

"Yes, My Darlin' Clementine."

"And you've just exceeded your quota of 'My Darlin' Clementines' for the day."

"Yes, My Darlin' Clementine." I heard her give him a raspberry.

He looked at me. "Alright, gal, here's what's going to happen: I'm going to drop all my own busy schedule— "

"Like the meetings he never attends."

"And I shall take you on as my own student— "

"If he remembers how to teach."

"She thinks she runs the place" he said in a loud whisper.

"I do." She called to me "It's *Sally* Osterhoff, isn't it? You're looking for a Masters?"

"Yes, ma'am. And a Doctorate. And I'd *really* like to teach, one day. College level? Hopefully?"

"If you're able, that hillbilly next to you will see you all the way through. Give me the rest of your schedule, and I'll check your records and see what needs to be done. Now, say 'thank you' to the bald-headed old fart, and leave him to all his profound thoughts of what to have for lunch."

Dr. Wheeler sighed. "Only the Good Lord knows how heavy my yoke is" and shooed me out the door.

sigh Oh, pity me in the depths of my great misfortune!

HA HA HA!

Anywho—

Oh, God, I'm starting to talk like him already.

Any*way*, I had finally found my Mentor: someone who DOESN'T look down on me (or down my neckline) or thinks I'm wasting his valuable time. He just loves math as much as I do and likes sharing it with people that are truly interested. He said the ideal classroom is a log with a teacher on one end and a student on the other, and it must be light enough for the teacher to pick up and pound the lesson into the student's head.

In case you haven't guessed, I really like Dr. Wheeler.

Marie had found her own Mentor: Dr. Evans. She (yes, SHE) teaches "Double-entry Accounting and Embezzlement, Tax and Insurance Fraud, Banking Vacations in the Swiss Alps and the Beaches of Bermuda, and Illegal Investments in Gold Ingots, Krugerrands and Mexican Pesos, and even guarantees that you can bribe your way to a CPA certificate, with absolutely no legal come-back." Or at least that's how Dr. Evans describes it.

She sounds like fun. Marie says she's a very tough grader as well.

CHAPTER SIXTY-EIGHT

House Building

Billy wrote that the aircraft carrier he was on picked up the next crew of Apollo astronauts when they came back from the Moon. Billy and the other Marines stood guard outside the quarantine trailer they stayed in until they got flown out, trailer and all, back to NASA.

Billy came home for a whole month's leave in March that coincided with Spring Break, and I "just happened" to misplace my car keys again.

Aunt Carmella says even though it's wrong, she understands Marie taking off with Billy and doing God-knows-what, but I should have held onto my car keys for at least a few days. Uncle Vince says that if this were the Old Country, he should be looking for them with a shotgun, but since he was the one who let them get away with it last year, he's going to pretend it's okay.

Granny Annie laughs and says what did they expect after all these years, and that they'd better not elope and cheat her out of dancing at their wedding.

It's funny. I'm happy for Marie and Billy, but I'm a little sad for me. Sometimes I feel lonely.

Billy told us that he'd been transferred to Midway Island for the rest of his enlistment. Marie's happy because now she knows for sure that he'll never go back to the war. Uncle Bill asked him what he had done to get sent there, but Billy just grins and won't say. I hope he hasn't gotten in trouble again.

We all made the Nationals, and Marie and I both Bronzed, and Doris Silvered. She says next year she'll complete the set and make the Olympic Team. Us too, we hope!

Summer came, and back to Ocean City and back to waitressing.

But this summer will be a little bit different. Okay, a lot different. I told Linda that I'd quit at the end of July.

Why?

I'm going to build three houses with Dad, for Marie's uncles.

I can't wait!

Marie still gets up to watch the sunrise and do her wedding imagining. We both know Aunt Carmella has her own plans about all the things that she wanted for her own wedding but couldn't have. I know that whatever Marie is working on, Aunt Carmella is going to hate it.

And I know Marie is going to win that fight when it comes, no matter what.

Thursday was still my day off, and Dad would come down and take me to all the different County offices to get permits and approvals, and to the electric and water utilities to set dates for them to bring electric, water and sewage to the site, and hire contractors for concrete and roofing. Dad kept reminding me that it's more than four walls and a roof, and I needed to learn what to do before the first nail went into the first board.

One other thing that Dad taught me to do was whistle—LOUD. Two fingers in the mouth, tongue just so, and blow! I didn't understand why, but he said I'd figure it out at the right time.

August came, and I traded my waitress uniform for work clothes and steel-toed shoes and reported for work "on-site" which was easy to do because we stayed at Aunt Carmella's cottage.

The first few days were the hardest. I had to toughen up my hands and build up my forearm muscles. The houses were going to be post and beam, and that meant lots of holes bored into lots of wood with a hand brace and bit. By the end of the first day, I wished Dad used power tools. At least he had blisters, too. Soaking your hands in saltwater hurts like Hell.

We stacked everything behind the cottage, and the utilities came and laid pipe, and the concrete contractors dug for the foundations. Dad and Mr. Joe and Mr. Mike went with the electric and water guys, and Dad told me to learn from the concrete guys how to do foundation work.

I found out why Dad taught me to whistle.

After being told "Honey, look out, you'll get hurt here, Honey, why don't you stay out of the way, Honey, this is man's work, Honey" THAT'S when I whistled.

I told them I was a MASTER Cabinetmaker; not an Apprentice, not a Journeyman, and I was taught by a MASTER Woodwright, and *I* was going to be building these houses, so knock it off and show me what you're doing, and don't look at Mr. Osterhoff, look at ME.

Dad was ignoring us and kept talking with the other guys.

The guys doing the foundations FINALLY looked at me, and said "Yes, ma'am" and began to explain and teach and let me work alongside of them. I know I'm always going to have to prove to men that I know what I'm doing, but it's always going to make me mad. At least with most professionals, I only have to prove it ONCE.

Stick bolts for the sill plates in wet concrete, cure the slabs for a couple of days, start making the roof trusses, place the sill plates, put up the posts, the beams, sheath the walls with plywood, mount the roof trusses (God, they were heavy), plywood on that, and on and on, and ONE house up after TWO AND A HALF weeks, and plenty more to do, but a least I already knew how to hang windows and doors, and lay floors, and raise inside walls, but there was no way that Dad and I could finish all three houses before I had to go back to UM.

Except that Marie's uncles and Uncle Bill and Uncle Vince and the Ocean City Fire Department all showed up, and Dad said we'd have an Amish Barn-Raising— sort of— and everything for the other two houses went up in ONE day.

At the end of the day, I asked Dad why didn't we do that for all three? I understood when he started to laugh.

I wouldn't have really learned if I hadn't done ALL the work myself.

So, Dad shook my hand and told me my apprenticeship was finished, and the rest comes from practice, and I am a MASTER WOODWRIGHT, capable of building everything from a box to a barn.

I was so proud, I stood there and cried.

CHAPTER SIXTY-NINE

Water, Numbers, and Plans

Back to UM, back to Dr. Wheeler, and back to swimming. I think all the work from building those houses built up my strength enough that I cut a whole 1½ seconds from my time for the 400-meter. Great, huh?

Until I took a good look in a full-length mirror in the locker room after a shower.

Nothing but muscles.

Oh, sure, I had nice boobs, and my hips and butt had nice, smooth curves, and a waist any girl would want, and NOTHING sagged...

But, God, ALL those muscles on my arms and legs and tummy and neck...

And those SHOULDERS.

I looked like Aunt Viv.

I stood there and stared, and all the other girls on the team walked by and went "WOOHOO!" and two of them (Marie was one) pinched me on my butt, and one girl said "It's 'CHARLOTTE' Atlas!"

I couldn't stop staring, and Marie came back and swatted me on my butt and said I picked the damnedest times to agonize over my looks and told me to get dressed and we'd go eat some pizza at Tony's and have a little vino (we're 21 now), and maybe a cannoli if there're any left.

We ate, and I whined that the way I look is the reason I don't have a boyfriend, and she said no, the reason I don't have a boyfriend is that I'm oblivious to guys asking me out. I said what about Dave? And she said I only heard him ask me out because I was teaching him and paying attention to him, just like it took a couple of years before I heard Joey asking me out.

God, am I that stupid?

Yeah, a head full of numbers and not much else.

Dr. Wheeler told me to give him a break so that he could catch-up on all the paperwork and meetings he's supposed to attend, and in the meantime, why don't I get all my tutoring organized and teach those illiterate drooling idiots on the sport teams in two big groups? Miss Clementine said she would do the scheduling, and find the empty lecture rooms, and that I should charge each one of them $25 an hour, and sock it away for those houses I wanted to build by the ocean one day. She was right, and those guys can afford it since they get more money than any academic program on campus.

"Amateur Sports." Nobody pays the women's swim team anything beyond our scholarships, and even that doesn't cover everything. It's a good thing we have our academic scholarships as well, and summer jobs (and like WOW, man, did I cleanup with those houses! They paid me UNION RATES!)

Marie and Doris and I have been pushing ourselves harder and harder at all the meets this year. The Nationals are going to be here before we know it, and there's only so many spots on the Olympic Team. God, I want it SO bad! I want to win for me, Aunt Viv, Adrienne, Mrs. Persky, Mrs. Thune, and everybody that ever helped me.

But mostly for me.

Marie has finished figuring out what she wants for her wedding, and I was right: Aunt Carmella is going to hate every bit of it. All the things that Marie wants sound beautiful and romantic, and if she can get it to turn out the way she wants, it's going to be far out! Some of it'll be easy. Karen Olejnik made us promise back in Junior High that when we got married, *she* would make the wedding cakes. And I'd sew Marie's wedding dress (and she wants a DRESS, not a gown), along with a dress for me— the Maid of Honor! She had something in her closet at home that was the style she wanted.

Aunt Carmella will be screaming at us at the top of her lungs.

Just wait till she finds out *where* the wedding will be. She'll kill both of us.

But Marie is my sister, and I'll be right there next to her, supporting everything she wants.

help

Marie and I missed another Thanksgiving because of a meet. At least the college rented a bus for us this time. We won every heat, and I'm getting close to setting a new record for speed in the 400.

Christmas was nice until after Billy's phone call. That's when Aunt Carmella wanted to talk about the wedding, and how *she* had it all planned.

It will be at St. Leo's. A High Mass. Marie's gown will be silk, satin, Philippine Lace and seed pearls, orchids for the bouquet, the reception will be at the Sons of Italy Hall and catered by Maria's 301, cake by Vaccaro's, this cousin and that cousin for Flower Girl and Ringbearer, and on and on, and then Marie said "Forget it, Ma. THIS is how it'll be."

Ocean City. On the BEACH. At SUNRISE. Sally makes the dress. A DRESS, Ma. No fancy gown. FORGET IT, Ma. And NO orchids. Daisies. I *LIKE* daisies, Ma. And instead of a veil, a circlet of those little wildflowers that look like daisies, whatchacall'ems.

Aunt Carmella took off like a rocket. "They're called WEEDS! You want some kind of Hippie Wedding! What'll the families all think? And you can't get married on a BEACH, it's gotta be in a CHURCH, or it's not real, and NO Priest is going to do it on a BEACH!"

Marie yelled back "Well, if I can't get a Priest to do it, I'll find some other Church that will!"

Aunt Carmella was crying, now. "You'd get married out of the Church?" and Marie yelled back "YOU'RE the one who always told us it's all the same God!" and Uncle Vince said, "It comes back to bite you, Carmella." "SHUT UP, Vince! And NOBODY is going to go all the way to Ocean City to see you get married on a BEACH!" "Anybody who *really* wants to see me get married'll be there!" and Marie stomped out of the kitchen, and Aunt Carmella starts telling *me* that I'VE got to tell Marie that she can't do this, and that this was the wedding SHE wanted but couldn't have, and now she wants it for Marie, and Marie yells "Yeah, that's YOUR wedding, NOT mine! I'm having MY wedding!"

I tried to calm Aunt Carmella down by telling her about the wedding dress. It was a shift, mid-calf, pure white linen, and embroidered around the neckline, and Aunt Carmella was crying louder now. "You made it ALREADY?" and SCREAMS out to Marie "I give up! You want your Hippie Wedding, FINE! You'll see! It'll be HORRIBLE!," and Marie screams back "GOOD! Then it'll be HORRIBLE! But it'll still be MY wedding!"

I don't know when Aunt Sally, Uncle Bill, and Granny Annie disappeared from the room.

I think we'll tell about having the reception at the Fire House another day.

CHAPTER SEVENTY

The Nationals

In February, right on St. Valentine's Day, Marie got a letter from Billy saying that he'd be home the end of July. His "C.O." (Commanding Officer) said he could use his accumulated leave and get home before his active duty ends and go to the nearest Military base and get discharged. That'll be the Coast Guard Training Base at Cape May, New Jersey, and that's just a drive and a ferryboat ride from Ocean City. He said the Major will have all his paperwork sent and received before Billy leaves the island. Billy says the Major is the best officer he ever served under and didn't deserve exile on St. Helena.

We got the thing about where Napoleon got sent, but you'd better believe that Billy's going to have a lot to explain about everything that happened to him in the Marines.

I think all I've done this semester is swim and learn with Dr. Wheeler. He's the only instructor I have now, and Miss Clementine has been sort of "diddling the books" so that it looks like I have a full schedule of classes and can still stay on campus in the dorm. Actually, I do have a full schedule because we're working all day, every day. I asked him how much longer it would be until I got my Master's, but all he said was "Never you mind, gal, I'll be sure to let you know when your brain is full."

At the end of March, we found out we'd made the Nationals. They were in Los Angeles this year, and we've got a good idea of who we're up against. Doris is a shoo-in for Gold, and Marie and I have to watch out for two girls from Arizona and one from Nevada. The rest of the field we've beaten in the past, so if we concentrate and give it everything we have, we'll make it (we hope.)

The day we left, we had everybody at Friendship Airport waving us goodbye. Some Alumnus paid for the Men's Team to fly First Class, but the Women's Team had to pay their own way. I didn't care too much; I was just happy we were going.

Okay, I was WAY bummed-out about *us* having to pay. *They* also got hotel rooms, too, while *we* stayed in UCLA's dorms wherever they could squeeze us.

The Nationals are always hard, but in Olympic years, it's even harder. Adrienne told us it all comes down to time. INDIVIDUAL time. Even in relay races, it's whoever has the fastest lap that will get picked.

Those girls from Arizona and Nevada are just as fast as we are.

All through our practices, there were about two dozen people sitting in the stands watching us with stopwatches. Some were other team's coaches, some were from the U.S. Olympic Committee, and some were what they call "touts." These were guys from the casinos, and they were recording the times for someone to figure the odds on who might win. I didn't think they should have been there, and our coach said definitely not, but "money talks."

There were only a couple of reporters. They came from the "Press Pool" and looked bored to death. Sorry, guys, we're not in bikinis and we're not built like Raquel Welch.

Everybody was feeling the pressure this year, and nobody was having any fun. I think we were all relieved when the heats started.

It was tough: every finish was down to hundredths of a second, not tenths, but we kept on winning, and kept on advancing. The touts got kicked out when the girl from Nevada told the judges she'd been offered a bribe.

Yeah, like any of us were going to lose a race on purpose and miss the Olympics. There isn't enough money in the world for that.

But the times are getting tighter, and the pee and blood tests are getting on everybody's nerves. What do they think we are, Russians?

We're down to the finals and just two more races. I'm in both the relay (breaststroke), and the 400m freestyle, and thank God there's a couple of hours between them. One thing happened that made all of us happy: Doris took the Gold on the 3m board! She's absolutely going to Munich!

I thought the relay went okay. We won, but right that minute, we couldn't figure out how our times were— Jeez, listen to me: for the first time in our lives, we couldn't do the numbers!

There were two false starts on the 400. It was the girl from Nevada. She was yelling at the starter, and someone came over and felt the top of the block, and someone else came and scrubbed it. We were whispering to each other, and we think someone smeared hair conditioner on it. I bet it was whoever tried to bribe her.

A clean start, and then it was back and forth and back and forth, just like Aunt Viv and Mrs. Thune and Mrs. Persky taught us, all those years of practice— almost my whole life! I remembered the best lesson that Mrs. Persky taught us: DON'T glide into the finish, STROKE to the last inch. REACH— STRETCH for that last inch. And if you bang your head, well, SOMETHING has to make contact.

I banged my head.

AND I WON!

It was worth the headache and the knot.

I'm on the Olympic Team!

But Marie... isn't.

That girl from Nevada beat her time by only three one-hundredths.

I was crying. It wasn't supposed to be like this. She and I were supposed to go together. How can somebody who lived in a DESERT be a better— no, *faster* swimmer than Marie?

Marie was telling me not to cry, and that it was always more my dream than hers, and besides, she was getting married, and this way she'd have a longer Honeymoon and wouldn't spend it swimming, and I wouldn't have believed her even if she hadn't started crying, too.

It's not going to be the same. It won't be like we'd always planned. It won't be *us*.

CHAPTER SEVENTY-ONE

Planning and Practice

We got home, and everybody congratulated me, and hugged Marie. Aunt Viv and Adrienne and Mrs. Persky came to UM on Friday, and said they knew exactly how we felt, and we knew they really did. They took us out for dinner, and we had four bottles of Champagne and got all wasted and had to go back to the dorm in a cab, and they slept on the floor.

The way I felt the next morning, I would *never* drink that much ever again. Everybody else was hungover too. Why do people get so drunk if this is what happens?

We went back to the wedding planning, back to practice laps, back to classes. I think we're both going to be a few credit hours short of our Masters. Marie says she'll finish her classes while Billy's in Fireman's School and taking Ambulance training.

Doris got her Master's in Chemistry, and will be going for her Doctorate in the Fall. Miss Clementine helped her get a grant from the United Negro College Fund. Doris says that Miss Clementine does that for a lot of the black students at UM. She also told me that Miss Clementine and Dr. Wheeler are married. Stupid me again, all numbers. They're both still telling me they'll let me know when I'm done, and if I keep bothering them, they'll stick a fork in me to see. Meanwhile, "just swim and don't fuss."

Marie's driving my car more than I am. She found out that some pizza and spaghetti joint on the boardwalk wants to expand into catering, and Marie's wedding will be perfect to show off what they can really do. There'll be breakfast, a little brunch, a big lunch, and lots of wine, and they even know a band that'll be okay with starting in the morning and playing till everyone stops dancing.

Uncle Vince says the families will dance till the wine runs out.

Aunt Carmella is still mad and says it's going to be a big disaster, but she took care of all the invitations, and made hotel reservations for the people that were coming (and some dropped out when they found out *they* had to pay for their rooms). She told them they'd have to bring lawn chairs to sit on the beach (and a few more decided not to come.) Uncle Vince says Marie was right: the ones that are coming want to celebrate with Marie and Billy and he might not end up in the poor house after all.

Karen is going to make the cake just like she planned. It'll be four tiers, lots of icing roses and garlands and candy pearls, and instead of the bride and groom figures on top, there'll be a pair of blown-glass doves from Poland. She'll bring the baked layers down and ice them the night before the wedding and keep it in the Firehouse refrigerator, and she'll kill anyone who sticks a finger in it.

I went with Marie on the weekend she ordered the flowers. We found out that those little daisy wildflowers she wants woven into a circlet for her hair really *are* weeds. The florist told her that if he can't find any, he'll take the smallest daisies he can find and weave those.

Other than sewing the dresses (mine is pale green), supplying the car, and giving "moral support," this Maid of Honor hasn't done much. Marie says that's fine, I'll be one less person to run around in circles screaming, like Aunt Carmella.

Billy came home on the 19th of July. The first thing he was told by everyone, including Marie, was NO Honeymoon until after the wedding. He said that's okay, but he wasn't going to turn her loose for at least a month afterward. Aunt Carmella said fine, he can pretend to be Superman *after* the wedding, not before.

He says he's being Honorably Discharged, but still won't talk about anything to do with the Marines, the war, or that Admiral. He did tell us that Midway Island is the most boring duty station you could get, and his only listed duty was to literally count the flagpole every morning. The only excitement he got was by getting his Major to have him assigned to the fire-fighting detail. There's a lot of fuel oil stored there for the Navy ships that sail by, but they're careful and they've never had a problem.

I guess everything else is his business, and he'll tell us eventually.

CHAPTER SEVENTY-TWO

Horror Movie

I spent most of my time in the pool at UM that summer, either spotting for Doris while she practiced, or her spotting for me when I did. I was practicing my dives off the platform, and turns at the end of laps, trying to get just a tiny bit more speed. The Wednesday before the wedding, I had dived so much that I was feeling sore, and I thought I had pulled an abdominal muscle. I tried only doing laps the rest of the day.

I still felt sore when we finished practice, and I didn't feel much like eating, either so I got a pail of ice from the cafeteria and kept filling up my grey icebag until I fell asleep. Doris and I had a long drive ahead of us tomorrow morning.

I woke up in the morning and felt horrible. My side hurt so much, and I knew I had a fever, and I was trying to figure out what I had caught when I heard Doris knocking on my door.

I tried to get up but couldn't. When Doris knocked again and called out "Hey, girl, you in there? We gotta get moving," I couldn't even answer. I heard Doris ask someone in the hall if I had gone to the cafeteria or someplace, and I heard Cynthia Smith tell her that she hadn't heard or seen me that morning, and she knocked and called too.

I finally managed to say "help" and Doris said, "Did you hear her?" and opened my door. Thank God I had forgotten to lock it last night. They both came in and took one look, and Cynthia Smith took off and said she was calling an ambulance. Doris felt my forehead and neck, and said, "Good Lord, girl, you're on fire!" and she ran and got a soaking wet towel from somewhere and patted my face with it.

Miss Eagers came into the room, and that fat rent-a-cop who was always hanging around the girl's dorms was right behind her. She was saying I must have given myself an abortion, and he was saying no, it's drugs, and Doris said I was sick and I needed a doctor, and the rent-a-cop told her to shut up or he'd arrest her, too, and I tried to tell them my side hurt, and Cynthia Smith came back in and said the ambulance was on its way, and she pushed that fat cop out of the way and said it might be appendicitis because she had had it, and that goddam fat cop pushed her out of the way and says no, it's drugs and poked me in my side and I screamed and threw up and...

And then I was awake, sort of, and in a bed, and Dad was sitting next to me, and my side still hurt, and I still felt hot. "Dad? Why are you here?"

Dad leaned over me as soon as I opened my eyes, and whispered "Shh, Kinder, you are alright now. You are in the hospital, and they took your appendix out. You are still confused from the anesthesia."

"My appendix? No, I had those with my tonsils."

"No, Kinder" Dad said "Your appendix. Not your adenoids."

"Appendix." I thought. "That's my insides." I thought some more. "Inside me. They had to cut inside me." I thought some more, and then I knew. "Dad! They cut me open! Will I be able to swim?"

He bit his lip. "No, Sally."

A nurse came in and I appealed to her. "Please?" I begged. "Will I be able to go to the Olympics? I won the Nationals! I'm supposed to go to the Olympics!"

"Um hmm" she said. "You and your horsey will be there in a little while. Why don't you go back to sleep now, and everything will make sense later."

"No! You don't understand! I won the Nationals! I've got to go to Munich in two weeks! Please! Listen to me! I've been waiting my whole life to go!"

She finished taking my temperature and blood pressure and left. I could hear her talking to someone. "National Velvet in there just won the race and she's off to the Olympics. I don't know what they give them in the O.R., but they come down here with the wildest dreams."

Dad kept stroking my hand, and saying "Next time, Sally. You will go next time."

Nobody understood. There wouldn't be a next time. This was it. My last chance. Gone. All gone. I would never go to the Olympics.

It wasn't fair.

it wasn't fair

it... wasn't... fair...

I woke up again later, and Dad was still there. It was dark outside the window. "What day is it?"

He jumped. I think he must have been asleep. He looked at his watch. "It is almost midnight. Friday morning comes."

Friday morning. Oh, God! The wedding! Saturday morning! TOMORROW morning!

"Dad." I pulled his hand. "You've got to get me out of here. Marie's getting married tomorrow morning. I lost the Olympics, but I am NOT missing her wedding. Help me get up, I gotta go Downeyoshun." I tried to sit up, and almost screamed.

"Lie down, Sally" Dad said. "You will not be able to go. The nurse said you will be here until Monday at the earliest."

"NO!" I told him. "I'm going to her wedding. I don't care if it kills me. I'm going." I managed to sit up, and I tried to pull the bedrail down.

"Sally, please" he said, and tried to push me down.

"No" I said. "I'm going. I'm getting out of here, and I'm going Downeyoshun one way or another. I don't care if I have to hitchhike. No, wait." I thought or tried to. "I'll drive. Just help me get to my car." I thought some more. No, I couldn't drive like this. "You drive. Get the station wagon. I can lay in the back."

"Liebchen, listen to me. I do not have the station wagon anymore, remember?"

That's right. He had a Dodge Dart. I felt like I was going to split open. I couldn't sit in my car or his car for three or four hours. "How much does it cost to rent one? Or even an ambulance? I can pay."

"Sally— "

"*No*, Dad." I figured out the bedrail, pushed it down and swung my legs over the side.

"Sally! Stop! Listen to me!" He kept trying to push me back down.

"NO!"

"Sally!" He said something in that Low German of his and took both of my hands. "Sally" he said. His voice was softer now. "I will take you to her wedding. I do not know how, but I will take you there. Please. Lie down now."

I looked at him. "You promise?"

He sighed and raised his right hand. "Before God, I swear this. I will find a way."

I lay down. He'd never broken a promise to me.

The nurses kept waking me up the rest of the night and shoved giant pills in my mouth and said I might have an infection, and here's some pain pills that'll make you woozy, but don't worry about that because you're not going anywhere.

It was almost noon before Dad came back. Doris was with him, and I remembered I was supposed to take her to the wedding with me, and I started to apologize, but Dad said he'd be taking her, and she had my Maid of Honor dress and a suitcase full of my clothes. I asked Dad how am I going?

It sounded so crazy I thought it was the pain pills freaking me out.

Dad had gone to work to see if he could borrow a station wagon from somebody he knew, but that he'd gone on his vacation a day early like Mother used to make Dad do. So, there wasn't going to be a station wagon, but some Boss had died in Ocean City last night from fooling around with his secretary, and his body had to be brought back to Baltimore.

That meant that somebody had to go down there to get him.

In a Hearse.

I was going to Ocean City in a Hearse.

I'm having a nightmare.

Dad said the Hearse was waiting for me.

This is like one of those Monster movies I hate.

Doris had a Dashiki from the girl that she rooms with, and she helped me get into it. A nurse came in and started yelling that I wasn't going anywhere, and Dad picked me up (I almost screamed), and Doris pushed the nurse out of the way, and we went down this hall and that hall, and it felt like a rat maze, and I wanted to wake up and have everything be okay, but I was already awake. We got outside, and this guy in a black suit opens the back of the Hearse and rolls out this platform thing that had a cheap, blow-up air mattress with pictures of seashells, and everybody helped me lie down. Some crazy person was waving papers at Dad and said sign it because they wouldn't be responsible for me leaving, and Dad tore it up, and the guy in the suit rolled me into the Hearse, and I fell asleep.

I woke up somewhere on the way, and called out "Hello? Can you hear me?" I felt the car swerve, and I yelled because it hurt. The guy in the black suit pulled over and turned around and looked at me. "Sorry, Baby Doll, I'm not used to the customers talking" he laughed. "What's up?"

I told him I had to go to the bathroom. Dad knocked on the window and asked what was wrong and if I was okay. I told him, and he said he had seen a sign for some drive-in just ahead.

When we got there, they slid me out, and helped me stand up. Everybody was staring at us, and the guy in the black suit told them: "I hate when the customer gets frisky."

This was the craziest dream I'd EVER had, and I knew it wasn't real, but I hoped I was going to Aunt Sally's, and not a graveyard. Maybe the next time I woke up, I'd be at the Olympics with Marie, Doris and Adrienne, and we'd all get Gold Medals.

It's so hot.

CHAPTER SEVENTY-THREE

The Wedding

I don't remember getting to Aunt Sally's, or her yelling that Dad and I were insane, or much of anything till morning.

Saturday morning.

Marie's Wedding Day.

I could hear people in the living room, and I got up and went into the bathroom with Aunt Sally and Doris and Granny Annie right behind me. I told them I was going to the beach and be Maid of Honor for Marie. Granny Annie said I should get some clothes on first, and Aunt Sally said I should be in the hospital. They all helped me get washed and dressed, and out to the beach. The walk up the hill nearly killed me. Doris sat next to me and held my hand, and we watched the sky getting lighter.

Father Perman from St. Mary's Star of the Sea and Uncle Bill and Billy came down the dune and sat next to us. Uncle Bill said he would help me stand where I was supposed to be, but if I couldn't, he knew Marie would understand. He also said I was nuts, and I should be in the hospital, not here. I told them all to worry about what THEY'RE supposed to be doing and leave me the Hell alone. Then I got up and walked to where I thought I should be. Uncle Bill got up right after me and guided me to the right spot and stood next to me.

Well, I said I'd be here, and that I'd die before I missed Marie's wedding. I just hoped I'd live long enough to see it.

People were sitting on lawn chairs and complaining about sand in their shoes, and what time is it, and is that a real Priest over there, and don't he know this is supposed to be in a Church for Chrissake, and what the Hell's wrong with Marie and Carmella and Vince; and kids were complaining they were tired. I started thinking it wasn't going to go the way Marie wanted.

Some lady came down the dune with a guitar case, and that started more people talking, and I felt so sorry for Marie.

Then a miracle happened.

The edge of the sun came up over the horizon, and there was a bright green flash. Everybody got excited and they were saying what was that, and did you see that?

Then the lady with the guitar stood up and sang Peter, Paul, and Mary's "The Wedding Song" and I don't think anyone there had ever heard it before, and everybody started crying.

Father Perman raised his hands, and everyone stood and turned toward the dune.

Uncle Vince and Aunt Carmella were walking on either side of Marie. She looked so beautiful! The florist had found those little wildflowers, and it looked like she was wearing a crown. Her bouquet was large daisies, and her feet were bare, and oh my God, I'd never seen anybody look that happy!

They came up to where we were waiting, and the lady finished singing. Father Perman said, "In the Name of the Father, and the Son, and the Holy Spirit," and everybody said "Amen." Father Perman started to say, "We are here today— ", but he stopped and looked up into the sky and said, "We are here, in God's OWN Cathedral, to witness and to share joy with William and Marie as they enter into the Holy Sacrament of Marriage." EVERYBODY was crying like it was a Funeral, and Father Perman asked, "Who brings this woman to be Wed?" Uncle Vince said, "Her mother and I do" and they both kissed Marie, and Uncle Vince put Marie's hand in Billy's, and everybody sat down. Father Perman read the rest of the service.

Marie was right, THIS was HER wedding, the way SHE wanted it, and it was PERFECT!

At the end, Father Perman whispered to them—

Okay, so, Father Perman and Aunt Carmella had both told them that the ceremony had to be in the Church, but they could do it on the beach if they would stop at the Church on the way to the reception and say their vows again, and it would be quick, only take a couple of minutes, and just the two of them, okay?

But now Father Perman was whispering that if he tried to make them do it again, God would probably strike him down with a lightning bolt, so, yes, you're married in God's eyes, and go on and kiss her.

Marie and Billy grinned at each other, and laughed and kissed, and they were MARRIED!

They walked up the dune, and everybody was cheering and applauding. Uncle Bill helped me to follow them. At the top of the dune, there was a surf fisherman standing there, holding his rod, bucket, and folding stool, and he stopped Marie and said he'd watched the whole thing, and was this a real wedding? Marie said yes, and he said it was the most beautiful thing he'd ever seen in his life. She kissed him and invited him to the reception.

I was feeling sick again, and I almost decided to stay at Aunt Sally's, but I got in Dad's car somehow, and we went to the Firehouse.

As soon as we got there, they were opening bottles of Spumante, and people were drinking and calling for Marie and Billy to kiss, and there were toasts, and I only managed to take the tiniest sip of wine, because I felt like I was going to throw up. They started serving food, and I couldn't even stand the smell without gagging.

I was at the Wedding Party table, and Marie's Godmother, Aunt Gina, was at the table in front of us. She kept poking her husband, Mr. George, and saying stuff about this one and that one, and the stories she could tell that no one else knew, and the more she drank, the louder she got. I tried to ignore her and looked around at all the other guests. Aunt Viv and Adrienne were sitting with Doris, and they were all laughing. They saw me looking, and waved, and Doris came over to me and sat in Uncle Bill's chair while he was dancing with Aunt Sally. She said "Girl, your aunt and cousin are hotter than a pair of pistols!" She told me she was having the time of her life. I finally noticed that she was wearing a beautiful bright Canary Yellow dress, and a big hat to match, and she said Adrienne had told her she was as pretty as Marie.

Aunt Gina was starting to get nasty. She said I looked like I was pregnant, and drunk, and on drugs, and then she started talking about Doris, and what's that jigaboo doing here, and if Marie has Daisies, Doris must be the Black-Eyed Susan and started laughing, almost like Mother. Doris was looking at her, biting her lips, and trying not to say anything. I told Doris that that was Aunt Gina and that she can't cook. Doris looked at me funny.

Then Marie's grandmother, Mama Loretta, came up behind Aunt Gina and started poking her. "Gina! You get up and come with me, I show you something."

Aunt Gina looked at Mr. George and said, "What the Hell's the old woman want now?" Mama Loretta poked her again, and said she wasn't deaf, and to get up and come outside.

There was a door behind our table, and I couldn't turn around to see, but Doris could. I heard Mama Loretta say "Go out there. Look up." I heard a scream, and Doris clapped her hands over her mouth and made a strangling sound, and grabbed my wine, put it down, and grabbed my water instead, and started sipping. Her eyes were shut tight.

"What happened?" I wasn't sure I wanted to know. Doris told me that Aunt Gina went outside, looked up with her mouth hanging open, and a big pelican swooped down— and she put her hands over her mouth again.

No, I didn't want to know.

I heard Mama Loretta tell Mr. George to take Gina away and wash her filthy mouth out.

I felt a soft cool hand stroking my cheek. It felt so good, I wished I could curl up and be held in it forever. It was Mama Loretta. I looked up at her. She was smiling at Doris and I, and she looked as happy as a little girl.

"Ah! La Bella Fiori! You two look so pretty!"

I smiled back and leaned my head against her hand and closed my eyes.

"So, you gonna go to those Olympics, hah?"

I looked up. She was talking to Doris, not me. I remembered that I wouldn't be going. She was stroking Doris' cheek.

"Yes, Fiorella, you go there, and people from all over the world, they gonna love you, and you make so many friends, and they always smile in their hearts when they remember you." She kissed Doris on the cheek. "You go, and you be happy, hah?"

Doris looked at her and grinned. "Did I just get my fortune told?"

I told her Aunt Carmella had Gypsy blood, and she looked at me again, but this time she looked worried.

Mama Loretta looked at me. "Ah, little Sally, you want to go so bad, but you can't. It's okay. If you go, you never be happy. No, you stay here, you do something better. Three week, you gonna save somebody's life. You gonna save *your* life, too." She kissed me on my cheek. "Ah, but you not gonna remember what I say, hah?" She looked deep into my eyes. "No, you gonna remember. But not for three years." She smiled. I didn't understand, but it didn't matter, so long as she kept stroking my face with her soft cool hands.

She turned to Doris again. "You go get her Papa. Tell him Sally gotta go to the hospital, right now." Doris jumped up and left.

Mama Loretta helped me stand up, and we walked to the door. Someone held it open for us, and she told him to take me to the ambulance, and I just floated away inside of it and went to sleep.

I woke up, and my side still hurt, but I didn't have a fever anymore. Dad was sitting next to my bed and holding my hand. I was in the hospital again.

"DAD!" I yelled, "I've got to get out of here! I gotta get Downeyoshun! I'll miss the wedding!" I tried to sit up.

Dad gently pushed me back down. "Sally, Sally, you *are* here at the ocean, you *were* at the wedding."

I started crying. "I don't remember it! And I'm still in the hospital!"

"A different hospital, Sally. We went to the wedding, but you got sick again, and now you are here."

A nurse came in. "Awake? Good timing. Dr. Flanaghan's making his rounds."

Dr. Flanaghan. Billy's doctor. I *was* Downeyoshun. I looked at Dad. "I was really at the wedding?"

"Yes, Sally. I promised I would take you there."

I remembered the promise, but everything else was crazy. "Did I come here in a Hearse?"

Dad laughed. "Yes, Sally."

"Did the sun turn green?"

Dad laughed again. "Yes, Sally. Both of your uncles say they have seen this before, on ships at sea. They say that the temperature of the air and water and the humidity must be 'just so' and then *maybe* it will happen."

"A fisherman came to the wedding?"

"That too."

"A pelican… and Marie's Aunt Gina…?"

He made a face. "I did not see it, but people talked about it."

I thought there was something else about Marie's Mama Loretta, but I couldn't remember. But it didn't matter if I was at the wedding.

Dr. Flanaghan and the nurse came into the ward. "YOU!" he shouted. "You ruined my weekend!" He pushed Dad out, and pulled the curtains around the bed, stuck a thermometer in my mouth, yanked the sheets down and my hospital gown up. I could feel him slowly peeling the bandages off. I tried to look down, but he yelled "Lay down! Don't be nosy."

I looked up at the ceiling while he complained. "I had my whole weekend set up. Half a dozen Dancing Girls and a quarter-keg of beer on ice, and just when I'm finishing my rounds and getting ready to go home, YOU get dumped on the parking lot by some clown in an ambulance, and I couldn't move my car around you, so I had to drag you in and see what YOUR major malfunction was, and by the time I got out of here, my beer was warm, and the girls were cold, and don't you think I'm not going to bill you for it!"

I felt him tug the rest of the bandages away. He turned to the nurse. "Get me a pile of sponges, alcohol, and more dressings." He was looking down at my tummy, and he looked mad. He took the thermometer out of my mouth and relaxed. "Fever's down. We're going to keep you on IV antibiotics for a few more days." I looked down at my left arm. It was in a splint, and a tube was poking out from under a bandage. He was frowning again, real this time, not pretending.

"Alright, shut up and listen. Whatever left-handed son-of-a… well, whoever he was, I'm going to track him down wherever he hides, and I'll get his damned license yanked, along with everyone else that was on that operating team."

He took a deep breath and calmed himself down. "Your appendectomy was botched. I think your appendix must have burst before you were even operated on. That 'butcher's boy' that cut you open couldn't even do McBurney's incision in the right place, and he couldn't find your appendix, so he sewed you up and probably went golfing."

"When I got you Saturday morning, I cut you open— the *right* place, this time— and found what was left of your appendix and removed it and scooped-out about a double-handful of pus."

The nurse came back in with a small cart of gauze and tape.

"I sewed you up and I had to put drains in you— speaking of which:

'There once was a lady, quite handsome,
Who was caught, in the nude, in a transom.
Though she begged and she pleaded,
Her cries went unheeded,
For the view was worth more than the ransom.'"

It wasn't funny, but maybe I just needed to laugh after all that had happened to me, and I did, and I couldn't stop, and it HURT! I could feel stuff oozing out, and him wiping my tummy, and saying "Sponge, sponge, sponge, keep 'em coming Esther, sponge, sponge..."

He finally finished wiping whatever was coming out of me and started bandaging me again. "You've still got gunk coming out of you, so the drains and the IV stay, and *you're* staying, too, until you pay off for my beer and girls." He put the last piece of adhesive tape on and smiled at me. It was the first time I'd ever seen him smile. "It's a good thing you're as healthy as a horse, otherwise you might not be here."

He put on his frown again. "You got a whole bunch of people lounging around the waiting room. After you see 'em, get 'em outta here. This isn't a bus stop." He grinned once more, winked, and left.

Everybody came in two at a time, and they were all upset because I had been even more sick than they thought. I said the wedding was more important, and they were all going to have to tell me what happened after I left (and everything BEFORE I left, I thought to myself.)

Dad and Doris had to go back to Baltimore, him to work, and her to... well, she was going to Munich.

I wished her all the luck in the world and then some (but it hurt that I was never going to go.)

She leaned over me and kissed me on the cheek, and said "Don't you worry, baby, I'm coming back with a suitcase full of medals, and if you behave yourself and get better before I get back, I just might let you hold one. I might even let you wear one, too."

I told her I'd hold her to that, and she and Dad said goodbye and left. Everyone had gone now except Aunt Carmella and Aunt Sally. They told me everything about the reception. Lunch came, and I was hungry, and that's when they told me it was MONDAY!

Somehow, someway, someone owes me a Sunday.

CHAPTER SEVENTY-FOUR

Lazarus

I stayed at the hospital until Friday and rolled out in a wheelchair and into Uncle Bill's ambulance and home to Billy's old bedroom. Aunt Sally and Aunt Carmella kept feeding me oatmeal, Cream of Wheat, Cream of Rice, soft-boiled eggs (which I *hate*), stewed prunes (GROSS!), and minced-up all the meat and vegetables until it looked like baby food.

After two weeks of that, I got up one morning and I was the only person there, other than Marie and Billy (still in bed). I figured that Aunt Sally and Aunt Carmella were shopping in Delaware, Uncle Bill was at the Firehouse, and Uncle Vince was down on the boardwalk drawing and painting.

Now's my chance... heh, heh, heh!

I pulled on a beach coverup, sandals, grabbed some of the "cold cash" Aunt Sally hides in a box in the freezer, and hobbled all bent over to the bus stop across the street.

I wanted food. REAL food. A training table. Fresh fruit. Steak and eggs. Hashbrowns. Toast with butter and jam. Orange juice, tomato juice, apple juice, pineapple juice, V-8— *anything* that wasn't the mush I'd been eating.

Where? The Sea Star, of course.

I went in and said hi to Linda and her dad and asked about James. Neither of them said anything about the Olympics, but they knew.

I had my breakfast, and tried to pay, and Linda said she'd smack me if I didn't put the money away and poured me another cup of coffee.

I sat there and dawdled and listened to our regulars complain about baseball, tourists, politics ("Nixon's The One" again), and just let my meal settle. Some tall, skinny guy with a limp came clumping in and sat next to me at the counter. He had motorcycle boots, jeans, a military-style jacket with the sleeves cut off, and two tattoos on his arms. One I recognized: the Globe and Anchor of the Marine Corps, and the other was a Bulldog smoking a cigar and wearing a WW1 helmet. Linda came over with a menu, and saw the tattoos, and called "Dad! Got a Marine here!" and gave the guy a big smile. Her Dad came out from the kitchen, looked at the back of the guy's jacket and started laughing. "I love the jacket, Buddy! WELCOME HOME, MARINE!" and grabs the guy's hand and almost shakes him off the stool.

I could see the back of the jacket when he got turned around. There was a big, embroidered map of North and South Vietnam, and across the shoulders it said "Vietnam" and at the DMZ border "If You Weren't There:" and at the bottom "Shut the Fuck Up."

Linda's Dad was still pumping the guy's arm. "Whatever you want is on the house, buddy. Just tell my girl." He pounded him on the shoulder a few times and went back to the kitchen.

When he turned around, Linda had already poured him a cup of coffee. He shook his head and said "All I need is a phone book. Every phone booth in town has books that're all torn up, and I can't find who I'm looking for." Linda gave him another smile, and said she'd get the one they had, but people tore pages out of that one, too.

I was staring at him. He looked familiar, sort of, but the look in his eyes reminded me of Billy when he had nightmares. The name above the pocket read MacTavish. I knew him! Mac from grade school! I hadn't seen him for four years, and I remembered I cried on him both times when the Kennedys got killed.

"Mac? I'm Sally Osterhoff. Do you remember me?"

He looked at me, and I could see the memories come back. "Yeah. Hi. Nice to see you." He tried to smile. "You still doing Math? And swimming?"

Linda came back with the phone book, and he almost grabbed it out of her hands, and started flipping pages. He got to a page that had been torn out and slammed his fist on the counter. His eyes looked like he wanted to start screaming and never stop, and he slumped on the stool. "Every book.

Every damned one. Always the same page gone. Jesus."

"Mac? Who are you looking for?"

He slumped even further on the stool and held his head in his hands. "I'm trying to find a buddy. At least I thought he was a buddy. Telephone operators won't give you a number unless you have an address, and I don't have a goddam address, just his name."

"If he's a local, maybe I can help" Linda said. "What's his name?

"Billy Palkin."

The first day of kindergarten came back to me in a rush. *Steven* MacTavish. His mother called him Stevie, but he wanted to be called Mac.

Steve.

I grabbed him by the shoulders. "Mac! You're *Steve*! Billy's my cousin! He told us you stepped on a land mine and pungi sticks and they took you away and they came back and took all your stuff, but they didn't take your gun or clothes and everybody thought you died from an infection, and he thinks you're dead but you're NOT! Mac! YOU'RE STEVE!"

He stood up slowly. "Where is he?" he whispered.

"We're all just right up Ocean Highway" I started to say, but he grabbed my arm and pulled me off the stool. I yelped, and grabbed my side, and he stepped back and looked scared and said he was sorry. He looked more and more like he was going to start screaming and never stop. I told him it was okay; I had just had my appendix out and I was still sore, and that he didn't really hurt me, and that I'd take him to see Billy right now.

Linda looked worried. "Sally, are you alright?"

I told her yeah, and I'd explain the next time I saw her.

We went out to the parking lot, and I asked where his car was.

He pointed to a big yellow motorcycle with "Triumph" written on the gas tank.

I tried to tell him I never had, and I couldn't, but he told me to spread my legs, and he picked up the whole front of the motorcycle, motor and all, with ONE hand, and leveraged me onto the seat.

He pushed his helmet on my head. I could feel it pull my hair and bend my ears, and the strap under my chin was too tight. He pointed down:

"Footpegs. Push 'em down and put your feet on 'em." He swung his left leg over the motorcycle, and I saw a brace on his boot that had been spray-painted black. He flipped a pedal down on the right side of the motor, and jumped on it, and it started.

"Which way?"

I pointed North, and he shot straight out into traffic.

I don't think they heard me scream in Baltimore, but I know they had to in Salisbury.

We ROARED up Ocean Highway until we came to a red light. He grabbed my hands and tried to pull them from around his waist, but I wasn't letting go. He finally yanked them loose and stuffed them in his jacket pockets. "How much further?"

"Just keep going. I'll let you know."

We finally got there, and I pointed, and he went across the yard to the front porch steps. For a second, I thought he was going to go up and inside. He got off, and I yelled for him to get me off, too, and he came back and lifted the motorcycle again. I thought that skinny as he was, he sure was strong. He clumped up the steps, and raised his fist like he was going to pound on the door, but stopped and pushed the doorbell instead, and pushed it two more times.

Billy opened the door in his boxer shorts, took one look at Mac, and fainted. Marie got there just in time to catch him and tried to pull her bathrobe closed at the same time. Billy came to, took another look, and fainted again. Marie yelled "Who the Hell are *you*?" and I said "Marie! It's Mac MacTavish! From school! HE'S *STEVE*!"

Marie turned pale. "But Billy said... Oh my God he thinks you're dead he said you were dead he told us, and he has nightmares and he— "

Billy snapped awake, looked up at Mac, got up shaking, and stared at him. Then he grabbed him and started crying, and I mean big, BIG sobs, and tried to say, "It's you, you're alive, you're not dead, you're alive, you're here."

Mac looked down at Billy, and then me, then Marie, then Billy again, and said "You *didn't* forget me. You thought I was dead." He wrapped his arms around Billy, and *he* cried.

I got up the steps and went inside with Marie. While she got dressed, I told her everything. We waited inside until they stopped crying. Marie took a deep breath and went to the porch.

"Hi, Mac. Sal says you didn't eat anything at the diner. You hungry?"

Mac made some huffing sounds, like he was out of breath, and I realized that was how he laughed now. I looked at him more closely. He'd changed a lot in four years. The same way Billy had changed. They were both… damaged.

I had never wanted to say that word around Billy, but yeah, that's what the matter was with both of them.

Marie started pulling food out of the refrigerator, and I put a frying pan on the stove, and she and I sliced, chopped and beat eggs, and we both carefully didn't watch Billy and Mac.

By the time we had food on the table, Billy had put some clothes on, and we all sat down, and Mac talked while he ate.

Mac didn't remember that Marie was my friend, and he didn't recognize her in that photo (yeah, I thought, you weren't looking at her face), and he didn't recognize me in that blurry picture she took, and Billy had only said it was his cousin Sally, and didn't say what my last name was, but he said he remembered me when we saw each other at the diner. He said he remembered that I was the prettiest and smartest girl in school, and that I loved swimming, and did I ever go to the Olympics?

Well, *that* slowed the conversation down. It was nice that he remembered all that about me, but what *we* all wanted to know is what had happened to HIM.

Aunt Sally and Aunt Carmella came rushing in then, and Aunt Sally said Aunt Carmella got the shivers and said they had to go home NOW, so what's going on?

When they found out who Mac was, they both started crying, and hugged him, and Aunt Carmella wanted to start cooking again. Then when Uncle Vince and Uncle Bill both came home, it started all over.

Mac told us a little about what happened to him, and I think it must have been worse than he said. He told us that whoever shit on those pungi sticks must have had every disease known to mankind, because it took months just to get the infections under control. The doctors all wanted to amputate, but he wouldn't let them, and there were a lot of operations for MONTHS to reconstruct his foot, but it was okay now, and it gets better each time he has an operation, and yes, he still needs some more surgery, but he's fine.

Something about the way he told it made me not believe it.

Mac said he was going to get a hotel room somewhere, and we all told him he's family, and that he was staying here, no argument. He got even quieter, and looked at the floor, and finally said okay and thank you.

He had ONE change of clothes in the saddle bags on his motorcycle, and he took a shower while Aunt Sally took his clothes to the laundromat. There was more talking, and more cooking, and then it was evening, and Aunt Carmella and Uncle Vince went back to their cottage. Uncle Bill brought out the roll-away bed, and Aunt Sally made it, and we all went to sleep.

Until 1AM.

I heard moaning, and I thought it was Marie and Billy getting it on again, but it got louder, and then the screaming started.

It was Mac.

He screamed "Billy, come back, don't leave me, *please*!" and howled like something that had gotten caught in a trap, and I remembered that was exactly what had happened to him. Billy started screaming next, and he woke up and got to Mac before the rest of us. They stood there shaking and hanging on to each other, and cried, and the rest of us stood there and watched.

Billy didn't have anything on. Marie went back to their bedroom and came out with a pair of boxer shorts. When Mac and Billy began to calm down, she said "Hey, Nature Boy. Put these on, you two look a little funny like that."

They looked down, and they both tried to laugh. Billy pulled his shorts on, and asked Mac if he was okay, and Mac asked if Billy was, and they hugged one more time, and we all went back to bed.

Until 3AM, when it happened again.

And again at 4:30.

And again, for the next two nights.

On the third night, they didn't go back to sleep. They took two lawn chairs, and sat out in the backyard, and started talking, quietly at first, but then louder as they relaxed.

Marie knocked on Aunt Sally's door and went in. I could hear her saying "Dad, I'm scared. He was doing so much better, he wasn't having the bad nightmares anymore, just the little ones. Dad, I don't want Billy to get lost in the dark again."

I heard Uncle Bill say, "Honey, don't worry. Billy went back in so he could bring his buddy out. They'll be okay."

She asked if he was sure, and he said yeah, and to go back to sleep, but she came into my room instead. We listened to Billy and Mac outside.

I guess I'd better start calling Mac "Steve." He's not really Mac anymore.

Steve talked some more about his foot and the doctors. He must have taken off all those socks he wears on his foot and showed Billy. Billy said... well, Billy always did have an extensive and expressive vocabulary.

Steve wanted to know what Billy had done after he'd left Vietnam and went back to "the world."

Billy told him that just before he got on the airplane in Saigon, they tried to give him a medal, and he threw it into a trash can, and they pulled it out and tried to give it to him again, and he threw it out the window. There was a whole lot of yelling, and he walked out on them.

When he got to that aircraft carrier a month later, the Admiral tried to give him the medal again, and ordered Billy to wear it. Billy told the Admiral that he didn't want it and wouldn't wear it. That's when Billy got his reduction in rank.

He said the Admiral wanted all his "Side Boys" to be HEROES, and that was why he got picked for that duty. He didn't like the Admiral.

When the astronauts came back from the moon, they were in that special quarantine trailer like the other astronauts had been. Billy was one of the guards that stood outside. He said that one of the astronauts kept calling him "kid" and wanted him to make a "geedunk run" (*), whatever that is, and to put it in the little door where all the medical stuff goes in and out of the trailer. (*note: "geedunk" is Navy slang for candy, soda, ice cream, etc.)

Billy told him "Sir, I believe you meant to say 'Sergeant,' not kid, and I will not leave my post, nor will I violate contact orders with you."

He said the astronaut kept calling him "kid" and "baby Marine" and Billy finally told him "Look, *AIREDALE* (*), I have my orders, and if you don't like it, complain to the Chaplain." (*note: Navy slang for a pilot)

And that's how Billy got sent to Midway Island to "count the flagpole."

Billy said his "fellow screw-ups" were all good men and didn't deserve "exile." There was another Sergeant that had just brought his men "out of the bush" with two men dead and two injured, and some 2nd Lieutenant fresh out of college told him to line his men up for "personnel inspection." The Sergeant told him... well, Billy said even *he* couldn't hold a candle to that guy's vocabulary.

Billy's C.O., the Major, got sent there because his men had been ordered to take some hill, pull out a day later, take it again and pull out, take it a third time, and that's when the Major refused a direct order, and got relieved and reassigned, and the next time his men got told to take the hill, nearly all of them got killed.

Billy said that after every war is over, they should hang all the Politicians and Generals and Admirals from BOTH sides, "as thousands cheer."

Right about then, the guy in the rental house next door yelled out the window to Billy and Steve "Why don't you two 'heroes' shut up and let people sleep!"

Wow, that fast, Uncle Bill was out in the backyard and... he sort of invited the guy to "come out and play." I'd never heard Uncle Bill get so mad or talk like that before. The guy didn't say anything back, and Uncle Bill told Billy and Steve to come back in and go to bed.

After that night, the nightmares still happened, but not as bad or as often. They didn't scream anymore, or at least only a little. I got up a couple of nights and sat with Steve till he calmed down and went back to sleep. He would tell me some "funny stories."

They weren't. They scared me to death. But I listened to them anyway. Sometimes there was more Mac than Steve, but not too often.

The day before the Olympics started, I went to see Dr. Flanaghan to get my stitches and drains taken out. Billy, Marie, and Steve all came with me. I didn't understand why, until we pulled into the parking lot of St. Mary's Star of the Sea, and we went in.

Father Perman was in his office, and he looked at Billy and Marie and said "What, didn't it take?"

Billy told him about Steve, and that he had always wanted Steve to be his Best Man, and he and Marie wanted to do it again, right then and there, with Steve.

This time, I'll remember ALL of it.

CHAPTER SEVENTY-FIVE

The Games

The 1972 Summer Games at Munich were finally here, but I wasn't there. That hurt.

I was happy for Doris, though, and Steve and Marie and I cheered when we saw her march in with the American team. Steve remembered how quiet she was in grade school, and he wanted to know what competition she was in, and how she learned that, and how good she was. I told him you don't get to the Olympics unless you're the best, and I felt sorry for myself again.

Having the cable gave us an extra ABC channel that had LIVE broadcasts of the games, more than you'd see at night. Very early one morning, we watched a practice session for women's diving. Jim McKay was talking and killing time before the American team came in, and right after they did, the Japanese team showed up, then the Soviets, and then the French. Jim McKay was saying that it looked like there was some confusion over who was supposed to practice, and all the teams were looking at each other and not smiling, and their coaches were talking, and they didn't look happy, either. Then the Australians came in, and the finger-pointing and hand-waving started.

That's when Doris climbed to the top of the 3-meter board, yelled "CANNONBALL!," and ran off the end of the board and made a huge splash.

ALL the coaches were yelling now, but the Japanese team started giggling, and two of them left their group, climbed the board, walked out together, and pushed each other off simultaneously, and made *two* cannonballs. The Australians were the next to go crazy, and one of their girls ran off the end of the board and kept on running like the Coyote in the

Roadrunner cartoons.

The French team walked out with their noses in the air, but one of them broke and ran back and jumped in the pool and started splashing everyone, including Jim McKay. He was laughing so hard he couldn't get away. The French coach SCREAMED at her, and she got out and left, but she was grinning ear-to-ear.

The Soviet coach blew her whistle, and everything stopped. She walked over to the edge of the pool and leaned over like she was going to yell at someone, but then she JUMPED and did a huge bellyflop that I knew must have hurt. NOBODY expected it. I never thought any of them had a sense of humor.

I was laughing so hard I was doubled-up, and I thought my incision was going to split open. Steve laughed that huff of his, and Marie was cheering "YAY DORIS!" Billy and Aunt Sally sat there with their mouths hanging open. I guess you had to know Doris to appreciate it.

They went to a commercial, and when they came back, it was sword-fighting.

I needed to get into water— any water. Dr Flanaghan told me no swimming until the holes where my drains had been healed completely, and that was a couple of weeks away, but I just had to go down to the surf and walk in it for a while. Steve, Billy, and Marie followed me.

I was still walking bent over a little and had a hard time keeping my balance on the soft sand. Steve got mad when Billy tried to steady *him*, so I asked Steve if he'd help *me*, and we held each other up. He couldn't come down all the way to the surf because he didn't want to take his boots off, so I went in by myself and slowly walked back and forth, and got my legs wet only a little bit above my knees. Even though I knew I'd never compete again, I'd still swim every day for the rest of my life, just like Aunt Viv. Marie says she will, too, so that she doesn't end up looking like a fat Italian Mama in a black dress like Aunt Gina.

Then I started crying on Steve, and I snotted-up his shoulder. I wished I was in Munich.

Two days later were the women's diving competitions, and every time it was Doris' turn, Jim McKay announced her as Doris "Cannonball" Johnson. He wasn't treating her like a clown, though. He said that she had her Master's in Chemistry after only *three* years of college, was going for her Doctorate, and had *always* been an "A" student and a member of the National Honor Society— all true! He also pointed out how popular she was with people on the other diving teams from all over the world, and that if she wasn't an example of the Olympic Ideal, he didn't know who could be.

Competition was very tight, and the judging very hard. It all came down to the last round of dives, but at the end of it, the U.S. won the Gold— but it wasn't Doris.

It was strange to watch. Everybody was congratulating the girls that medaled, but everybody was hugging Doris, too, and they all looked disappointed that she hadn't made it to the stands. One of the Japanese girls was crying when she hugged Doris. I think Doris made a lot of friends at the Games, and I thought I should have remembered something about that, but I didn't know what.

We all went back to Baltimore. Classes would be starting again for me at College Park, Marie was transferring to the Baltimore campus, Billy was starting Fireman's training, and Steve had to go back to work. He had a job with the Johnson Controls Company's apprenticeship program to be an air conditioning and refrigeration mechanic. He says there's good money in it, and lots of jobs around. He was living on South Conklin Street too, in a little apartment a few blocks away, so we'll all get together at weekends.

When I got back to the dorm, there was something I had to do, and I wasn't sure how. I had to thank Cynthia Smith for calling the ambulance. I had never liked her, but it wasn't as if I had ever made some kind of decision long ago *not* to like her. I finally walked down the hall to her room and knocked on the door. I thought I had better step back, too, in case she still felt nervous about me grabbing her that day when Billy came back from Vietnam.

Who was I kidding, *I* was the one who was nervous.

She opened the door and twitched when she saw me, but she said hi and said Doris had told her all that had happened, and was I okay? I said yeah, and thank you for calling the ambulance, and I was glad she had been there for summer session, and that I was sorry for that day I almost beat her up, and the time I yanked her bikini top open. She laughed and said don't ruin her opinion of me and closed the door. When I turned away, she opened it again and said you're welcome, and that she was honestly sorry I didn't go to the Olympics so she could "boo" me. We both laughed then, even though I think she meant it.

Okay, and I'm avoiding important stuff again. Back at the Olympics, Palestinians had broken into the Israeli dorm rooms and kidnapped and killed eleven of the Israeli athletes. It looked like the police didn't even try to do anything to stop it or to save anyone, and they even let them get away. The TV showed the whole thing like it was some kind of movie. Uncle Vince said anybody who expected the Germans to do anything to save Jews was simple-minded. People thought that the Games should be cancelled or something, and they were stopped for a day, but Avery Brundage, the guy running the Olympics, said that "the Games will go on, and not be affected by politics."

I wished I was there just so I could kick him in his balls, like Adrienne did. "Politics" my sweet pink ass!

Doris came back on the 14th. She brought me a jacket, and team pins from all over the world. I said thanks, and I tried the jacket on, and we sorted all the pins, but it felt wrong. Doris felt the same way. She said it was like someone stole all the bubbles out of the champagne and left poison. I said I felt sorry for the people who won. Every time they'd look at their medals, they'd remember what else had happened. I'd always wanted to go to the Olympics, but now I was almost glad I hadn't. I don't think I'd ever have felt happy again if I'd won. I told her about Mac MacTavish and how I found him and brought him home to Billy, and she grinned and said, "I guess you saved his life."

She told me she had been "summoned" to Avery Brundage twice. The first time was for "embarrassing" the U.S. team with her "clowning around" at that practice, and it was all "YOU people" this and "YOU people" that, and she should "learn her place." When he got to that part, she walked out. The second time was for being "too popular" with the other athletes and trying to "worm her way" into getting some award for being a good sport, and that he didn't want her at the Games anymore. She told him he should be more concerned over what had happened with the Israelis, but he said "THOSE people" always bring trouble on themselves. She told him that he was all "YOU people" and "THOSE people," and that if he wanted her gone, "You OLD people" can get on TV, and tell the whole world that she was out and why, and that he was lucky she was raised a good Christian, otherwise she'd be throwing his Honky ass out the window, and walked out.

I put the jacket in my closet, and the pins in my puzzle box, and we went swimming together that evening— the first time since my appendectomy. God, it hurt! But it felt good, too. It made the other hurts go away for a while.

CHAPTER SEVENTY-SIX

Puzzle

The second week of October I asked Dr. Wheeler how I was doing, and he told me it was "going to be like cooking Sunday Dinner on an old woodstove. Everything's got to be done to a turn at the same time, and we have to wait for the rooster to come a'struttin' in and ask for a trim. Meanwhile, gal, just to keep you occupied when I'm not teaching you, howsabout you take a crack at this here thing that I haven't had time to fiddle with? It's like one of those little puzzles you see on the back page of Reader's Digest. No rush. But don't dawdle."

This *never* came from Reader's Digest.

It was a theory about Prime numbers, and... well, it was pretty convoluted, and it would probably bore the rest of the world to tears, but to me, and to other mathematicians, it was interesting. Okay, EXTREMELY interesting, but also frustrating as Hell! Every time I thought I had a solution, somewhere it wouldn't apply.

Miss Clementine gave me a key to the offices, and told Security I might be working late, or coming in early. Doris would come at suppertime and drag me off to eat and take me to swim for a couple of hours, but I'd find my way back to the office afterwards.

One evening, right in the middle of a lap, I got out of the pool, and ran back to the offices, and "got all het up" as Dr. Wheeler says, and worked the whole night through, and did it! I solved the damned thing! It was beautiful! It was elegant! It was... it was... it was "slicker'n eel snot!" as Dr. Wheeler would say, and I was "a'snortin' like a hawg in a waller," and "a'grinnin' like a mule eatin' briars," and "John, when is she going to come back from wherever it is that she goes to?"

That's when I realized it was morning, and they were both standing beside me.

And that I was in my bathing suit.

Dr. Wheeler said "It could have been worse, gal. You could've been like Archimedes in the bathtub and ran around in your birthday suit."

I went back to the gym (and did I get some stares— it was the end of October!); got showered and dressed, then back to the office. Miss Clementine was writing all my work down as Dr. Wheeler was reading it to her, and they both turned and told me to get out, go eat breakfast, get some sleep, take the day off, take TWO days off, take the WHOLE WEEK off, in fact don't come back till we call for you.

Halfway to the cafeteria, I realized I was dead on my feet, and went back to the dorm and slept until Doris shook me awake that evening and said she was going to take me to the Rustler Steak House and buy me a Prime Rib, her treat.

When we got there, Dr. Wheeler and Miss Clementine, Dad, Marie, Billy, Steve, Aunt Carmella and Uncle Vince were all there, and I wondered what was going on.

I found out.

I felt like Rip Van Winkle. A lot of things happened today while I was sleeping.

First off, that "little puzzle" I'd solved was Staszkiewicz's 3rd Theory from two hundred years ago, and I had refuted Yaskov's negative proof from one hundred years ago. Miss Clementine hand-delivered a copy of my solution to Johns Hopkins University and mailed copies to a bunch of other colleges. She also typed it up as my Doctoral Thesis.

Secondly, that's right: my "Doctoral Thesis"— my "original contribution to the field of mathematics." I asked what about my Master's? and Dr. Wheeler said "Oh, didn't I tell you, end of last Winter? Well, you had a lot on your mind then, and I didn't want to fret you." Bald-headed old fart. I'll get him for that.

Third, it seems that Dr. Collins had been making his annual "threats" of going to another college that would give him the tenure he deserved, and what did Dr. Wheeler and the University intend to do? After all, it was mid-semester, no one to take his place, blah blah blah blah and blah.

Dr. Wheeler shook his hand, wished him luck at his new position whatever that might be, Campus Security will be along shortly to help you carry all your old Playboy magazines out to the parking lot for you, don't let the doorknob catch you on your fat ass on the way out, and SO LONG!

Fourth, there was now an opening for a new instructor, and would I be interested? No tenure being offered, *yet*, but be patient. After all, someone of my stature in the lofty field of higher mathematics would certainly bring a large measure of prestige to the University of Maryland.

Can you dig it? *DOCTOR* Sally Osterhoff. B.S., M.S., PhD. (We in Academia know that that means Bull Shit, More Shit, and Piled Higher and Deeper than yours.)

far freakin' out

I started giggling, but then I was crying, and all over Steve as usual. Everybody was looking at us funny. I probably would have cried on anybody sitting next to me, and Steve made a joke that he was my human Kleenex, and he didn't mind. Steve's a really nice guy, and I kinda like him a lot. He sort of balances us out when we hang out with Marie and Billy.

Oh, there was a fifth thing.

I had to start teaching in the morning.

So much for "take the whole week off."

Miss Clementine had already typed out my schedule and had even managed to still set up times and places for me to tutor all my Jocks.

As far as lesson plans are concerned, she and Dr. Wheeler would help me with that, just as soon as I straightened out the mess left behind by Collins and his so-called teaching, and don't you worry, gal, you can do it.

I did, too.

I still lived in the dorm for a "small, nominal cost" until Christmas, and then I was sent to UMBC to teach. I'd miss John and Clementine (and it felt strange to call them that, but that's what they wanted), but Clementine said we would see each other at all the big Faculty meetings and conferences, and she would make sure John would attend them, like it or not, if only just to see me.

I moved back in with Aunt Carmella and Uncle Vince, and we had a big argument over how much rent I would pay, and we all found out I knew a lot more Italian besides swear words.

Marie finished her Master's in December and started working at USF&G. Billy had completed Fireman's training and had almost finished all those special courses for his Ambulance Certification. He said the Fire Departments and the State are pushing for even more training nowadays, and they want them to be called Emergency Medical Technicians, just as soon as the hospitals stop dragging their feet. He says they act like the Fire Departments are business competitors.

CHAPTER SEVENTY-SEVEN

Changes

When Marie and Billy moved to Ocean City, Steve and I visited them on weekends. If it was cold or rainy, I'd drive, but if it was sunny and warm, I'd ride on the back of his motorcycle. He gave me a helmet and leather jacket, so it's like I have to do it, or I might hurt his feelings. Steve's nice, so I wouldn't want to do that.

At the end of the Spring semester, I had to decide whether to go down to the ocean and waitress or teach the summer session. I lost all my Jocks when I came to UMBC, so if I wanted money for my house, I'd better teach. Thank God for the weekends and thank God for Steve when we didn't go to the ocean. We'd hang out together "to fill the empty hours of our existence," as Billy would say. I like Steve, he's fun. Although he can be a real jerk, sometimes. No, sometimes he's a real pain in the ass, like when he had more surgery on his foot and didn't tell me about it.

He called me at Aunt Carmella's when he got out, and we went to dinner and a movie. He was clumping around with the brace again, and when I asked about it, he got all touchy and whiny, and finally admitted that he'd had another operation. The trips down to Ocean City weren't too comfortable the rest of the summer. On my vacation in August, Marie and I would run in the mornings at the surf's edge, and even she got on my nerves one day when she said that Steve and I should patch up our "lover's quarrel." I told her there was nothing going on, and all she did was smirk. Just because she's married, she thinks I should be, too.

Steve and I finally apologized (HIM first), and things went back to the way they were, but we were NOT dating and NOT a couple, we just hung out, and it wasn't anybody else's damned business.

Thanksgiving was at Aunt Carmella's that year, and the families went crazy when Marie stood up after dinner and patted her tummy and said, "Guess what I have in here besides turkey?"

I don't know if it's a good or a bad thing that liquor stores are open on Thanksgiving, but the only two people that were sober were Marie and I. We finally got to be alone in my bedroom with the door locked.

She was due in June, and I was going to be Godmother, and the best Aunt in the world, and they were going to ask Steve to be Godfather when we all got together on Saturday, and don't forget, Sorella, you're going to be building two houses for all of us to live together sometime soon, and yes, she was going to hold me to that.

I have to admit I felt a little relieved when she said that. I'd been feeling that we weren't as close as we always had been, and I missed her. I wasn't sure what she meant by *all* of us, and I very carefully didn't ask.

It feels like everybody wants to play matchmaker.

Christmas came, and New Year's, and Easter, and I found out that I was expected to organize a baby shower. Thank God Aunt Carmella "offered" to help, along with every other woman in the families, and it ended up that the only thing I had to do was mail the invitations.

It was at the Sons of Italy Hall, and Maria's 301 catered, and Vacarro's supplied the cake, so I guess Aunt Carmella made up for the wedding.

And the presents! My God, you would have thought Marie was having a litter! And it was all girl things because Mama Loretta said it was going to be a girl, and she was never wrong.

Aunt Viv and Adrienne were there, and Doris and Adrienne were head-to-head the whole party, and I guess they talked about the Olympics all afternoon, and they left together afterwards.

The closer Marie got to her due date, the more nervous I got. Aunt Carmella told me to knock it off, and that she was doing all the worrying for everybody. She finally had enough and called Dad and told him to come and pick me up on Saturday morning, and have me build a house or *something, anything*; and somewhere, anywhere but home with her.

Dad had been let go by the railroad after their latest merger, but with the severance package and all the pay from his accumulated vacation time, he had bought a tiny little lot with an even tinier little building on the edge of a farm in Strasburg Pennsylvania. "Osterhoff Furniture" is a small business that will repair or make exact reproductions of fancy antique furniture. We spent a day working together just like we did when I was growing up. Dad finally feels happy.

CHAPTER SEVENTY-EIGHT

Stopwatch and Clock

The Spring semester ended, and I had a couple of weeks off before the summer classes. Aunt Carmella told me to go see Marie and give *her* the benefit of my worrying.

I got to Ocean City about six o'clock Thursday evening, just in time for supper— at the Diner. Linda's dad asked where Steve was, and when we were going to "get off the dime." I'm getting tired of explaining to people that we're just friends. Steve doesn't say anything when people ask him, so maybe I should start doing the same.

I went home to Aunt Sally's, and my bedroom was filled with baby stuff. I didn't know how they were going to find room for the baby. I found out that Dad had come down and bumped-out the bathroom to make room for a washer and dryer. I was a little hurt that he didn't ask me to help, but Aunt Sally said all I would've done was fuss over Marie.

Marie looked more beautiful each time I looked at her. That Little Orphan Annie hair of hers was thicker than ever, her face was round and smooth, and her boobs looked like something out of Playboy magazine. Her tummy— no, her belly— looked like she was ready to explode. She said, "At least my tail never spread." She'd been wearing halter tops and men's shorts, and I wondered why maternity clothes tried to cover everything. She was pretty!

Of course, *I'm* never going to be doing this. I'll stick with trying to be a nice Aunt.

On Friday morning, Aunt Sally went to school, Uncle Bill and Billy went to the Firehouse, and I made breakfast for Marie, and was probably annoying her. She looked irritated and asked me to rub her back so that I would calm down.

A couple of times, I felt some muscles tighten up, and she'd grunt. I asked if I was rubbing too hard, and she said no, and just ignore it and don't worry about it, it was just the baby trying to get comfortable, and she asked me to move the alarm clock to where she could see what time it was.

Then she wanted to get up and walk. Not down at the beach, but just back and forth in the living room. She had a pocket watch on a lanyard, and twirled it on her finger, and looked at it a few times. I was starting to worry. She stopped pacing and looked at me.

"Alright, listen up!" she said. "Are you listening to me?"

I nodded. My mouth had gone dry.

"Then shut up and stay quiet." She took a couple of deep breaths. "I think I'm in labor, and-if-you-open-your-mouth-I-will-slap-you *SO* hard, you'll think your mother was here. So, *shut up*."

I nodded again.

"Dr. Julia says first babies take a LONG time to get here, so we are NOT going ANYWHERE. Are you still listening? This isn't TV, it's not the movies, it's going to take a looong time. Did you hear me? We are BOTH going to relax, okay?" She handed me the cheap stopwatch, and she showed me which buttons to push. "Get a piece of paper and a pencil. When I tell you, you will start the stopwatch, and write down the time on the kitchen clock. When I tell you again, you will stop the stopwatch, write down the time on the kitchen clock, and write down the time on the stopwatch. Got it? You want me to repeat it?"

I started to nod, shook my head, and nodded again.

Marie sighed and repeated everything. Then she hugged and kissed me. "Relax, Sorella, everything will be fine." She laughed. "Maybe you should take notes for when it's your turn."

Not me, I thought. "Should we call anyone?"

"I'll call the doctor. Nobody else." She closed her eyes and rubbed her arms. "Ma knows. I can feel it." She shook her head and laughed again. "Ma's probably on the phone right now, trying to get in touch with Pop. It's going to be a long time before they get here, 'cause it's a Friday. Poor Pop."

Oh, God, I thought, Aunt Carmella will have gone crazy by then. Wait a minute— "Marie... are you... I mean, do you get... 'feelings' like your Ma?"

"Sometimes" she said. "Not a lot. Nothing like Ma. Or Mama Loretta. Just since I got pregnant." She started walking again and stopped. "Okay" she said. "Now. Stopwatch and clock."

My hands were shaking. "Stop shaking" she told me. I stopped.

We did this all morning, and into the afternoon. I calmed down after the first few contractions. The magic number was FIVE minutes apart, and we weren't there yet, Sorella, not by a long shot.

But they *were* getting stronger. About 3 o'clock, she was hanging off my neck while a big one came. When it was over, she straightened up, looked at me, and kissed me— harder than we usually do.

"I want you to know something— just in case something happens— and *NOTHING* is going to happen— but just in case." She looked very serious. "I still honest-to-God believe that me and you were supposed to be sisters. It was never just some little-kid thing."

I looked into her eyes. "I've never believed anything else— Sorella Mio." I kissed her back, just as hard.

We looked at each other. "Okay, then" she said.

"Okay."

We laughed a little and held each other close for the next two contractions.

Uncle Bill and Billy came home at 3:30. Billy called out "Twins! Dr. Palkin once again saves the day for the tourist industry!" Then he saw Marie. "How far apart?"

"About six minutes" I told him and showed him my notes.

"Water broke?" he asked.

"No" she said.

He went into their bedroom and came out with one of those blood pressure things, and wrapped it around her arm, while Uncle Bill took her pulse. They relaxed. "Okay" Billy said. "You ready to go now?"

We heard Aunt Sally drive up.

"Yeah" Marie told him, and grinned. "Ma's probably there waiting for us."

She was.

"You couldn't call and let me know?" she cried, and hugged Marie. "*One* phone call?"

"Ma. Did I need to call?"

Aunt Carmella stroked her face and arms and belly. "You still should've. We coulda been here *hours* ago."

Uncle Vince hugged her. "You okay? No problems?" I could see that he was trying not to show how worried he was.

"I'm fine, Pop. Sal's been taking care of me."

Sure, I thought. Marie's been keeping *me* from running around screaming.

Billy came back from the Registration Desk. "Dr. Julia has another birthing going on right now, so we'll go back, and she'll be around soon and do an exam. We'll go to the Delivery Room when it's time."

"They're letting YOU go in?" Aunt Carmella asked.

"Yeah, Ma. Dr. Julia says it's better if a family member is there. It's something they do over in Europe."

Aunt Carmella had crossed her arms. "Sounds like more of that Hippie stuff to me. Why you? Why not her mother? Me?"

"Billy knows what to do, Ma" Marie told her. "He's delivered five babies since January. Twins today."

"I don't know" Aunt Carmella said. "I don't like it. Why can't I be there? Jeez, they'll be bringing back having them at home next." She was twisting her hands together. "Women DIED then. No. I'm coming with you."

"No, Ma."

"Marie—"

"NO, Ma."

"No, you listen to me— "

"*NO*, Ma! And that's IT, Ma." She placed Billy's hand on her belly. "My husband is going to be with me." Then she looked at me. "And my sister."

I stood there with my mouth hanging open. I didn't want to be there! I started to say "Marie— ", but Uncle Vince said "Carmella! Leave the kids alone!"

Aunt Carmella snapped at him. "It's none of your damned business, Vince! Stay out of this!"

"NO!" he said. "It's none of YOUR business! You go in there, you'll try to run things, and Christ knows what'll happen. Leave the kids ALONE."

Aunt Carmella was crying. She turned and started to walk away. "Carmella!" Uncle Vince snapped at her. She looked at him, and then us. "Alright" she said quietly. "I'll stay here and pray." She kissed all of us, and whispered to me, "Don't let this doctor do anything crazy."

Like I really know what's going on.

Billy and Marie and I went with a nurse to an exam room and waited. I still had the notepaper and watch. A few seconds later, another nurse came in.

"Okay, Marie, a quick peek, and I'll get back to you in a little while." She and Billy helped Marie get up onto the exam table. "Peel 'em off, Marie. Billy, get gowns and things for everybody, and show that one" (pointing to me) "how to scrub." She tugged the stirrups out and put Marie's heels in them, and I got a look at something I'll *never* forget.

"OHMYGODMARIEWHATHAPPENEDTOYOURTHING!?"

Then all this water just POURED out of Marie and splashed the nurse, and I thought it was my fault, and I was apologizing, and Billy was laughing, and Marie told me to shut up and calm down or she'd kill me, and then she'd kill Billy.

The nurse was down there feeling around and looking inside, and I was wondering when this Dr. Julia was going to show up, and for a change I thought before I opened my mouth. She was Dr. Julia.

She stood up. "Okay" she said. "Let's get you a room, and you let Billy take care of you, and YOU—you stand at the head of the bed, and don't say anything, just be with your—what? Girlfriend? Relative?"

"Sister," we said.

"That's fine. Just be quiet." She looked at Marie. "About another hour or so. We talked about spinals. You want one? Better decide now. Like I told you, it won't hurt the baby, but it might slow the contractions, and make this last a little longer."

Another contraction came. I was still keeping track. "Three minutes."

Marie closed her eyes. "The Hell with it. Let's just get this over with. No spinal."

"You're sure?"

"Yeah." She squeezed my hand and looked at Billy. "I'm sure."

Dr. Julia nodded and left. A nurse came in, and Billy took me outside to a set of big sinks and showed me what to do. He grabbed some towels and went back to Marie. Some old man, I guess he was a doctor, came over and said "Who the Hell let you in here? Probably that damned woman that thinks she knows more than a man does. Get out, or I'm throwing you out."

"Stop interfering with my cases, Doctor." Dr. Julia had come up behind him. "You" she said, looking at me, "Scrub." She turned to the old man. "One more time, Doctor. Just one. I don't think the Medical Ethics Board of this hospital– ". He turned away and stomped off. She mumbled something I didn't quite hear, looked at me, and said "Hurry along."

I finished washing, and we both went back to Marie's new room. She was in a bed, now, with a hospital gown, and her legs propped up. I didn't look this time. I went to the head of the bed and started toweling her face and neck. She was sweating more and more. Billy went out to wash. Dr. Julia was down there doing something, and said it'll be over faster than she thought. I hoped so. Marie looked terrible, and she was squeezing my hand so tight my fingers were numb. Dr. Julia and Billy were telling her to push and breathe and bear down and breathe and relax and breathe.

Dr. Julia patted Marie's foot. "Okay, Marie, it's time. Billy, get the gurney, and you -" she pointed to me "- you'll follow us, alright? By the way, what's your name?"

"Uh... Sally?"

She sighed. "You sure? Never mind. Let's go."

We got to the delivery room, and I was terrified. It didn't look like the kind of place you'd want to be born in. Marie took one look and almost crushed my hand.

Billy kissed her. "Don't worry, Felix, it's almost over."

Two nurses came in with this tray thing on wheels with knives and scissor things and stuff on it. They helped slide Marie from the cart onto the operating table. Dr. Julia started with the push and breathe again, and I wasn't looking, and I wasn't going to look at all, either. Dr. Julia said she was crowning, and the head was out, and the shoulders and here we go and it's a girl and the baby was crying, and Marie was crying, and Billy was crying, and I was crying too. They weighed and measured the baby and put her on top of Marie, all greasy and slimy looking. Marie was shaking so hard I was afraid the baby would fall off, but Billy said the shaking was normal. I hoped so.

Dr. Julia was still between Marie's legs, saying one more push and the placenta is out, and I really, REALLY didn't want to look.

Marie and Billy were moving the baby around and put her mouth on Marie's breast. That was weird—it wasn't a boob anymore. God, her nipples were HUGE.

Dr. Julia said Marie did great, no tears, so no stitches, and Billy made a crack that it would fit more comfortably now, and Dr. Julia jabbed him in his ribs for it. Then she did something I didn't understand.

She had this syringe with silver stuff in it, and a cotton ball, and the nurses turned away, and Dr. Julia squirted it into the cotton, and said left eye, right eye, and dropped it all into a steel pan. I looked at Billy, and he whispered that it's supposed to prevent syphilis from blinding a baby, and he put his hand over my mouth before I could say anything. Billy said it was all something about an old law, and some doctors just go through the motions, but it's still the law. He held my mouth until I nodded.

Dr. Julia said "Sally. Write this down: 6 o'clock on the dot, 8 pounds, 20 inches."

"And her name is Anne with an 'e,'" Marie said. "Little Annie Palkin. You can tell Granny Annie she's a Great-Granny, now."

I wrote it all down. "Okay" I said and waited.

All three of them rolled their eyes at me. "Waiting room. That way. Down the hall. On the left" Dr. Julia said. "Go. Now."

"Oh. Yeah. Right." I left.

Everybody in the waiting room looked up when I came in, and I remembered I still had my mask, head cap, and gown on, and maybe I looked like a nurse. So, me acting like a smart-ass, I went over to the family and said, "Mr. and Mrs. Giametti, Mr. and Mrs. Palkin, Mrs. Granny Annie, it's a girl, born at six o'clock, 8 pounds, 20 inches, and named Anne—with an 'e.'"

And that's when I fainted.

CHAPTER SEVENTY-NINE

Smoke and Mirrors

Marie came home in a couple of days, and Granny Annie almost moved in. When Marie wasn't feeding or changing her, Granny Annie was holding little Annie, and talking to her, and singing hymns to her (I'd never heard her sing before.) You would have thought Granny Annie was her mother.

Marie would sit all snuggled up with them, smiling and happy. Everybody except me was telling her to give someone else a chance to hold her, but Marie said it was okay, and that Granny Annie was happy and little Annie was happy. Uncle Bill said "Mom, you never made this much fuss with Adrienne or Billy."

Granny Annie hmphed at him, and said "Now, Bill, I knew I was going to have them till they grew up. But I'm 74 now, and I don't know how much longer I'll be on this Earth. I want little Annie to know she had a Great-Grandmother, and that I loved her. Now, YOU stop fussing."

I thought that so long as someone else was holding her I wouldn't have to. She SCARED me. They were all saying how big she was, but to me she was so tiny, and I knew if I dropped her or did something wrong, and she got hurt, I'd never forgive myself. No, sitting on the other side of the room was close enough. At least until she's big enough to walk over to me. I didn't know how long that would take.

Classes started, and I went back to Baltimore to teach. It would be a few weeks until little Annie's Baptism, and Steve and I went down to talk to Father Perman about what we were supposed to do as Godparents. According to the Church, we're supposed to be Catholic, but Aunt Carmella's saying "God won't care" again, and that she wasn't going to tell Father Perman.

Everything was going well, and everybody that had come to the wedding would be there for the Baptism.

But then we had to postpone it.

The Wednesday before it was supposed to be, Aunt Carmella woke Uncle Vince and I up at 4 o'clock in the morning, and said she smelled smoke and to get out fast. When we went out on the porch, she said she didn't smell it anymore, but she was shivering. We thought about Uncle Bill and Billy.

The phone finally rang at 8:30.

There had been a fire at Granny Annie's. Uncle Bill said it had started inside her car, and then the garage, and then the house. Her neighbors broke in and pulled Granny Annie out of her bed, and called the Fire Department and –

It was too late. It was the smoke that had taken her.

I went back upstairs and cried for my Granny Annie.

The funeral was on Monday, and the service was at St. Paul's By the Sea Episcopal. Granny Annie had wanted to be cremated (which felt a little creepy when you thought about how she died), and have her ashes taken out to the ocean. One of the big fishing boats took us out, and a lot of other boats followed. Granny Annie had a lot of friends, and many of them were fishing boat Captains. I had never known that Granny Annie was the Route 50 Bridge Keeper from World War 2 up until the State forced her to retire. She had raised and lowered the bridge every day, Tuesday through Saturday, 3PM till 11PM. Sally Oblivious Osterhoff, that's me.

Uncle Bill and Billy were quiet all day. They hadn't had the night shift when it happened, but Aunt Sally said they felt like things would have turned out differently if they had. Aunt Viv reminded them that Granny Annie hadn't wanted to go in her sleep, she wanted to be awake for it and see what all the fuss was about.

Yeah, that was my Granny Annie.

I hoped that little Annie would have a memory of her.

Annie's Baptism was two weeks later, right after Sunday Mass. It still felt sad. Everybody crowded into the dim Baptismal Nave in front of a big stained-glass window of Jesus and John the Baptist. I held Annie, and Steve stood next to me. Father Perman was about to start but the sun started to shine through the stained-glass and painted everyone in Technicolor. Father Perman looked at the window, and then at Marie. He grinned, and we all did what we were supposed to do, and said what we were supposed to say, and when it was over and everyone was leaving, Father Perman went to the window and peeked through a cracked pane and laughed. I went over to him and asked what was funny.

He said that the sun had shone through the window.

The window faced NORTH.

One of those trucks that carried big sheets of glass on their sides had pulled into the parking lot of the Florist store that was next to the Church and reflected the sun into the window.

Father Perman told me to tell Marie "No more signs from Heaven" because his heart couldn't take any more.

CHAPTER EIGHTY

The Naughty Lady

Summer ended, and I found out that Steve had had more surgery, and hadn't told me again or let me visit, even though he'd only been there for a week. I got mad and everybody started that "kiss and make-up" crap again. He finally apologized, and I did too, even though it wasn't my fault.

Thanksgiving came, and Aunt Carmella invited Steve to come with us, but he said he was spending it with his mother. I was annoyed that he didn't ask *me* to come, not that he should have, or that I would have, but still ...

Steve really irritates me sometimes.

Christmas came, and home to Ocean City. Annie's getting bigger, and not as scary to hold. Steve didn't come.

The day after Christmas, Aunt Sally and Aunt Carmella took off for the sales in Delaware, and Uncle Vince, Uncle Bill, and Billy went down to the VFW Hall to watch football.

Marie had put little Annie down for a nap, and she and I were sitting in front of the heater with our feet propped up. She stood and said, "Give me your car keys."

I told her I'd go anyplace she wanted me to go, but she said no, just give her the keys, because she was going stir-crazy, and needed to get out of the house for a while, and Annie's asleep and won't wake up for a couple of hours, and PLEEEZE give her the keys and let her go out and thanks and she'd be right back.

I was alone in the house with Annie.

I kept going into her room, and checking to see if she was still breathing, and not suffocating under her blanket, or was too cold, or getting ready to fall out of the crib, or –

She woke up and started crying.

I stood next to the crib and told her that Marie and everybody would all be home soon, and PLEASE don't cry, but she just got louder, and TEARS were coming out of her eyes and she held up her arms to me, and I picked her up for the first time all by myself, and what do I do NOW?

The radio started playing a really old, *old* song called "The Naughty Lady of Shady Lane" that I remembered from when I was a little kid, and I started singing to her.

Annie stopped crying and was watching me. Her eyes were wide open and so was her mouth. Yeah, Honey, your crazy Aunt Sally has totally freaked-out. Annie was smiling now, and that was better than crying, so I sang the next verse, and started swaying back and forth, and she started to laugh. I held her a little closer and danced with her around the living room, and she wrapped her arms around my neck. And then she SANG! Honest, she sang "EEEEEE," and I said "Yes! You're harmonizing! Okay, BIG finish! Ready?" and everybody was smiling at us, and we both sang the last stanza, and... wait... *everybody* was smiling?

I s-l-o-w-l-y turned around, and, yeah, EVERYBODY was smiling at us. They were waiting for me to say something.

I said "uh."

I tried again. "uh."

Okay, Sally, once more: "She ..."

Keep going: "The baby ..."

Be specific: "Little Annie ..."

I took a deep breath. "She woke up. I'm singing her a lullaby."

Even Annie went into hysterics.

Marie came over with her arms out, and I felt myself step back and hold Annie closer, and heard myself say "No, it's okay, I've got her" and they all laughed harder. Marie said, "I've got to feed her" and I backed up some more, and said, "I can do that" and Aunt Sally and Aunt Carmella were on the floor. Marie patted herself, and said "Uh uh, yours are still for show."

Oh. Yeah... I forgot.

I looked down at Annie, and she looked up at me with this absolutely adoring look in her eyes, and I thought, well, maybe one day, *maybe* I might want one, but then she frowned, and I felt her legs move, and she grunted and had a wet fart. I tried to hand her back to Marie, but now *she* backed up and said, "On second thought, you can have her a little longer."

I heard myself whine "Marie ..."

"C'mon" she laughed. "I'll talk you through it. This is what you get for playing carpenter instead of playing with baby dolls."

So, I did, and it was *everywhere*, and I mean EVERYWHERE, and why was it YELLOW? I got her cleaned up, and... YUCK! GROSS! And then after I got the clean diaper on her, she PEED, and I had to do it all over again, and the whole family couldn't breathe from laughing, and I really DON'T want one of these!

But then Annie smiled at me.

That smile. God, that beautiful, beautiful smile.

Maybe. One day. Maybe.

CHAPTER EIGHTY-ONE

Steve

Uncle Vince didn't want to be on the road too late on New Year's Eve with all the amateur drunks, so we closed the cottage for the winter and headed back to Baltimore right after lunch. We got home, unpacked, started the laundry, Uncle Vince got sent to the store, we had spaghetti olio for supper, and were in bed and asleep by 9 o'clock—the excitement never ends in our family!

I got up New Year's Day at seven, put on jeans, sweatshirt, and my sneakers, bounced down the stairs and into the kitchen, said "Happy New Year," hugged Uncle Vince from behind and kissed him on his bald spot. He growled and tried to swat me with the newspaper. I went around the table and said "Ma, I'm going out for a run, I'll be back in about an hour" and gave her a hug and a kiss.

Her head snapped up and she looked at me. "What did you say?"

"I... said I was going out for a run." She had a funny look on her face. "Ma? Are you okay?"

Her mouth moved, and she stood up and said in a rush "You haven't had anything to eat. Sit. I'll make you breakfast."

I took an apple out of the fruit bowl and held it up. "That's *not* breakfast. Sit."

I sat. She started with a thick slice of panettone, stuck it under the broiler to toast, spread some mascarpone and raisins on it, and put it on a saucer. She put a dollop of oil in a frying pan, cracked an egg into it, added diced salami and roasted peppers, poured me coffee, sat it all in front of me, wrapped her arms around me and kissed me.

I leaned back into her arms. Dear God, I loved her. If there was anyone who had raised me, it was her.

I ate my breakfast and tried to clean up, but she pushed me away from the sink, and said "Go. Run."

"Okay, Ma." I snagged that apple again, held it up, and grinned. She shook her head and rolled her eyes at me.

I grabbed my jacket and was closing the door behind me when I heard Uncle Vince say, "I don't think she heard what she said."

It must have been something on the radio.

Down the porch steps, some leg stretches, up Conklin, left on Eastern, into the park. I kept a steady pace and was making my third go-round when I saw this guy clumping along the path. Steve.

I slowed to a walk, and I told him about Christmas and little Annie, and we were just enjoying each other's company when he tripped and fell.

His left foot was twisted funny, and I leaned over to help him, but he drew back and yelled "Get the Hell away from me!"

I stared at him. "What the Hell is wrong with you? And don't you yell at me like that!" I leaned over again, and he yelled "Leave me alone! I'm fine, alright? Just go away!"

I looked down at his foot. "That is not 'fine.' And stop yelling!"

He managed to stand up on his right leg. His left foot was bent and twisted about 90 degrees from where it should be. Why wasn't he in pain? "You can go" he said. "I can walk now." He didn't look at me when he said it.

"If I help you over to that park bench, I can get my uncle and we can take you to—"

"Goddammit, I don't need any of your help! I'm not a cripple!" He tried to hop and fell over again.

"Oh, to Hell with this" I said, and grabbed his left arm, yanked him up, ducked, tucked my arm between his legs and got him in a Fireman's Carry across my shoulders.

"Put me down, dammit! I can do it myself!"

"Right" I said. "And if it snows tonight, do you want me to dig you out or wait till the Spring thaw?"

I carried him out of the park and put him on one of the benches facing Eastern Avenue. The Highland Bar was across the street from us. I looked at him. "If you move, or try to, I'll stomp on your other foot when I get back."

The Bar was open, and there were plenty of customers trying to drink their New Year's hangovers away. I went back to the phone booth and called home. "Ma, Billy's friend Steve just hurt his foot here in the park. Can Uncle Vince take us to the hospital?" I told her where we were, and went back to Steve, and told him we'd take him up the street to City Hospital.

"I can't" he said. "I have to go to the VA hospital."

"Then that's where we'll take you," and I sat there and listened to more crap that he was fine, and he tried to tell Uncle Vince the same thing. We slid him into the back seat, and I sat up front with Ma and Uncle Vince. When we got there, Uncle Vince ran in and got a nurse with a wheel chair, and then we had to listen to even more crap that we could go now, and we didn't need to be there, and Ma asked if there was someone he needed to call, and he said he'd take care of it and he didn't need any more help that he never asked for. Uncle Vince looked ready to punch him and asked if they taught "Jarheads" any manners in the Marines.

A nurse came over and told him that Dr. Chatterjee was in today and would be down to see him. Now he REALLY got mad, and wanted us out, NOW. I told him I wasn't going anywhere until I knew he was going to be alright. Before he could start yelling some more, Dr. Chatterjee came in, and introduced himself to us, and looked at Steve's foot and frowned. "No brace again." He had an accent.

Steve wasn't looking at any of us. "I don't need a brace" he mumbled. "I'm not a cripple."

Dr. Chatterjee looked disgusted. "I will cut off this boot and see how much injury you have caused again." He asked the nurse for shears.

Steve got all wound-up again, and said they were Frye boots, and they cost him $60. Dr. Chatterjee said well then, he'd just pull it off and cause even more damage. Steve didn't say anything else. The doctor cut the boot and all those socks he wore off.

It was the first time I'd ever seen his foot. It was horrible. There was only one toe, and everything else was nothing but scars.

"My God, Steve! If that's what it looks like AFTER all the reconstructive surgery, I'd hate to have seen what it looked like BEFORE!"

Dr. Chatterjee looked at me and Steve. "Reconstructive surgery?"

Steve said it wasn't any of my business, and for Christ's sake go home. The doctor told him to be quiet and not talk to his girlfriend in that tone of voice. The doctor told me there hadn't been any reconstructive surgery since Steve had been discharged from the Marines and said Steve should always be wearing his brace, because he kept damaging his foot when he didn't.

Now *I* got mad and yelled at Steve that he'd been lying to Billy, as well as me, and Billy kept thinking he was getting better, not worse, and he was going to break Billy's heart when he found out. Dr. Chatterjee and I took turns yelling at him, and we finally just ignored him, the selfish jerk.

Dr. Chatterjee told me everything about Steve's foot. He said that all the doctors in the Marines and the VA had been telling him since it happened that his best option was amputation. His foot was always getting damaged because he couldn't feel anything in it, and it was getting worse each time; all the bones in his foot including his ankle were like rotten toothpicks, and even fusing them didn't do any good. I looked at Steve's foot. "So, you can't fix it anymore?"

"No."

"And an amputation would be better?"

"HEY!" Steve yelled.

"Shh! I'm talking to your doctor."

"Yes" Dr. Chatterjee said. "He would actually have more mobility than he has now, with a prosthetic."

"I'm not giving up my bike!"

"SHH!" I asked the doctor "Would he be able to drive his motorcycle?"

"If he is riding it now, he will be able to ride it with a prosthetic."

"I won't feel to shift!"

"Shh!" Dr. Chatterjee poked his foot. "He feels nothing now. What he does feel is the resistance of the pedal in his calf muscles."

"You don't know that for sure!"

"SHH!" We both shushed him. "I DO know that for sure. I have another amputee patient who rides, and I have told Steve this, but he will not hear it."

"I DON'T WANT TO BE A CRIPPLE!"

I'd had enough now. I pointed at his foot and yelled back. "You think THIS isn't crippled? God, Steve, why don't you DO something about it instead of LYING to us?"

"It's MY foot!"

"STOP WHINING, DAMMIT!"

Steve had his eyes closed tight, and I could see tears trying to come out. "Alright, goddammit" he whispered. "Cut the fucking thing off."

"Yes!" Dr. Chatterjee said. "You will do this! I have witnesses!" He almost RAN out of the Emergency Room. "I will schedule the surgery!"

"So, your girlfriend can talk you around when nobody else can." A woman about Ma's age was next to Uncle Vince. She had a helmet in her hand, a heavy parka, and those damned motorcycle boots. She looked at me, and then Steve. "Well? Are you ever going to introduce us?"

Steve didn't look at either of us. "This is my mother. This is Sally" he mumbled. "What are you doing here?"

"Hospital called. As usual. 'Next of Kin' remember?" She shook my hand. It was as hard as mine. "Agatha MacTavish. Call me Aggie. He talks about you all the time."

Steve finally looked up. "Mom. Don't."

We all stood around the exam table he was lying on. She laughed. "Don't he look natural?"

"*Jesus*, Mom!"

I thought that was an unbelievably bizarre thing to say to her own son. Uncle Vince tried to hold it in, but he laughed with her.

Ma and Uncle Vince said they were going to get some coffee somewhere, and Steve's mother said "Yeah, let's leave little Stevie alone with his girl. I think your kid can handle his bullshit."

Steve and I sat there and didn't look at each other, but I could see out of the corner of my eye that his face was as red as mine.

"Steve? Did I... talk you into getting your foot... you know... amputated?"

"No." he said. "Maybe. I don't know. No. I always knew I'd have to one day. I mean, I'm not as stupid as I act sometimes. No. Maybe you just helped me decide. Maybe earlier than I wanted, but, yeah, I should do it." He was quiet for a few minutes. "I hope he's right about riding my bike."

I hoped so, too. I didn't like it myself, but I knew that if he couldn't, we'd never be friends again. I changed the subject. "Your Mom still calls you Stevie? Like in Kindergarten?"

Steve huffed that laugh of his. "Only when she thinks I'm being an asshole."

I asked, "What does your dad call you?"

"He doesn't. Mom produced me by parthenogenesis."

I laughed. "You've been hanging around Billy too long."

He grinned. "Yeah, he could insult Top Sergeants and Officers to their faces, and they'd swear they'd been complimented."

Dr. Chatterjee came back. "We will do this tomorrow morning. I hope no one will still be hungover by then."

Steve turned pale, and I grabbed his hand. "You've got one Hell of a bedside manner!" I snapped.

He chuckled. "Why waste it on Marines? They are 'rough and tough and no creampuffs.'" He took Steve's other hand. "He and I have been fighting for a long time. And now, *I* have won." He smiled at me. "I do not operate in the small hours of the day. When you do not have enough sleep ..." He shrugged, and Steve gripped my hand tighter. "If you are here at 8 o'clock, you will have an hour with him before surgery. Please tell his mother." He looked at Steve and frowned. "You already know what to do. No food after dinner. No water after 'Taps.' And no trying to escape. That is most important." He patted Steve's hand and started to walk away.

"Hey!" I called. "What about his foot?"

He came back, grabbed the foot and yanked it straight. Steve didn't blink, but I almost jumped across the room. He laughed at me. "I told you he feels nothing in this foot." He leaned over Steve's face. "And NO walking." He left.

We spent the rest of the day getting X-rays, making sure his blood type was correct in their records, and signing a whole bunch of paperwork. Along about supper time, I remembered we'd left our families behind somewhere, and they managed to catch up with us, or we to them, when Steve got a bed on one of the wards. Everybody looked worried, but Ma and his mom had that "aren't they a cute couple" gleam in their eyes.

Uncle Vince went to Pixie's Subs and Pizza and brought back a cheesesteak and sodas. Steve only picked at his half. He was looking more and more scared. I held his hand until visiting hours were over, and I promised I'd be there in the morning at eight. I leaned over to kiss him on his cheek the way I always do, but he turned and started to say something, and I landed on his mouth.

It lasted longer than I thought it would.

Not bad, either.

Both of us blushed, and we left right after.

When we got home, I thanked Ma and Uncle Vince for everything they'd done that day and got started on my worrying. I sat at the kitchen table and rolled an orange back and forth until Ma took it away from me and told me to go to bed. I hugged and kissed her and said "Goodnight, Ma" and stopped dead and looked at her.

She was smiling, and her eyes were wet. "So, you heard what you said, huh?" She touched my cheek. "You've been saying it all day."

I hesitated. "Is… is it… okay?"

She almost squeezed me in half with that hug.

I passed Uncle Vince in the living room, and I kissed and hugged him, too, and I wondered …

Before I could say anything, he said "You know, Sal, your father's a good man. Tried to be as good as that woman would let him be. He's pretty damned proud of you and how you turned out. Yeah" he said, "Freddie's a good man."

I stood there.

"Alright" he said. "ONCE. And ONLY once."

"I love you, Pop" and hugged him tight.

"Right" he said and turned away. "Go to bed." His voice was shaking.

I went upstairs.

CHAPTER EIGHTY-TWO

Aggie and Motorcycles

Dr. Chatterjee had said I could be at the hospital by eight, but I got there at six, and Steve's mom was already there. Steve was pale, and his hands shook when I held them, and he kept asking if I'd stay and be there when the operation was over. I kept telling him yes, and I'd tell Billy about the operation, but *he* was going to have to tell Billy the rest of it when he came to visit; and then they came for him.

We both kissed him and promised again that we'd both be there when he got back, and his mom told him she loved him, and I said I'd see him in a little while, and I kissed him one more time.

We went to the waiting room and waited.

And waited. We stared at the walls, out the window into a crummy little garden with frozen weeds, at the TV, at old magazines, newspapers, and each other.

I tried to make conversation, but it only lasted a sentence or two until I asked her what kind of motorcycle she drove. She stared back at me like I had just fallen out of the sky.

"Christ, you're a cool one" she said. "Your boyfriend is getting his foot chopped off, and you want to talk about BIKES?"

"Mrs. MacTavish, honest to God—"

"It's MISS MacTavish."

"Okay, sorry, *Miss* MacTavish, honest, Steve and I aren't going together or anything like that—"

"Then what the Hell are you doing here?"

I swallowed. "He's my cousin's best friend, and I—"

"I asked why YOU'RE here."

I took a deep breath. "Steve's my friend, too. I mean, you know, we're not... but we—"

"Aren't you missing work?"

I was watching her hands knot around themselves. I spoke very softly. "The Spring semester doesn't start for a couple of weeks, and I don't have anything I need to go in for, but even if I did, I'd just call Clementine and tell her my boyfriend was in the hospital and I needed to be with him, and he needed me– "

I stopped and thought. Steve and I were going out all the time, Steve and I holding hands, and I remembered that I'd been doing that a lot longer than just yesterday. Steve and I kissing yesterday, and how nice that felt even though it was a surprise. Steve and I always being asked about what was going on between us, and Steve never saying anything, but always looking kind of sad when I'd say that nothing was going on, and –

His mom was sitting there watching me. Waiting.

"Sorry. Everybody tells me I've got a head full of numbers and not much else, but sometimes my mouth lets me know what's going on." I tried to smile. "I guess it– "

"I *ride* a Harley-Davidson model WLA U.S. Army Courier's Motorcycle. It's a single seat, 45-inch flathead with a suicide shift and a hardtail frame." Her hands had relaxed. "It was built in July of 1942, and I rode it all over England, Scotland and Wales, and later in France while I was in the Women's Army Corp."

The abrupt change threw me, but I listened. "I didn't know girls did that during the war."

"*Girls* didn't" she said. "I was a WAC. Not a Girl Scout."

If anyone should have known better than to have said that, it was me. "Oh. So, when you came home, you bought one like it?"

"No" she said. "It's my bike from the war. When I got my orders to go home, I gave a Mail Clerk 11 pair of nylons to crate it up and send it home with me." She grinned. One of her teeth was chipped. "Parts and repairs are no problem. I'm on the Force. A Meter Maid. Those three-wheeled scoots still have the same engine and a lot of other parts as mine." She laughed.

"'Your tax dollars at work.'"

Suddenly, I liked her. She was—what? Wild? Bold? No, I knew: she was like Aunt Viv. She and I talked (well, *she* talked, I listened.) Her father had been a motorcycle cop and had taught her how to drive—I mean, *ride* his "Indian," which was another brand I'd never heard of. After she came back from the war, he got her a job as a meter maid ("Sorry, Agatha, that's all you can get"), and she used to patrol the Dundalk area around Fort Holabird.

There was an Army Lieutenant that always parked illegally off the Base, and after she gave him about a dozen tickets (which he always challenged in Court), they started dating, got married, she got pregnant, and everything was all roses until the day the baby was born. Her husband never came to the hospital, and never came home, and transferred to another Base, and she never saw the "lousy, scum-bag son-of-a-bitch" ever again. She changed back to her maiden name, changed the baby's name to Steven MacTavish (for her father), and that was that. He wouldn't divorce her, and she still gets a check every month from the Army under her married name, and she writes "For Deposit Only" on it and banks it. "The no-good bastard is a two-star General now, so the checks got bigger, but that's all he's good for, so screw him and the horse he rode in on."

She started telling me about Steve. Good student, good mechanical aptitude, gets whiny about his foot, and he absolutely ADORES me, and always had. "Oh, he never held a torch for you; dated other girls, got serious about a couple, but he never dated after his foot got messed up until he bumped into you again. Swears you saved his life."

Oh, wow.

I started to tell her about me, but she laughed. "Honey, every time I see him, you're all he talks about."

That's when Dr. Chatterjee came into the room, all smiles, and told us the operation was over, Steve was fine, but still coming out of anesthesia, and we could go back to see him soon.

A nurse took us back, and Steve was lying there with his eyes closed and asking "Sally? Where's Sally?"

Oh, Jeez.

I told him I was there, but he said he couldn't see me, and Aggie grabbed his head, tilted it towards me, and pulled his eyelids open. "She's right there, dummy."

His eyes focused, and he smiled at me.

Steve got off the painkillers pretty quickly. He and Dr. Chatterjee both said it was better to have a little more pain than to become an addict. He started physical therapy right away, even before the stitches were out.

My classes had started, and I was going from home to the pool, to classes, to the hospital, and back home, and all day at the hospital on weekends. One Saturday, I was there with him when he got a charley-horse. It hurt so much he bent the handrails on the bed. I whipped the bedsheets off, grabbed his... well, his stump, and started to massage it, hard and deep, until the muscles relaxed, and he calmed down. I kept massaging, trying to figure out how the muscles changed and how they were attached now. I kept concentrating on that, until he asked, "What do you think?"

I laughed.

It was the wrong thing to do, and I tried to explain in a big rush.

"I'm sorry, you just reminded me of a joke back in, oh God, I think maybe Junior High? Anyway, there was this guy with a wooden leg and he got married and his wife didn't know he had a wooden leg and on their wedding night they got undressed in the dark and they got in bed and she reached over and felt his stump and he said what do you think and she said get the Vaseline and we'll give it a try, and that's why I laughed."

Steve stared at me, and another guy on the ward said "Lady, you can't tell a joke for shit."

I felt embarrassed and stupid, and Steve was still staring, and I was still massaging his stump. I said "Okay, it's soft now. Does it feel better?"

Every guy on the ward roared.

One weekend when Billy, Marie and Annie came up, we all had a long talk before we went to the hospital. I knew that when Granny Annie died, she left the house to Aunt Viv and Uncle Bill, and her money to Adrienne and Billy, but I didn't know how much.

Marie said she had had everything in Bonds. Savings Bonds, War Bonds, Liberty Bonds, and even Stamps Aunt Viv and Uncle Bill bought at school that you used to buy Bonds with. It took a long time for all the lawyers and bank people and tax people to straighten everything out.

And it was worth a LOT.

Billy's share was enough to buy the land that the house had stood on from Aunt Viv and Uncle Bill. Marie talked about sub-dividing, loans, mortgages, and how about it, Sorella? You gonna build our houses?

I'd been saving as much as I could, but I had nowhere near enough to buy into this.

Marie said "Trust me, Sal, I learned from the best. We can do this."

Ma said to do it like she did and rent it out all summer until the mortgage is paid off.

I took a deep breath, hugged her, and said "I'm in!"

I'M GONNA GO LIVE DOWNEYOSHUN!!

I wonder if Steve will want to?

Steve got out of the hospital at the end of February, and Dr. Chatterjee and Aggie and I nagged him into going back to work on a temporary adjustable prosthetic and got fitted for his new foot by mid-April. He kept bugging Dr. Chatterjee to get the other biker with a prosthetic to teach him how to ride again, and on the last Friday in April, we took off from our jobs and went to a Drag Strip in Howard County.

The biker's name was Peg-Leg Eddie, and he was about the grungiest, greasiest guy I'd ever seen. Aggie knew him from "runs" that different motorcycle clubs did for "Toys For Tots", and children's cancer charities. Aggie rode Steve's bike, and Steve rode with me in my car, and whined the whole trip.

Eddie showed Steve what to do while his bike was turned off, and then they both started up their bikes and slowly drove up and down the drag strip, and then did turns on the empty parking lot. Steve started riding by himself and went faster and faster and did tighter and tighter left turns until he almost tipped over. Then he slowed down again and came back to us. Eddie called him an asshole and rode off.

I didn't want to do it, but I got my helmet and jacket out of the trunk, gave my car keys to Aggie, and told him he could take me home *if* he didn't drive like that.

He stuck to the speed limit, and I didn't crush his ribs.

We dropped Aggie off at her place, and they went inside, and I could hear her yelling at him. I sat in my car with the heater set to "Roast." April is too cold for motorcycles—for me at least. When he came out, he looked embarrassed, but he came over and asked me out for dinner, my choice, to celebrate.

I told him I'd cook for him in his apartment instead, and we both drove there. I'd never been to his place before, and he only had a frying pan and one pot, and he suggested we do carry-out and figure out what to do afterwards.

We did.

Figure out what to do, I mean.

It was my first time.

He was surprised.

So was I.

Marie was right, it wasn't like those stupid romance novels that were always lying around at the dorm. It wasn't the "Grand Passion", or the "Blood and Agony", it was just... new. It worked, but it'll take practice like she said.

BUT EVERYTHING ELSE HE DID WAS *GREAT*!

He walked me home. Sunday. Night. 9 o'clock. Almost 10.

Ma and Uncle Vince were watching TV, and looked at us and didn't say anything, so Steve kissed me goodnight, and said he'd see me tomorrow if that was okay, and Ma said, "Here. For dinner", and he nodded and kissed me again, and left.

Ma looked at me, stood up, crossed her arms, and said "Vince. Take a walk." He got up, grabbed his jacket, winked at me, and left.

Ma just stood there.

I was probably as red as a Fire Truck.

"So, you jumped the fence just like your sister."

I couldn't help it. I snorted, laughed, giggled, you name it. I thought I'd never stop.

"THREE DAYS!" she said. I tried to say I was sorry, but I was still laughing.

"Do you love him?"

I stopped laughing and thought. "I don't know."

"Oh, jeez", she said. "Does HE love YOU?"

I was quiet now. "I don't know that, either."

"Were you at least *careful*?"

I snickered. "I'm a good Catholic Italian Girl."

"SALLY!"

"Yeah, Ma" I said. "EACH TIME!" and I started laughing again.

She sighed and threw her hands up in the air. "Well, I'm not going to get any sense out of you, tonight." She hugged me and drew back with her nose all wrinkled up. "Does he have a bathtub or a shower in that place?"

I remembered. "OH, YEAH!" I was still laughing.

She shook her head. "You kids all think you invented sex." She hugged me once more and pushed me towards the stairs. "Go take a bath, for God's sake. You smell like Payday at Tilly's, and the Fleet's in town." I went upstairs giggling.

Maybe I'll cook for him next weekend.

CHAPTER EIGHTY-THREE

Our House Is A Very, Very, Very Fine House

I didn't get to cook for him.

Over in Vietnam, Saigon fell. The TV showed all these South Vietnamese soldiers and other people who worked for us trying to get out—and most of them not being able to.

There were a bunch of helicopters flying people off the top of the U.S. Embassy, and Steve said that those were Americans. Walter Cronkite said that other helicopters were flying some Vietnamese people to American ships, and other country's ships, and others were getting onto fishing boats and smaller boats and sailing away to God knows where.

Steve had come over after work on Wednesday, and we watched it all on the TV at Ma's. When Steve started crying, she and Uncle Vince went out into the kitchen. Marie called later, and said that Billy had cried, too.

It had all been nothing but a huge waste.

All the people that got killed or hurt like Steve.

All those years.

All for nothing.

When Marie called, she said it was time to come down this weekend and figure out what kind of houses we wanted. She said to drag Steve down with me, and while she and I worked, Steve and Billy could play together, and little Annie would keep an eye on them and make them behave.

We went to Granny Annie's and took a good look at the land. With Assawoman Bay in the backyard, we'd still mount the houses on pilings. The old pilings that her house had been on were still sticking up out of the ground. They'd have to be cut off. The little pier—we thought about taking that down as well, but Marie said if we rebuilt it, and went a little further out, it would be a selling point for renters: "Sail to Ocean City! Dock at your own private pier! Stay in a beautiful, spacious home instead of some cheap motel!" She'd check with Ma's rental agent.

I was more concerned about how much more it would all cost, but Marie said she'd do all the money stuff, and not worry.

Marie had a pile of magazines that sold building plans, so we went home to read them. I found mine pretty quickly—three bedrooms, 1½ baths, eat-in kitchen, a big everything-room, a simple roof with no fancy angles, and NO garage. Marie picked something like it, but with four bedrooms (she wanted an office) and two baths.

Steve got interested and said we had to go back to Granny Annie's. He paced-off distances, and asked about the new pier to see if we would want a "heat pump" that would have a "heat exchanger" in the water under the pier to make cheap heating and air conditioning. He explained how it worked and said he could do the work and get the heat pump machine "at cost" from where he worked.

What I liked best was that he had cheered up.

Marie started nudging and whispering about "wedding bells" again, but this time, I thought about it.

Spring semester ended, and I told Clementine and John that I wouldn't be teaching that summer, packed my new steel-toed shoes and work clothes, and drove home to Ocean City!

It was the busiest summer of my life. Permits, Approvals, Allowances, scheduling, getting all the materials delivered on-site, supervising (and thank God I've dealt with most of those people before. The only new ones were the people from the pile-driving company, and they'd heard of me from the others.)

Dad came down and helped, and the Fire Department came when it was time, and we raised both houses. Plumbing with Mr. Mike, electric with Mr. Joe, ductwork with Steve and Mr. Sal, drywall with Mr. George and Mr. Vic, and cabinetry with Dad.

Mr. Mike came back for rest of the plumbing installation, and asked me just when the Hell was I going to start calling *him* Uncle? Oh, wow, like that was the surprise of the year! I gave him a hug and a kiss, and he said it was about damned time, and that I had better have left him enough room to mount the sinks and shower (no bathtub for me, thank you. Showers are cleaner and save water. If—and I do mean *if*- there's a baby one day, I'll give her a bath in the kitchen sink until she can stand.)

Mr. George and Mr. Vic (whoops, I mean Uncles George and Vic) came back and did the painting, and it was all done except for Steve's heat pumps. He came down the last weekend of August, and that Saturday was the hottest it had been all summer—102 degrees, high humidity, and NO breeze. Marie and I did all the work under the water beneath the pier (and stupid me, I should have waited to plank it over until we had done all this.) Billy filled in the trench from the pier to the houses, and Steve installed the outside part of the heat pumps. Little Annie "supervised" from her playpen, sitting in front of the fan.

The only thing left was hooking up two "vacuum pumps" to the heat pumps to suck all the air out of them, so Steve could put the Freon in. He wanted them to run at least six hours, and then see if they would "hold a vacuum" after that for another two hours.

In other words, EIGHT more hours until we could have air conditioning.

Billy was sitting in his boxer shorts, Marie and I had peeled down to halter tops and loose shorts, and wondered how much more we could get away with, little Annie was sitting on a diaper with her arms raised in front of the fan ...

And Steve was standing there in heavy work pants, a long-sleeved shirt, and those GOD-DAMNED BOOTS!

I said "Steve, do you have *anything* else you can change into? Something cooler? You're making me hot just looking at you."

He leered at me.

"That's *not* what I meant, and you know it."

He shrugged his shoulders, said that was it, no other clothes except another set "all same-same."

The sweat was pouring off me, and I was tired and irritated, so I told him I'd take him out and buy him a pair of shorts and a tee-shirt and a pair of sneakers or whatever he wanted, just come on and let's go.

He started mumbling about how his foot needs to be specially fitted. I told him that I could do that; God knows I can build or sew anything, but he said "No."

I yelled at him "WHY NOT?"

"Because people will look at me like I'm a cripple."

That did it. I'd had enough of that crap to last me a lifetime.

I yelled "NO, you IDIOT, they're going to look at you and think I've got a good-looking husb—hus—h ..."

Marie scooped up Annie and grabbed Billy and said "outoutoutout" and rushed out the door.

Steve stood there with an ear-to-ear grin. "A good-looking what?"

"Nothing."

"A good-looking husband?"

"It was a slip of the tongue!"

"You're gonna slip me the tongue?"

"STOP IT!"

He leaned against the wall. "So, you want to marry me, huh?"

"Is that supposed to be a proposal?" I snapped.

"Oh, I thought that *you* were proposing to *me*."

I stamped my foot. "Steven MacTavish, I will be damned and gone to Hell before I ever let you tell our kids that *I* proposed to *you*!"

He was laughing now. "Oh, we've got kids, too?"

ARRRGH!! MY MOUTH!! I took off *out* the door, *up* the driveway to my car, I had left my keys *in* my bag, *in* the house, and I started walking towards the street. I heard Steve clumping up behind me. He got in front of me, went down on his left knee, reached into his pocket and pulled out a wad of Saran Wrap.

"I was going to do this tonight" he said and started picking at the plastic.

"When we were in 'Nam, we were out on patrol one day—not *this* day (he reached down and tapped his boot), and I found this chunk of rock with a red dot in it. I saw a travelogue in the movies when I was a kid about Burma and Thailand and Cambodia and Vietnam and all that, and the guy in the movie said that the best rubies in the world came from there, and he showed this rock that had a red dot just like the one I found. I mailed it home, and wrote Mom what I thought it was, and she took it to the jewelry store—"

He finished unwrapping a little box, opened it and pulled a ring out.

"She said the jeweler told her that it was a ruby, and that the color was called 'pigeon's blood,' I don't know why, and he told her where to go to have it cut."

He took a breath. I was holding mine.

"Sally Osterhoff, I love you. Will you marry me? Will you have me for your husband?" He grinned again. "Will you let me be the father of our children?"

I looked at the ring. It was a deep red, and it almost did look like blood, but not in a gross way. I remembered Aunt Viv's ring with the yellow diamond that her husband had found for her.

OHMYGOD! I remembered something else! Mama Loretta told me I was going to save someone's life! And I HAD saved Steve's life that day at the diner, he said so! And MY life, and the Olympics and being happy and she said I wouldn't remember what she said for THREE years! And that's NOW!

"Sally?" I looked down at Steve.

"Huh?"

He took my hand. "Will you marry me?"

"Oh" I said. "Um. Yeah. Okay. I mean YES! YES, I, I, I *will* marry you! I'll, I'll be your wife, and, and, and the mother of our children." I pulled him up from the driveway. "And I love you, too."

The ring fit my finger, and he kissed me, and I could hear tiny bells chiming.

I screamed "MARIE! HANG UP THAT PHONE!" I could hear her giggling. "BILLY!"

“Hey!” she yelled, and Billy called out “The phone has been secured” and Steve laughed. A *real* laugh, not that huff he’d been doing since he came back from Vietnam. I kissed him again.

“There’s something I need you to do for me” I told him. “I want you to go and ask my father for my hand.”

“Your hand?” He was laughing harder, now. “I want a few more parts than just your hand.”

“Steve!”

“Okay, I’ll ask him.” He frowned. “No, wait, I can’t.”

I was getting annoyed again. “Why not?”

He kissed me again. “Because first, you’ve got to take me out and get me a pair of shorts and a tee-shirt and sneakers. I used to wear Jack Purcell’s. Black. Size 10½.”

I could hear Marie. “Oh my God, she tamed him.”

When Steve and I came back from shopping, we all went to Aunt Sally’s. Dad had been staying there just in case I needed him. He looked down at my hand and smiled. Steve told him that he loved me and wanted to marry me, and would he give us his blessing? Yes, of course he would, and he shook Steve’s hand and kissed me, and we let Marie phone everyone.

Ma took over the planning, Dad paid the bills, and I made my gown and Marie’s.

But there was something else that only I could do.

I went to the “Buttons and Bows Gown and Bridal Shop” on Eastern Avenue to talk to Mother.

She had gotten a job there when she divorced Dad, and when the lady who owned it retired, she bought the business. I’d heard she’d done quite well, but not much else.

She looked up at me when I came in. “May I help you?” still in that cold, quiet voice of hers.

“Hello, Mother” I said.

“Mother? I thought that woman was your mother, now.”

I really didn’t want to go through with this.

“I’m inviting you to my wedding” and handed her an Invitation.

"Yes" she said. "You're marrying that crippled motorcycle gangster you've been sleeping with. I suppose you're pregnant, just as my sister was." She dropped the Invitation into a wastebasket beside the sales counter.

I said "It's Saturday the 26th of this month. Botz's Church. 2 o'clock."

"Your father left me destitute. I have to work every day." A mother and daughter walked into the shop, and Mother turned to them. "May I help you?"

They looked at me. "We're finished" Mother told them.

"My girl wants that gown in the window" the mother said.

Mother looked at the girl. "No" she said. "Her skin is too muddy for pure white. She cannot wear anything lighter than Pale Champagne. And she's too fat for that style."

The woman looked like she wanted to punch Mother, but then she dropped her eyes and asked, "What do you think she should wear?"

I suppose Mother's admittedly well-known and well-deserved fashion sense must make up for her nastiness. She was right about us, too: we were finished.

The wedding was small, but it was everything that Ma had planned it to be: the music, the flowers, the guests all seated "just so." Reverend Lehmann came down from the little township in Pennsylvania he had retired to and did the service, and when he asked "Who giveth this woman to be wed?" Dad said, "Her family and I do!" and that made me cry.

We had the reception at Hausner's Restaurant in their upstairs banquet room. Karen made the cake, of course; and there was music and Steve DANCED with me!

Our wedding night was at his apartment, and the next day we moved all his things out of his apartment and into Ma's basement. We both went back to work on Monday morning.

Not much of a Honeymoon, right?

Wrong.

I couldn't've been happier.

I was surprised that Steve and I seemed to fit together so well. Oh, we had our arguments, and sometimes he got stubborn or lazy, and sometimes

I nagged, and it wasn't always comfortable not living on our own (Marie had warned us about that), and only having ONE full bathroom for all of us is something I should have given a *lot* more thought to when I built my home. Oh well, I can remodel one day.

Steve finished his apprenticeship and doubled his wages, Clementine always made sure I got steady increases in my salary, and Marie was hitting the renters for every penny she could squeeze out of them while she, Billy, and Annie lived at Aunt Sally's during the tourist season (Ouch! More crowded than we were.) We were hoping to have the mortgages paid off by 1980, and would have, except for two things:

In April of '77, I got a notification through interdepartmental mail from John and Clementine that a tenured position had opened, and it was mine if I wanted it, but there was a condition:

I'd have to relocate to another UM campus.

The University of Maryland at Eastern Shore.

Less than an hour's commute to Ocean City.

Oh, and there would be a big raise, too.

IF I wanted the position.

Silliest question of the year.

Steve asked for a transfer to his company's offices and shop in Salisbury and got it, and how soon could he start?

And that other thing?

Last Thanksgiving, Marie and I BOTH stood up and announced we were pregnant.

We're due in June.

Spring semester ended, and we packed. Not a lot, just a TON of baby girl things from the shower (Mama Loretta says it's going to be a girl.) We rented a U-Haul truck, and Ma and I sat in the backyard while Steve and Uncle Vince loaded it.

I looked around me. A square block of plain rowhouses, the same as nearly every other block in Baltimore. Brick, concrete, and asphalt. Grey, gritty air you could taste in your mouth and feel in your eyes. Smells from the brewery, the steel mill, the filthy harbor, and the garbage cans in the alley. Hot, humid, and no breeze in summer, and cold and damp in winter.

No, there wasn't anything I ever really liked about Baltimore. I always knew where I belonged.

I stood up, went inside and to the bathroom one more time, kissed my Ma and my Uncle Vince, and promised I wouldn't have the baby until they came down next week. Steve's bike was strapped to the back of the truck, and my car was hooked up to tow. I climbed into the front seat next to my husband.

"Let's go home."

EPILOGUE

Aunt Sal's Downeyoshun, Summer 1980

Sitting at the kitchen table and grading final exams is always tedious, but it has its' good moments. Right now, I was looking at a *perfect* test score from Rachel Blue.

I didn't need to check my notes. Rachel came from Crisfield, and after this one year of scholarship, she would go back there, to a life of picking crabs, shucking oysters, or plucking chickens in some packing plant.

Not if I could help it.

It was Saturday, and first thing Monday morning, I'd call Clementine and get the ball rolling for more scholarship money from the UNCF, and when Doris and Adrienne came down the week after, I'd take Doris to Crisfield and we'd find whatever Church Rachel attended, and any other place we could shake tuition money from. Former Olympian Doctor Doris "Cannonball" Johnson is well-known and respected, and always persuasive. If there's a dime to be had to help Rachel, Doris will find it.

Of course, I'll have to listen to Doris rant and rave about "that stupid, useless, Cracker from JAW-JUH" for pulling us out of the Olympics that summer; and her friend Ludmilla from Moscow says—

Clunk. Splash. "MOM! I spilled the milk!"

It was Carrie. The kids were having lunch outside on the deck I built last summer. "Well, no use crying over it" I called, and heard her complain to her cousin and partner-in-crime, Loretta, "She always says that." I grabbed a dish towel and went outside.

"Ah-Roo, Roo, Roo, Roo!" I sirened. "Alright, Kitchen Police! Nobody moves!"

"And she always says that, too" Loretta complained back to Carrie.

"Well, that's because of the high rate of recidivism around here" I told them.

They turned to Annie, who lifted her eyes from "Charlotte's Web" and sighed with all the world-weariness a six-year-old could muster. "I'll look it up."

I bent over to sop-up what I could of the milk that hadn't gone between the deck boards when the baby kicked (#2 and the last.) Annie jumped up, took the towel and patted my "big baby belly", and said "I'll get it, Aunt Sal."

We all looked up when the car horn beeped. Marie jumped out, yelling "Head for the hills, the Dam's gonna bust!" and tried to run as fast as she could for the bathroom with her legs clamped together and holding *her* belly with #3 and *her* last.

The guys started unloading the groceries, and Steve walked past us with full arms, but still managed to toss me one of the "Slim Jim Foot-Long Spicy-Hots" that I'd been craving since December. Dr. Julia only allows me one a week.

I had it peeled and half of it crammed into my mouth before he came back for the rest of the groceries. He kissed me and made a face and intoned "The Wages of Slims is Breath!"

Annie whispered, "And HE always says that."

We smile, and we are happy.

end

About the Author

Baltimore born, the author is a U.S. Navy / Vietnam / Agent Orange veteran and cancer survivor. He was once "with it" as a carny in a traveling gadget show, and has worked as a fire extinguishing systems installer and serviceman, route delivery sales for a brewery, flexographic press operator, licensed boiler plant engineer, and story teller. He much prefers the last.

Apprentice House is the country's only campus-based, student-staffed book publishing company. Directed by professors and industry professionals, it is a nonprofit activity of the Communication Department at Loyola University Maryland.

Using state-of-the-art technology and an experiential learning model of education, Apprentice House publishes books in untraditional ways. This dual responsibility as publishers and educators creates an unprecedented collaborative environment among faculty and students, while teaching tomorrow's editors, designers, and marketers.

Eclectic and provocative, Apprentice House titles intend to entertain as well as spark dialogue on a variety of topics. Financial contributions to sustain the press's work are welcomed. Contributions are tax deductible to the fullest extent allowed by the IRS.

To learn more about Apprentice House books or to obtain submission guidelines, please visit www.apprenticehouse.com.

Apprentice House Press
Communication Department
Loyola University Maryland
4501 N. Charles Street
Baltimore, MD 21210
Ph: 410-617-5265
info@apprenticehouse.com • www.apprenticehouse.com

www.ingramcontent.com/pod-product-compliance
Lightning Source LLC
Chambersburg PA
CBHW060632310726
48982CB00003B/744

* 9 7 8 1 6 2 7 2 0 6 0 2 0 *